AMERICAN
GHOUL

AMERICAN GHOUL

MICHELLE McGILL-VARGAS

BLACK
STONE
PUBLISHING

Printed in the United States of America

First edition: 2024
ISBN 979-8-212-22456-7
Fiction / Horror

Version 1

Blackstone Publishing
31 Mistletoe Rd.
Ashland, OR 97520

www.BlackstonePublishing.com

For Jackson and Madison

ONE

I can't kill somebody who's already dead.

That's what I told them white folks sitting out there, judging me. Of course, they didn't believe me. For months, they saw Simone walking and talking like a real living person. But she wasn't. Wasn't living at all. Her heart didn't beat none, and if they paid close attention, they'd notice she never took a breath and rarely blinked them baby blues of hers. No, Simone wasn't one of us, but none of that mattered now. All they saw was me, some colored woman, standing over what they thought was Simone's freshly dead body.

Hell, ain't been three years since old Uncle Abe freed me and my ilk. But here I am, shackled again, except this time I'm in an Indiana jail, waiting for my date with the hangman's noose for supposedly killing a dead woman.

"What are you going on about, Lavinia?"

I flinch at the jailer's familiar use of my name. Like he knows me. I fought hard for my name, but hearing it come out of his mouth is like sticker bugs scraping against my legs. Reminds me how getting familiar with the wrong folks got me into this mess.

Martin, the jailer, makes his way to my cell. Doubt he can hear me over all the shouting outside. I can't make out the words, but I ain't gotta guess the whole town's out there demanding my head. Martin turns his ear toward the noise, snorts quietly, then smiles. Even though it's late in the afternoon, the July heat has him sweating like a fool and I can smell the tobacco plug steeping in his mouth. The whole jail isn't that big. Just two side-by-side cells, each barely large enough to hold a cot and a pot. Takes Martin only a few strides across the wooden floor to get to me from his desk. His hand grips a battered tin cup for collecting shots of muddy juice from his stained mouth. He shifts the mound around in his jaws before settling on a comfortable corner in his cheek. Then he leans against the bars of my cell, spits a glob into the cup, and licks brown dribble from his bottom lip.

"What did you think was going to happen? You killed a white woman."

"She was *dead*," I say loud enough for him to hear despite the noise.

"Of course, she's dead. You killed her." Martin removes his hat and scratches his thinning gray hair. He spits into his cup again.

I regard my hastily bandaged forearm and cover the bindings with my hand. "I ain't killed nobody," I say, knowing it's only technically true. "Don't matter. Y'all gon' hang me no matter how many times I say it."

"We found you with the body."

"You act like I was the only one out there." I place a finger to my lips and glance at the corrugated tin ceiling. "Oh wait. I *was* the only one out there."

"This has nothing to do with you being colored," Martin says, shocked that the accusation came from my mouth.

"Doesn't it? The whole neighborhood was outside. And there wasn't a mark on Simone. Yet everybody somehow came to the conclusion that, outta *all* them people out there, I was the one who killed her. But sure, it ain't got nothin' to do with my being colored."

"It doesn't. I got no ill will toward you people. And Miss Arceneau treated you just fine. Why you would go and do such a thing—"

"I told you, I didn't—"

"Kill her. Right. Because she was already dead."

"She was!" Then under my breath, I add, "You'll see. Don't be surprised when she shows up tonight and busts me outta here."

Loud thumps rain against the jail from all sides, causing both of us to jump. Martin hurries to the door and cracks it just enough for several stones, clumps of dirt, and louder threats to make their way inside. I test the strength of the metal bars of my cell with my body. They oughta keep me safe, for a time. As fast as this town turned on me, I wouldn't put it past Martin to hand them the keys.

He finally gets enough sense to shut the door once a few of those rocks knock him back. "And here we thought you were different." Martin closes his eyes and shakes his head.

"If you only knew how different I really was," I mutter, noticing a thin red line emerging on the bandage around my arm. All that jostling getting me here from the courthouse must've got it bleeding again.

Martin sighs and tilts his head as if he's tired of hearing me talk. "*If you only knew how different I really was?* Now what's that supposed to mean, Lavinia?"

"I'm a ghoul. Or at least I was one."

"A what now?"

"A ghoul," I say, surprised by the wave of sadness that hits me. I stroke my injured arm, remembering how, at first, I hated being a ghoul. But now, with only Martin standing between me and that mob, I'd give anything to be one again.

The constable bursts in and for the first time, I hear only a few voices shouting my name. "Damn fools," he says as he slaps a set of keys onto his desk. "All that hollering, for what? As if I understand anything they're saying. You'd think if folks want something that bad, they'd tell you in English!"

"These Germans sure love a hanging," Martin says with a smile. "You get 'em calm, boss?"

"For now. And let's keep it that way. No drinking tonight. You think you can handle that this time?"

Martin's face falls. Then he notices that I notice. He adjusts his pants and then sidles over to the constable. "Ain't nothing but the grace of God gonna keep her safe." He lowers his voice while staring at me. "She killed a white woman."

"I didn't kill nobody!" I remind them.

"Had you not gotten so stinking drunk," the constable continues as he reaches for the door handle, "they wouldn't have gotten inside and strung up the last fella we had in here. And he turned out to be innocent!"

"What do you want me to do, boss? I'm one man against a whole town."

"You've got a badge and a gun. Use 'em." He listens at the door before opening it, then swears. "Look, Martin, mind the door this time, will ya? Somebody's going to Hammond in chains tomorrow morning. If I come back and find her dead 'cause you couldn't keep your eyes open, I'll settle for you."

And with that, he leaves me at the mercy of an armed drunk and a town itching for a necktie party. Martin mumbles something as he wears a path in the middle of the floor. Then he finds his way back to my cell.

"What were you saying earlier?" he spits out, brows all crinkled together as if I'm the reason he's mad.

"I didn't kill—"

"No, not that. Ghoul. What the hell is a ghoul? Some fancy French word Miss Arceneau taught you?"

I raise an eyebrow. If he's talking, he ain't drinking. And if he ain't drinking, I just might survive long enough for the constable to get me on the train outta this town. Not like the law in Hammond will believe me any more than these two. But swinging from a tree for something I didn't even do ain't how I want my story to end. And even though I owe Simone a good skinning for what she did to me in the end, I sure hope she ain't *dead*-dead. Could use a little help getting outta here when night falls.

I gently press down on my bandage; more crimson blooms. "You really wanna know?"

He shrugs. "Nobody here but me and you." He takes out a pocket watch and checks the time. "Be a couple of hours before the constable gets back from the post office to send that wire. And the Michigan Central won't be by 'til the morning to carry you to Hammond. A story'll keep me occupied." He spits the entire wad of tobacco in the tin cup and wipes his mouth on his sleeve.

I sigh and sink down to the earthen floor of my cell. This jail re-minds me of the sod dugout me and Simone lived in when we first arrived here last fall. The cave, as we called it, was dark—had to be for Simone's sake—with only a door to let in a few rays of sunlight. This jail got one door and a tiny window in each of the two cells. The wood along the bottom of the walls is worn away—or has been chewed by vermin. I quickly climb onto the thin, straw-filled mattress on the cot.

"You gonna tell me the story or what?" Martin opens the drawer of his desk and takes out an oval pewter flask. He shakes it and I can hear liquid sloshing around.

Shit.

But he approaches the cell and hands it to me. I narrow my eyes at him before taking the flask. I unscrew the lid and sniff. Not that it matters much if it's poisoned . . . or that it smells like tobacco and stale breath. I pour a swig in my mouth without letting the rim touch my lips. Martin's always jawing on tobacco, so I don't doubt the stuff is crusted all over the top of it. The whiskey warms my innards and my shoulders lower. For a second, I don't even feel the throbbing pain in my arm. Didn't know I was that tense.

"You really wanna hear it?" I ask.

"Already said yes, didn't I?"

A smile crawls across my face. He ain't ready for this story. But I got nothing else to do. "You ever heard of vampires?"

Two

Vampires.

Yeah, I'd never heard of them either until last summer, right after Uncle Billy came through Georgia with his Yankee army, burning everything in sight on his way to the ocean. I'd been slaving for Miss Tillie on her plantation since I was a little girl, and on account that she was the only family I had, I stuck around when the war was over. Miss Tillie wasn't about to be like these other women: standing in the road, crying over everything they lost. No, she took her dead husband's whiskey and gin recipes and opened a saloon inside one of the abandoned slave shacks. Even ran a brothel in the big house. Wasn't like there was a slew of folks coming by, though. Mostly soldiers returning home or men wanting to forget that the Rebs got their asses whupped. Miss Tillie never asked me to work the brothel; I was glad of that. I guess she figured her clientele wouldn't be interested in dark meat. But I had to clean up the saloon and get Miss Tillie and her girls ready for another day once all the fighting and drinking and cavorting was over at sunup.

That morning, I woke up with a tickle in my throat and a cough that got my head to aching. Now, I ain't been sick in forever, and with me being the only set of work hands around for miles, the last thing I needed was to be laid up for any amount of time. There was a whole mess of greenery growing in this thick forest right off the main road. Any time one of us got sick, we went out there to gather tree sap, bark, and whatever else we needed to get through the day. So, I took the quarter-mile walk from the plantation to gather the star-shaped sweet gum leaves I needed to make a quick tea to get my body right.

I stopped in the middle of the road, wondering if anybody would be passing by like they used to. I'd seen whole families of colored folks, some with nothing but the clothes on their backs, heading anywhere north of here. Most of them left when Sherman came through. Others held on as long as they could until the food ran out or the plantations started crumbling around them. With my handful of sweet gum leaves, I stood on that road, eyes trained north, listening to mourning doves sing the song of my life. The northern horizon swallowed up one end of that main road leading to town where the military handed out weekly rations. For me, anything past that point was like wondering what happened after death. Ain't nobody ever come back from the dead to tell me they'd seen the pearly gates. And ain't nobody ever come back from past the ration point to tell me if it was worth sticking more than my toe on that road.

Daylight was burning, and I needed to get this tea in me before I started my rounds.

I got the indoor and outdoor ovens going. One was for my tea and breakfast—or lunch, depending on when Miss Tillie and her whores got up—and the other was to boil the mess outta all them bedsheets. The big house greeted me with the usual musky, sour stank of last night's work. With a copper pot and wooden spoon in hand, I climbed up the rickety stairs to the second floor and rang the morning alarm.

"Alright, y'all!" I yelled above the clanging of the copper pot. I stomped up and down the worn green carpet in the hallway and waited for the five bedroom doors to open. One by one, various faces swollen from sleep and topped with nests of disheveled hair made appearances. Leaving the pot and spoon on the floor, I grabbed a large wicker basket, ready to collect all the soiled sheets.

"Uh-uhn, don't hand me none of them nasty linens," I commanded.

"Y'all know the routine: dump 'em in the basket. You drop 'em on the floor, they stayin' there!" This I repeated until I got to the end of the hall where fresh sheets were waiting for distribution. All the girls, except ole redhead Ginny, complied. Ginny's ass balled up her sheets and tossed them against my back when I turned around. The sweet gum tea hadn't kicked in yet, so I left them dirty things in the middle of the hallway.

Then on to Miss Tillie's room. It was the grandest one, of course, about the size of three slave shacks put together. Hot and darkened by thick, dusty curtains, I held my nose against the stench of stale liquor leeching from her skin. The whole place would probably go up if I lit a match in there. "Get on up, Miss Tillie," I said. "Your girls made a right mess down there in the parlor last night. You best get on up so I can get the place clean 'fore this evenin'."

Miss Tillie threw a pillow at me. "Why are you so loud, Vinny?"

"I ain't loud, Miss Tillie," I said, throwing the curtains and the window open to air the place out. "It's all that whiskey you drank poundin' 'round your head." I went over to the bed and threw the sheets from her. The old woman still had her face painted up from the night before. Most of it had smeared onto the pillowcases. At least this time she'd actually made it to the bed.

Still lying on her stomach, Miss Tillie stretched her arm out to me. "Can you help me up, Vinny?"

I sucked my teeth and planted my hands on my hips. "Time's a-wastin'. I got fifty million things to do and liftin' you outta the bed ain't one of 'em!"

I left her there wailing about her pounding head. I hauled the soiled sheets to the tub of water boiling on the outdoor stove, and then set a platter of vegetables, eggs, and what the military claimed was meat out in the dining room. All the silver and china were taken when the Yankees ran through here, so Miss Tillie had to use the tin and wooden pieces the slaves left behind. With the sheets boiling and my tea finally kicking in, I was ready to tackle the saloon.

And that's where I found Simone.

I didn't think she was real at first. She just stood there, stock-still in a dark corner with her eyes closed, sweating like the dickens. She balanced on her bare tiptoes like she was avoiding the sunbeams coming through the walls where the chinking had worn out. A black curtain of hair falling almost to the middle of her chest hid her face. Sweat spots and dark brown streaks dotted the frock she wore, as gray and washed out as her skin. Reminded me of when Miss Tillie's husband died and they let him set up in the parlor too long before putting him in the ground.

"Hey, miss?" I called to her from across the room. "Place is closed."

She didn't move. I couldn't tell if she was drunk or what. I crept closer to her, thinking maybe the floorboards creaking beneath my feet would get her attention. That didn't work either. So, I poked her in the chest with my broom handle. Nothing happened.

"Hey, miss," I said again. "Unless you plan on helpin' me clean up this mess, you gotta go!"

When she still didn't move, I grabbed her arm to drag her out. Didn't really care that she was a white girl. I'd thrown lots of them out like that, and Miss Tillie always turned a deaf ear to their complaining about it.

But when her arm passed through a shaft of light, you'd have thought ham was frying in there. Her cold, clammy skin started bubbling, blistering, and stanking to high heaven. And she let out a scream that sounded like a cat with its tail caught under a rocker. I let her arm go. The poor thing sank to the floor and tried covering herself from the sunlight with that raggedy dress she had on. With all that screaming and writhing she was doing, I snatched a tablecloth—really, only a bunch of burlap sacks sewn together—and threw it on her. I ain't never seen nobody smoldering before, and the smoke from her body was coming right up through the stitching. I stood there until the screaming died down to a whimper, hoping Miss Tillie and her girls all the way over in the big house were too drunk to have heard the noise.

I had no idea what to do with her. She wasn't one of Miss Tillie's girls. She looked young, about fifteen or sixteen. Not that it was too young to be working at Miss Tillie's whorehouse, what with the world turned upside down after the war. Folks were broke down to the lint in their pockets. Hardly nobody around here had a pot to piss in and, with us slaves taking a much-deserved leave from servitude, probably couldn't even find the pot to piss in on their own. But I couldn't just leave her there, smelling like she was. Bad enough it took forever to get the regular stink out. I didn't need her cooking skin added to the air. So, I dragged her, still wrapped up in that burlap, out of the saloon, across the yard, and into the shack where I lived. Couldn't do nothing about the sun hitting her on the way over. I covered up the two windows in my place and left her there, expecting her to be gone when I got back.

"Sunburn," Martin says, cutting into my story. He's been sitting at his desk, entertaining himself by trying to spit his tobacco juice into the tin cup he's placed an arm's length away. Several brown circles dot the desk, the floor, and his shirt. He rolls his eyes at what sounds like a two-man posse demanding he bring me outside. "She got sunburned, is all. I don't expect you to understand what a sunburn is. You see, if regular folks like me stand in the sun too long—"

"I know what the hell a sunburn is, Martin," I snapped.

To prove it, I stick my good arm out into a sunbeam streaming through the tiny window in my cell. Dust motes float down the beam, disappearing into the shadows. My skin ain't that dark, about the shade of a finely-baked pecan pie. And since I worked in the big house at Miss Tillie's, I spent most of my time indoors. Wasn't until after the war and I was the only one there that I had to work outside. If nothing else, my forearms got a bit dark. Sometimes the back of my neck, too, if I had my hair secured in a kerchief. But the skin only dried and peeled off in white flakes.

"What Simone had wasn't no sunburn," I continue. "Your skin don't burn as soon as the sun hits it, does it? Well, that's what happened to Simone. Happens to all vampires."

"Right. Vampires. She had a sensitivity to the sun, so what? That doesn't mean she was dead. We all got quirks."

"Really?" I swipe the invisible dust from my arm. "You ever recall her bein' outside before last week? Ever see her walkin' 'round in the daytime?"

Martin looks up, as if turning the thought over in his brain. "No. Can't say that I have."

"That's 'cause vampires can't be out in the daytime. The sun cooks 'em in a second, like that." I snap my fingers.

Martin returns his focus to the tobacco in his mouth. The lump in his jaw slowly migrates from one side to the other. With the cup in his hands, he walks to the door and opens it. "Don't you fellas got somewhere to be?"

"About time for you to take a little break now, ain't it, Martin?" one of the men shouts.

Martin says nothing. Just chucks the contents of his spit cup out the door and then ejects the wad from his mouth. After slamming the door, he paces, scratching at his chest. "You're saying the sun killed her?"

"No, not exactly," I say, thankful Martin remembered the constable's threat. "But I ain't done with my story yet. That was jus' the first inklin' that somethin' was off with her. There's more to it."

"Fine." Martin approaches my cell and points to the flask on my cot. I'd only taken a couple of sips from it to ease my mind, then hoped he'd forgotten about it. Guess them fellas outside got under his skin. Bet that's how they strung up the last prisoner in here. I look at the flask then back at Martin whose arm is extended into my cell through the bars. His hand trembles in midair. I hand him the flask, holding on to it longer than necessary. Our eyes lock, and I'm hoping he catches what I'm throwing at him.

He snatches the flask away from me. "Well? Get on with it."

Well, after hours of cleaning the saloon and the big house, and then cooking what little supper I could find for Miss Tillie and her girls, I fell onto my mattress dead tired, thankful I could sleep the whole night without being disturbed. The effects of my tea had long since worn off.

My body ached worse as the day wore on, and the tickle in my throat had grown to a constant scratchiness. I couldn't wait to lie down. The cords of rope holding up my mattress groaned and squeaked beneath me. Didn't even bother to blow out the lantern I'd used to light my way here in the dark. I'd forgotten all about the smoking girl until I felt something nibbling on my big toe. It was her sucking on it like it was a chicken bone.

"Jus' what the hell you think you doin'?" I asked, kicking her off me.

"Hungry," was all she said from the foot of the bed. Her face was still horribly scarred from the sunlight. The drops of my toe blood on her lips only made her appear paler than before.

"What's that gotta do with my toe? I look like food to you?"

"Yes," she said. "I need—"

"To leave." I wrapped a piece of cloth around my now-throbbing big toe and stood to throw her out again. "This what I get for helpin' you? Should've left you smokin' in the saloon!"

"But you didn't," she said with an accent I'd never heard before. "You weren't afraid of me."

I looked her up and down. She was shorter than me and probably didn't weigh more than a sack of potatoes. Looked more poorly than folks around here did after Sherman left. Worse than me even, and I'd been wearing the same calico dress with the frayed sleeves and tiny moth holes since Christmas. "Worse things around here than you. Where were you when I came home anyway?"

"Under the bed."

"Why?"

"The sun. It hurts my skin. I need . . . food, to make me better."

"Don't we all," I said. I hobbled over to the window and moved the covering aside. "Moonlight won't hurt you, will it? If you wanna eat, we gotta go to the big house. After that, you leave."

Simone nodded and followed me out. Didn't have to worry about running into Miss Tillie. By this time of night, she'd be sitting on the bar, crowing to a bunch of fellas too drunk to care that she couldn't carry a tune. All the whores would be holed up in their rooms, making enough noise to wake the dead. And with the way Simone was looking, wasn't no man about to pay any amount of money to be with her. But we walked around back to the kitchen anyway.

"Look out for a mean, redheaded woman named Ginny," I told Simone while I searched the pantry.

"You don't like her?" Simone asked.

"I stay clear of her, is what I do. She thinks colored folks should still be in chains. Besides . . ." I turned with an apple in my hand to find Simone gone. Damn girl must've gotten curious and took a tour around the house. I wasn't about to follow her. Though the regulars knew who I was, these were desperate times, and I didn't wanna catch the eye of someone with a hankering for chocolate, if you know what I mean.

Some yelling and a high-pitched scream outside got my attention. Though such noises weren't unusual in this place, there was never much ruckus *outside* the house. I got to thinking maybe that smoldering girl done found herself in some trouble. With the apple in the pocket of my dress and a lantern in my hand, I went outside and saw two black blobs wrestling in the darkness. The closer I got, I found it was Louis, a regular to the saloon, tussling on the ground with Simone. Now Louis wasn't one to visit the whorehouse; he usually got so drunk he could barely keep his head up, let alone any other part of his body. Half the time, we found him laid out in the yard the next morning. That smoldering girl must've said or done something real stupid to upset a drunk like him. But as I held the lantern out in front of me, I saw Simone straddling him. Looked like she was kissing him on his neck.

"Well, I'll be," I said. With her skin all burned like that, I thought the girl would've been in too much pain to wanna mess around with some man. And Louis didn't seem to mind, laying there with his arms spread out to his sides and one of his legs twitching. The girl must've heard me coming because, all of a sudden, she lifted her head, jumped off Louis, and dashed into the darkness.

"Now, you know you ain't s'posed to be doin' that stuff out here," I said, approaching Louis. Whatever that girl did to him must've been real good, because he was still laid out, moaning and twitching. "She ain't even one of Miss Tillie's girls." I stepped closer until I was damn near on top of him. "Mr. Louis?"

Even in the dark, I could tell there was a hole about the size of my fist in his neck. The ground around his head was moist from the blood pouring out of the wound. The moaning changed to a gurgling sound from deep in his chest. Though his eyes seemed to be looking at something in the distance, he must've noticed I was there. He stretched his arm out to me before his body shut down. His arm dropped, head lolled off to the side, and his leg finally stopped moving. I stared off toward the darkness where the girl had run off, then shook the notion from my head. Louis must've gotten bit by a coyote or something and that smoldering girl must've been trying to help him. I mean, what other explanation could there be?

I raised my lantern and searched the darkness. Maybe that wasn't even the girl I saw hovering over him. Didn't have time to ponder that one. If it had been a coyote, I knew a chunk of neck wouldn't satisfy it. I listened for growling, howling, footfalls coming toward me. Nothing. Just chirps and croaks from animals that couldn't do the sort of damage I saw on Louis.

A coughing fit took over. I was in no shape to tarry long in the darkness with that dead body. Wasn't nothing I could do for Louis nohow. And I wasn't about to get caught with a dead white man at my feet. When I got back to my shack, I found Simone sitting on my bed, smiling at me like I was an old friend come to call. Smooth alabaster skin with a hint of rose underneath had replaced the slick, red burn patches on her face and arms. A swath of bright red, glistening like it was still wet, stained the front of her dress all the way down to the hem. A flicker from my lantern played across her face, like something feral and demented, and for a second, she looked like a wild animal about to pounce. But then the shadow fell and she was just a girl. My eyes hadn't played tricks on me; she had been out there. And of course, she'd have Louis's blood on her; she was out there helping him after all. Was probably trying to bandage the wound or something. Except I didn't notice any strips of fabric missing from that nasty frock she had on.

I pointed a finger at her ruined dress.

Simone closed her eyes. "The man outside," she said. A smile teased at the lips she was tracing with her forefinger.

"Yeah," I said, remembering the screaming I'd heard earlier. "You see what happened?"

Simone released a smile that curled all the way up to her ears. "A late supper."

"What's that gotta do with Louis?" I asked with a raised eyebrow and a hand on the door handle. "Thought I saw you out there. What happened?"

"I savored him." She licked clean her red-stained fingers. Then she flashed a smile that would've made the boogeyman shit himself. "I never seem to tire of Irish fare."

I wasn't quite sure what she meant by all them fancy words, but I gathered it had something to do with her acting like she'd just eaten a greasy piece of chicken. That, and the blood splattered all over her.

Then Simone pointed at the apple I still had in my hand. "Is that for me?"

I glanced at the forgotten fruit and lobbed it over to her so she wouldn't come near me. Ain't like the shack was that big nohow. She could've reached out and grabbed it if she wanted to. The girl caught the apple in midair with one hand and then took a bite. Lemme tell you: I ain't never seen nobody eat an apple like that! Running her tongue down the fruit to the spot she'd chosen, then letting her lips slide over the skin as she bit down. All done real slow like.

Faint brightness at the window caught my attention. What had been a pitch-black sky faded to a purple rose. Simone sat there on the bed, eating that apple, core and all. Then she stood and sauntered over to me. Must've seen the look on my face because she stopped, took a step back, and looked down at her clothes.

"Oh! Is this bothering you?"

I wanted to tell her no, that my brain was still trying to reckon what had happened to Louis. Or maybe this sickness was getting worse. Instead, she went to pulling the soiled fabric over her head.

I stopped her with a hand on her chilled arm. "Wait! I don't need to be seein' all your goodies." I scurried over to a small wooden box that contained the only other stitch of clothing I had: my yearly hand-me-down from Miss Tillie. I kept my distance and tossed the rumpled fabric to her. "Put that on. You can wash in that bucket over there."

She stared at the dress in her hands for a long time, fingering the material. Wasn't like it was some gown Miss Tillie would've worn to a ball. Simply a brown short-sleeved cotton thing I was grateful to have with lace tatted on the sleeves, hem, and around the high collar. Without the petticoat underneath, it dragged on the ground like a death shroud. I wasn't sure if Simone found the gift beneath her. Dirty as it was, I could still tell what she had on was once something she could've worn to a cotillion, even if the underskirts and petticoat had long since lost their fluff.

"Really?" she finally said.

"What? Ain't nobody ever gave you nothin' before?"

"Not since I became . . ." She looked up at me with a different face, one that recalled a past tragedy she'd probably carried with her from wherever she'd come from. This thing, whoever or whatever she was, was now merely some innocent girl, softened by my simple gesture.

"Became what?" I ventured to ask.

"Well," Simone went to biting on the nail of her pointer finger while musing over my question. "First, you should know that I'm not like normal people."

"That part I got."

"What I did to that man . . ."

I craned my neck toward her and raised an eyebrow. Did I just hear her right? I figured a fever must be coming on, but I asked anyway. "What you did to Mr. Louis?"

"Didn't you hear what I said? I ate him." She said it like I'd asked her what she'd planned on doing with that apple I'd given her. "That's what I am. That's what I do." She took a step closer to me. "I'm not like you," she said as if she were talking to the wind. "Blood is all I think about. I need it like you need food or water or air."

I'd seen the Yankees do some right terrible stuff during the war. Seen what bullets and cannons can do to the body. But I'd never known one person to do what Simone claimed to have done to Louis with her bare hands.

I damn near threw up I laughed so hard. "You almost had me there," I said, followed by another coughing fit and pounding at my temples. "Thank you for that. I ain't had a good laugh in a while."

"You don't believe me?"

I opened the door. "Girl, I ain't got time for this. Sun's 'bout to come up and I ain't had a wink of sleep. Pick a shack and stay there if you want, but you ain't stayin' in here."

When the girl didn't move, I pushed her out and shut the door. Not that I believed all that foolishness she was spouting. I had a fever coming on that had my ears hearing stuff that wasn't true. All the same, I figured it wouldn't hurt to place the table up against the door before settling down for some shut-eye.

THREE

Between the coughing and keeping one eye on the door, I barely got a wink of sleep. Before I knew it, the sun had come up. Now my body ached all over. My head felt like it was full of cotton. I'd used all the sweet gum leaves yesterday, so I needed to get more if I planned on making it past lunch. I was winded by the time I reached the main road. Bent over and panting out painful breaths clogged with sickness, I turned an eye toward the freedom road. No time for wishing. I needed a potion, quick. In addition to the leaves, I grabbed a pocketful of monkey balls, the round and spiked fruit of the sweet gum tree that littered the ground, and a chunk of that white skin underneath the bark. With all the rotgut Miss Tillie was brewing, I ought to be able to make me a tincture to knock this sickness right out of me.

It took a while before I roused the whores, mostly because I needed to get my tea made first, and also because I stopped to watch two men load poor old dead Louis onto a wheelbarrow. Somehow, I'd managed to forget all about him. As I walked past, the men, both musicians at the saloon, nodded in my direction.

"Got a dead body out here, Vinny," Billy, the saloon banjo player, said, as if I hadn't noticed the pale skin, blackened fingertips, and a faint stench of rot.

"Old Tillie's not gonna be too happy about that," said the piano player as he laid a horse blanket over Louis. "You see anything last night, Vinny?"

I shook my head and averted my eyes. While I recognized these men, it was common practice not to invite any additional conversation from white folks. Some don't care if you talk to them or not. Some only want you speaking when spoken to. Problem was, you never knew which was which, even with the same person. Billy was one of those people, especially after Miss Tillie's rotgut got in him.

"What you think, Vinny?" Billy asked.

"Coyote, maybe?" I ventured.

"Why would a coyote just chew at his throat?" Billy asked. He counted to three and they lifted Louis onto the wheelbarrow.

"Then what do you think could have done that?" the piano player asked.

"Maybe it was one of Miss Tillie's girls," I said after coughing into my hand.

The two men looked at each other, then back at me.

A cloud settled over Billy's face as he glared at me. "What did you just say?"

Did I say that out loud? Lord, I must be sicker than I thought. I lowered my gaze and said, "Nothin', Mr. Billy."

He spat on the ground, the glob of spittle landing right at my feet. He eyed me for a long second and then turned back to the piano player, mumbling something about me talking out of turn. Then he added with a chuckle, "Maybe it was one of Tillie's girls."

Didn't I just say that? I rolled my eyes and backed away toward the big house, slowly, in case Billy wasn't really giving me permission to leave.

"Yeah, I guess if you get one of them mad enough, they could tear your throat out!" Billy wiped his hands on his trousers. "Knowing Louis, he probably pissed somebody off." He glanced at the body and then spit right in its face.

The piano player furrowed his brow. "Damn, Billy! What you spit on him for?"

"He was always eyeing Ginny," Billy said.

"Ginny the whore? You're mad 'cause he was eyeing a whore?" The piano player snorted through his nose and shook his head.

"Still, she was my girl."

The piano player tossed his head back and laughed. "For the right price, she was everybody's girl, you dumb sumbitch! Don't mean you gotta spit on him."

"What's it to you?" Billy said. "He's dead. They're gonna dump him in a hole anyway. Got no kinfolk around, far as I know."

The two men hauled the body away, making more ridiculous guesses as to who the culprit might be. I hurried into the kitchen to make my tea and get my bearings. But then I found out all the rations were gone. And with Miss Tillie unwilling to even get out of bed, it was up to me to hitch the horse up to the wagon and ride to town to get them. I'd only gone to get rations by myself once, and let me tell you, it wasn't no picnic. Forget that I was sick as a dog riding out there today. Soon as I took my place at the end of the line (and kept going to the end whenever a new person showed up) dozens of eyes stared me down with scowls on their faces. Either they were hungry for food or retribution for being on the losing end of the war. Folks who'd known me for years spit and hissed at me like I'd personally destroyed their lives.

As I handed the military man the paper signed by Miss Tillie indicating how much food she needed, I made sure to cough as loud as I could all over everybody so they would stay as far away from me as possible. The food was packaged in round tins or wrapped in butcher paper. I knew riding back could be even worse, so I directed them to place all of it in this long box kept in the back of the wagon. Funny how this measly food was placed in something that looked like a coffin, given how it was hardly enough to live on.

With the rations in the box, I let the reins go slack in my hands and the horse moseyed on back down the road toward Miss Tillie's. Piles of rubble lined the wide dirt road where two- and three-story brick buildings used to be, the businesses they housed long gone. Then I tightened the reins and my head swiveled in the opposite direction. I had food, enough to last one woman for what, a couple of weeks? By the time Miss Tillie realized I wasn't coming back I'd be . . . where? I had no idea. Wasn't nothing waiting on me back at the plantation but the same work I'd been doing my whole life for a bunch of people who only noticed me when they needed something. A click of my tongue and a tug of the reins, and I could be halfway through the county by nightfall . . .

Something hard struck the side of my head that sent sparks of lightning in front of my eyes. Before I could turn to see what it was, I heard, "Move that wagon out the road, nigger!" Another knot of something struck my shoulder. As I shrank to protect myself, I saw a gathering of men and women with rocks and clumps of dirt clutched in their hands and standing by a pile of rubble about as high as I was sitting in this wagon. Beside me was a man on his own horse, an old friend of Miss Tillie's husband and the one I presumed was doing all the yelling. Why he didn't just ride around me instead of hollering like he didn't know me, I couldn't tell you.

"Get on outta here!" a shriveled old woman in a moth-eaten black dress growled. Whatever she had in her hand came flying at me.

I slapped the reins of that horse and hightailed it outta there before the next round of rocks knocked me to the ground. If this was what awaited me with people I knew, what would a town of strangers offer?

When I finally got back, my neck was sore from checking for any foolishness that might befall me. Of course, now I was way behind on my chores. Didn't have enough time to make my tea, so I was moving slower than usual. Wasn't even done cleaning the saloon by the time folks started showing up. Billy the banjo player and the fiddler began their racket, while Miss Tillie served her potions from behind an overturned horse trough she used as a bar. Even with everybody there, she still expected me to clean up. For what? Today's stains just covered up whatever was left from last night. And nobody seemed to mind that the floors weren't swept. All they cared about was the pint of poison filling their guts to forget their current circumstances.

And nobody but me seemed to notice the only other female in the place: the smoldering girl who stood off in the shadows like a statue, except this time instead of sunken cheeks and oozing blisters, her white-as-a-sheet skin seemed to glow. Her hair was still a mess, but at least she'd changed out of them bloody clothes she had on last night.

I swept my way over to her. After coughing from the dust or maybe just moving the broom around, I asked, "Your mama know you here?"

"My mother is dead," she said.

"Sorry to hear that. Your daddy then?"

"He's probably dead by now, too." She hadn't looked at me yet. Her eyes stayed on the rowdy group of men. I don't even think she blinked.

"So, what you doin' here? Lookin' for a job?"

"Looking at the menu."

"Menu?"

"Yes. I believe the banjo player is Scottish. A couple of Norwegians in the corner there. I'm not quite sure what I'm in the mood for tonight."

I coughed again. "Um, alls we got here is gin, whiskey, and some mess brewed from potatoes."

The girl finally looked at me and turned up her nose. "Are you sick? You look sick."

"I'm alright," I said. This time I tried to hide my cough in my sleeve. I took long, slow breaths to keep the next fit away. The longer the girl spoke, the longer I could stay still and catch my breath. "Must be all this stink makin' me sick."

She returned my weak smile. "You're funny. What's your name, funny lady?"

"Lavinia."

"Lavinia. That's pretty." She nodded her head. "It fits you."

I let the broom go lax in my hands. Ain't nobody ever said anything about me was pretty. Never thought it myself. Never even bothered with any of the looking glasses Miss Tillie's old vain behind had all over the house. And it was the first time I heard someone use my proper name. Almost shocked me when she repeated it.

"I'm Simone Arceneau of Montreal," she said, making her words sound like her tongue was wrestling with itself in her mouth. "Now, if you excuse me, I think I've made my choice."

Now, remember how small I told you these slave shacks were? Well, in two seconds, Simone had Billy the banjo player's wrist in her mouth. The man jumped up, but Simone had latched on like a hungry babe to its mother's teat. With all the noise in there, nobody seemed to notice the banjo player wasn't playing no more. I watched Simone swinging from the man's arm as he tried to shake her loose. When Billy finally got her off him, he started pounding her face with his fist. Simone snapped back like a turtle trying to catch the blows. Now, everybody jumped into action: shouting, holding back Billy and Simone (except she tried flailing at whoever was touching her at the moment.) With chairs and curse words flying every whichaway, Miss Tillie finally decided to step in. Did no good since the place was too small, the noise was too loud, and she was too drunk. Her slurred words disappeared into the air.

I wasn't gonna let Billy beat on the girl like that. I did the only thing I knew would catch everybody's attention: tipped over a whole barrel of beer. The room froze with chairs, tables, and bottles still in midair. All eyes watched that bubbly brown liquid disappear through the cracks in the floorboards. In the sudden quiet, I coughed out, "Alright now, Mr. Billy. That's enough."

He lowered the chair in his hands. He grabbed his bleeding wrist as if it finally dawned on him that a whole chunk of it was missing. Then he motioned toward Simone with his head. "Did you see what she did? She bit me!"

I looked at Simone. I'd watched Billy hit her about a dozen times but wasn't no bruising or bleeding or nothing anywhere on her. Only blood I saw was the smear on her mouth from the bite. I thought back to Mr. Louis's wound from the other night. That fool girl was telling the truth about eating people?

A pair of arms held Simone as she raged. I touched her shoulder and shushed her like a baby until she complied.

"You know her?" Miss Tillie asked, her brow all crinkled with doubt.

I searched the crowd. "Do I know her?"

"That's what I said." Miss Tillie stumbled toward me with her hands on her hips.

"Well, I . . . She was here the other day, but I don't *know* her."

"You called her by name."

"She jus' told me—" I bent over coughing again, but Miss Tillie grabbed me by my ear, yanking me up.

"You bring some hussy in here to destroy my business?" she growled in my stinging ear. "Why would you do this to me, Vinny? Why? After everything I do to keep a roof over our heads. You want us all thrown out on the street with nothing?!" She was screeching and sobbing now. Somebody pulled her away from me.

I cleared my throat and rubbed my ear. Anger, and probably a bit of fever by now, kept my eyes to the floor. "I'll take care of this, Miss Tillie," I said, holding my ear. "Never you worry. I'll take care of this." I pushed Simone by the shoulder toward the door and led her out.

When we got a ways from the saloon, I fell to my knees, letting this mighty cough wrack every bone in my body. I thought a lung was about to spill out. By the time I caught my breath, I felt a hand gently patting my back.

"I guess I made quite the scene back there," Simone said. "Thank you for not making it worse."

"You think?" I said with a roll of my eyes. Blood rushed to my head, sending me to the ground on my side.

"You're burning up, Lavinia." She placed an icy hand under my elbow and lifted me up.

Weak as I was, I let her lead me back to my shack.

"Good thing I was here," Simone said as she goaded me along. "Those awful people would have left you out here all night."

She was right. I imagined Miss Tillie out here the next morning, wondering why my dead body wasn't up fixing her breakfast. Then a thought struck me. I stopped my shuffling and pushed myself away from her cold body. "What you helpin' me for?"

"You're sick."

"Don't explain why *you* are helping *me*." I hoped she got what I was throwing at her without me having to explain. The fact that she was touching me at all was surprising enough.

"Would you rather I left you there?" she asked.

"No, but . . ."

"I guess it would seem strange to you. But I'm not like *those* people. Papa always complained about them: plantation owners who think they can rule over everyone because they have money. Even though he was a great chef—not a cook, mind you, a chef—they still treated us like we were beneath them." Simone spit out her disdain, then wrapped her cold arm around my waist, and urged me forward. "I won't give them the satisfaction of treating us that way."

I snorted out a soft laugh that made me cough even harder. Only company Miss Tillie and her husband ever took were rich landowners like them who never seemed to do anything other than sit around drinking, planning parties, and talking about all the money us slaves were making for them with our labors. I never had a notion that there were white folks not like that.

My shack was only a few yards from the saloon, but it took forever to get there. Probably because I was shuffling along and leaning on Simone's little self for support. I must've been getting sicker by the minute because a chill shook my bones whenever my body touched hers. And I thought I smelled a bit of rot coming from her skin.

"You know how to . . . make tinctures?" I asked when I finally fell upon my bed, shivering like a fool. My chest hurt with every breath. "I got . . . I got the stuff here . . ." I reached into my pocket and pulled out the leaves and monkey balls I never had a chance to use.

Simone sat on the bed next to me. She pulled my threadbare blanket up to my neck. When she took my tincture ingredients from me, her hand touched mine. It was ice-cold. You know what they say: cold hands, warm heart. But how her palm was as cold as it was in the middle of a Georgia spring, I couldn't tell you then.

"I appreciate you stepping in back there, but you didn't have to. That man couldn't hurt me."

"You don't even look like you been in a fight."

Simone shrugged. "I'm used to it by now. Always happens. That's why I can never get a proper feeding in."

"Right, 'cause you eat people." I pursed my lips and tried sitting up, but only managed to fall back on my pillow, panting.

"Count yourself lucky that you've never experienced the kind of hunger I do." She lowered her voice to a whisper. "You know when your monthly visitor comes, and you get those awful, throbbing pains in your legs and right under your stomach?"

My lip curled. What woman didn't feel the effects of the curse in some form or fashion? Before Miss Tillie's monthly bleed dried up, she'd be balled up in her room for days, crying for the good Lord to put her outta her misery. She'd have me up there changing her soiled rags and rubbing on her belly with steaming towels I'd heat in a large black pot of water kept in a burning fireplace. Then I'd put a few drops of some clear tincture on her tongue that finally knocked her out for a little while. What she didn't know was that I'd kept that tincture for my own pains once I saw how well it worked for her. What she'd been getting was only drops of watered-down gin, but I don't think her brain knew the difference. Still worked.

"Now imagine feeling that all over," Simone continued. "Every part of your body pulsing in hot pain, from your scalp to your toenails. That's what it's like for me when I go too long without blood. I once went a whole month without feeding after getting chased out of a soldiers' camp. The pain drove me to the point of insanity."

I snuggled in and closed my eyes. "Ain't no wonder you got your head busted tonight if that's what you call eatin'. You gon' get yo'self killed one of these days, girl."

"Maybe you could help."

I wanted to laugh, but a cough beat me to it.

She laid a cold hand on mine. "I'm serious."

"Look, if you need food, you could work 'round here. I could use an extra hand, 'specially if I keep feelin' like this." I tossed the blanket from me and willed my aching body to sit up. Had to take a breath after that.

"Where are you going?" Simone asked as she pushed me back down.

I was so tired, I didn't even fight back. "Well, if you ain't gon' make me a tincture, I gotta do it myself. Plus, I need to make things right with old Miss Tillie for what you did at the saloon."

Simone scrunched her face up in confusion. "After the way she talked to you back there? In front of all those people?" She shivered like a cold wind had crept up on her. "We don't have to put up with that." Simone rose from the bed. "We could go anywhere!"

"Who is 'we'?"

"Me and you! If you helped me get my . . . food . . . you'll never have to worry about a Miss Tillie or anybody treating you awful ever again."

"How's that?"

Simone smiled, and for the first time, I noticed her eyeteeth were long like a wolf's. Long and sharp enough to cut through somebody's neck or wrist.

"There's a whole world out there. You've probably never gone as far as this plantation, have you?"

"No." I shifted my shoulders around in the bed.

She twirled around, arms stretched wide. "I've been everywhere. I'm from Montreal, you know, up in Canada. I've visited my aunt's château in France. I've been all up and down the Eastern Seaboard here in America. There's so much to see! You tell me where you want to go, and I'll get us there. No problem."

"And get myself lynched out there?"

A mischievous grin spread on her face as if a naughty secret lay right on the tip of her tongue. "I wouldn't let them live long enough to lynch you. Think about it."

I recalled those nasty folks at the ration point, attacking me when I ain't said word one to them. Not that I would've anyway. A smile tugged at the corner of my mouth as my mind inserted Simone into the scene. The slightest signal from me, a tilt of my head or a whistle from my lips, summons her from my wagon, and her chewing on every one of their throats. Like she did with Louis and Billy. Then I'd ride back to Miss Tillie's and dare that two-faced witch to grab my ear again. I'd never heard of people doing what I'd seen Simone do. But she did it. And maybe, just maybe, a creature like her was what I needed to get out of the South in one piece.

She readied herself to leave until I told her the sun was coming up.

Best wait until later, I said. From beneath the bed, she happily pulled those pieces of burlap I'd dragged her in and seated herself back on the side of my bed. Went on and on about all the places she'd been and all the girls back in Montreal she hated because they'd been mean to her in some form or fashion. Something about her father owning a restaurant, too, I think.

I don't remember much about her ramblings then. What I do remember was Simone tearing out Miss Tillie's throat over and over again in my dreams.

FOUR

Been a long time since I had a witches' ride: when you're half awake and half asleep listening to what you think is happening around you, but you can't move. Can't even open your eyes to know if what're experiencing is real. Your mind starts filling in the missing pieces, painting a picture so vivid, you can't tell if it really happened or not. I used to have them a lot when I was child. A waking nightmare I called them because the sounds I thought I heard were never pleasant. This time though, I just knew Simone was eating somebody right there next to me. A lot of slurping and growling like a rabid dog. Though I couldn't see her, I recognized Ginny's voice begging for her life. Then I felt someone crawling on the bed, first at the foot, then inching up until they were crouched over me.

Simone.

Her cold body chilled me to my bones, and her horrid breath made the hairs in my nose curl. And the rot. Like something had crawled into the walls and died. Simone sniffed all around my face, in each ear. Then she licked my neck—even her tongue was ice-cold.

"I've never had one of your kind before," she whispered in my ear. "What flavors will your blood unleash on my tongue? Will I experience a spice pallet from the dark continent, or the garbage your German mistress feeds you?" She sniffed again, then licked the tip of my nose.

"Never fear, my chocolate savior. I shall not feed on you . . . yet." Then she kissed my nose and slunk away into the darkness.

I awoke with a start. Sunlight cut a large swath across the shack, cluing me to the fact that I'd slept too long. I grabbed the blanket and pulled it up to my chin; my body shook. Must be from all that talk about Simone eating people. And Louis's dead body. And Billy's missing wrist. Crazy girl done got in my head.

A fever dream. That's all it was.

Except the rot still lingered in the air and it was starting to churn my stomach.

Slowly, I coaxed my aching body to sit up and I slid my legs over the side of the bed. The handful of monkey balls I'd shown to Simone the night before tumbled to the floor. I groaned. Leaning over would only make my head hurt worse. But I needed the seeds hidden inside the balls to make a stronger tea. With the way I was feeling, I'd probably eat them raw. On my hands and knees, I felt under the bed for the stray monkey balls and my hand swept across something wet and sticky and hard. I drew my hand back and saw it was smeared red. I sniffed my palm. The metallic scent of blood was unmistakable. Where on earth did this come from? I lowered myself to peer beneath the bed and saw a thin white arm. I sat up and then skittered as fast as I could to the other side of the shack. The hairs on the back of my neck perked up. With the side of the burlap-covered body in view, I realized it was Simone. That horrible nightmare I had last night done showed up under my damn bed.

After my initial fear calmed down, I crawled back over to the bed and shook her.

"Simone?"

She didn't move. Wasn't even making a sound. I tried shaking her and calling her name again, but still nothing. Either she was the hardest sleeper I'd ever met, or something awful done happened to her.

I summoned as much strength as I could and pulled her halfway out from under the bed by the arm. She still didn't move. Didn't even open her eyes. I figured the blood on my hand came from what was smeared on the front of her frock. Fresh blood. And a lot more than before. I checked myself, leaving red palm prints all over me. Despite what I thought I heard on my witches' ride, she hadn't taken a bite outta me. When I leaned over her, I smelled something wafting from her still body, a thick stink of meat that had gone bad. Before I could get my bearings to figure out what the heck happened, someone busted through the door.

Miss Tillie appeared with the constable and a couple of other whorehouse regulars. "There she is," she said, pointing at me still on the floor with Simone lying next to me. Billy and another man walked inside and dragged me to my feet.

The constable grabbed my hand and examined my bloody palm. "You killed Louis, too, didn't you?" the constable asked.

"What . . . I . . ." I couldn't catch my breath fast enough to answer. If the room stopped spinning and those men quit yanking me around, I might be able to say something.

"Then what's this?" He pointed at Simone.

"I don't know what happened, sir. I found her like that."

Billy grabbed me from behind the neck and shook me. "Then where'd all that blood come from?"

"It was on her! I only touched her to see—"

"Maybe you're the one bleeding," the constable said. He bent down and yanked up my skirts. Then he shoved his hand between my legs, his nails scraping my thighs. I looked to Miss Tillie, but she simply turned her head away. Tears welled in my eyes, but I blinked them back. I'd be damned if I let them see me cry.

When he was done with his examination, the constable, rubbing his probing fingers together, looked at me and smiled. "I guess not."

"This is the girl who killed Ginny," Miss Tillie finally said.

I frowned. "She killed Ginny? You saw her?"

Billy shook me again. "That's the bitch who bit me!"

"What's she doing in here with you?" The constable's voice thundered right in my face, making my headache worse.

"She brought me back here," I said. "Must've stayed here the whole night."

The constable bent down and touched Simone's neck and then pressed two of his fingers against her wrist. "This gal's ice-cold," the constable said. "She's dead." He turned to Miss Tillie. "You sure this is the one that killed Ginny? She couldn't be this cold that fast."

"I just saw her!" Miss Tillie said, tapping the side of Simone's head with the toe of her boot. Then she turned to me. "What did you do to her?"

This witches' ride was getting crazier by the minute. All these people in my dream . . . my head was so heavy . . . a stack of bricks piled on my shoulders. I couldn't tell if the world was spinning or if my head was wobbling around on my neck. If I could just rest my eyes for a moment . . .

Damn this pneumonia! When I came to, I was sitting in the town jail.

FIVE

"Aha!" Martin says, jumping to his feet. "So, this isn't the first time you've been accused of murder!"

I narrow my eyes at him. "Bein' accused and actually doin' it are two different things. And that don't mean I killed Simone. If I had any ill will toward her, don't you think I would've turned her in then?"

"Why didn't you?"

I shrug my shoulders. "What did it matter? They thought she was dead. Who else was they gonna blame but me? Besides, they wouldn't have believed me anyway. At that point, even I couldn't imagine that itty-bitty thing taking down a woman who looked more like she should be choppin' wood, instead of screwin' it. Guess I was too sick for any of it to make sense then, like how she'd cured herself so fast or didn't look like death no more after that attack on Louis. Why her eyeteeth were long like a wolf's. All I knew was Simone wasn't your average white person, not your average person at all, for that matter. But I wasn't 'til that night in the jail that I really knew what she was."

"Well, I know what I am," Martin says, scratching at his stomach. "About to burst. Gotta make water."

"Wait!" I yell, grasping the cell bars. "You can't leave. Constable says you gotta stay here."

"Constable said to make sure nothing happens to you. Didn't say I couldn't take a piss."

"You comin' back, ain'tcha?" I purse my lips together and watch him leave with the damn flask.

We'd been talking so much, that for the first time, I notice the quiet. I climb onto the mattress in my cell and peer out the barred window. Nothing there but the whisper of the wind blowing through the prairie grass and the faint whistle of a train. Too bad it's not the one taking me away. But at least nobody's looking to get in . . . for now. Might as well relieve myself while I have privacy.

In the corner of my cell is a bucket of water that looks like it's been in here longer than I've been alive. The other bucket is empty, but one whiff tells me what once was inside. I ready to lift my skirts when the door to the jailhouse opens.

"That was quick, Martin." I groan but figure I can hold it for a minute.

Instead, I hear German-accented shouting. I pause with the hem of my skirts still bunched in my hands. I'm clutching the fabric so tight my wound starts bleeding again. The pain in my arm throbs in time to my panicked heartbeat. I look toward my cot. They'd see me if I slid under there. As quietly as I can, I lower my skirts and shrink back into the corner, as if I could hide myself in this tiny place.

"If Martin is anything," one of the men says, "he's predictable."

I can see them now, scanning the other jail cell. There must be ten of them here, and the rope in their hands confirms they're not here for visiting hours.

The youngest looking one of the group laughs. "Told you he'd be heading to the outhouse. The drink runs through him like water."

"There she is!" A man with a thick, black mustache that curls on the ends stands in front of my cell. He wasn't one of the men who ever came calling on Simone, not quite genteel enough for her company, but I recognize him from the local saloon. A smile causes his black eyes to disappear into the folds of his ruddy wrinkles, like his whole face was sucking on a lemon. He pulls on the bars then orders his companions to search for the keys.

"Looking for these?" Martin returns and tosses the keys onto the desk.

The younger man goes for the keys, but Martin covers them with his hand. "Constable'll be by any minute. He expects her to be in one piece when he gets back."

"She'll be in one piece," Mustache Man says.

"And alive," Martin adds.

"What's it to him if she's dead or alive?" another man asks.

Martin shrugs. "That's what he said. He was awfully hot about the fella who got strung up out there the last time."

"Town's calling for her head," Mustache Man says.

"She says she's innocent," Martin shrugs again. "Been in here spinning a yarn all about it."

"'Spinning a yarn'? This ain't the time for tales, you drunk idiot!"

Martin whips that pistol out of his holster and points it directly at Mustache Man's face. "What'd you just call me?"

Mustache Man raises his arms and whole crowd takes a step back toward the door. "What's with you?"

"Guess we got here too soon," the younger man says. "Drink ain't had time to do its thing."

A sprinkling of laughter adds to the thickness in the jail. Martin's face falls for a second time. But then he straightens his shooting arm and lifts his chin. "Until the constable gets back, I'm the law in this place, understand? Now, you all get!"

The men laugh louder as Martin's voice cracks. The hope I had of staying alive long enough to plead my case to a judge quickly fades.

Mustache Man simply pushes the barrel of the pistol from his face. "That quiver in your arm tells me you're gonna need some of your liquid medication real soon." He smiles and returns his companions' agreement with nods. "Give it a minute, boys. We'll get justice for Miss Simone before the day is over." Justice for Simone? Sure, as though she would have given him a second glance.

Mustache eyes Martin coldly for a second, then motions for his men to follow him outside. Once the posse clears the jail, Martin shoves his pistol back into the holster. I try to take in a gulp of air. I don't even think I was breathing that whole time. When Martin tossed them keys on the desk, I just knew he was gonna let them at me. But surprisingly, he plops down onto his chair with a burst of swear words from his mouth. Guess those fells rattled him as much as they rattled me.

"How'd you hurt your arm anyway?" Martin asks, his eyes narrowing.

"You don't want to know," I say, thinking about how the flash of silver met my flesh and hoping that Martin is too disinterested—or drunk—to press. Sure enough, what does Martin do? The very thing those fools expected: drink away his anger. Problem is, for some folks, alcohol fuels the rage instead of tempering it. I knew Martin, but not well enough to know if that flask in his hands is a good or bad thing.

He smacks his lips after draining whatever was left, leans his chair back and, as if all that other stuff didn't just happen says, "Finding Miss Arceneau under the bed, you must've thought your chance at leaving Georgia went out the window."

"I did," I say slowly, playing along with Martin's desire to forget the confrontation. Mentally, I shrug it off. He did just save me from a mob. "And after Miss Tillie thinkin' I had somethin' to do with Louis and Ginny, I figured I was as good as dead in that jail. But then Simone showed up."

"And this supposed killing machine busted you out," Martin says.

"That she did."

He snorts and shakes his head. "And I bet you think she's gonna rise from the grave and bust you out now. Come on, tell me. What should I expect to happen if she waltzes in here now?"

SIX

A few rays of moonlight bled into my cell through the bars on the window. Wasn't a soul in the jail, not even the constable. Had me laid up on some wooden bench in the darkness with a threadbare blanket. But even that did nothing to keep my teeth from chattering and my body shaking like a leaf in the wind. Sounded like rocks rattling around in my chest when I breathed. Hurt so much I didn't even want to breathe, or wheeze, which was what I was really doing. I suppose they'd be carrying a pine box out of here by morning. Damn this pneumonia. Damn my life. I cursed myself for not leaving when I had the chance. Cursed myself for letting that foolish girl get me mixed up in a murder.

I could smell death coming on me. Death and fresh Georgia clay. The wind whistled outside, sending shadows of gnarled, leafless tree branches against my cell wall. The world waving goodbye to me. A dark shadow moved closer, and my heart sank. Thought God would've sent an angel for my soul after everything I'd been through. Old Scratch had come instead. The last few days had sho' nuff been a nightmare if I ever had one.

"C'mon," I managed to rasp out. "C'mon and gimme my due."

Then I heard a female voice, soft but insistent, whisper, "I'm so sorry!"

Simone emerged from the shadows and stood within a shaft of

moonlight. She knelt beside me, looking healthier than I'd ever seen her before. Her pale, youthful face scrunched up in confusion.

I reached for her, but my arm fell to the side, hanging off the wooden bench. Now, this time I knew I wasn't asleep, but that still didn't explain how this girl was dead and had come back to life.

"What hap . . . ?" If only I could finish a sentence without coughing and gasping for air.

"I'm so sorry they put you in here! When I go to sleep—well, I wouldn't call what I do sleep." Her shoulders relaxed while she gathered her thoughts. "It's more like a spinning wheel winding down to a complete stop. I can't hear a thing once that happens."

"Go to sleep?" I said, attempting to raise myself up on my elbows to get a better look at her. "You was dead. I saw you. We all saw you."

Simone covered my hand with her chilled one. She leaned in closer and said, "Lavinia, I am dead. I've been dead, for about a year . . . maybe less. I'm not too sure."

"But you—"

"I know," she said with a smile as if she'd pulled off the greatest trick of all time. "I'm right here talking to you. But I am dead. Whoever found me under your bed must have thought so too, because I woke up in a mound of dirt."

"How'd you . . . ?"

"Remember when we first met? Me sucking on your toe? Those few drops of blood were the sweetest things I'd ever tasted. Like buttercream. I've never had a colored person before. Indians, yes. They leave a little zing in the back of the throat. I wonder if all Negroes taste—"

"Simone!"

She snapped out of her food trance. "Oh, well now I can smell you from a mile away."

"They say you killed Ginny."

Simone furrowed her brow. "So? You said you didn't like Ginny. I told you no one would bother you again with me around. And see, Ginny won't ever bother you again. If I had known they would blame you for it all . . . Oh, Lavinia, you just can't die!"

I tried my hardest to keep my eyes open, not sure if this would be the last time I'd see her if I closed them. I was too tired to give her advice. Too tired to tell her to get outta here before the law showed up. Why I was worried about her surviving when death was knocking at my door, I couldn't tell you. Sure, she was a few pecans short of a pie, but she had taken care of Ginny for me. I inhaled one last, painful time. If Simone could cry, I'd suspect she would. Instead, she leaned over and kissed me . . . like a man.

Lemme tell ya, that jolted me awake. Simone's tongue got to swimming all around my mouth like an eel. Her spit was like ice water dripping down my throat. I figured, hell, ain't nobody gonna kiss me like that, ever. So, I laid there and let her.

Then the wench bit me. Clamped down on my tongue like she was biting into a roast. Guess she couldn't help herself.

Something wrenched my stomach so that I rolled off that wooden bench and fell to my knees. Felt like a fist had reached down my throat and was trying to pull my ass up through my mouth. Then all that sickness in me poured out. I coughed up thick globs of green molasses that stank and sizzled when it hit the ground. I couldn't control it as it flowed outta me like a lazy river on a Sunday afternoon. When all the sickness was gone, I stayed on all fours catching my breath. Then I stood and wiped the goo and blood on my sleeve.

"What the hell, Simone?"

"Lavinia! Look at you!"

"Look at me? Look at you! I swear, you got about as much self-control as a horny dog! Ain't no wonder people always chasin' after you."

"Lavinia," Simone said, like she was trying to calm down a child. "You're not sick anymore."

I was so mad at her for biting me, I didn't even notice. The heaviness in my head and chest were gone. Was like how her burnt-up skin healed after she said she bit Louis . . .

I narrowed my eyes at her. "What d'you do to me?"

"Nothing! I mean, I bit you—by accident! But I—"

"You didn't turn me into a whatever you are, did you?"

Simone shook her head. "No!" Then she bit at her thumbnail. "I don't think so."

I stretched out my arms in front of me, turning them over and shaking them. No pain. I rolled my neck around and took a giant gulp of air. Still no pain. I could breathe without wheezing. Could smell the coming of rain in the air. I thought back to her talking about blood being her food. When she bit Billy, I thought she was crazy, like old Woody who used to sit outside the big house kitchen barking like a dog to get outta doing field work. Then I remembered why I was in jail in the first place.

"All that blood on you tonight," I said, pointing up and down her body. "That was from Ginny?"

Simone lowered her shoulders and sighed. "I told you—"

"Yeah, yeah. You drink blood. Was that what you were tryin' to do? Drink my blood?"

She stood there with her mouth pinched all tight like she was trying to keep herself from bursting. "I couldn't help it!" she blurted out. "I get so hungry sometimes."

"You wanna eat me?" My eyes widened and I stared at her like she'd punched me in the gut.

"What do you want me say, Lavinia? When I tasted your blood that first time . . . It was just soooo good! Like the sweetest dacquoise melting in my mouth." She closed her eyes and stroked her neck. "I wonder, do all Negroes taste so decadent, or is there something special about you? Those few drops I'd gleaned made my thighs quiver. Imagine how orgasmic an entire feeding would be!"

"So, you do wanna eat me."

Simone lowered her head and opened her eyes like she wasn't just sex-eating me in her mind. "No! Not now. I mean, I . . . won't," she said, her pleading eyes tinged with a lie even I could detect. "You're nothing like the other humans I've encountered. I know my appearance can be a bit off-putting. But you gave me refuge anyway. You spoke to me like . . . a human. You aren't even repulsed by what I did to Ginny. And Louis. And that bartender—"

"Bartender?" I said. "When did you eat a bartender?"

She eyed me blankly. "What bartender?"

"You jus' said . . . Never mind. I didn't say I wasn't. I ain't wrapped my head around me havin' to eat blood like you."

"I don't think that's going to happen."

I cocked my head to the side. "How you know?"

"Because." She nodded her head as if putting a period on the discussion.

"You don't know, do you?"

"I know that never happened with Etienne."

"Eighteen?"

"*Eh-tee-enne*," Simone said, exaggerating the word. "He was a sous chef in my father's restaurant. For weeks, I fed on him as he slept. A few little bites he attributed to rats sneaking in his bed. He didn't turn into anything."

"Your parents knew what you were?"

"No," she said, a bit of fear shrouding her face. "That was after something like me bit me."

"Uh-huh. And all that bitin' did nothin' to Eight—however you say his name?"

"No, no. Not . . . really. I mean, he didn't die or anything like that. He slowed down. A lot. After a few days, he'd simply lay there with his eyes open, staring at the ceiling and not saying a word." She smiled and twisted a lock of hair around her finger. "Easiest feedings I ever had."

"That information ain't helpful."

"Well, you haven't seen that Irishman I ate walking around, have you? And the banjo player, the Scot. He didn't change into anything."

I wasn't convinced even though none of their wounds healed up like mine did.

Simone smiled. "He was just an hors d'oeuvre anyway. They all are, actually. I can't remember the last time I had a real meal. There were even leftovers with Ginny."

I winced at her words. "You talk about this stuff like you're at a dinner party."

She shrugged. "It's my only joy since becoming a vampire. Now,

I've taken to comparing the nationalities of my meals to food. Canadians taste of wine, whether red or white depends on where they live. Prussians, of beer. Scandinavians provide a gamey finish. The English, of boiled broccoli—my least favorite."

Waving my hands in the air to get her to stop, I said, "Alright, I get it. I'm gonna turn into some crazy-ass woman who drinks blood from people."

"A crazy-ass woman no one will trouble again."

I plopped myself down on the cot and held my head in my hands, pondering what she said. Simone sat next to me, copying my posture. She had a point. I was healed, that was a plus. But drinking blood? The sun burning my skin? That was the trade-off?

"It's not as bad as it seems," Simone said softly.

"No? What was all that about how hard it is for you to get a good feedin' in? I'm gonna be out here starvin' if I gotta eat people."

The vampire took my hand and squeezed. "That was me, all alone, trying to figure this out. With two of us putting our heads together, imagine what we can do!"

I wasn't so sure of that. Even if I had the ability to tear out people's throats if they crossed me, how close would they let a colored woman get to them? Would I have to rely on sneaking into houses at night, nibbling on toes? What kind of life was that? Being with a white woman who had the ability to do the same sounded more attractive than what awaited me when the sun came up. But I couldn't ponder long. We had to get outta this jail before somebody learned that the dead body they carted out of my shack had come back.

SEVEN

Martin has pulled his chair up to my cell, his dirty boots propped up on the bars. Guess I'm getting his attention with my tale. He's been sitting there, still jawing on his tobacco, and hasn't spit not once into the cup since the last time he interrupted me. He chews like it's spruce gum in his mouth. I hope he ain't swallowing that mess.

"So, she's a . . . vampire?" Martin finally asks when I take a breath from my tale. "She drinks blood from other people?"

"That's what she said."

"And you saw her do this?"

"Jus' with Billy at that point 'cause we were all there when she bit him. I didn't see what she did to Ginny."

"Huh." Martin moves the tobacco around in his mouth and glances down at the tin cup as if remembering he's supposed to spit the mess out. He does, and then scoots his chair closer to the bars. A few more inches, and he'll be right in here with me. "How'd she become a vampire? Is it a disease? Something she likes to do?"

"Somethin' she *likes* to do?" I glare at him like he's crazy. "Who you know likes drinkin' blood?"

"Well . . . nobody. But you're making some crazy claims here."

"Trust me, I know how crazy this sounds. I lived it for a good while."

I walk the few paces back to my cot. With Martin back to spitting in the cup, I don't want any of that juice getting on me. "Simone was never one for talkin' 'bout her past. But after she bit me, our minds got connected somehow. Sometimes I could see her thoughts and memories, even see her doin' things in the moment, without her even sayin' a word."

Martin leaned forward. "What did you see?"

"She'd been attacked by some vamp that looked like he'd been around to help Noah build the ark. He was a dumb one, too, so old that all the energy he used turnin' her killed him. Dropped dead with his fangs still in her arm. If anybody needed a ghoul, it was him. Simone simply happened across his path. He drained her all the way, then died. Left her without knowin' what she was or what to do about it. I almost felt sorry for her. All alone in the world with not another vamp to teach her anything."

Martin crinkles his brow and shakes his head. "How sad."

"Don't get too mushy 'bout her predicament," I say. "Simone wasn't exactly truthful with some of this stuff she told me. Anyway, I was really still pissed about the bite, wonderin' what was gonna happen to me."

"Turning into a vampire."

"Right."

"But you didn't." Martin tilts up the brim of his hat and scratches his sweaty forehead. "And what are you again?"

"A ghoul," a quick glance at my bandaged arm reminds me to add, "I mean, I was a ghoul." I didn't like thinking about circumstances that had reverted me back to normal.

"Vampire, ghoul. What's the difference?"

I raise my palm to him. "Hold your horses. I'm gettin' there."

EIGHT

Back to my situation at the Georgia jail, the constable took his sweet time coming in to check on me after supper, giving Simone plenty of time to wrap herself in that blanket and slip under the wooden bench. He milled around for a minute, lit the wick on his desk lamp, and then sat his fat behind at his desk with his feet propped up and read a newspaper. Didn't say a word to me until I approached the bars of my cell.

"Well, looky here," he finally said from across the room. "See you managed to sleep it off."

"Sleep what off?"

"All that drinking you must've been doing! I told Tillie about giving you free rein in that saloon of hers. You passed out right there in that shack."

I had no idea what he was talking about. I remember watching them drag Simone out from under my bed, then I woke up here. Must've collapsed from the fever.

"I wasn't drunk. I was sick."

"Don't look sick now."

I didn't feel sick either. The bite on my tongue didn't even hurt anymore. I glanced back at the pile of blankets tucked neatly beneath the wooden bench. Simone's kiss had healed me. In fact, I hadn't felt this good since I heard old Uncle Abe emancipated us. My mind was another story. Even with her sleeping under that bench, it was like Simone kept sending me the jumbled mess that was her life. 'Cept none of it made any sense.

I saw her arguing with a man with long yellow hair, dressed in all black. Then I saw her digging around in mounds of dirt, pulling out detached arms and legs. My mind flashed, and there she was, surrounded by a bunch of colored folks, one young woman in particular seated at her feet looking up at Simone like she was Jesus's mama or something. In another flash, a group of men chased her with a pointy stick.

The pictures in my head went on and on until I finally shouted, "Alright! I get it!"

"Glad to see you're so accepting of your sentence."

The constable stood in front of my jail cell. He'd been talking to me the whole time I was watching Simone's mind pictures. "My sentence?"

"Didn't you hear me? You're gonna hang in the morning. Sooner, if anybody else gets wind of what you did."

"But I didn't kill nobody!"

So, what are you going to do? I heard Simone ask.

What *was* I gonna do? Either I was gonna hang, or the sun was gonna burn me up. I don't know how Simone got in here, but she obviously couldn't get me out the way she got in, or we would've been outta here hours ago instead of arguing like a couple of old biddies. Had to resort to the only weapon I had.

"Mr. Constable, sir?" I summoned him closer with a crooked finger. "There's somethin' in here with me." I pointed to the pile of blankets in my cell. "That dead girl y'all hauled outta my shack?" I lowered my voice to a whisper. "She's back."

The constable pursed his lips in disbelief. "Sure, she is. Maybe you're not as dried out as I thought you were."

"Please, sir!" I hissed. "Don't leave me in here with that thing!" I rushed to the blankets and lifted them, exposing Simone in her dead state.

The constable scratched his head. "Now wait just a dad-blamed minute! How'd she get in there?"

I kept my voice low. "I told you. She got in here right after you left and slipped through the bars like smoke. Stood right there in the corner, jus' starin' at me with the devil in her eyes like she wanted to eat me alive! But when she heard you comin', she took my blanket and went under there. I've been too scared to move 'til you got here."

He fumbled with all these keys he had hanging from his belt. A whole lotta keys for two jail cells. He pushed me aside once he finally got the gate open. I held my breath as he bent over and snatched the blanket away. Simone lay there, still and stiff as a log. The constable grabbed his collar with one hand and started crossing himself with the other.

My plan was starting to work. Get him in the cell, take the keys, and then lock him in. If only there was something to knock him over the head with . . .

Too bad you can't get up and make a meal outta him, I thought with a smile.

Right then, Simone's eyes opened. Her head turned sharply toward the stunned constable. With her wolf teeth all showing, Simone flew from beneath the bench and pinned the constable against the wall. Her mouth clamped down right in the center of his throat so he couldn't scream. The constable's legs and arms twitched like he was having a fit. I stood there, frightened, horrified, and amazed at what was happening before my eyes. She could've been sucking on his neck like a lover for all I knew. Only difference was there wasn't a lot of blood this time. Nothing spraying. No body parts or chunks of flesh flying. It wasn't until a quick shot of blood sprayed against the wall that I told her to stop. She released him, letting the body fall to the floor with a thud. There was hardly any blood on her at all, only a few drops at the corner of her mouth that she wiped away with her pinky finger. The poor constable wasn't dead yet because his blood was still flowing. Even the wound looked different than the others.

I clasped my hand around my throat and took a few steps back. "Not the usual mess, I see." A nervous chuckle left me.

"What's the rush?" she said with a wicked smile. "There's no one else here, and I was leaving some for you."

I turned up my lip. "No, thank you. I'll stick to plants and animals, if you don't mind."

A confused frown sprouted on her face. "You don't want any? Really?"

"No!" I stuck my tongue out.

"Interesting." She drew the word out like she was disappointed.

"Why? What d'you do when you turned?" I said with a chuckle. "Jump on the first person to cross your path?"

"I don't remember." Of all the talking she did, this was the flattest I'd ever heard her voice. But then she suddenly perked up and said, "See! Told you I didn't turn you into anything."

That didn't make me feel any better. Something had happened to me when she bit me, but I wasn't sure what at the time. Then I saw a portion of Simone's memory when she got turned. Her killer didn't leave any blood in her at all. She was as pale then as she was now. Louis and the constable were a little bit alive when she was finished with them. All Billy had was a nasty flesh wound and was well enough to see me hang the next day. Simone hadn't taken much from me either. What I decided was that whoever Simone bit had to die all the way with no blood in them before they turned into a vamp like her. Not sure about Ginny, though. That thing might turn, but she was one angry creature when she was alive. Wouldn't wanna run into her as a vamp.

"We best get outta here 'fore night wears thin," I said. Feeling this good about getting out of jail would be meaningless if we got burnt up on our way out.

Simone smiled. "You're ready to leave? For good now?"

"Got no choice, do I? Though I do want to settle some business 'fore I do."

Simone and I sprinted back the two miles to Miss Tillie's from the jail. Was surprised I didn't get winded or tired. Didn't even have to stop. I also noticed that I could see clear as day in the darkness. Not as if my eyes beamed a bright light at whatever I was staring at; more like looking through a dirty window at dusk. Maybe that had something to do with me getting cured from Simone's bite.

Since dawn hadn't peeked its head over the horizon yet, I knew I'd find Miss Tillie stumbling back to the big house to sleep off another night of drinking. I left Simone in the barn to hitch up the horse and wagon (of course, I had to show her how) while I went to see Miss Tillie.

"Vinny!" she said, like she was happy to see me. The saloon was dark and quiet, save for Miss Tillie and a lantern swinging from her arm. She stumbled into me. "We missed you tonight! Where were you? I had to serve these people all by my lonesome."

Had she really forgotten she had me hauled off to jail only a few hours before?

"Sorry 'bout that, Miss Tillie," I said as I threw one of her arms over my shoulder and guided her to the door. Kept my head turned so I wouldn't smell her stank-breath with all the nonstop talking.

Then she started weeping. "You know, Ginny's gone."

"So I heard."

"Somebody ripped her to shreds." She spread her arms wide, hitting me with the lantern so hard I thought my dress was gonna go up in flames. "Should have heard her screaming and flopping on the floor with that girl on her neck. You know that girl. The one who bit poor Billy. Didn't have any good music tonight, what with Billy having only one functioning hand. Matter of fact, he wasn't there either." She pointed a finger at me and whispered, "What is the wagon doing here?"

"You too heavy for me to carry all the way over to the big house," I said, certain her drunk brain didn't notice anybody at the reins.

She willingly got in the wagon with my help. Laid her out in the back with the ration box since her sitting up straight in the driver's seat wasn't happening. She talked and sang the whole twenty minutes we rode until we came to one of those burnt-out buildings, out of earshot from folks still milling about the saloon. My retribution fantasy came true. Simone emerged from the box once we stopped and sank her fangs into the old woman's neck. Miss Tillie didn't scream, only low moans until she realized her life was leaving her. The old woman reached out to me, her pleas for help bouncing against the empty walls. Miss Tillie struggling to get away soon slowed to her twitching like she was catching the Holy Ghost. Arm outstretched, she said, "Help . . . me."

After everything we'd been through, Miss Tillie wasn't all bad. She never beat me. At Christmastime, she gave me a dress she'd worn only once. Would even call the doctor for me and the other Negroes on the plantation whenever we got sick. But looking back, it was probably because a dead slave meant lost income. Even still, until Simone came along, Miss Tillie was the only person who even bothered to speak *to* me instead of *at* me.

"Vinny?"

"Lavinia." My brow furrowed. I bent beside her body still cradled in Simone's arms. "My name is Lavinia."

I had nothing but my name and she wouldn't even give me that.

Her death rattle was the shackles of slavery falling off me. For the first time, I felt free. Like Saul when the scales fell from his eyes, I had new sight. I stared at Simone leaning against the side of the wagon, looking like she finally got hold of an itch she couldn't reach. She licked away the few traces of blood from the corners of her mouth. Then she stared at me, her blank expression a bit unnerving because I had just witnessed her eating two people.

"Happy now?" she asked with a raised eyebrow.

"Very." I was hugging and thanking her before I could wonder if she'd had her fill of blood for the night.

"I should be thanking you," Simone whispered as I held her, "after everything you've done for me." I wasn't afraid when she rested her head on my shoulder and her cold lips pressed softly against my neck. "What shall we do now, Lavinia?"

My name—*my name*—never sounded so sweet. Looking down at Miss Tillie's open, dead eyes, I said, "Live."

NINE

"So, you up and went with her?" Martin asks. The wrinkles and crinkles in his sallow face have steadily increased as I recall my tale. "She killed three people, in front of you, and you decided to leave with her? That doesn't make any sense."

"You think I wanted to stay on that plantation after what they did to me?"

"But Miss Tillie was gone," he says, as if her death touched him in some kind of way. "If Miss Simone was what you say she was, and you thought you were like her too, why not take over the brothel? Hell, the two of you could've killed everybody and had the house all to yourselves."

"And explain all them deaths and us bein' there, how?"

"I don't know," he says with a shrug. "Sickness? You said everybody was pretty bad off after the war."

I shake my head and walk over to the bars of my cell. "She would have to eat the sheriff, too. And no tellin' who all he told after he arrested me. Naw, that would've been too much work. Plus, Simone didn't always act like she was dealin' with a full set, if you know what I mean."

He brings the pewter flask up to his lips, tilts his head back, and accepts the trickle of brown fluid dribbling into his mouth. Then he lowers his head. "But she killed people, according to you. Weren't you scared of her?"

"I already told you I wasn't. I guess I was so eager to leave, and I'd gotten so comfortable with her, it didn't really dawn on me that she'd do anything. Since I believed I was like her, she wouldn't bother me."

"Maybe she was saving you for later," he says with a smirk.

"You always think the worst of folks, don'tcha?"

"You're the one describing her as a killer." Martin scratches the graying scruff on his chin. "How the hell did you end up here, in Tolleston, Indiana, of all places? Town's only a decade or so old and in the middle of nowhere. Shoot, you could ride past the place and not even know it's here."

"Tell me something," I say, letting my arms go slack through the bars. "You from here or did you come from someplace else?"

"From Detroit."

"And what brought you here?"

He looks up and frowns. "I'm asking questions about your crazy story, not the other way around."

I chuckle, figuring there's a reason why he doesn't want to answer such a simple question. I turn my palms up in surrender. "Come on, Martin. You're so certain I'm gonna hang, what difference does it make if you tell me? If it's somethin' awful, who am I gonna tell?"

He sucks his teeth, looks toward the door as if checking for eavesdroppers and says, "My boy was killed at Antietam, in the war." He regards the flask in his hands. "This was the only thing that kept me from remembering my only child was dead." He chuckles. "After a while, I couldn't stop."

"So, you left all that pain behind and moved here?"

He doesn't answer, just presses his lips together and stares at the flask. At least I know why he drinks so much. "But when you got here, you got back on your feet, right? Opened that smithy shop you got over on Martha Street. Even got a star on your chest."

He nodded.

"Think I could've done the same thing? Restarted my life in some new town like you did?"

"What?" he says with a laugh. "Open a business?"

"Why's that so funny?" I ask, a little miffed that the thought tickles him so. "Mrs. Gibson runs an inn. Mrs. Schneider got the dry goods store."

"That's different," he says, rising to hand me the flask, and I wonder if he's sharing because of that confession he just made. "They got 'Mrs.' in front of their names."

"And they ain't colored," I add. "You just proved my point. My best bet was Simone. She was all I had. If you didn't wanna stay in a place that caused you pain, why would I?"

He scratches his forehead. "Guess you're right," he says with a bit of reluctance in his voice. "Still doesn't tell me how you ended up here of all places. It's just miles of sand."

"We talked about it for a minute. But we didn't come here on purpose. The plan was Chicago. But as you can imagine, travelin' with a vampire can get you sidetracked."

The journey north was bittersweet. To my back: Miss Tillie's place and the only life I'd ever known. Ahead of me: God only knew. Simone had described all the places she'd been. But a white girl like her could go where she wanted with no problems. I knew there were folks who still wanted the world to go back to the way things were, where people who looked like me weren't even regarded as such. Would the same be true once I got north?

I reasoned that traveling in a wagon would be better than a train because one, we could keep to ourselves in a wagon; and two, I ain't never been on no train before. I'd seen them rumbling through the countryside over them thin rails, belching clouds of smoke up to the heavens. Like some big steel dragon coming at you. Couldn't imagine what it must feel like being in its belly. Loud as it was on the outside, I'd probably go deaf riding in it. No, thank you! Simone tried to convince me otherwise, that riding on a train was like being pulled by a thousand horses, so we'd get out of the South a whole lot faster. I didn't care. Told her I'd have to be dead like Uncle Abe if she wanted me in one of them things. Plus, we had nothing but the clothes on our backs. How she thought we'd pay for train tickets, I don't know. So, the wagon it was.

After getting rid of Miss Tillie's body, Simone joined me in the driver's seat. In her hands was a wooden ball with lots of colorful shapes on it.

"Where are we going?" she asked, spinning that ball between her hands like a speckled pumpkin.

"North."

"What's up north?"

I lifted my shoulders. "That's all I heard when I was growing up: *Go north to freedom.*" I pointed up to a bright star in the sky. "You see that star there?"

Simone followed my finger. "Polaris?"

"Right." As if I knew it had a name other than the North Star. "That star guided my people to freedom. We'll jus' ride in that direction 'til we get somewhere to settle."

Simone raised the ball up to one of the two lit lanterns hanging on poles on either side of the driver's seat. "There are lots of places 'up north.' Where specifically are we going?"

"What about where you're from?" I asked.

Simone frowned, bit the corner of her bottom lip, and started spinning that ball again. "You pick a place," she said.

I squinted my eyes to make out the tiny shapes in the darkness. Besides all the colors, there was scribbling on it that I couldn't decipher. As important as my name was to me, I wouldn't know it if I saw it. Didn't know my numbers either. All I knew about the world was Georgia, Montreal on account of meeting Simone, and Africa because all the slaves here used to talk about going back there. She showed me France, a little shape in the middle of a bunch of other shapes where her people lived before they arrived in Canada. Simone could trace her family all the way to some little town there, back before anybody even heard of North America.

I wondered if Simone was funning with me by telling me to pick a place, or if she really thought I could read the words on that thing. I shrugged and asked, "Where's Africa?"

Her face turned serious. "No sea travel. I don't do boats."

"I thought you said you been to France."

"No boats."

"Fine. I jus' wanna know where Africa is, is all."

She turned the ball and pointed to what looked like the side profile of a long wig with a bunch of colors on it. Africa was so big! Where would I even go if I decided on Africa? With all them shapes bunched together, I wondered which one of them my great-grandparents might've come from. Were any of my people still there? Were any of my people still alive here? I never met no Negro straight from Africa. Anything I knew about the place came from what somebody had told me, and what somebody else had told them. At that moment, looking at that giant patchwork of shapes on that colorful wooden ball, I felt like an orphan. Like a light in me had been snuffed out. I had no home, no nothing. Right now, all I had was Simone.

I collected myself and asked, "Where are we now?"

She pointed again to this little orange piece next to a lotta blue. I spread my hand across the ball; my thumb and pinky finger connecting the two places I'd just learned about. Seemed kind of far.

"What do the blue spots mean?"

Simone laughed, and a chill ran up my back. I didn't know what made me madder: Miss Tillie never respecting me enough to call me by my name or Simone laughing at my ignorance.

She placed her cold hand on my shoulder. "All that blue is water. Oceans, rivers, lakes."

"You seen these big ole oceans before?"

"This one," she pointed to a large blue section that separated Georgia and Africa. "The Atlantic Ocean. You have to cross the ocean to get to France."

"I thought you said—"

"That was before I was turned."

I huffed at all the secrecy. "Well, what was it like?"

"France?" Simone's face lit up. "Wonderful! I stayed in my aunt's château, and—"

"No, the boat ride. Was it a big boat? Was the water blue like on this ball?"

I must've sparked an awful memory because her face fell, and her eyes got all narrow like I'd cursed her mama. "Let's forget about going anywhere that involves a boat, okay?" She forced a half smile.

I rolled my eyes. "Fine."

And she went to reading off the names of all these places and making me repeat after her like we didn't just have that awkward exchange. I wondered what that was about. Whatever it was, going over all the words written on the ball seemed to ease her mind. I'd never seen an ocean. Never seen more than a creek, let alone a Great Lake. One of them Great Lakes looked like God had pressed His finger against the world. And it was north of here. Way north of here. Far enough to put my old life behind me. And I didn't see nothing more than them little squiggly blue lines she said were rivers between here and there.

I pointed to a black dot beneath the God-spot. "Let's go there."

Simone flashed that wide smile of hers making her face look like it would split in half. "Chicago it is!"

I nudged the horse along with a click of my tongue and a soft slap to her back with the reins. My mind conjured all kinds of images about what the place might look like. Might be a few Negroes living there I could meet. Maybe even a handsome blacksmith. I let my thoughts mosey along like this horse, content in the fact that, no matter how long it took to get there, I'd be starting my life anew.

Then I recalled what had happened back at the jail. When I thought about her eating the constable, she actually did it, as though she heard me thinking.

"I did hear you," Simone said. "I can also hear your heart beating when I sleep. It must be the result of when I bit you."

"Must be. Wonder what that means."

"It means we can communicate with each other without being in the same place. You don't ever have to worry about me doing something stupid when I'm away. You can simply tell me, with your mind, and I'll hear you."

"Too bad you didn't bite me before I got locked up in jail."

"Good thing I found you when I did." Simone smiled and nudged my shoulder with hers. "And I did hear you, about wanting to settle down. I hope your plans include me."

Honestly, I hadn't even seen Simone in my future because I figured she'd go off doing her own thing. "Include you? What, to fetch and cook and clean for you? Had enough of that back at old Tillie's place."

Simone smiled. "Well, what else would you be doing?"

I widened my eyes and scoffed. Twice. She was right, but I didn't want her to assume I'd be running up behind her just because she said so. "I figured you'd go off and find your family in Montreal or something."

She faced forward and I noticed her jaw tightening. "I told you. My parents are dead."

"Well, ain't you got no family or friends still alive that wanna see you? You said your daddy was a chef. Surely you got something to go back home to."

"I was an only child, so, no. There's nothing back in Louisiana for me except heartache and memories I want to forget."

"Montreal."

"What?"

"You said, 'Louisiana,' but you meant Montreal, where your people are from."

She started messing with her braid again. Plaiting and replaiting the same four turns at the end. "Yes, Montreal. Sorry. I must be thinking of something else. Either way, I don't want to go back there."

I didn't say anything for a minute, glad she really didn't mean Louisiana. Miss Tillie's cook was from there and she didn't have nothing nice to say about her time there. I said I wanted to get out of the South and I meant it. "Well, if I had family somewhere, I'd go to find them. Don't care how crazy they might be."

"Well, that's you," Simone said with her chin lifted. "I assume you had family or friends at Tillie's place. Why didn't you leave when everybody else did?"

I sighed. "Scared, I guess. Didn't trust them or myself enough to think I could make it with no money, no food. Thinking the Rebs were gonna snatch you up and send you back someplace worse than where you ran from." I glanced over at Simone, who sat quietly and still. "You don't have a clue as to what I'm talking about, do you?"

"I've been chased out of my fair share of places," she said. "Even you put me out of that shack of yours."

"I didn't know you then," I said with a playful nudge to her arm. "You've been all over the place, seen all kinds of things. Even if you wasn't as well off as Miss Tillie used to be, I bet your worst day was better than any good one I had 'cause you could do what you wanted."

"You think so?" Simone finally said. "You think I had it that great where I was from?"

"Look, all I'm sayin' is, I only knew that plantation and the couple of miles around it. The devil you know, you know?"

"You knew what to expect from Miss Tillie, even if she treated you badly," Simone said. "Sometimes the devil you know is worse than the one you don't."

"You can get away with traipsin' all over the place. I ain't got that luxury."

Simone turned to me and smiled. "Well, now we have each other. You don't have to worry about any Rebs or Miss Tillies with me."

"And don't think I'm gonna be yes-mammin' you. You help me get outta the South. I keep you from gettin' your head bashed in with your feedin's. Either we equals or you can walk to wherever you're tryin' to get to."

"Okay, funny lady." She linked her arm in mine and leaned her head against my shoulder.

I looked at her. With a full body of blood, she appeared normal. Her skin had plumped with a bit of color. It had been kind of nice having a friend, and a white girl at that. Simone was shaping up to be someone I could tell anything to, any way I wanted to. But I didn't want to expose everything about myself like Simone did. But now she *would* know. Every thought I had. Every thought about her. I remembered Uncle John and Aunt Mary, the old couple I shared a shack with when I was a girl. They loved each other, but they had their share of arguments. Talking bad about the other when they thought I wasn't listening. They left when the war was over. I wonder if they'd have stayed together if they could've heard what the other was saying about them when they got mad. What if Simone turned on me if she heard something she didn't like?

"That would never happen, Lavinia," Simone said, doing the very thing I was afraid of. She held my arm and snuggled against me. "Like you said, we need each other."

"Yeah," I said, pressing my head against hers. "We'll see."

We sat there for a minute, our bodies rocking along with the wagon wheels rolling over the uneven ground. A soft wind whistled through the trees. Coyotes howled messages to each other. Then a thought hit me. I still couldn't get over what had happened back at the jail. How my sickness got cured. How Simone got herself inside the jail in the first place.

"I just walked in, silly," Simone said, hearing my thoughts. She lifted her head from my shoulder and looked at me. "The entrance was unlocked. I mean, what is there to steal in a jail of all places?" She shook her head like the answer was obvious.

"But how'd you get in my cell?" I asked. "It was sho' nuff locked after they put me in there."

"With the key hanging on the wall. Did you think I turned into a puff of smoke and went through the bars?"

It took me a moment to process what Simone had told me about the key. I glared at her with a frown on my face. "You mean to tell me you had the key the whole damn time?"

Simone was sitting there, fiddling with that braid again. She nodded, humming out an "Um-hmm."

"A key. That could open the cell. The cell I was in?"

She nodded again, innocence lighting her eyes.

I threw my free hand in the air. "Then why the hell didn't you jus' let me out?"

Simone stopped braiding and raised her head in thought. I don't know what startled her more, my yelling or all the noise from the night animals. Then her face crinkled in confusion making her look like a baby who'd gotten a taste of something nasty in her mouth. "I don't know. I guess I was so happy that I found you that . . ." She shrank into herself, and her voice got all soft. ". . . that I forgot I'd left the key in the lock when I opened the cell door. Sorry!"

I closed my eyes and shook my head in disbelief. "Good Lord, chile! You couldn't figure that out? How you lasted a year on your own, I don't know. Infants and fools, like they say. Infants and fools. I can already see, you gon' be a lotta work."

Simone smiled her apology, then hooked her arm into mine again. "But think of the fun we'll have!"

I hoped she was right.

TEN

We rode all night. The excitement of travel had my eyes wide open. My cheeks were sore from smiling so much. A million thoughts zipped through my mind with things I wanted to do, like getting a new dress and new shoes. Learn to read and write. Have my own house where I could fix the food I liked and not just eat whatever was left over. And since I didn't have any family, starting one of my own was a priority. Of course, all that after I found a place that didn't care that I was a Negro woman on my own.

That happiness faded with the approach of dawn. Simone wasted no time scrambling back into the ration box. All that talk last night about "us" and "we," and here she was, leaving me to figure out what to do with myself. I could've continued riding since I must have left sleep back at Miss Tillie's, but I couldn't risk being out in the daylight. All I'd need was for somebody to stop me and find Simone's dead-asleep body in the ration box. I also wasn't looking forward to my skin bubbling and blistering once the sun hit it. My nerves were a right mess until I found a patch of forest with a canopy thick enough to keep the sunlight to a minimum. To be safe, I crawled under the wagon and sat there, studying that wooden ball, or globe, as Simone called it. She'd used our time traveling last night to teach me the names of all the continents and oceans. Whether I said the right names when I pointed to the shapes was anybody's guess at that point. If nothing else, I could at least recognize Africa when written.

The horse whinnied softly. I held my breath, listening for voices, the crunch of boots against the ground, or the crack of branches as moving bodies broke through them. Squirrels scuttled from tree to tree. Then the horse tapped the ground with her hoof, shifting the wagon slightly forward. A beam of sunlight burst through the wooden slats of the wagon bed, landing right on my arm. I shrieked, snatched my arm away, then clasped a hand over my mouth. My scream frightened away several birds nesting in the tree above me. The horse signaled her displeasure with a snort. Once the chirping and flapping ceased, I listened again for possible travelers. Then I braced myself for what the sunlight did to my arm.

Except there was nothing. No bubbling, no blistering, no pain. Slowly, I placed my arm back in the bright beam and breathed a sigh of relief. I wasn't whatever Simone was. I wouldn't be drinking blood and running from sunlight after all. I used my mind to tell her this, but I heard nothing back from her. I tried poking around in hers, only to check if she was listening, but all I saw from her mind was blackness. I wondered if it didn't work during the daytime or if her being in the box had something to do with it.

I slid from underneath the wagon and walked to a spot where a break in the treetops allowed the rays to rain down. Arms spread wide, I tilted my head back and let the sun bleed through my closed eyelids. My first day of freedom, real freedom. I didn't have to fetch nothing for nobody, clean body fluid–stained sheets, or make any meals. I wrapped my arms around myself. This body was mine, finally mine, to do as I pleased. I belonged to no one but the Almighty.

I wasn't even hungry myself, though it had been a couple of days since I'd eaten. Instead of waiting for my stomach to start growling for food I didn't have, I decided to explore the forest for something I could eat. I made marks on the tree trunks I passed to make sure I could find my way back to the wagon. Took my time—all I had was time since I was wide-awake—stepping slowly over the blanket of leaves, branches, and grass to make as little noise as possible.

Over my shoulder, I glanced at the box in the back of the wagon. Sooner or later, Simone would be wanting to eat, too. What if we were so deep into these woods that we couldn't find anybody? I'd wind up like that Eighteen boy she made a meal-puppet out of. Might as well have been half dead, the way she described him. Kill or be killed by the thing that sprung me from jail. Were those my only options now?

I turned my head away from the box and peered through the curtain of foliage in front of me. Maybe there was one last alternative that didn't involve hauling around a dead body that drank human blood. I took a step forward and then before I could think too deeply on it, sprinted away.

I didn't get far.

A pain in my head brought me to my knees. Felt like the whole forest had collapsed on my skull. Couldn't hardly open my eyes for the throbbing across my forehead and down the back of my neck. This was worse than the sickness I had a day ago. Blind and clutching anything on the ground to transfer my pain to, I eventually turned around. When I managed to open my eyes, I spied the wagon. Had poor Simone gone through this very thing when she got bit? If this had something to do with her bite, I figured I'd best stick around for an explanation. Then just as suddenly, the pain stopped.

I didn't tell Simone about the head pain, and we continued on. If not for the horse needing to eat or rest, we probably would have driven straight to Chicago without stopping at all. It was days before I got hungry or sleepy. Even Simone wasn't hankering for blood. A couple of times, she didn't bother coming out of the box unless I roused her, but by the end of that first week without either of us eating, Simone had turned back into the dead-looking thing I found in the saloon. Whatever rosiness had been in her skin faded to an ashen pall. Dark circles rimmed her eyes and sunken cheeks. Gave me a fright when she climbed outta that box! And of course, she was hungry. Silly girl had it in her head that she could go find something to eat while I waited for her.

"And how you plan on doin' that?" I asked. Of all the biting I'd witnessed back at Miss Tillie's, it seemed like Simone operated on pure instinct . . . no planning at all.

"Find person, bite person. Simple."

"So, you're jus' gon' walk up on the first person you meet and bite 'em? What if somebody sees you?"

"I have to feed."

"You shit out in the open, too?"

Simone frowned at the question. I'd forgotten she'd been dead about a year. It had been a while since her innards worked. She was dead after all, no heartbeat, no breathing, no nothing.

"What I mean is, you don't let everybody know your business. Some things you gotta do in private."

"Private," Simone said, frowning again like she still didn't understand or was turning the thought over in her brain.

I sighed and shook my head. "I'm supposed to be helpin' you feed, remember? You want us to get caught?"

"Do you have a better idea?"

I thought for a moment then said, "Follow me."

Since no one back at Miss Tillie's saloon had seemed to notice when Simone went after Billy, I concluded another gathering of drunkards should be easy pickings. We left the wagon and wandered into town. A few folks were still milling about, probably leaving the shops that were closing up one by one. You would have thought some two-headed elephant had appeared, given how all them folks stopped in their tracks to gawk at us. At first, I thought they were focused on me pulling Simone back by her collar to keep her from chomping on them. But when she finally calmed down and just walked like a normal person, the gawking didn't stop. They still stared as we passed. And given the sameness of the faces that evening, the only obvious elephant on the road was me.

"Am I eating or sightseeing?" Simone pouted.

"Jus' wait," I said, as we stood in front of a general store. "You can't go yankin' somebody off the street with all these witnesses. Wait 'til it thins out a bit."

A woman and a little boy exited the store. Simone about tore off my arm trying to follow behind him.

"A child?" I whispered when I finally got control of her. "You can't eat a child!"

Simone lowered her head like she was looking at me over the rim of a pair of imaginary glasses. "Why not?"

"Don't be stupid! His mama's right there."

"No, dessert is right there."

I pursed my lips and shook my head. Lord, I was gonna lose my mind if this was what I had to deal with.

"What are we looking for?" she whined.

Wasn't quite sure myself. A fat man? A short woman? Somebody wearing green? Simone had talked about how different people had different flavors. How she knew that before she bit them, I don't know. But I couldn't have her sampling each passerby until she finally found the one that suited her. Especially not with me standing beside her.

We were so busy fussing at each other under our breath that I accidentally bumped into a man—or rather he bumped into me. Hard. Before I could apologize, he spat right in my face.

I stood there, letting anger and shame wrestle within my soul. I closed my eyes, not wanting to see the expression on Simone's face. Walking with her, I'd completely forgotten who and where I was. How stupid was I to think that Simone's presence would shelter me from stuff like this? I turned to Simone, expecting to see either laughter or pity on her face. Instead, a snarl curled on her lip.

"That one?" she asked. "Please say it's that one."

I narrowed my eyes at his back. "That one."

We followed him to, where else, a saloon. Poor Simone was about to come outta her skin the whole time as I laid out my plan to her. We let him enjoy the last drink he'd ever have, then when he left, Simone was to act like she was some loose hussy and convince him to follow her back to the wagon. Men with only one thing on their mind ain't gonna be worried about some itty-bitty thing doing them any harm. And with it so dark, they'd hardly notice her appearance.

I bet he thought he was special, some nameless whore choosing him for a private romp.

Simone followed my directions to a T: get him in the wagon bed, start unbuckling his britches and, when his eyes get to rolling in the back of his head, expecting to have the best night of his life, have at it. Get him in the throat like she did back in the jail so he can't scream. And don't get to gnawing all over the place like some greedy dog. Wasn't enough explaining in the world to keep two bloodstained women outta jail. So, I stopped her before the man's skin got all pale and bloodless and his body stopped twitching. Then I started rifling through his pockets.

"You're robbing him?" Simone asked with a look of shock on her face.

"What he gon' do with it now? Can't buy stuff with money we ain't got."

In addition to the few coins and a pocket watch I managed to fish out, I found a gold wedding band. My heart sank. I sat there, staring at the items in my hand.

"What's wrong?" Simone asked. "Not enough for you?"

"The ring," I said, showing her my find. "I think he's married."

"So?"

"So? That means he's got a family. Children, maybe. Somebody who's gonna be lookin' for him."

"And they will find him, right here, with his trousers around his ankles."

I studied the ring. "He did spit on me for no reason."

"There, see?" Simone said. "He should have gone home instead of spending his money at the saloon. Are we done here?"

We got away clean that night. From then on, I chose prey to not only feed Simone but also folks who really deserved to be eaten. Like the man who nearly ran over a little boy with his carriage and then had the nerve to scream at the mother for not controlling her child. But if I'm being completely honest with you, sometimes I also looked for things I needed when selecting her meal: a pair of boots when the soles of my old ones wore out or to replace a dress ruined by my monthly visitor.

Other times, the best option was some lonely soul living in a crowded rooming house who no one would miss.

But with Simone, it wasn't always that easy.

Once, we tried staying at an inn. Simone got a room and had no problem when she explained her servant girl—me—would be rooming with her. She played the role of a mistress, ordering me around with an ease I didn't recognize. After two comfortable days of sleeping in a real bed, I made the mistake of leaving to get myself some food without telling the innkeeper not to bother us. I ain't gotta tell you the commotion the maid caused when she found what she thought was a dead body under the bed. She didn't holler long when Simone's fangs got in her throat. Good thing I found Simone before she got drained. I simply hid the bite marks underneath her high collar, waited until the coast was clear, and then posted the maid up in the hallway like she'd fallen asleep or something.

Like with that married man at the saloon, the maid tugged at my soul. From what I could tell, she was nice. Didn't throw her nose up when she saw me in the room for the first time. She'd even brought the towels we'd complained about not having. And, since she appeared to be the only maid in the whole place, someone would be looking for her. Sticking around wasn't an option.

In the in-between time, Simone taught me my letters and numbers, and how to write and recognize my name by drawing in the dirt with our fingers. I saw the seasons change from summer to fall. Leaves of colors I'd never seen in the South fell around us like the world was throwing a parade.

Martin whistles through his teeth. "Damn! You were thieving, too? Keep talking; you're only digging your own grave."

I thought I was making some headway with Martin. But instead of focusing on parts about Simone *eating* people, he's up in arms about my light fingers. According to him, I have no "moral compunction," whatever that means. Not that an admission of my thieving will lessen my fate. Any old excuse to see me swinging from a tree will do, it seems.

"Martin," I say for the tenth time, interrupting his rant. "You're missin' the point."

"Which point? The one of you planning a murder or the one where you're robbing the people you murdered?"

"Ain't you hearin' the difference?" I stand in the middle of my cell with my hands on my hips. I stare at him like I'm scolding a child. "Simone had no control when it came to feedin'. If I could've put her on a leash I would've. Best I could do was be there and make sure she didn't pick the wrong person."

Martin scratches his chin. "You mean like a child or something?"

"Lemme tell you about *that* one!"

ELEVEN

Since then, we'd been chased outta our share of towns, either because Simone couldn't control herself unless I was right on top of her the whole time, or her chosen dinner wasn't always alone. One evening, despite my repeated warnings for the girl to stay put, the minute I went to relieve myself, the fool took off. I couldn't find her nowhere. Not in her box, not under a thicket. Nowhere. I rode around until I came upon a town. A little sandy place with two-story wood-frame houses shaded by all those colorful trees I'd fallen in love with. Even in the darkness, I could make out all the golds and reds rustling in the evening breeze. Seemed strange, all these houses bunched together so closely—though they were several yards apart. Guess all them years I'd spent in Georgia had me spoiled. Miss Tillie's place was almost a mile from the main road. Couldn't even see any other houses. Don't know that I'd want to live where somebody can just look out their bedroom window right into mine.

Anyway, with it getting so late, I expected everyone to be inside readying for bed. So, I was surprised when I found Simone kneeling on the ground talking to a little girl. The child must've been in the front yard tending to her dog that was chasing its tail. I jumped down from the horse, ready to give Simone a good tongue-lashing for having me out here like this. But before I could blink, she had the girl in her arms and her teeth in the child's neck. Didn't stop either the girl from screaming or the dog from attacking. A kick from Simone sent the dog yelping back to the house as she continued to squeeze the poor girl to her chest.

I yelled for Simone to stop. She turned to me and those thundercloud-black eyes of hers made me take a step back. I could see the child was limp, blood dripping down her back. The first thing that came to my mind was the sloppiness and sheer stupidity of it all. Then, I noticed the purple flowers embroidered on the girl's reddening skirt and my chest tightened. I'd stitched enough back at Miss Tillie's to know these weren't no lazy daisies. Someone had put a lot of time and effort into this skirt.

From the corner of my eye came a flash of brightness. A woman screamed. I turned my head to see the girl's mother standing in the open doorway of her home. I ducked down near the horse's front quarters. Peering around the horse's leg, I spied a man emerging from the doorway and now both he and the woman were rushing toward Simone, who continued to feed as though she had all the time in the world. Why wasn't she running?

Why wasn't *I* running?

People began to gather with candles and oil lamps in their hands, shouting and sobbing. Then a blast from a rifle. Simone finally dropped the child but still didn't break into a run. The idiot just stood there like her dead brain couldn't process what was about to happen. Well, believe you me, my brain knew *exactly* what was gonna happen if I stuck around here. Simone's foolishness wasn't gonna get me strung up. So, I made to take off . . . but something pinned me to the ground. This time, it wasn't the pain. I couldn't just leave Simone here at the mercy of this gun-toting mob.

"You!" came a man's gruff voice. "On your feet!"

Ain't gotta tell me twice. I stood as fast as I could, but kept my arms raised and back to the fray. Didn't even look over my shoulder to see what they were doing to Simone. Or what she was about to do to them. Even if she wasn't hungry, she was usually happy to go in for seconds when the opportunity arose, and she was always strongest after a good feeding.

I heard the mother's gut-wrenching wail followed by a bunch of words I couldn't understand. Either what she was saying got lost in her weeping or she was speaking another language, but it didn't take a genius to understand the agonizing pain in her voice.

The hard metal of the gun barrel jabbed my back several times.

"Are you with that woman?" a man asked.

Just a bunch of stuttering nonsense left my mouth. The man grabbed me by the shoulder and spun me around. It was then that I got a full view of the scene. The wailing woman was on the ground, clutching her dead daughter while a dozen or so people had pounced on Simone.

"Her!" The sobbing mother pointed to me. She was still seated on the ground rocking her dead child in her lap. "I saw her," she said in English. "Out here. With that monster."

A man with a lantern in his hand approached. He stood in front of me and lifted the light. I had to turn my head away from the brightness. "Who are you? Never known no colored folks to live in these parts."

Now, I had a couple of options here. I could admit that I was with Simone or I could do a Saint Peter and deny everything . . . except that didn't turn out all that great for ole Peter. I swallowed hard and surveyed the crowd. The anger and shock on their faces was evident, even in the darkness. They wanted answers. Whatever I told them, the plain truth, or the truth I wanted them to hear, might make no difference at all. They were out for blood.

Two men had their hands on me in seconds, the cold metal of the gun still up against my back. So, this was how my story was going to end. Shot. Beaten. Hanged. All because that damn vamp couldn't keep her fangs to herself until we found a suitable meal.

"What do you want to do with this one?" The man dug the barrel of the gun between my shoulder blades and looked to the mother for direction. Her wailing had softened to a bit of whimpering, but there was fire in her eyes when she turned her head up to me.

"She's dead!" One of the bystanders examined Simone. He looked up at the fella who'd been guarding me. "Your shot got her."

"Huh? I fired my rifle in the air," the man protested.

"Well, something got her, 'cause she's dead."

The guy with the gun pushed through the crowd and the other two men released their grip on me to go follow. Someone nudged Simone's foot. "How do you know she's dead?"

"She's not breathing and she's cold as ice . . . like she's been dead for a while."

I wasn't fool enough to draw attention to myself with folks I knew, so I for sure wasn't about to do it around strangers. Still, I wanted to run to her, hold her hand, and check to see if she was really dead. You see, with Simone, dead didn't mean anything. When she rested during the day, that's exactly how she seemed: dead. Simply lying there on her back, not moving a muscle. If she rested right after a feeding, she looked freshly dead. But after about a week or more, even I hated to go and rouse her at nightfall. She'd be back to that gray, washed out, stanking thing I first found at Miss Tillie's. Eyes would be all sunken into her skull. Sometimes her mouth would be hanging open with them fangs showing like she got scared to death.

I closed my eyes, searching for Simone's voice. A thought, a memory, anything.

Run.

Everyone straightened their backs and started mumbling among themselves. The crowd was too busy consoling that poor mother and wondering how they had two dead bodies in the middle of the road to bother with me. I took the opportunity to crouch behind a tree.

"Well, she's dead now," the man said. "Best call the constable."

The man with the rifle approached. "And tell him what? How do we explain that this woman is dead?"

"And my Nadia?" the girl's father asked. Then he rattled on in their language. Whatever plea he was making quieted everyone and caused the men to lower their heads.

The spokesman for the group nodded toward Simone, and the crowd drew together around her pale body.

Run, Lavinia.

Again, don't have to tell me twice. Simone didn't move when the men wrapped her up in a horse blanket and carted her away. I kept to the shadows and ran as fast as I could. I figured at least I wouldn't have to worry about Simone frying in the sunlight if they stuck her in the ground. She'd be back in no time.

But by the next morning, Simone still hadn't popped back up. All I got from her was a bright, white light. What did that mean? Was she for-real dead?

I had no idea where I was. It had been months since we left Georgia, but we could have traveled all the way to the moon for all I knew. I didn't have a drop of fear traveling with Simone. But now, I was alone. Again. I wasn't even sure I could make it to my Great Lake by myself, but what was going to happen when the two of us arrived there anyway? Maybe it was for the best that we end this partnership now. If Simone was still alive or undead or whatever you want to call it, she'd be fine, I told myself. Hell, she managed to make it without me before, and I wasn't sure how many more accidents like this one with the little girl I could even stomach. I couldn't stop thinking about the mother collapsing onto her daughter's small, limp body.

It's for the best, I repeated to myself. I'd wait until the sun went down, find that North Star, and follow it to my Great Lake. No sooner had that thought come to mind than the head pains started up again, growing in intensity until I could hardly see. My knees buckled, sending me crashing to the ground. An invisible vise squeezed my temples to the point I thought my eyes would burst from their sockets. I was blind, out here on a road in the middle of nowhere. All I could hear was a loud ringing sound in my ears. Somebody could've wrapped a noose around my neck, and I wouldn't have even known it.

"I can't leave like this," I yelped. On my hands and knees, I panted as if I'd run a thousand miles. Clouds of dirt from the road puffed up with each breath. "Jus' make the pain stop!"

And with that, the stabbing in my brain ceased.

Now I knew it must have something to do with that damn bite. Like they say, fool me once. The pain was gone, but the questions it left behind rattled around my skull uncomfortably. I needed to talk to Simone and figure this whole thing out.

Fortunately, I didn't have to wait that long. Simone came waltzing back to the wagon as soon as night fell, like she just took a trip to the outhouse. I grabbed her dirt-speckled arm like Aunt Mary used to do when I was little and got to smelling myself. "Girl, where you been?"

And like I used to do, Simone stared at me like I'd just slapped her. "What?"

"It's been two days! Where were you?"

"Two days?"

Another thing I learned: Since Simone only came out at night and could go so long without feeding, she had no concept of time. A week for me felt like only a day to her.

"I got so hungry," Simone confessed, "I chomped down on the first person I saw."

"Yeah, I know. A little girl. Simone, we talked about this—"

She raised her palm in defense. "I know, I know. You always say, 'Don't shit out in the open. Don't choose the innocent. If they ain't got what we need, don't eat it.' But you're the one in charge of all the details. What did you think was going to happen if I was left to my own devices?"

"Nobody left you nowhere. I told you I was goin' to relieve myself. And if anyone is leavin' anybody, it's you. This is the second time you jus' went dead, leavin' me to figure out how to get out of the mess you caused. If that's how you lasted this long on your own, what you need me for?"

Simone's face fell like she was about to cry. "What are you saying, Lavinia? You want to go off on your own and leave me?"

Honestly, I didn't know. Did I want to live with the threat of going to jail or getting hanged because Simone couldn't control herself? There was no guarantee that the threat would disappear without Simone, not with these Northerners acting like I was some kinda unicorn. "I didn't say that. All I'm sayin' is—"

"I don't always 'go dead,' as you call it. I've been shot, stabbed, and trampled by horses from people chasing me. Almost got staked by some soldiers once. I'm not immune to the pain of it. It's fleeting, but it still hurts. With you around, I can bypass the pain and just get buried."

I crinkled my face in confusion. "But that doesn't help me, Simone. Any number of terrible things can happen to me in the time it takes you to come outta the ground. Them seein' a white woman fallin' out don't mean they're gonna forget about the Black woman left standin' there they can blame."

She hoisted herself onto the back of the wagon and watched her legs swing back and forth. "I guess I didn't consider that."

"I guess you didn't." I stood there with my arms folded, not sure where we went from here. "Maybe we should go our separate ways." And the minute the words left my mouth, a sharp pain in the left side of my head squinted my eyes closed.

"Are you okay?" she asked.

"Just a headache is all," I said, attempting and failing to rub the pulsing sting away. "All this craziness with you is workin' my nerves."

Her voice came softly, almost a whisper. "I don't mean to do that to you, Lavinia." She raised her eyes and forced a little smile. "You can't fault me. I'm an only child. I'm used to having my way."

"And what, you jus' blamed the person closest to you to get out of trouble?"

She shrugged. "It worked for those silly rich girls I used to see. When my father was hired to prepare lavish meals for the rich landowners, he would take me along. Balls, cotillions, summer parties. I'd sneak off to watch the dancing and all the beautiful Parisian dresses. I can't count the number of times I saw those horse-faced girls dropping like flies to take the attention off the fact that their dance cards were empty. So, I tried it a few times at home with the help."

"Did any of them hang for you?"

Simone grunted and rolled her eyes. "Now, you're just being dramatic. Of course, no one died."

"Well, you're gonna have to get over that," I said. Now, I was tapping the side of my head with the heel of my palm.

"So, you'll stay?" She jumped from the wagon bed and folded her hands in front of her.

"I guess." And with that, the pain ended. I opened my eyes and blinked, surprised and relieved. "We need to set some ground rules. No more wanderin' off on your own. You eat only when I'm with you. And I'll choose when and where you get your 'food.' Got it?"

Simone snickered as she finger-combed clumps of earth from her hair. "That's quite the switch, isn't it? You telling me what to do? Bet you never thought that would happen in your lifetime, huh?"

I pondered what she said and wanted to smile. The tables had turned, and a surge of excitement grew in my chest, a sense of power I'd only felt when something foreign ended up in Miss Tillie's meals when she made me mad. As I watched the clumps of dirt fall from her hair, I asked, "What d'you do? Jus' crawl outta the hole?"

"How else was I going to get out?"

I pursed my lips together and asked, "Did you at least cover the hole back up?"

"Why would I do that?"

I don't know if I was madder at her recklessness or selfishness. And I didn't think anything I said was gonna make her see how stupid everything she just did was. Hopefully, I could lessen those occurrences. What I wanted to do right now was get as far away from this place as possible before the town found that empty grave. I took a calming breath and lowered my voice. "Look, no more talk of leavin' each other. Every time that happens, my head starts hurtin'."

"Really?" Simone pressed the back of her hand against my forehead.

I smacked her hand away. "Yes, really. Noticed it that first day after we left."

"Wonder what that means."

Saying it out loud, I realized what it meant: I could never leave this girl, couldn't even consider it. I'd struck an unholy bargain by agreeing to help her find food . . . I should simply call it what it is: helping her kill people. My heart pinched. If she cooperated, I could get her to make better decisions, but no matter how you cut it, I realized that I'd simply traded one form of slavery for another, my mind shackled to a fool who couldn't see past her own nose.

TWELVE

I soon learned that I had at least some control over this connection Simone and I shared. If I was doing something, or if my mind was occupied trying to figure something out, I could ignore Simone's voice. It would also block out my thoughts. I could be thinking about blowing up the world with her in it, and she wouldn't hear me. All that time I'd spent sitting up in the wagon by myself in the daytime, I had nothing else to do but think. She had nothing else to do but listen when I let her. But once we landed near that Great Lake I'd longed to see, everything changed. What ended up occupying my mind and time nearly ripped my relationship with Simone to shreds.

By the time we made it to Indiana, I barely felt the chilled October air on my skin. Over the months, we'd amassed quite a collection of goods to trade once we settled down. Knowing I had a vampire to care for, finding a nice, quiet, private place would be difficult. But I carried on, passing through miles of prairie grass about as tall as me, until I came across a soggy, swampy area dotted by mounds of sand. Getting through all that stuff took about three days. All that to travel six lousy miles. The wagon wheels kept getting stuck in the muck and it was almost impossible for us to ride over the sand hills. Carrying that big box was out of the question, so we had to go around the sloughs and dunes until we found level ground.

It was like I was in another world. One minute, we were in a wood-
land forest and the next it was like we were in a desert. All this sand with
a few stunted bushes and grasses growing out of it. The wind here was
something else; about nearly blew me from the driver's seat. Couldn't
imagine a soul being anywhere around here for miles. That would be a
problem for Simone.

I set up camp right beside one of those sand piles to block the wind.
I reckoned I had about an hour or so before Simone rose at dusk, so I
used the time to figure out what we were gonna do next. I hadn't eaten
in about a week, and even though I didn't have a taste for nothing, I
had a powerful ache in my stomach from it being so empty. While I
wasn't sure how far we were from Chicago, I'd grown weary from all
the traveling we'd been doing. Got tired of sleeping on the hard ground
and running from folks. Even with all the beauty of this strange place,
I longed for four walls and a roof.

I'd hitched the wagon up to an anemic tree that didn't have a leaf
left on it. A rushing sound up ahead caught my attention. Like someone had a big ole broom trying to sweep away all the sand around us.
I'd thought the change from red Georgia clay to the thick black loam
we'd encountered further north was a miracle. All this sand really
knocked me for a loop. Reminded me of Moses leading the Israelites
out of Egypt and into the Promised Land. I knew this was my promised land when I crawled over a sandy ridge and saw what had to be
my Great Lake. It wasn't blue like on the wooden globe. Almost a steel
gray, the massive sheet of water blended perfectly with the overcast
October sky. If not for the few scattered clouds and the sun playing
peekaboo between them, I wouldn't have been able to tell the difference between the two. The air was crisp and fresh. I took a big gulp
and held it in my lungs. Blew it all out, cleansing myself with a bap-
tism from the inside. I looked left, right, then straight ahead. Not an
end to the lake in sight. And the wind kept pushing the waves toward
me, like it was asking me to step in.

"Beautiful, isn't it?"

The lake was speaking to me. Figured it would be a man's voice, all deep as this lake had to be. I walked to the water's edge, right where the sand turned into a bed of pebbles. I squatted down, scooped up some of the water, and brought it to my ear.

"What's that you say?" I asked as it slipped through my fingers. "You want me to come in? Feel you all over me?"

"Might be kinda cold this time of year."

I dropped my hands and stood. The voice wasn't coming from the water, but from a man standing about five feet from me. He was almost as beautiful as that lake. Reddish-brown skin and long black hair, straight like a horse's mane, hung in a ponytail down his back. Thick hair framed his eyes and mouth. Wasn't another body in sight. Only me and this man who appeared out of nowhere. Was this God come to call me out about all the stuff me and Simone had gotten into? I was so glad I'd changed into the green cotton dress I'd been saving—I took that off a woman about a month ago—before I ventured out here, else he would've caught me in that raggedy calico frock I'd been wearing since we left Georgia. Managed to wrangle a couple of pairs of shoes, too, so I wasn't standing here in my old brogans stuffed with straw to avoid feeling the ground through the holes in the soles.

The man lowered his head and smiled before approaching me. I found his moment of shyness quite attractive.

"Don't get too many Negroes up this way. You must be new here." He extended his hand. "King Jones."

"*King* Jones?"

"King David Jones." He lifted his shoulder. "My daddy was a preacher. And you are?"

"Lavinia."

I didn't have a last name like he did. Folks usually took their master's name after the war was over, but I didn't wanna do that. I didn't need nothing to remind me of that part of my life. I wondered if "Jones" was the name of his people or the folks who'd owned them.

He hugged himself and rubbed his hands against his arms. "What brings you out here? You're not looking to buy any fish are you? Because I sold the last of it in town. If you come back tomorrow . . ."

"Not looking for fish," I said. "Been wantin' to see this lake. Ain't never seen nothin' this big in my life."

He was standing so close to me now that I could smell the beach coming from his skin. Beach and fish. Could he smell death on me? Ever since Simone bit me, I had this whisper of stink following me around, like the first hint you get when you realize something had crawled into the walls of your house and died. I took a step back and began spilling all this information about me that I didn't remember him asking for. I told him about coming up here after the war. Told him about Simone, my sickly young mistress, who'd recently lost her poor Aunt Tillie back in Georgia. That she was looking for a new place to settle for the winter before she made her way back to Montreal.

King tilted his head to the sky. "Now where have I heard that story before?"

"You think I'm lyin'?" I asked, a bit put off.

He blinked, looked at me, and smiled. "Of course not. It's just something you said that sounded familiar, that's all."

King David turned my attention to the northwestern horizon and pointed out a gray blob that was Chicago. I didn't know which was better: living in a big city like that or waking up every morning and seeing it set next to such a beautiful man.

"There's an old stagecoach road that'll take you right into the city," he suggested.

"Any places around here that'll take us in for a spell?"

"Lots of places to stay around here," King said. He pivoted on his heels as he pointed to and named nearby towns like Tolleston, Miller Station, and Bradford.

"What's closest to you . . . I mean here, this beach?" We both laughed at my slip. "I wanna be as close to all this as possible."

"Gets awfully cold around here in winter," King warned. "Not sure a Georgia girl like you would enjoy that too much."

"I'll manage."

Truth was, I couldn't feel a thing, not the chill in the wind or the coolness of the lake when I scooped it in my hands. I'd learned that

Simone's "kiss" did more than simply link our thoughts. Changes in the weather didn't affect me. I could go days on only a couple of hours of sleep. I could still eat food, but my appetite was next to nothing. My body had changed to serve Simone. I needed to always be on call for her. Make sure her rest wasn't disturbed or the place discovered. Had to make sure she was fed properly and stayed out of the sunlight. And I needed all my energy to stalk her prey. Couldn't do that if I had to worry about my own needs.

Yet, here was someone helping me.

Even offered me a meal in the tiny sod dugout he called home a few steps from the beach. Fried sturgeon and beans. The taste of the food was lost on me, but I would've eaten the driftwood his furniture was made from to spend a couple more minutes in his company. His voice was as soothing as the lake licking the shore. And he sure talked up a storm! I didn't mind. Being all lonesome out here, I reckon he was happy to have somebody to talk to.

King David Jones was born a freeman, the son of a Potawatomi girl and a slave who'd run off during the War of 1812. King had spent his life on the lake up north in Michigan, helping his daddy supply fish to folks coming through from Detroit on their way west. How I envied how free he was! Never knowing the shackles of slavery. Coming and going as he pleased. Doing whatever he got a notion to do. Glad he didn't ask about my former life. Not that I had tales of rapes or beatings and such, but slave life ain't glamorous by no means. I didn't know nothing beyond the little town Miss Tillie's plantation was in because I wasn't free to come and go like King. Betcha he could read and write, too.

I asked him about the sod house, thinking this would be best for me and Simone while we were here. It was cool like a tomb, with only a door to let in the sun. His place was nestled right between two large ponds teeming with all kinds of fish. With the tall reeds and prairie grass, you wouldn't even know it was here. Was surprised there weren't more Black folks living out this way. Runaways could've hidden for weeks before a paddy roller found them with this mess of brush growing everywhere. But according to King, wasn't nobody here but him. His place was set

up with a jackleg bed, a table and two chairs (guess he did have company every once in a while), and a potbelly stove with the pipe snaking
outside to vent the smoke. Though he kept feeding the fire in the stove,
I couldn't tell the difference. All I felt was the warmth of having another
living human to talk to for once.

I didn't realize how long I'd set up in King's dugout until two sharp
raps at his wooden door made us pause.

"Who on earth could that be?" King asked as he rose to answer the
door. The slight irritation on his face made me smile.

But I prepared myself anyway. I was expecting a woman. Couldn't
no man as handsome as him be alone on purpose. I was right. King
took a step back when he opened the door. Simone stood on the other
side. The lantern in her hand and the black night made her white skin
glow like a candle.

I jumped to my feet and hurried to the door. I stood between the
two. "King, this is Miss Simone, my mistress." I'd forgotten all about her.
Either I had blocked her out by being so occupied with King, or she had
been sitting out there, listening to us the whole time, waiting to make her
entrance. "Miss Simone, this is King Jones. We'd jus' been talkin' and—"

Simone crossed her arms and raised an eyebrow. "King Jones." She
laid her long, pale fingers on his chest. "Don't you look . . . delicious."

I pushed Simone back outside. "He's not for dinner," I hissed in her
ear. I turned back to King. "Forgive her. She ain't been well."

"I can see that," King said, doubt clouding his dark eyes.

I grabbed Simone's hand and dragged her back to the wagon as fast
as I could, running through sand. I didn't say a word to her. Tried re-
placing King's image and voice with the sound of the lake now behind
us. But I let my anger at Simone come through. That I couldn't control. Had she not shown up, I'd have been there all night, asking him
more questions about stuff I cared nothing about. Of all the times for
Simone to rise from her box without me rousing her first. Bet she had
a good old time watching me through my thoughts.

"You put them eyes of yours back in your head," I said when we got
to the wagon. "King is a nice enough man. He can help us."

"Of course, he can," Simone said, plopping herself onto the edge of the wagon bed, her legs swinging like some child on a tree branch. "I'm famished."

"No, not him."

"Why not him? If he tastes as sweet as you . . . Wait a minute. Has someone caught my Lavinia's fancy?"

"Ain't nobody caught nothin'," I lied. "Before you interrupted us, King was tellin' me about this huntin' area not far from here. Out in the swamps or somethin'. Lots of folks from all over go there, 'specially at night. That would be the perfect place for us to hunt, too. Thought maybe we could go out there, see what's what."

"But that's not what you were thinking the whole time, was it?" She raised an eyebrow. "How do you think I found you?"

I'd been paying so much attention to King—the way he smelled, how he stroked his facial hair before answering a question. His perfectly straight teeth . . .

"You're thinking about him right now!" Simone said with a punch to my arm.

I couldn't help but smile. "Look, after months in a wagon with nothin' but the world passin' by, my eyes deserve a little break. That King Jones was sho' a handsome thing!"

"He's only a man," Simone said, with a hint of disgust in her voice.

"A whole lotta man!" I added, my thoughts wandering back over to memories of his face.

Simone turned to me with her arms folded across her chest. "Have you forgotten what your life was like in Georgia?"

I swatted the air with my hand. "What's he gotta do with that?"

"Don't you wonder why he's out here in the middle of nowhere? Up to no good probably, hiding from a wife or the law."

"You got all of that from the two seconds you saw him? Or is there another reason why you think I can't trust him?" I didn't want to believe it was because he was a Negro. Simone had no problem with me, but in all the stories she'd told me, I'd never once heard her talk about being around any other Black folks. I was a bit miffed that she was turning my wonderful day into something dark. Almost had me thinking twice about King with all her assumptions. Can't nothing evil be packaged in something as beautiful as him, right?

"Beautiful or not, you can't trust him because he's human."

"You trusted me."

Simone rolled her eyes and stared out into the darkness. "He'll break your heart. They all do."

I jumped down from the wagon, wanting to end the conversation since, knowing Simone, she wasn't gonna tell me why she had her hackles all up about King. I'd simply wait until dawn and find out for myself. This time, though, she surprised me.

"There was a priest at my parish, Father Henri. He arrived from France with his thick head of auburn curls and hypnotic speech that calmed colicky babies with only a word. Why the monsignor would send such a seductive creature who looked like that . . ."

"You had it bad for him, huh?"

Simone finally turned away from the darkness and looked at me. "It was because of him that I found myself in the clutches of that thing that turned me into what I am."

I let her confession hang in the air for a minute. She usually rambled on about the good times of her life. I didn't want to pry too much, at least not then. As much as we give of ourselves, us women are entitled to a few secrets, something that didn't belong to husbands, children, or slave owners. Problem was, with my mind connection to Simone, I had to work extra hard to keep it that way.

"You act like we're jumpin' the broom tomorrow," I said, trying to change the mood. "The point is, that place out in Tolleston sounds like a nice private spot for us to hunt."

"So, we're staying? Right here, on the beach?"

"Why not? It's quiet, and according to King, not a whole lot of people around here, either."

"According to King, huh?"

I could hear Simone's eyes rolling to that question. "Until I learn more about this area, we're gonna need King. Alive. Got it?"

"Got it. I'll stop thinking about King . . . if you can."

Leave it to her to ask me the impossible.

Yeah, right, I stopped thinking about King. That would've been like me trying to ignore the sun shining every morning.

The next day, I returned to his dugout with all the apologies for Simone's behavior I could muster. He was nice enough to take time out of his fishing routine to help me find a dugout of my own. Conversation came easily between us during the search. Almost forgot who I was until he mentioned a story in the papers about some little girl south of here getting eaten—his words, not mine—by a strange woman whose dead body went missing from her grave. An "Oh, yeah?" was all I could manage for fear that something stupid and incriminating might spill from my mouth.

"Said there was a Negro woman with her," King added. He stared at me for a long minute.

I swallowed, searching the area for something my eyes could focus on other than King's accusatory expression.

"I guess I better not anger you or your mistress."

A nervous snort left me as I bent down to fiddle with the hem of my skirts, but then King laughed. A throw-your-head-back-and-clutch-your-belly laugh. Had tears streaming down his face when he was done. "Guess you weren't the only one with the idea of traveling with a white woman to get out of Georgia."

I tried to push the pitiful image of the girl and her mother out of my mind and match his humor, but I was too focused on not shitting my britches. A weak chuckle was all I could manage, but it was enough for him to nudge me with his elbow and continue his trek among the dunes.

Another reason to stay close and keep my eye on him.

The dugout I settled for wasn't that far from his. Instead of being right on the beach, it lay more inland where wetland grass, fruit-bearing bushes, oak trees, and white pine thrived. Less than a quarter mile south of the lake, I had the Grand Calumet River and dozens of ponds with their own fish supply as my backyard.

"This is the one," I proclaimed, standing at the entrance to the sandy cave. It was at the base of a larger hill sparsely covered in wispy grass. I wouldn't have known it was there if King hadn't pointed it out. The cave wasn't completely empty. A bed of cattails and branches covered the floor, and it smelled like a zoo. Could fit a whole family of bears with room to spare. Just right for two women . . . and that old ration box we now used as a coffin. Whatever called this place home would have to find somewhere else to live.

"Way out here by yourself?" King asked as he wiped sweat from his brow with a handkerchief. Though a cool breeze blew off the lake for most of the afternoon, all that crawling and climbing over them sand dunes had him sweating like a runaway slave. If he noticed I wasn't sweating, he didn't say nothing about it. "Where's your mistress staying?"

In a box, in my wagon, I almost said. I was so at ease around him. I couldn't remember the names of all the towns he'd told me about, so I merely pointed west. "Over there."

"Tolleston?"

"Yes," I said with a straight face.

"You're not staying with her?"

Back at Miss Tillie's, I'd learned that telling a fib helped me survive, so now lying came easily to me. "She ain't found a place yet," I said while kicking apart the animal nest. "Some church folks took her in. She don't need me jus' yet."

"Awfully far for you to be traveling—"

"I don't mind. Better than stayin' where folks don't want you nohow."

He sighed at some faraway thought. "I know what you mean."

Did he? Couldn't imagine anybody not wanting this man around.

"No need in setting up this place if you're only going to be here for a little while," he said after a long pause. "You're welcome to stay with me, if you like . . . until you get on your feet."

What I wouldn't give to say yes to that! But I had a vamp to care for. "Don't think Miss Simone would take too kindly to me settin' up house with a man." Don't think King would take too kindly to a coffin right outside his dugout either.

It took us a whole 'nother day to get the wagon to my new home, what with the wheels getting stuck in the soggy sand every couple of feet. And since the horse couldn't pull the load up the dunes, we had to take the long way around, until we found level paths to travel on. Of course, he asked about the box in the back. Mind you, it wasn't coffin-shaped like something you see posted up at the undertaker's. It was nothing more than a regular ole rectangular box big enough for a body.

He rapped on the lid. "If we took some of this stuff out—"

I stopped him before he opened it. "Can't. Got lady stuff in there."

I didn't know what lady stuff that could be. Miss Tillie had an oak box about half the size of Simone's at the foot of her bed. Called it her hope chest. I think the only thing she was hoping for was that her husband wouldn't go in there and find the stash of booze she kept beneath her wedding dress and a bunch of quilts. King simply shrugged, took off his shirt, and lifted the thing like it didn't have no dead body in it at all.

Must've seen the look on my face because he chuckled and said, "What's the matter? Never seen a shirtless man before?"

Not one chiseled like you, I wanted to say. Thinking on my feet again, I pointed to the wooden cross he had around his neck. My fingers "accidentally" grazed his solid chest as I examined the cross. Slightly bigger than the palm of my hand, someone had taken the time to carve fancy swirls and patterns into the creamy tan wood.

"African white mahogany," King explained after he set the box back on the ground. He got that faraway look on his face again while he fingered the cross with me holding it, his hand cupping mine. "The wood came with my great-grandfather from Nigeria. He kept some and passed them to his children to remind them where they came from. 'Stay strong, like this wood,' he told them. When it passed to my daddy, he turned it into this. It was the only thing he took with him when he freed himself." He stared at the cross for a while then shook his head. Then he quietly carried Simone's coffin into the dugout.

Africa. I'd held something that'd come all the way from Africa. King had history, stories to tell his children's children. What was I going to tell mine? That I lugged a dead body with me all the way from Georgia?

After we—or rather King—unloaded what little belongings I had from the wagon, I boiled up some sassafras tea from all the plants growing around the place. He trapped a couple of rabbits for supper. Roasted them over an open fire and we ate sitting right on top of Simone's box. I didn't rouse her that evening. Was glad she didn't bother waking herself, either. Don't think I could've explained my way out of that. King and I didn't talk much while we ate. Most of the time was spent chewing and smiling at each other. The silence between us felt perfectly natural, like an old married couple used to each other's company. First bit of normal I'd had since leaving Georgia. Hated to see him go, but he'd lost a whole day of fishing and needed to get up early the next morning to make up for it. I stood at the cave entrance until the night swallowed him up. And then, like a normal human, spent the remainder of the night imagining what our babies might look like.

I didn't have to walk far to see the smoke spiraling out of King's dugout. Only a five-minute climb over a sand dune about as tall as a two-story house, was all. I used my experience stalking Simone's prey to map out his daily activities. He spent his early morning hours fishing out on the lake with three white fellas. They seemed friendly enough; laughing and joking with King like he was one of them. Wouldn't see that down South. They'd return before noon with a whole mess of sturgeon. I was glad to see that when they split the catch, King got the same amount as they did. I also learned that they sold their fish in different towns so as not to compete with each other. Good thing King's territory was east in Miller Station, and not west in Tolleston where I'd told him Simone lived.

Then he'd be out gutting and drying his catch, getting it ready for sale in neighboring towns right before folks got ready for supper. I'd pick my way through the huckleberry bushes and slide down a mound of sand toward his place and wave hello. A few days a week, I'd invite myself over to help gut and dry, hoping the fish smell covered my own rot. Felt strange, me doing all the calling and courting. But he didn't seem to mind.

With him so busy and me sitting around waiting until Simone needed to feed, I had time to think up other reasons to go by and see him. I'd ask him questions I already knew the answers to, like if the leaves I'd picked on my way to his place were poison ivy. Or if he knew of a better way to trap rabbits. Or if he could fix the wagon wheel I'd purposely spent all morning tearing up with my bare hands. Stupid stuff that I'm ashamed to admit now. I cooked him meals, too, mostly to show off my culinary skills: squirrel, rabbit, and a variety of fish from the surrounding ponds. I even made bread from the Canadian rye that grew among the wetlands. My efforts weren't for naught. Whenever I got ready to leave, he'd think of something else to say, another reason for me to stay longer. At least, that's what I liked to think he was doing.

"It's always about King, isn't it?" Simone asked me one evening in the dugout.

I huffed and rolled my eyes. While I wished Simone would quit invading my brain whenever I wanted to soothe my loneliness with thoughts of King, I was glad she decided to get out of her box and confront me. Not that I wanted to hear what she had to say. Even when I wasn't with her, she didn't hold back expressing herself through her mental connection to me. But I hadn't seen King in a week and was kinda feeling sorry for myself now.

"Can't you jus' leave me to my thoughts?" I asked from beneath my jackleg bed. Since I needed a distraction, I took to organizing all the stuff I'd pilfered from Simone's victims. My dugout was packed full of crap: brass buttons, belts, coins and folding money (if we were lucky), rifles, pistols, pocket watches, parasols, and brooches. One fella even had a gold front tooth. Took a minute to get that out. Having light fingers was another skill us slaves needed to have, and I was the queen of lifting things that didn't belong to me. Since I was always in the big house with Miss Tillie, the other Negroes figured I had access to things they wouldn't otherwise have. If somebody needed an extra bit of cornmeal for ashcakes, a brandy-soaked cloth for a teething baby, or even just to spit in Massa's tea once in a while, they came to me.

"I would," she said, as she plopped on the bed above me. "But that's all I hear now."

"Ain't nobody makin' you listen." I bumped my head on the sagging part where her behind was when I scooted myself out. I stood and straightened my back.

Simone was sitting on the bed fashioning her hair into a long braid over her shoulder. A habit I realized she had whenever she was about to say something crazy. "I wonder, would his blood have a fishy taste," she said as if she were thinking aloud and I wasn't standing there listening. "Or maybe his Potawatomi side will make his taste even better than you." Then she flashed a smile at me, showing off them wolf teeth of hers.

I said nothing. Just turned on my heel and walked toward the door.

"Where are you going?" I heard her say from close behind me.

"Out." I walked out the door, pushing closed the ill-fitting wooden thing behind me.

"You almost hit me with that!" she said. "Lavinia! Where are you going?"

I increased my pace, heading toward the tall dune I usually sat on to watch King during the day. From behind, Simone's increasingly angry pleas for me to stop were met with silence. The breeze blew against my face as I rushed toward the dune, and eventually breaking into a sprint, the wind soothed me. It gave me something to feel other than my irritation. Thought I was gonna burst. Even as the climb up the dune slowed me down, but didn't get me winded, I pressed on until I reached the top.

And of course, she was right behind me.

I turned to her and held my arm out. "Stop, Simone."

"Why are you ignoring me?" she said with a muted stomp of her foot against the sand.

I took a deep breath and said, "I'm not ignorin' you, Simone. I just need a minute to myself."

"Why?" she pouted. "Because you haven't seen King? I'm here."

"Yes, you're here. And I'd have been perfectly fine sittin' there talkin' to you tonight. But you up here raisin' sand about King when I ain't said a word about him."

"You were thinking about him."

"So what? What's wrong with me thinkin' about him? I do nothin' all day while you're sleepin'. King's the only person around here I can talk to durin' the day."

"I don't have to sleep, you know," Simone said with her lip poked out. She started messing with that braid of hers that must have come undone while she was chasing me to the dune. "I can stay up."

I sighed and placed my hands on her shoulders. "I'm with you all night, Simone. I like spendin' time with King." When she pursed her lips and lowered her head, I added, "That don't mean I don't like spendin' time with you. Sometimes I jus' need a minute. Didn't you ever jus' wanna be by yourself with your own thoughts sometimes?"

She closed her eyes, and shook her head as if to dismiss the thought. Given what I know about Simone, I can imagine her just a ball of energy, only stopping when her nursemaid or somebody forced her to sleep. "You said you were an only child, right? You had to have spent some time by yourself."

She shrugged again. "I never liked it."

"I can imagine."

"You wanting time to yourself," Simone started as she sat on the sand. I joined her. "My mother always wanted time for herself. I'd spend all morning with the tutor on lessons. When I was done, I wanted my mother. She always shooed me away. I don't know why. All she had to do was manage the house and the servants and the accounts."

I puckered my face in confusion. "I thought you hated rich landowners. Sounds like you had plenty of money."

"Anyway. Mother would retire to her room the minute I emerged from my lessons. I wouldn't see her again until supper."

"What was she doin'?"

"Laudanum. I peeked through the keyhole once."

I smiled. "I ain't up here takin' laudanum, Simone." Though if I knew where I could get some . . . "Listen. Here are the rules. I know I can't stop you from pokin' in my brain whenever you want. But when I come up here to think, you gotta leave me be, hear? No pokin' in my brain. No commentin' or gettin' mad 'cause a thought or two of King might pass through."

She folded her arms against her chest and mumbled, "Way more than two."

"This here thinkin' dune is off-limits," I continued. "Okay?"

"Fine." She stood and wiped the sand from the back of her frock. Then she raised her head to the sky. "Look at all those stars."

I stood next to her. "Close your eyes and listen. You can hear the earth breathe."

"It's just the lake rolling up on the beach, silly!"

I yanked her by the arm to make her stand closer to me. With her cold hand in mine, I urged her to listen to the lake. Enjoy the quiet. Take a minute to forget about King and killing folks.

"Once I figure out how to make some money, we can go on to Chicago like we planned," I said.

"And what about King?"

"King's jus' a friend helpin' me out. Helpin' *us* out. I couldn't leave you if I wanted to, so we both gotta make this work. Constantly irritatin' each other over silly things don't help."

"Fine. Let's pick a new place to hunt." Simone closed her eyes and twirled about with her arms outstretched. "Waiting to pick one of those hunters out in the woods takes too long." She spun several times with one pointer finger extended. When she stopped, her gaze followed the digit. "Let's go there."

I squinted my eyes toward the western location she'd randomly chosen. "Only see a few lights. King mentioned some places to me. Have to ask him what's there."

Simone lowered her arm to her side with a slap. "Of course, you do."

"Well, I can't jus' mosey on over there, walkin' around like ain't nobody gonna notice me. King said . . ." I stopped when she tilted her head and eyed me. "I *heard* people been talkin' about what happened with that little girl you ate."

"What's that have to do with us?"

"They're tellin' folks it was a white woman and a Black woman travelin' together that did it. And according to . . . *some folks*, I'm the only Black woman here. Folks might put two and two together if we ain't careful."

"That town is three days from here," Simone said. "And that was weeks ago. Surely more things have happened since we were there." She took my hand in hers. "You ready?"

I yanked myself away. "Not tonight. Lemme get my bearin's first. I don't even know how far wherever you jus' pointed is. You'll be fine for the next couple of days. Come on," I sat back down on the dune and patted the space next to me. "Let's listen to the earth breathe for a while."

Thirteen

Since Simone had no concept of time, she had no idea that it was three days since that night on the thinking dune when we finally got out to what I learned was a little town called Clarke Station, northeast of Tolleston and about a day's journey away. And yes, it was King who told me all about it.

He was sitting right outside the door of his dugout the afternoon I decided to stop by and inquire. At his feet was a pile of prairie grass, the onset of colder weather fading the once-green blades to pale, brown wispy spears. Several braids of grass were draped along his lap and stretched to the ground like skinny brown eels. His forearm atop the pile kept them from blowing away in the intermittent gusts off the lake.

"First time seeing you in a whole week," he said without looking up. How he knew it was me, I don't know, given he couldn't have heard me walking across the sand. Must've seen me before I saw him. Or he was waiting on me. Either way, his greeting caused a smile to erupt on my face. "Missed you while I was out visiting my mama."

"I missed you, too," I said, trying to hide my giddiness. "I'm sure she enjoyed the visit. What you workin' on?"

He bent down and retrieved a white net from the sand. Holding it up in the air, he stretched it to reveal several openings big enough for his fist to go through. "My net's no good. Until I can sell a few more loads of fish, I gotta make do with this."

"Makin' your own net?" I asked. "Need some help?"

He looked up at me, eyes narrowed by the sunlight. A fist on his hip, he sighed and said, "Was hoping you would say that."

King gave up the wobbly, three-legged stool he'd been sitting on, and plopped down on the sand at my feet. I took a few strands of grass, knotted them together on one end, then started plaiting them while King laid out the finished ones into a large lattice. I spied the rest of his gear strewn all over the beach. Wooden poles with long cracks snaking down the shafts. A tangled mess of frayed fishing line discarded in a pile as if a frustrated King had given up on releasing all the knots. Rusted hooks that looked about ready to snap in two if I so much as picked them up.

"You're quick," he commented as he took a few of my finished pieces and added them to his array in the sand.

"I've braided my fair share of heads," I added.

"Your dainty little things are better than these sausages I got." He held up his hand and wiggled his thick fingers.

I studied my hands. Dainty wouldn't be the word I'd use for these rough claws. Even my nails were worn down to ragged nubs. I turned my body slightly away from him and continued to braid. "How's your mama?"

"Fine." He stopped arranging the strands and stared out toward the lake. "We spent the whole time arguing about my moving with her to Chicago."

"And you don't want to?"

"One day. Right now, I'm testing out a new adventure that's fallen in my lap."

"What's that?"

"Oh, this young Georgia girl who keeps spying on me every morning."

My face grew hot. My eyes went everywhere but to his face. Lord, I was just as bad as Simone. Her stalking my brain, and here I was stalking this poor man. I didn't think he noticed, except when I purposely made my presence known. But he laid his hand on mine and squeezed.

"I like knowing you're there," he said softly. "Gives me something to look forward to when I get back from the lake."

"You do?" More than my face was aflame at this point.

He smiled. "What brings you by today?"

I almost forgot why I was there, trapped in his eyes, his voice, the lingering touch of his rough hand on mine that he had yet to release. I imagined Simone raging now if she were awake, probably vomiting—if she could—at me swooning over this man. At least I knew the sunshine would keep her in the dugout. Should she find her way into my thoughts, I'd deal with her colorful assessment later. Right now, I'm gonna soak this in as long as I can.

When I finally remembered myself, I turned from him and said, "I was wonderin' what town was over that way." I pointed to the spot Simone had picked.

King released my hand and trained his eyes west. "Well, you've got Clarke Station . . ."

"How far away is that?"

"About a day's journey. Why?"

"Oh, my mistress was wonderin' about it. Told her I'd see if you knew anything."

"You aren't thinking about moving, are you?"

"Well, if my mistress goes . . ."

He released a loud breath and scooted his bottom across the sand so that he was looking right up at me.

"What's wrong, King?"

"Don't take this the wrong way. I realize we've only known each other for a few weeks, but I think I can say this to you." He placed his hands on my knees and said quietly, "You're free. You don't have to go with her if you don't want to."

I ain't as free as you think, I wanted to say. Simone's hold on me, this invisible thing connecting us, was almost as bad as the one that tethered me to Miss Tillie my whole life. His words bore a glint of truth. Legally, I was free. I should be able to stay with King if I wanted, part ways with Simone if I wanted . . . Can't even ponder long on that lest my head pains get to roaring. "I know, King. But startin' over for me ain't that easy."

"I can't imagine what life was like for you before the war. And you don't have to tell me about it now or ever. I just want you to know you have choices now and your mistress can't hold you to a status that doesn't exist anymore. Besides, two women traveling alone just invites trouble. Trouble you, of all people, don't need. If you decided to stay, I wouldn't let you suffer out here on your own. The invitation to stay with me is still open."

As quickly as the image of me playing mistress in his dugout crossed my mind, I brushed it away, along with a brief stab of pain at my temple. "I couldn't crowd you outta your place like that," I said, hoping my mild refusal goaded him into saying more.

He pursed his lips and gave his head a quick tilt to the side. "We'd get a bigger place. Wouldn't have to be this here dugout. Wouldn't have to be on this here beach, either. It can be anywhere you want."

I smiled and tried to resume braiding the grass on my lap. But my fingers forgot what to do, awkwardly bending and scratching over each other until the neat plait I had going turned into a knotted, twisted mess curving to one side. His was almost the same proposition Simone had given me back in Georgia. Except he ain't out here murdering anybody. "You makin' plans, Mr. Jones?"

King matched my expression. "Not if you're leaving."

"Well, I didn't say I was. Miss Simone just wants to get out of Tolleston for a while."

He turned to me with a devilish grin on his face. "You two going after another little girl?"

For the third time my face ignited, and I thought my eyes were gonna pop out of their sockets. "What you goin' on about?" I said with a nervous chuckle.

"That story I told you about, remember? The little girl that was attacked in Crown Point. Heard that, in the past couple of weeks, two hunters were found out in the Tolleston woods with their throats torn out and all the blood drained from their bodies. Just like that little girl."

I think I left my body at that point. Next thing I knew, he was gently shaking me.

"You okay?" He looked genuinely worried. "I'm only joking."

"Oh, I know," I said, fanning myself. "It's jus' so awful, hearin' about all them killings. Jus' awful."

"I didn't mean to upset you, Lavinia. I'm sorry. Guess I'm getting too comfortable with you."

"Get as comfortable as you like." The words fell out of my mouth.

"You sure? I can be pretty blunt."

"I'm still here talkin' to you, ain't I?"

"And making this work go by a lot faster. Finish this pile, and I'll tell you what you wanna know about Clarke Station."

"What a bunch of horseshit!" Martin says. "I'm supposed to believe Miss Simone, little dainty Miss Simone, was capable of doing that kind of damage to those hunters?" He shook his head. "No way."

"That's what I'm trying to tell you," I say, rubbing my bandaged arm. At least it's stopped bleeding, as the crimson bloom hasn't grown in a while. For a minute, I thought my ghoulness returned, but the throbbing hadn't subsided. "She wasn't like the rest of us."

"And she could tear out a man's throat like a coyote? Drain their blood like a . . . like a . . ."

"Vampire?"

"Ain't no such thing as a vampire!" He bangs his fist on the desk. But he's smiling at the same time, a laugh tickling his words.

"So, just because you haven't seen it means it ain't true?"

"Yeah."

"That makes no sense, Martin. You don't see the sun shinin' in France, but you know it's daylight there at some point."

"Maybe you should tell this story to the judge in the morning. He might think you didn't have all your faculties when you killed Miss Simone and show you some mercy."

"Huh, you think I'm talkin' crazy? Lemme tell you about crazy: a pair of folks who lived right here in Tolleston believed in vampires and knew Simone was one."

"And who would that be?"

FOURTEEN

Other than King, the only people I'd met since coming to the area were the few general store owners I sold or traded my stolen goods with. I doubted being friendly ever crossed their minds. Hardly anybody in the area would do business with me. I was free to walk into their establishments, but I couldn't sell or trade nothing. Half of them acted like I wasn't even in the store. I had to take Simone with me to get anything done, which was a pain, because that meant I had to find places that operated after the sun went down. And when Simone guessed why I was taking her with me, she always wanted to make a meal outta one of the store owners.

Then I came across Victor and Valerica Radut.

Now, Victor was this fat, squat, balding thing who owned a little general store out in Miller Station. His wife, Valerica, was a sickly reed compared to him. Thinner than a blade of grass, that one was. Ole Victor couldn't speak a lick of English, so he needed his wife to do all the talking. He'd stand behind her, waving his hands and hollering in their language; she'd be flinching all the while. Seemed like everything she did made him mad. Even when she secured a trade that favored him, his eyebrows would be all knitted together like couldn't nothing make him happy. I guess I brought in good stuff, because Victor didn't holler no more or less at me than he did at everybody else. Still, my skin color didn't escape him. He'd make me wait until all his customers were gone before he even looked in my direction. Then he'd cross his arms and mumble under his breath while I showed him my wares. Dealing with Victor, I learned I could recognize the word "nigger" in any language.

Anyway, I had all day to wait. If another person who spoke all crazy like him came in, he'd do the deal himself, leaving Valerica time to talk to me. She'd glance at him over her shoulder and sidle over to me, messing around with whatever was in arm's reach, acting like she really wasn't talking to me at all. Her accent was so thick, by the time I ciphered out what she was saying, Victor was ready for me. After a while, me and Valerica got to understanding each other just fine.

"I see you've made a new friend," Simone said one evening. "The shopkeeper's wife. The one you're trying to hide from me."

I was sitting on the jackleg bed, knitting a blanket with some yarn and needles I'd gotten from the Raduts' store. "I ain't tryin' to hide nobody," I lied. "Jus' wasn't no reason to mention her. Like you said, she's jus' the shopkeeper's wife, is all."

"You spend a lot of time there."

"How else you think we get these new frocks and such? I gotta sell off all this junk we got lyin' 'round here. Can't hardly walk out the door for stubbin' my toe."

Truth was, I didn't want her to know about Valerica. I'd already reduced my interactions with King to keep him alive, and I needed to have some human contact during the day or I was gonna lose it. And I didn't trust Simone. She hadn't said much about King since I started going to Radut General Store. I didn't know where the Raduts were from, but I could tell it wasn't anywhere in America or Canada. All I needed was for Simone to start craving exotic food again—the two hunters she'd eaten in the Tolleston woods were Germans, according to her taste buds.

I thought I'd succeeded in keeping Valerica to myself by reading the newspaper out loud whenever I went to the store. With my reading skills, it took me forever to sound out the words, but the more I did it, the better I got. Instead of thoughts of Valerica, Simone was supposed to know about what the government calls reconstructing the South. I skipped over the reports of dead hunters found in the woods. She'd think it was some kind of competition, not a warning that we needed to be more careful disposing of the bodies.

Simone plopped on the bed with me. "Your friend. Why is she so afraid?"

"Her husband's crazy. Be shoutin' all the time at nothin'."

"He's not so nice to you."

I lowered my knitting and eyed Simone. I knew where she was going with this, and I didn't stop her. Valerica had told me how she had to leave all her people behind in the old country because of Victor's superstitions about haints and vamps. Sometimes I'd catch her sniffling and wiping her eyes when I came in the store. I'd imagine Victor being the source of her tears, and me being the one to stop them. Then I'd have a friend for life. All it'd take was a word to Simone.

Simone heard my musing.

"You can't have him," I said, after she begged me to let her eat him. "He's the only one around here who don't mind doin' business with me."

"He might be nicer . . . if I came with you."

"Uh-huh," I said. "You ain't foolin' nobody, Simone."

"What?" she said, eyes all wide like I'd insulted her. "I don't want to teach *her* a lesson!"

"You ain't teachin' nobody nothin'! I mean, good grief, you can't go after every human I befriend. Don't you ever wish there were others like you?"

"Why? I'm doing fine all by myself."

"You mean fine with me helpin' you?"

Simone smiled, showing those deadly fangs of hers. "See! I don't need anyone else. Especially not another vampire."

"But still . . ."

Simone sighed and fell back onto the unmade bed. She laid her arm across her face in a fake swoon. "Is this about King again? We could solve that problem very easily."

"You can't have King," I said.

"Apparently, neither can you."

I groaned and resumed my row of purls. She didn't understand. Loneliness will kill you faster than a vamp at your neck. Too much time by yourself, and your mind starts taking trips to places you don't wanna go. The devil parks himself on your shoulder, tricking you into thinking you're doing something to get rid of it, but you're only making the loneliness worse, more powerful. Before you know it, it's too late. Loneliness ain't what turned you into a fool; it's you, allowing it to make you do foolish things. To be fair, Lord knows the things I'd done for Simone were right foolish, too.

Anybody else would call me a thief, a hermit, or a bit touched in the head with this new life I had. Another ghoul, for example, would understand. They'd understand the connection I had to Simone; the reasons why I couldn't go where I wanted, when I wanted. Why I craved another human sometimes like my next breath.

"That's what you want?" Simone asked, wandering around in my thoughts again. "Another like you?"

I shrugged. "I don't know. Maybe? Don't you ever want another like you?"

"No!" Simone sat up. "You think I want to be this thing that I am? To be around others like me? I had a good life before that happened."

"I know," I said, lowering my work.

"I had a family, friends, suitors. Parties to attend. You're the only thing making this life bearable."

"You went a year without me."

"And do you know why I was in that saloon when you found me?"

"Too stupid to leave?"

"Too tired of this existence. I was working up the nerve to walk out into the sunlight when you found me."

I wasn't sure how I was supposed to feel after hearing that. Loneliness had almost driven her to kill herself, and then I came along and extended her misery. At least I knew she understood how I felt. Curled up on the bed, she looked more like a lost babe than a ruthless killer. Almost thought I saw tears in her eyes even though I knew she couldn't cry.

"Simone, jus' 'cause I wanna be around other people don't have nothin' to do with us. We gotta bond, you and me, and ain't nothin' I can think of can change that. But you can't go thinkin' everybody I meet is food."

"Fine," Simone said with a roll of her eyes. She waved her hand at me. "Go find somebody to befriend. But make sure they're worth it. I won't hesitate to get rid of anybody who hurts you. And I don't have the patience to train another Lavinia."

I don't know who was training who between the two of us, but Simone coming with me the next time I went to the Raduts' store wasn't an entirely bad idea—long as she understood the rules before we went. Simone was good at haggling. I'd seen her get more money for stuff that wasn't worth half of what we got for it.

"You can come with me," I told her. "But only after you've fed. Need you focusin' on the deal, not food."

I thought *I* had issues being Black. The stares, the nasty remarks, being treated like a child or completely ignored. None of that was new to me. Victor and Valerica's reaction to Simone was, though. We weren't in the store for two seconds before Victor shrank behind his wife, mumbling in his strange language, and crossing himself. The constable back at the Georgia jail had done the same thing. Like they knew what Simone was.

Valerica's wide eyes stayed on me. She pointed a shaky finger at Simone. "*Nosferatu*," she whispered. "My Victor was right. The nosfer-atu . . . they want him!"

I didn't know what a "nosferatu" was, but it must've meant "crazy, half-dead girl looking like she was ready to eat." Simone stood there with her hackles all up, licking her chops like somebody rang the dinner bell. I couldn't give up the only business establishment that made me feel like a person. I didn't have to do the "Yassir, no sir" routine with them and they didn't kick me out before I even opened my mouth. All Victor saw was green. And in my lonely mind, I believed Valerica saw a friend in me.

I jutted a thumb over my shoulder at Simone. "Who? Her? She ain't with me!"

"Romanian," Simone said with a moan and a lick of her lips. "It's been so long since I had Romanian."

Hands on my hips, I wagged a finger at Simone. "You listen here, missy! Don't be botherin' these fine people in this here establishment. Now you get on outta here with yo' crazy self!"

You owe me, Simone's mind said as she sank back through the doorway and into the darkness.

Victor ran to the door and kicked it closed. After bolting it with a thick slab of wood, he gathered an armful of garlic from one of the crates of vegetables they sold and crushed the cloves against all the windows.

"What's wrong with your man?" I asked Valerica. I set my bag of goods on the payment counter, fully expecting Victor to return to his senses and do business.

"Nosferatu," she repeated. "The undead. They kill all Victor's family in Marotinu. And now they will kill him."

I followed Victor's frantic race around the store with my eyes. Now he was up on a stool trying to hang a string of garlic bulbs in front of the door. I turned back to Valerica who was pacing behind the payment counter.

"You mean vamps?" I asked.

"Vamps? What are vamps? They drink blood of living like nosferatu?"

If I had a normal life, I would have thought the woman was a bit touched in the head. But I knew the truth. Vampires were real. They did suck blood out of the living. But I couldn't imagine Simone chasing her prey across state lines, let alone across the world. Couldn't nobody's blood be that good. Vamps must be different in different places. If they were as crazy as Valerica seemed to think they were, I don't blame Simone for not wanting another one around.

"So, you got vamps—vampires—where you're from?"

Valerica nodded. Then she shook her head. "We did. I never see them."

I don't know what, if anything, these crazy Raduts had seen in their home country. But somehow they knew what Simone was. "Then how d'you know they're even real? What makes you think Sim—that girl was one?"

"Victor tell me."

I frowned. "He seen one?"

Valerica shook her head again. "But he made sure they never came back to the town."

Victor started up with all his hollering and Valerica raged back, gesturing toward me. Whatever she said calmed him. He threw his hands in the air and spoke to me in English for the first time. He spread his arms as if introducing everything in the store. "Anything. You take."

"He serious?" I asked.

Valerica's hand covered mine. "We are friends, yes? You will help?"

"Help with what?"

She pointed toward the door. "Kill nosferatu."

The Raduts wouldn't let me leave.

They set me up in a tiny room of their house, which was the upstairs part of their general store. Though the place was simply a glorified log cabin lit with kerosene lamps, their home was ten times better than my old dugout. They had a parlor with a big ole rug in the middle and a kitchen with one of them cast-iron stoves, not a potbelly. The floors were wood, not hard-packed sand. There was a porcelain washstand and matching chamber pot in my room. They probably had the same in theirs. Guess we'd all be using them since I doubted the Raduts were going to the outhouse tonight.

The big double bed got me. Wrought-iron frame with two big fluffy pillows. I just about died when I sat on the mattress. Lord, it was the softest thing my behind ever touched. Better even than the ones at Miss Tillie's place. I didn't know these kinds of beds existed. I wasn't the least bit tired, but I couldn't wait to lie down on this!

Valerica told me about her nosferatu while Victor smeared that god-awful garlic all over the one window in my room. He took a couple of the bulbs and crushed them with his foot on the door threshold and then hung the leftovers right over my bed. Since none of this would actually deter Simone if she were after somebody, it was going straight out the window when they finally left.

Her story was mostly stuff her grandparents had told her, nothing she'd seen with her own eyes. She described her vampires like they were walking skeletons that spent nights feeding on folks. Some of what she said sounded like what I knew from Simone: needing blood, couldn't be in sunlight. Other stuff sounded downright made-up, like them turning into bats or controlling the weather.

Valerica tapped the side of her head with a finger. She frowned as she spoke, either because she was serious or pissed about the whole affair. "You know nosferatu is near when family gets sick. Victor's uncle die, then all family got sick. Pale, no color in the face. They cough up blood all the time. Their teeth like this," she placed a hand on either side of her mouth and extended her pointer fingers.

"Coughin' up blood? Sounds like wastin' disease to me."

"No!" Valerica said, now with a finger pointed to the sky. "No disease. It was nosferatu. So, we go dig up uncle. He was fat with blood." She puffed out her cheeks and gestured at her waist. "His nails long, and teeth, like the nosferatu here tonight. He feed on family. Kill everyone until only Victor is left."

"That why y'all came here?"

"Yes. But first, we kill uncle."

I smiled and threw my hands up in the air. "Well, then. Ain't nothin' to worry about."

"We kill uncle; not nosferatu uncle made. The chief nosferatu they could not find. He must die to kill all."

"How d'you know he made other vamps?"

"B-because . . ." Valerica waved her hands in front of her like she was searching for an answer or the right English word to use. "That's what they do. On and on, feeding and feeding."

Even though I wanted this conversation to end so I could get this stanking garlic out of my room and roll all over this bed, I couldn't help asking more questions. "Then wouldn't there be a whole bunch of vamps around, like all over the world? Wouldn't everybody know about vamps?"

"No," she said with conviction. "In Old World only. They can't cross water to get to the New World."

Nice try, Valerica. "So, where'd this vamp tonight come from?"

She fingered the silver cross hanging from a chain around her neck, completely ignoring my question. "So, you will help?"

"Kill Sim—the vamp? She ain't even related to you." At least I didn't think she was. Simone was French Canadian and, from what I knew, had only been to France and up and down the East Coast of America.

Valerica began to pout. "You will not help?"

"You jus' said they kill family. If she ain't related to you, then you ain't gotta worry about nothin'. She for sure ain't related to me."

Valerica sat quiet for a while, nodding like she was turning a thought over in her head. Then she clapped her hands together. "No. She must be destroyed. She will kill. You want nosferatu all over this place?"

"No, but—"

"Then you help?"

I agreed, for no other reason than to stop this stupid conversation. Despite what I'd seen with Simone, Valerica's experience with vamps—if you wanna call it that—was beyond ridiculous, and when Valerica explained what had to be done to kill the nosferatu, I almost fell outta my seat. At least Simone killed her prey with some style. Not much blood unless we're trying to beat the sun home. But cutting off heads, burning hearts, and then drinking the ashes . . . these people were crazy.

"How you gon' find her?" I asked. "They only come out at night, right?"

"You know nosferatu?!" Victor finally chimed in.

I glared at him. "She was here. At night, wasn't she?"

A thought occurred to Valerica. "We get horse, a white horse. Find nosferatu grave."

"Need virgin," Victor added.

They both turned to me. Not that it was any of their business, but

I said, "I ain't ridin' through no cemetery on no horse. All these people you know 'round here, somebody got a virgin."

"We don't want panic," Valerica explained. She pointed to her head again. "People will know why we ask for these things."

"Well, I ain't cuttin' off nobody's head."

Victor shook his head and waved his arms as if to finalize his words. "Only way." Then he drew a finger across his throat.

I frowned at his gesture. "Why I gotta do it?"

"You face down nosferatu tonight," Victor said. He pounded on his doughy chest. "Strong heart needed. And you run faster than me, yes?"

Good grief! What could I do to make them feel better? These folks were genuinely scared; they had a reason to be since that fear had shown up on their doorstep. But Simone wouldn't do anything to them if I asked her not to.

What I didn't want to do was let on that me and Simone were friends. Victor seemed to think I had some magic power that got her to leave so quickly. And he did let me take anything I wanted from the store. Got some high-quality fishing gear I thought King might like to replace that old stuff he had. If Victor kept thinking I could keep the two of them safe, I might never have to pay for anything ever again.

I slid beneath the covers of the mattress, hoping they'd get the hint. A few black-and-gray feathers floated out as the entire bed seemed to swallow me whole. I'd been so wrapped up in this nonsense, I didn't even check to see if Simone made it to the dugout. Good thing she'd already fed. I didn't have to worry about her getting herself into a spot without me tonight. I wonder if she found all this as funny as I did. At least I hoped she did. Ain't gotta guess what she would do to them if she didn't.

"How 'bout you leave it to me," I said. "I'll find that nosferatu for ya."

Valerica pushed her husband out of the room. "Then you come get Victor and," she slid a finger across her throat like her husband had done.

I winced at how that slicing motion made her smile. She acted more like a hunter of vamps and less like one scared of them. "Right. See y'all in the mornin'."

I didn't get any sleep that night at the Raduts', what with Valerica popping her head in every twenty minutes asking if I needed anything. Once I tossed that stanking garlic out the window, I stripped down to my underthings and then sank into the bed, thinking I was lying in the palm of God's hand. Watched as a tiny dusting of snow—the first of the season—drifted across the windowpane. Scenes from the life I'd lived for the past seven months flashed in my brain with each snap and pop from the fire Valerica had lit for me. I'd gone from whorehouse chambermaid to keeper of the undead. I'd finally gotten out of the South, something I thought would never happen. I'd learn to read and write. Had a home of my own, even if it was only a cave. And here I was, an honored guest of some white folks, sleeping in a big ole bed fit for a queen.

I thought of King, wondering if anything might come out of this new friendship of ours. As much as I'd love to get to know him a lot better, I wondered how that would even be possible. Could I ever tell him about Simone? Would he even believe me if I did? Simone certainly didn't help the situation. She didn't have to show up to King's that first night. She knew where I was, what I was doing, and why I was doing it. Could have left well enough alone. Didn't have to act all vampish at the Raduts' either. Would she always be there, waiting in the shadows, disrupting any chance I had at being human?

I half expected her to come through the window right then. I closed my eyes and located Simone in a saloon. Lord, that girl's attraction to juice joints was beyond me. Guess it was because folks were generally too drunk to pay much mind to what was going on around them. Seemed she'd found a place down the road from Radut General Store. Close enough that I could get to her if things got out of hand. To people not expecting an undead girl to be among them, Simone would appear as normal as you and me, especially in a dark and smoky saloon. White as a sheet, but normal. Though I'd had more than my fill of the Raduts, I wasn't ready to leave this bed yet.

Valerica knocked on my door again. Had it been twenty minutes already? Lord! Might as well be back at the plantation as much as these people were hounding me.

"Please come," she whispered. The candle she carried with her seemed to highlight the dark patches under her eyes, making her look sicklier. The fear in those eyes didn't escape me. "We need you."

I groaned, quickly dressed, and followed the glow of her candle down the narrow stairway that led to the back of the store where they kept all their stock. I made note of all the stuff I could trade for. Victor stood there talking to a man with the tails of his nightshirt hanging out from under his coat. There were scratches across his face like he'd fallen in a thicket . . . or been in a fight. Words trilling and spilling out of their mouths, like they were stabbing at something. At least that's what it sounded like to me. Couldn't make heads or tails of half of what people around here said, even when they spoke English. When Simone spoke in French, it was smooth, like satin ribbons winding through the air. Whatever the man told them caused Victor to embrace him.

"His wife," Valerica said to me in English. "Find her in the barn. Dead."

"Nosferatu!" Victor said, and all three of them crossed themselves.

"But Victor told him of you; that you chase off undead tonight."

Couldn't have been Simone. She'd fed the night before, though she did seem awful excited about getting her fangs into some Romanians. Right now, all I could see in my mind was blackness, the same blackness I saw whenever Simone was safe in her box.

"What makes you think that girl killed his wife?" I asked.

Valerica translated what I'd said to the man, who touched the side of his neck with two fingers. "He say she had marks on her neck."

"Nosferatu!" Victor chanted again. And again, they all crossed themselves.

"How you know it wasn't a rat or somethin' that bit her?" I asked.

The man shook his head. "No rat. Undead. Many people missing. Hunters go to Tolleston. Never come back! We must fix. You," he pointed at me. "Fix."

Funny how these folks suddenly know English when it suits them. "Look, I don't know what Victor told you—"

The man removed a silver chain from around his neck. He grabbed my arm and pressed the chain in my hand. Attached to it was a tiny colorful picture of a blond-haired angel. My first thought was what in Victor's storeroom he might give me for it.

"Saint Michael the Archangel," Valerica explained. "He will protect you."

"From what?"

She pointed to her head. "You know." Then she bared her teeth. "Come. You help."

Valerica placed a shawl over my shoulders as we walked east to the man's farm. About a dozen folks had gathered to pay their respects to the family. The grieving spouse led us into the barn where a woman was laid up on two bales of hay. Only six folks had lanterns to light the darkness, so for a moment, I wasn't sure what I was supposed to be looking at. Valerica took my hand as we waded through the crowd. The woman was sure enough dead. Whatever happened to her, it wasn't an easy death. She was whiter than the snow that had started sticking to the ground. Eyes and mouth were wide open like she'd been scared to death. Still clad in her nightgown, her arms were folded across her chest. Fingers bent into claws. I'd seen Simone's victims after they'd breathed their last. The bite wasn't always on the neck. But I wasn't about to go feeling about a dead body to be sure. What I do know is none of them ever looked like this.

Women stood around weeping and wiping their noses. A couple were mumbling while fingering strings of beads with crosses attached. Six men surrounded the body. Everyone stopped what they were doing and glared at me like I had two heads. After the Raduts' royal treatment, I'd almost forgotten who and where I was.

The man pushed through the crowd, dragging me with him. He got to gesturing and trilling in his language. Then the Raduts chimed in, saying my name over and over again. The crowd nodded their heads and patted me on my shoulder. I looked to Valerica to tell me what they were saying:

"She will wake up and kill until her whole family is dead. We must end this now."

"What's that gotta do with me?"

"You stand watch, for other nosferatu. Protect these people here while they do what must be done."

I did what they asked. A simple job, standing by the barn door as what seemed like the whole neighborhood gathered inside. Heard the lot of them chanting and praying, but on the way over, the Raduts had told me what they had to do to prevent more vamps. I refused to watch. The head chopping, the heart stealing. If this was what they'd planned to do to Simone if they ever got their hands on her, they had another thing coming.

I should leave. Staying here meant I was giving these folks the impression that I was with them in their gruesome task. That I agreed with all of this. Yes, there was a vamp in their midst. But they didn't understand how Simone lived, how and when she fed. She wasn't a monster, at least not in my eyes. We killed for a purpose. Depending on the circumstances, you might even call it a public service.

Yet standing with these folks gave me something I'd been missing for a long time. Here I was with people—a whole lot of them—who actually wanted me here. Sure, these folks were crazy, but I was one of them, part of a community. This brief sense of belonging had my feet glued to the ground.

When the deed was finished, they all thanked me for keeping them safe. Their fear faded with the rising sun, so I guess they didn't need me no more. I returned with the Raduts to their place, thinking they didn't need me no more either. They trudged back to their bedroom, the bags under their eyes showing the exhaustion from the ordeal, or relief that they could sleep without worrying about a vamp attacking them. I could've left then, but that bed was calling me. Might not ever be another time I'd get to lay in something like this.

"We have breakfast for you," Valerica said with a smile a few hours later. She handed me a hand towel and poured fresh water in the porcelain basin. Breakfast and housekeeping services? Maybe these Raduts weren't as bad as I thought they were.

They had an eat-in kitchen off the little parlor in their upstairs house. I watched Victor wolf down his food like it was either the first or last meal he'd ever have. Even brought out the good china. I recognized some of what was on the plate: fried eggs, a thin slice of what I thought was ham, some garden vegetables, broken-up pieces of moist cornmeal they called polenta, funny-smelling cheese, and coffee. Wasn't so bad, even though I wasn't hungry, as usual. I wondered if this was what Simone would taste if she ever got her fangs into the Raduts.

"Eat," Victor said with a mouthful of cornmeal. He aimed his fork in the air at his wife, sending sprays of wet grain everywhere. "She take you home. Rest. Tonight, we hunt."

"Hunt for what?" I asked. "You already got rid of that man's wife last night."

"Still hunt for nosferatu that made her."

"Maybe she moved on," I suggested.

Victor shrugged and returned to his plate. "You wait and see. More dead in Tolleston woods, nosferatu is still here."

"And if the killin' stops?"

"How killing stop if we don't stop nosferatu?"

"The vamp could leave," I offered. "Maybe she'll get bored and move on."

Victor and Valerica glanced at each other then laughed. Couldn't dodge the polenta spray coming from two directions.

"They live forever," Victor offered. "We don't."

"We won't," Valerica chimed in. "We hunt. Tonight."

FIFTEEN

Martin throws his head back and laughs so hard he knocks himself out of the chair and onto the floor. "Wait a minute! You mean to tell me there's a whole village of idiots just east of here who believe in this stuff?"

His tumble doesn't stop his laughter. He simply rolls on his knees and coughs a bit. Some of that tobacco juice must've gone down the wrong pipe. On his hip are the keys to my freedom. I squat down on the ground and stick my hand through the bars just to see if I can reach them.

He stands and sees me on the ground. "What're you doing down there?"

I smile and release a light chuckle from my nose before standing up. "Yeah, sounds crazy when you say it out loud."

Martin sets his chair upright and posts up by my cell again. "Are you saying they're the ones who gave you the idea to kill Miss Arceneau?"

I wave away his question. "No. I mean, no one gave me any ideas 'cause I didn't kill her. They're the ones who wanted her dead."

"And what about the dead woman in the barn? Miss Arceneau did that?"

"Ain't no vampire kill her. She had bruises on her neck like this," I grab my neck with one hand in a choking fashion. "And I guess nobody but me noticed the scratches on her husband's face and the bruisin' on his knuckles. Naw, a livin' person killed that woman."

"If you knew all of that," Martin says, "why didn't you say anything? Why let them desecrate her body like that? Makes you an accessory after the fact, in my book."

I just blink at him. "Still findin' a reason to blame me for somethin', huh? Why not go out and check on them poor women out there in Miller Station gettin' abused by their husbands?"

"Not my jurisdiction."

"What's that mean?"

Martin stands up and begins opening and closing all the desk drawers. "Means that's not my business over there. You killing people in Tolleston is my business."

"I'm going to say it again. I didn't kill nobody," I tell him.

Not finding whatever he was looking for in the desk, he stands in the middle of the jail and scratches his head. Then he perks up, goes over to a cabinet, and locates a green bottle among the mess of papers and books. He smiles, toasts the air, and then uncorks it with one yank. "What about those hunters over in the Tolleston woods? Even you said that would be a good place to hunt for Miss Arceneau."

"I might've been huntin'," I say. "But I ain't killed nobody. When you're deer huntin', the one who shoots the thing gets the credit, not the one out there jus' stalkin' it."

"You still helped. That's bad enough."

"You're right." I snap my fingers and point to the bottle sitting on his desk. "I did help her. But that's all I did. Helped you, too, if you think about it."

He hands me the bottle. "How's that?"

"I bet in the last eight months, these cells been empty. Am I right?"

"What's that have to do with you?"

I tap the side of my head with the half-empty bottle before I pour a stream down my throat. Was like lightning running down my gullet. "Think about it for a minute," I choke out.

Martin shakes his head as he reaches for the bottle. I hesitate to return it, partly because it's relaxing me enough to get through the night, and mostly because I don't need Martin running to the outhouse again and leaving me at the mercy of the next band of fools who decide to stop in. But he is attending to my tale. I hand him the bottle.

I saunter back to the cot and stretch out with one of my hands clasped behind my head. "Let's jus' say nobody out in Miller Station was gettin' abused for a good while."

Despite my protests, Valerica hitched up her wagon and drove me home. I could've gotten there myself in about an hour, but I couldn't carry the free fishing gear Victor had given me all the way to my dugout, and I sure as hell didn't want Valerica to know where I lived. Plus, I'd hoped to catch King before he got out on the water. Valerica let her horse mosey on along the road like she didn't have nowhere else to be. She talked nonstop about nothing, but I have to admit, I didn't mind.

Since it was so early in the morning, King had to still be out on the lake. So, I had Valerica drop me closer to his place than mine. My plan was to leave the fishing gear somewhere safe, then come back later and surprise him. A thank-you for everything he'd done for me so far.

"You live here on beach?" Valerica asked after I'd climbed down from the driver's seat.

"Um, yeah," I said. I hurried to the back of the wagon to retrieve the stuff and get Valerica on her way.

Her head swiveled on her shoulders. "Where? I see nothing."

"There," I said, pointing to King's dugout a few yards away. Wasn't nothing else out there, so what was I supposed to say?

"I help." She jumped down from the wagon before I could stop her.

As we trekked over the sand with our arms laden with fishing poles, nets, spools of fishing line, and a small box of hooks, I tried to locate where I could leave the stuff without Valerica knowing I didn't really live here. But wouldn't you know it, King came around from the other side of the dugout with the collar of his duster pulled up around his ears. I froze. What the hell was he still doing here? And what was I gonna say to these two?

King shielded his eyes from the sun. "Lavinia? What's that you got there? You two need some help?" He jogged over to us and whistled at all the stuff at our feet.

Valerica stepped so close to me that our shoulders were touching. "Who is that?" she asked.

"King." My voice sounded breathier than I wanted. I shook her hand away when I realized she was squeezing it. This woman was frightened by a solitary man running over to us, but not a knife-wielding crowd chopping off heads? I took a step to the side, but she followed right along like a shadow.

"Ma'am," he said with a nod of his head to Valerica.

"I go now," Valerica said. "You remember later, yes?"

"Yeah, yeah. Later." I swatted my hand in the air then gave my head a quick tilt toward the wagon. Thankfully, Valerica took the hint—or was really that scared of King—and she scurried back to her wagon. I didn't want to present this stuff to him in front of an audience anyway. Fine if he rejected my offer, but not in front of Valerica. I would've melted right into the sand from embarrassment.

King squatted down and surveyed the gear. "What's all of this?"

"It's yours."

"Mine?" He shot me a questioning eye. "Where'd you get all of this stuff?"

"My mistress. I told her what all you did for me, and she wanted to help me thank you."

He stood and folded his arms across his chest. "Is that right?"

"You don't believe me?"

"She seemed a bit . . . off when we met."

I shrugged. "Told you, she's sickly. Sometimes she don't know how crazy she be actin'. But she's as nice as she can be once you get to know her. That's why she let me get this stuff for you; to make sure somebody was keepin' an eye out for me. Hope you can use it."

King scratched his head as if turning the thought around. "Sure, I could use it. But you didn't have to do this, Lavinia. Your company is thanks enough."

I made like I was gonna gather the equipment. "Well, if my company is all you need—"

He grabbed my hand and stood me up. "Now, now. No need for all of this to go to waste." He smiled, holding my hand longer than he needed to. "How about I catch a nice fat piece of sturgeon you can carry over to your mistress later?"

I bit my bottom lip, wishing he would kiss me. Instead, I nodded. "That'd be jus' fine."

"Good." He squeezed my hand and drew me closer to him. Then he leaned in and pressed his chilled lips against mine. "Thank you for the gear," he whispered before taking a step back. After insisting I not help him carry the gear, he walked backward to his dugout with the promise to call on me soon.

By the time I got to my little hole in the dunes, I was ready to burst. Could still feel his lips. I let out a squeal right when I opened the door.

"Did you have fun?"

Simone's voice, low and heavy, startled me. She slid out from under my bed and took the posture of a parent angered by a missed curfew. I wasn't surprised she was there. Could smell her when I first walked in. All the joy I'd felt at seeing King suddenly melted down into my brogans. "Thought you were in your box."

"Thought you'd be home last night."

"Had stuff to do."

Simone crossed her arms. The corner of one of her eyebrows lifted. "Human stuff?"

I let out a deep breath. I hoped she hadn't seen everything I'd done last night. Or heard all my thoughts about the whole affair. Thank God I didn't watch their little ritual in the barn. Didn't even wanna think about what Valerica told me they did *after* all the other stuff. Buried the poor woman with a huge rock in her mouth even though the head wasn't connected no more.

"Are these the types of humans you want to be with?"

"I didn't know what they was gon' do, honest." I said with a shake of my head.

"You barely know these people and you're already sleeping in their house, and joining their little vampire hunting social club!"

"Now, that wasn't my fault," I said, with a chuckle. "They wouldn't let me leave." If she'd laid in that fluffy bit of heaven they called a bed, she probably wouldn't have left either. "Look at it this way: me entertainin' their notions will keep 'em off your scent, see?"

"And what happens when they learn we know each other?"

"They won't," I said, mostly to convince myself.

To keep Simone happy and my friends off her menu, I kept my distance from them for a while. But over the next few days, folks from that barn found out where I lived—ain't gotta guess how—and would stop by, thanking me for this phantom protection I'd given them that night. It was only the women, bringing me weird food I'd never heard of. Since they were certain a vamp existed in their midst, they never came after dusk. Irritated Simone to no end. She had to stay in her box or under the bed whenever they called, even though I never let them inside. Part of me looked forward to their visits. Part of me was terrified they would find out what else was in that dugout and lynch us both.

SIXTEEN

The Raduts hounded me about Simone every time I went to their store. I started making up stuff, like I'd seen her turn into a bat and fly over the lake, or I followed her into a cemetery in Tolleston. They even insisted I go with them once at dusk—white horse, virgin, and all—to a Miller Station cemetery looking for Simone's resting place. Victor led the horse and some young boy over and around the headstones. Me and Valerica followed behind, both armed with an ax and a knife. I was irritating the hell out of them by calling for the vamp like it was a lost cat. That horse didn't wanna be there no more than I did. It bucked and whinnied at every grave, knocking over loose markers until it finally got that boy off its back. Victor swore it was because a vamp was nearby. But the horse ran off, leaving a nasty red burn in Victor's palms from the rope he was holding. Almost made myself sick from laughing so hard. Of course, the Raduts didn't find any of it funny.

"I don't either," Simone said after I'd recounted my tale. She'd made her way out of the coffin and into the dugout. For someone who preferred sleeping in the ground, she sure took a liking to setting up on my bed every time she came to call.

"You should've seen their faces when that horse acted like it found a vamp." I bugged my eyes out and raised my hand over my head like

I was holding the ax. "Nosferatu! Nosferatu!" I said, with my best Romanian accent. I had to fan myself after that fit of laughter.

"They're dangerous."

"They crazy, that's what they are." I located a carpetbag I'd taken off one of Simone's victims and filled it with a few items I'd intended to sell to the Raduts.

"Why not tell them you can't find me?" she asked. "Why keep feeding into their delusions?"

"Well, for one, they ain't delusional. They saw you and you're real. All that other stuff about Romanian vamps is a bit suspect, but they knew what you were the minute you walked into their store. And two, because they *know* there is a vamp around, they ain't gonna stop lookin' for you. As long as I know where they are and what they're doin', you're safe."

Simone's face hardened again. "Or we can end this quickly." She rubbed her throat. "I've had nothing but Germans since coming here. A Romanian would be a nice change of pace. What about Chicago? The original plan was to go there. Maybe now's the time." She licked her lips. "A nice big city teeming with a smorgasbord of flavors."

"And leave this place?" I caught Simone's raised eyebrow of doubt and quickly corrected myself. "I mean leave this place with what? We got lucky coming up on King and the Raduts. Ain't no guarantee we gon' find people nice enough to help us out. Plus, we ain't got the money to be livin' in no big city like Chicago nohow. Not yet."

"If not now, when? After you've married King? After those demented Romanians cut off my head and shove a rock in my mouth?"

"They're harmless." I weighed the bag in my hand, hopeful it would be enough to buy me the shells I needed for a shotgun I'd taken from a hunter last week. "Plus, with them thinkin' I got some power over vamps, they let me take whatever I want from the store."

She sat her fists on her hips. "Have you forgotten how awful Miss Tillie was to you? After all the work you did, she wouldn't even call a doctor for you! She threw you in jail, remember? All because you were protecting me."

I waved her off. "Look, I didn't choose Miss Tillie. I mean, what's the problem? You don't like King. You don't like the Raduts. You don't give nobody a chance. 'Sides, King and the Raduts have been helpful. We got this cave and supplies from the Raduts. Give 'em time."

"And how much time did you give to Miss Tillie?" Simone asked with her chin raised in the air. "How much time did you waste on that plantation after the war with a woman who, in the end, essentially threw you away?"

This girl was not letting up! I said I wouldn't pry, but I had to ask. "I get you not trustin' folks. Must've been hard fendin' for yourself, not knowin' if somebody was gonna find out what you were. Lord knows I've had my share of disappointments in people. But you took a chance and trusted me! Can't be too much of a stretch to think there are other folks out there who you can trust. Somethin' awful must've happened for you to be like this, huh?"

Simone stared at the ground and bit her bottom lip. I thought she had fallen asleep or something because she didn't move at all. "My father," she finally said without moving. "He turned on me. His only child, and he turned on me."

"Turned on you? How?"

She suddenly straightened her back and smiled. "Let's not talk about that."

God, this was like pulling teeth. I could probably find out the whole story myself in two seconds if I simply looked into her mind. But I hated it when she went wading around in my thoughts. And she was sneaky about it, too. Would climb outta her box at night and stand outside the door, just a-listening to my thoughts. Then would have the nerve to walk in, commenting on what she'd heard like we'd been having a conversation the whole time.

"You're the one who brought it up," I pointed out. Come to think of it, I'd never even seen Simone's daddy in all those pieces of memory I saw.

"Well, forget I did." She stood and walked over to the door. "Mark my words: these people may seem nice now. But just you wait. When push comes to shove, they'll turn on you." Simone pointed at me one last time before walking out into the night.

I didn't follow her. With my mind's eye, I knew she was sitting on the thinking dune, up there thinking about whatever had her behind chapped about her daddy. Given what I knew about Simone, it was probably something minor that a spoiled rich child like her would believe was the end of the world. I glanced around the dugout—as if anybody else would be there—and then closed my eyes. Relaxed my shoulders as I thought of Simone, thought of where she was, what she was doing. The keys to her mind. Once I was in there, I let her thoughts carry me wherever they went. As expected, she was out there, thinking about the night her father hit her.

Darkness. It was night in the streets where Simone had wandered, barefoot and dressed in only stockings, a camisole, and an underskirt. She scratched at her neck where that old vampire had attacked her. A thin, pale man with foul breath and sharp teeth biting her neck. Modesty kept her pressed closer to the buildings she passed and out of the shafts of moonlight and gaslit streetlamps lighting her way home. Every few steps, she'd drop to her knees, the pain consuming her body manifesting in intermittent screams, howls—scrowls—that caused a chorus of dogs to join her mournful plaint. The clop of horse hooves against the road brought Simone to her feet. She scrambled back into the shadows of the closest building, waiting until the coast was clear. Then onward, stumbling through muddied streets and puddles from the early evening rain toward the safety of her home.

Every door in the Arceneau manse was locked. Even the windows from the housemaids' third-floor residence were darkened at this late hour. Beneath her parents' window she climbed the white wooden trellis hidden by an overgrowth of lemon-scented moonflower vines. As expected, the balcony doors were slightly ajar, welcoming the rain-soaked night air through gossamer drapes. Simone crept in, her footfalls mimicking the rhythmic thrumming coming from somewhere in the room. Father was such a heavy sleeper, so she ventured toward her mother's side of the bed. The closer she got to the bed, the louder the thrumming became. Simone covered her ears, but the thrumming grew, so much so, that she could feel it in her temples, wrists, and the bottoms of her bare feet.

Then came the fragrance of blood. She'd never found the aroma appealing before, but this time, the metallic scent wafted through her nose and into the back of her throat. Hunger pains and that horrific scrowl emerged again, startling Simone's mother awake.

"Mama?" Simone reached for her mother, who was now shaking her husband awake.

"Simone? *Mon enfant!* Where have you been?" Madame Arceneau rose from the bed and gathered her once-missing daughter in her arms. "Jacques! Wake up! Simone has returned."

The phantom thrumming deafened Simone. Her stomach churned as her head rested against her mother's neck. As she fell into the welcoming embrace, her mother's green throat veins burgeoned with fresh blood pulsing in time to the thrumming in Simone's ears. Her lips brushed against the invisible peach fuzz on her mother's neck. The blood summoned her closer to its source, igniting white-hot pain all over her body. In response, the girl's mouth opened. Teeth sank into soft white flesh, releasing the sweet, crimson fluid from its chamber.

Simone didn't hear her mother's screams. Other than the hot liquid streaming down her throat and the sides of her mouth, the next sensation she felt was the blow to her forehead. Simone stumbled back several feet, taking a chunk of her mother's throat with her.

What Simone drank from her mother wasn't enough to sate the hunger. She scrowled again and charged toward the rhythmic call now emanating from her father. But before she reached him, Monsieur Arceneau raised a candlestick and struck his child several more times.

Simone retreated to a darkened corner of the bedroom, whimpering like a wounded animal. He'd hit her. Her father had actually hit her. But could she blame him? The attack was swift, a matter of seconds between biting her mother and the first blow of the candlestick. Her mother. Had she killed her? She'd done the exact thing that monster had done to her. Had consumed her mother's blood like it was a fine merlot. But of all the cuisine she'd sampled in her short life, that blood was the best thing she ever tasted. Some of it still stained her fingers. She licked them clean and wanted more.

I jumped out of Simone's memory with a start. No wonder the girl didn't wanna talk about it. It wasn't just that her father had struck her; that was bad enough. It was the reason why. Simone swore up and down that she didn't remember what happened to her after she was bitten by that old vampire, but apparently, she did. And after everything we'd gone through, Simone had the nerve to lecture me about trusting folks when she didn't even trust me enough to explain why she felt that way. To be fair, I probably wouldn't want anybody to know I'd eaten my mother, but it did make me wonder what other traumas haunted her mind and affected her reasoning. Trusting the wrong people will get you in trouble, and usually there are warning signs of what's to come. But so far, the only one in this town who had given me any reason to believe I couldn't trust them was Simone.

SEVENTEEN

With winter approaching, the days got increasingly shorter. Good news for Simone. By four o'clock, the sun was damn near set, meaning she was up outta her box and in the cave a lot longer. While I liked the company, and Simone was a hoot with all her crazy stories, sitting in that cave for fourteen-hour stretches got me claustrophobic. As much as Simone needed the night, I needed the warm rays of the sun. Got tired of living like a mole.

I made the mistake of telling all of this to Simone one morning when we heard a knock at the cave door. We froze, unaccustomed to anybody calling on us. King and I met either out on the beach or at his dugout. And the Raduts' crazy friends never dared approach unless they saw me outside. Even that slowed down once the cold weather kept most normal people inside. But somebody had come calling nonetheless. Since we weren't prepared for the visit, we sat there, me holding my breath and Simone testing the sharpness of her fangs with her tongue.

"Who could that be?" I whispered to Simone.

"You're the one out there meeting the locals," she countered. "It's probably your Miller Station entourage dropping off food again."

I turned up my nose. Their tasteless fare looked bland on the plate: lots of yellows, greens, and earth tones from the cornmeal, vegetables, and boiled mystery meat they cooked. "Can't be them. It's too early in the morning for that."

"Lavinia!" Valerica called from the other side of the door.

"Under the bed!" I ordered. We quickly cleared a space among the stolen property. I made sure Simone's whole body was covered with her ever-present burlap before I opened the door, allowing only the weak sunlight in.

"Valerica!" I said with a forced smile. Couldn't be mad. I'd talked her up while complaining about getting out of the cave. A wicked wind from the lake sent streams of sand right in her face. "What brings you out here on this fine mornin'?"

I'd have thought she had a snake for a neck as bad as she was trying to get a look inside my dugout. "You have a caller?" she asked.

"No." I pulled my shawl tighter around my shoulders. Whether it was cold out or not, I couldn't tell. But I had to remember to act like a normal person. Eat when they eat, yawn when they yawn, comment on the weather like I was as hot or cold as they were. Otherwise, folks get to wondering why they're about to die from thirst and exhaustion while I could still go a few rounds.

"I hear you talking to someone."

"Ain't nobody here but me," I said, angling my body so she couldn't see inside. "Who else am I gonna talk to by myself?"

She pushed past me anyway. Standing in the middle of the small, dark space, she scanned the whole place with two turns of her head. I thought I'd gotten everything under the bed, including Simone, until Valerica bent down and retrieved something from the floor. "Ivory smoking pipe," she said. She walked to the door to get a better look at one of the most treasured items I'd taken from a victim. "You smoke?"

"No."

"Why have then?"

"Took it," I said, taking it from her. I tossed it on my bed. "From the plantation I worked on before I got here. Think maybe Victor'll give me something for it?"

"He would like," she said with a smile. "You come," she said, pulling me through the door by my arm. "I have work for you."

I protested, digging my heels into the ground. "I told you the other day I ain't diggin' up no bodies."

"Not that. Real work. A job for you."

"Who said I needed a job?"

Valerica called me closer to her with a bend of her finger. "You out here alone. Victor say not to worry, that the vamp-girl is afraid of you. But you help us hunt, so I help you live. Otherwise, you freeze this winter. This place, you like living here? In a hole?"

I was a mite offended by her characterization of my home, but honestly, I didn't like living there. Only thing benefiting me was my proximity to King. But this was all for Simone. How could we live in a real house with no money? Ain't like somebody was gonna sell one to me nohow.

"I have friend who needs someone to cook and clean," Valerica said.

"Well, I can't jus' up and leave—"

"What you do now? In cave, what do you do?"

"That ain't none of your—"

"Come," she said, this time guiding me toward her wagon, which she'd parked on a flat strip of land a ways from my dugout. "She needs help, and you help, yes?"

What could I say? I was bored outta my mind, and it was early. The sun was out, so I didn't mind riding with Valerica to her friend's house. Except she wasn't driving toward Miller Station where I thought all of Valerica's crazy friends lived. She coaxed the horse on a southwest route, the same route Simone and I took to get to the Tolleston woods. I held on to the sides of the wagon and looked back at my dugout disappearing in the distance.

"Where we goin'?" I asked.

"Tolleston."

I figured as much. Lips pressed together, I glanced back in the direction of my dugout, now absent along the northern horizon. I'd never gone to Tolleston without Simone, so I made sure to send her thoughts that I would be coming back. Didn't wanna have to explain to Valerica why I thought my head was exploding.

"That's awfully far, Valerica, don'tcha think? I mean, if I get a job, how you expect me to get there every day?" And how did I expect to leave Simone every day, all alone, that close to King?

"I said, you live there," Valerica called. "No need for hole anymore."

I groaned. The wagon wasn't going that fast. I could jump out. But what would my explanation be? I'd left something on the stove? I got a vampire waiting on me back there? Valerica talked the whole hour as we rode. Shouldn't have taken that long, but she seemed to be in no hurry. A couple of times I had to remind her that I didn't speak Romanian when she got on a tear about something. I never saw Valerica without Victor. I wondered if she was enjoying this brief bit of freedom herself.

At least her nonstop talking kept my mind from thinking about my head exploding. Before I knew it, we were on the main road into town. I'd never seen Tolleston in the daytime. There had been no need to visit the town proper, or any of the surrounding towns for that matter. Folks from all over, even Chicago according to King, came to the Tolleston woods to bag their share of deer, ducks, fish, and muskrats. Simone and I had been here a little over a month, so the five times she's had to feed, we went to the woods.

From the looks of it, Tolleston was a nice little town. The wide dirt-packed roads were set up in perfectly straight lines. The houses were situated on identical squares of property, each one separated by fences that came up to my thigh. Folks were out visiting with their neighbors or strolling along the raised wooden sidewalks lining the stores in the town's business district. Tall trees, now naked from the onset of winter, towered over every building we passed. We stopped in front of a white two-story house on a quiet street. Behind the house was a wilderness of naked trees and leafless, overgrown bushes that resembled our hunting grounds.

Mrs. Wiltshire was a plump, wrinkled old woman with hair as white as her skin. I was surprised Valerica didn't think this woman was a vamp given how pale she was. She paused in her sweeping of the front steps and waved. I sighed and plastered on my best smile and readied myself to listen to yet another tale about a dead relative the woman suspected of being a vampire.

"Is this the woman you told me about, Valerica?" Mrs. Wiltshire asked. "My, you brought her by quickly! It was only yesterday that you mentioned her."

"Lavinia," Valerica said. "I tell her how you helped us with our problem," she widened her eyes and spoke slowly. "She has work for you. In her house."

My shoulders lowered a bit, knowing I wouldn't have to listen to yet another Romanian vampire tale. I noted Mrs. Wiltshire didn't have the same accent as Valerica did. "That's mighty kind of you, Valerica," I said. "But I don't think—"

She pulled me to the side and whispered, "You want to live in dunes alone with that demon on the loose? Who will help if vamp finds you? That man? Mrs. Wiltshire, she has a place for you. You work in house and stay there. I do this for you." Then she goaded me toward Mrs. Wiltshire with her hands. "You, Jane," Valerica said, this time motioning to Mrs. Wiltshire, "tell her of the job."

Mrs. Wiltshire smiled, her cheeks reddening. She reminded me of these white, cone-shaped mushrooms that grew in the sweet gum forest back in Georgia. "Merely the normal cooking and cleaning. We had a young man help out around the house, but he works at our business establishment now."

"Uh-huh," I said, not quite sure I was interested, though having something to do during the day would be nice.

"You'd have your own private room where you'd sleep and take your meals," the mushroom lady said.

"My own room?"

She looked at Valerica and then added, "And we'll pay you, of course."

Pay me? In real, hard currency? I'd be able to buy my own things, like a respectable woman. Maybe save enough to buy a new dress out there in Chicago. Or go to Chicago for the day. And working a real paying job would allow me to save up funds in case we had to hightail it out of there at a moment's notice.

Mrs. Wiltshire gave me and Valerica a tour of the house. It wasn't as grand as Miss Tillie's, but it was miles better than that dugout me and Simone had. Except it didn't have no hallways. Every room opened up into another one. Once you walked in from the covered front porch, there was a narrow foyer that led into a parlor with a set of sliding doors on opposite walls. One set of doors led into the library chock full of books which sent my eyes to bulging.

"Do you read?" Mrs. Wiltshire asked as I walked past the books, my fingers sliding across the bindings.

"Some, but I haven't had much practice."

She patted my back as we made a circuit around the room. "Maybe we can work on that during your free time."

The other door led into the dining room, which led into the kitchen with a pantry, porcelain washbasin, and a wood-burning stove. Upstairs were three bedrooms, again one room opening into another. No privacy at all. Could probably hear Mrs. Wiltshire farting from all the way downstairs. The room that would be mine was right off the kitchen.

"This was Nathan's room," Mrs. Wiltshire said after I poked my head inside. No more than a large closet, it was already furnished with a narrow bed, bureau, washstand, chair, and an end table. "The young man I told you about who worked here," she continued. "Quiet as a mouse, that one was. Kept the place spick-and-span." It was far enough from the rest of the house that my leaving in the evening wouldn't be heard if I was quiet enough.

But the best part was the indoor outhouse on the ground floor. It was close to the kitchen and big enough to hold a commode and copper tub. Even had a hole dug beneath the tub so all you had to do was pull a plug and drain the water straight into the ground. And wouldn't you know it, the wooded area behind the house was the eastern edge of the Tolleston woods. Mrs. Wiltshire joked how I could grab a deer or duck right from the back door. A covered crawl space beneath the house, and hunting grounds a stone's throw away. This place might be perfect. With winter knocking on nature's door, I wasn't sure what effect the change in weather would have on me or Simone's menu. Maybe I could convince Simone a close safe haven would benefit us both.

Restlessness took over and I jumped into work while Mrs. Wiltshire and Valerica visited in the front parlor. Got to beating on a couple of rugs hung on the clothesline. Refreshed all the bedroom water basins from one of the sloughs in the woods. Swept out the ashes from the upstairs and downstairs fireplaces and got them roaring again with fresh wood from the barn. Rummaged through a full pantry, the likes of which I hadn't seen since before the war, and prepared a meal of roasted duck they had hanging in their icehouse and garden turnips stored in their root cellar. Valerica stayed there the whole time and carried me back to my dugout supposedly to retrieve my things. I let her go once she dropped me at the cave, assuring her I'd get to the Wiltshires' just fine tomorrow on my own.

"You must have been doing something awful with that vampire hunter to hide it from me," Simone said, greeting me inside the dugout once I returned.

The sun hadn't set yet, so I was more than surprised to see her. Before I could ask how she got in, I spied a large hole in the middle of the cave. "What the hell is this?" I asked, pointing to the hole.

"A project," she said with her chin lifted, and crossed her arms. "I was trapped here—alone—waiting for you all day. I got bored."

"So, you dug a damn hole?" I got down on my hands and knees to peer into the black tunnel. The thick scent of rot swirled around like two-day-old meat festering in the sun. "Guess you been in here stewing the whole time, huh?" She was so preoccupied with her anger that she couldn't hear my thoughts.

"What were you doing, Lavinia?"

"Nothin' to hide about. Cookin' and cleanin'," I said, looking around for where the displaced dirt might be. Betcha she filled her coffin with it on purpose to keep from going back in there. I tsked and kicked a thin dusting of earth from the floor into the hole. "And what'd I tell you 'bout lookin' in my mind without askin'? Do I go around peekin' in your thoughts?"

"Not that you've told me," Simone said. "How do you do that? Block me from your thoughts?"

I shrugged. "Didn't know I could on purpose. What makes you think that?"

"Once you got into the wagon with the Romanian, there was nothing. It was like staring at a blank white wall."

"Well, that's what you get for pryin'," I said, sticking out my tongue at her. I was surprised and kind of happy that she hadn't caught on to my little trick. Since Simone was mostly dead-asleep in her box during the day, she couldn't invade my brain while I visited my small pool of friends. Half of that was to keep them safe. The other half was for me to have something of my own, even if it was hunting for a vampire, part of the time.

"So, what *did* you do today?" Simone asked.

"Cemetery with the Raduts again," I said as if announcing the weather. Simone had just proven I needed to keep some things to myself, and it wasn't like she didn't have her own side hobby. I pointed to her little digging project. "Wanna show me how this little tunnel of yours works?"

EIGHTEEN

Though I didn't miss slaving at Miss Tillie's, I did kinda enjoy working at Mrs. Wiltshire's. The lady was old, over sixty, I think she said. Too old to be trying to keep up with a whole house on her own. Childless, and her husband, a local saloon owner, was hardly ever at home. And like the Raduts, their whole family was back in another country. A stream of neighbors and church members stopped by throughout the afternoon, and she proudly introduced me to every one of them. I knew she was simply showing off, but I poked my chest out anyway, especially since she called me by name.

"Lavinia!" Mrs. Wiltshire sang from the second floor of her home. Though the house had two stories, it was small and narrow, so I knew from the sound of her voice that she was at the window of the bedroom that faced the road out front.

"Yes, Miss Wiltshire," I said as I left the kitchen and stood at the foot of the stairs.

She appeared with a bundle of freshly cleaned sheets in her arms, despite me telling her I'd put them on once I finished in the kitchen. A smile plumped her already chunky cheeks. "What time is it, Lavinia?"

She asked this question every day at the same time. "It's four o'clock, Miss Wiltshire."

"And what does that mean?"

This woman sang everything she said. I closed my eyes and returned her smile. "It's time for tea. Already got the kettle goin'."

She tucked the sheets under her arms and clapped her hands. "Brilliant! I'll get the book."

Mrs. Wiltshire took tea three times a day: first thing in the morning, at four o'clock, and right before bed. I assumed she was used to taking her tea with visitors. But since the weather had turned cold—a foot of snow had been on the ground for weeks and more had been threatening all day—nobody called on her except this young circuit preacher named Reverend Norquist. I guess she still wanted the company, so every afternoon at four we sat in the parlor, drinking our tea out of a pink-and-yellow porcelain set that had been a wedding gift. Sometimes I made little sandwiches for us. Other times she asked for biscuits, which, at first, I didn't know meant "cookies" where she came from. While she nibbled, I'd read aloud from a book with these short stories. Even though I stumbled over most of the big words, she was real patient helping me sound them out.

"Why you got me readin' these awful stories, Miss Wiltshire?" I asked after closing the book. I slipped a sugar cookie—these ain't biscuits no matter how many times she corrects me—from the serving tray and sat back in the plush armchair. "The witch that tried to eat two little lost children in the forest, people poisonin' each other, lockin' 'em in towers. Today, it's girls cuttin' off pieces of their feet to fit in a shoe that ain't even theirs."

"Whatever do you mean?" she said, the teacup at her lips. "The evil stepsisters received their comeuppance."

"But her daddy made her a slave in her own house," I argued. "None of that other stuff would've happened to her if he paid attention. I bet the reason why her mama died was 'cause that mean ole daddy of hers killed her."

Mrs. Wiltshire covered her mouth to keep cookie crumbs from spraying everywhere as she laughed. "Oh, Lavinia! You tickle me to death with such entertaining insights. I never thought of the father being as equally evil as the rest of the family."

A knock at the door interrupted our tea. It was Reverend Norquist again. Wasn't he just here? He must really love preaching to ride all the way out here from Chicago to call on folks, especially since it had started snowing and the sky was now one big nasty gray cloud. I escorted him into the parlor with Mrs. Wiltshire and went to fetch another teacup.

"Lavinia is a dream!" I heard Mrs. Wiltshire gush to the reverend. "I don't know how she does it. Not a speck of dust anywhere in the house!" Then her voice lowered to a whisper, but I could still hear her like she was standing right next to me. "I don't think the girl sleeps. She's up at cockcrow and is still working when I retire for the evening. Hasn't had a day off yet."

She had a point. I'd been dragging my feet to get back to Simone, but it'd been almost a week since the girl's last meal and I couldn't put it off any longer.

"Miss Wiltshire?" I said upon returning to the parlor with the extra teacup. "Was wonderin' if I might take me a day tomorrow? I still have some things over at my old place I need to take care of."

"Of course!" she said. "I was just telling Reverend Norquist—"

"And I was wonderin' if I might leave a mite early today."

Mrs. Wiltshire glanced toward one of the three windows in the parlor with the drapes partially open. "Early? Why, the sun is about ready to set. I'm not sure it would be a good idea for you to ride back alone at night in the cold."

A storm was brewing and getting stuck here when Simone was due for a feeding wasn't a good idea, either. "This way I can get everything done and be back first thing the day after tomorrow."

She pursed her thin lips together and set her teacup down. "Well, if you must. Though if something happens to you—"

"I'll be fine," I said, already removing the white apron tied around my waist.

"See that, Reverend?" Mrs. Wiltshire said. "Never sleeps."

Their laughter at her comment stopped when the front door blew open with a brisk gust of air. Mr. Wiltshire and another man burst through, a thick stream of snow following behind them. That weather sure took a turn!

Mrs. Wiltshire ran to the foyer and clapped her hands like somebody was delivering a pie. "John! You're home! Look who's here."

"Reverend," Wiltshire grumbled as he wiped snowflakes from his hat and coat. "I only brought Nate by to fix that hinge on the stove while business was slow."

"Nathan!" Mrs. Wiltshire sang. She grabbed the man by his arm and dragged him into the parlor. "Reverend Norquist, you remember Nathan, the young man who used to board here. He tends the bar at our business."

This Nate fella simply nodded and kept his head to the floor. Not like anybody could make eye contact with him. He had a face full of thick, wiry brown hair. The curly stuff on his head was bound in a ponytail like King's. Wiltshire tapped Nate's shoulder and then pointed at me. "Follow her into the kitchen and hurry up."

The bartender rolled his eyes before staring at his feet again. He didn't say a word to me as he tinkered with the stove, not even when I asked if he wanted tea. I only knew he wasn't English like the Wiltshires after he told them the job was done. The slight Southern drawl in his speech chilled me.

When Wiltshire and the bartender made to leave, Mrs. Wiltshire stopped them.

"Aren't you staying for supper? Surely, no one is coming to the saloon with such wicked weather."

"A little snow's not going to stop anyone from drinking, Jane," he said, pulling his coat over his shoulders.

Mrs. Wiltshire chuckled nervously. "Why, I can't remember the last time we had supper together."

"It's supper, not a tea party."

"But John—"

"Dammit Jane!" His nostrils flared. Then he checked his pocket watch. "Nate, come!" Wiltshire was out the door and behind the curtain of snow, leaving Mrs. Wiltshire with her mouth hanging open. Even Reverend Norquist said his goodbyes after getting a look at the weather.

Alone in the parlor, Mrs. Wiltshire plopped onto the sofa and stared straight ahead. Her constant blinking did nothing to stop the tears from silently flowing down her face.

"I guess you'd better leave before it gets too bad out there, Lavinia." Poor woman spoke as if she were waking from dream.

I sat beside Mrs. Wiltshire and took her hand in mine. "I can't leave you in such a state. How 'bout we go in the kitchen and get supper ready for us?"

The old woman's eyes brightened as she turned to me. "Oh, Lavinia! You'll stay?"

"One more day ain't gon' kill me."

At least I didn't think so. That one day turned into three because of the snow and I spent the whole time attempting to check on Simone. I could see nothing in her mind, so I knew that meant she was still in her box. When the weather finally broke, I hightailed it back to my dugout, keeping my thoughts on the weather and not the guilt—and fear—I felt for leaving her alone for so long.

I know I'm supposed to feel bad about blocking my thoughts from Simone. Or even worse—not thinking about the girl, period. If someone had my life in their hands, I'd want to know their whereabouts, too. Difference was, Simone wanted to eat everybody I met. And she constantly warned me about trusting King and the Raduts, even when I didn't bring them up. Almost like she was trying to find a reason to eat them. At least now, I'd been so busy working at the Wiltshires' every day that I didn't need to concentrate on blocking her out. It just happened.

Not only that, but I still couldn't see her or any of her thoughts. I can't think the worst, that the girl had gotten so hungry that she left her box and feasted on the first and only person she'd encountered out there on the beach. Maybe she'd guessed how to block me from her, too.

Even in the darkness, my old cave appeared undisturbed. No smoke came from the makeshift chimney. But there were footprints in the snow leading from the beach, to my dugout, and back again. After securing the horse, I used the lantern I'd carried with me to light my way to the door. I sniffed for rot in the air. If Simone hadn't eaten in over a week, she was gonna be an awful fright. The door creaked open and nothing but cold air and an empty cave greeted me. I walked around to the other side of the cave where Simone's box was buried. No footprints there. No indication that the box had been opened and what lay inside had crawled out. My shoulders relaxed. From what I could tell, she was still there. All I needed now was to steel myself to rouse her for the evening.

Once I got the fire in the stove going, I sat down on the bed, thinking back to the two weeks I'd been gone. Working at the Wiltshires' was nothing like working at Miss Tillie's. Mrs. Wiltshire, used to cooking and cleaning the fifty years she'd been married, continued to work beside me. And like Simone, she talked to me like I was someone she'd known all her life. Talked to me like a person and didn't take liberties with calling me any old name she preferred. Once my work was done and the Wiltshires were sound asleep, I'd go out and play in the snow before making the trek back home. I loved seeing it melt in my hands or getting lucky enough to have a single flake fall on the tip of my finger like miniature frozen lace. Curious to see how cold it was, I stripped naked and rolled around in it. All I got was wet, but it was fun anyway.

"Lavinia?"

King's voice, and the sight of his head poking in my cave, startled me. I brushed past and pulled him outside.

"I came by a few days ago to see if you were alright in your first winter here. It can be rough if you're not ready for it."

"How thoughtful!" I sang, hearing Mrs. Wiltshire's influence on me. "I got a job over in Tolleston. Been stayin' there. I only came by to check on the place."

"Well, I don't want to keep you—"

"Okay, thanks!" I said louder than I wanted, hoping he'd get the hint.

"I thought to come by and ask you over for supper—"

"I'd love to."

Neither of us hid our disappointment when supper came to an end. I lingered for a moment, not wanting to leave, but knowing Simone's feeding was well overdue. I promised to call on him again the next time I was back at my dugout. He held me against the door, his lips covering mine, and showing little to no desire to get me out of his house.

Then he finally released me with a whispered invitation to stay. When I politely and begrudgingly refused, he offered to walk me back to my place. That brought me out of my reverie. Couldn't have him accidentally coming face-to-face with a hungry and angry vampire. So, I made the lonely, painful, five-minute trek back to my cave.

The rot hit me before I even got to the door.

Like the first time I met her, Simone, almost as white as a sheet, stood in a corner of the dugout. Her head was tilted downward, but her narrowed eyes glared up at me.

Did she know almost two weeks had passed?

"Two weeks?" she said, taking a step toward me. "You left me in there for two weeks?"

"Well since you insist on listenin' in on my thoughts, you already know it ain't been a full two weeks yet." The scowl on Simone's face told me this wasn't the best approach. "Look, I'm sorry. I lost track of time 'cause of the snow."

"How, Lavinia? How does one lose track of time sitting in a dugout all day?"

Is that what she thought I'd been doing? Each word out of her mouth exposed those fangs of hers. I swear, either her gums must shrink while she sleeps, or those things have grown since the last time I saw her. "I . . . got a job."

"You have a job?!"

I jumped back. "I know. I know. But this job will let me stop pocketin' things when we go huntin'. We'll finally be able to move to Chicago."

She folded her arms across her chest. "Is this a job with the fishmonger? I saw you over there with him this evening."

I hadn't realized how close she was to me—or how much I'd been backing away from those teeth until I was standing out in the snow again. "I'm cookin' and cleanin' for a couple in Tolleston. You know I can't sleep like regular folks. I jus' lost track of time. But I'm here now. We can go huntin' if you like."

"If I like?" She held her head like I'd spoken to her in a foreign language. "Because of you, that pain I've dreaded has returned. The pain of not feeding." She pressed one hand against her stomach while the other reached out to me. "I can hear your heart beating." Her steps toward me quickened. She sniffed the air. "I can smell the salt in your blood. Did you know your blood can speak? It has a voice, a soft voice, that calls to me when I'm hungry. Right now, I'm very hungry."

She was on me in a second. I tumbled backward into the snow, my forearm up in front of my face to stop her snapping mouth from biting me. Simone latched onto my arm, pushing it down so that it nearly crushed my nose. I turned my head, mostly not to see this wild creature attacking me, but also to keep her rot-stink outta my face. A stream of blood from my arm dripped onto my lips. I screamed, then punched her in the face until she let go. Then I jumped to my feet, ran back into the dugout, and barricaded the door with my body. Simone tried knocking it down with hers. All the growling and shouting she was doing, I feared King would come checking on me and find himself on the wrong end of those fangs. But I couldn't risk opening the door and having her make a meal outta me.

Then the banging stopped. Did she leave? I pressed my ear against the door, listening for her feet crunching against the snow or that god-awful snarling she did before she bit me. Nothing but an intermittent gust blowing from the lake. I exhaled loudly, gritted my teeth, and cracked open the door. Then the rot returned.

I spun around and saw Simone standing next to that hole she'd dug. She made to charge at me again, but I managed to grab a chair and keep her at bay. Didn't stop her from snapping and growling at me anyway. I ran forward with the chair and pinned her against the wall. One of the chair legs splintered and sliced into her neck. No blood flowed from the deep wound.

"Simone! Stop!" I had to call her name several times before the frenzy stopped. "If I give you some of my blood, will that calm you 'til we get to the woods?"

She screamed her response, a loud, shrill kind of holler that made me think the cave was gonna fall in on me, and clawed at the air.

"Simone. It's me, Lavinia. Look." I raised the arm where she bit me, only to find the wound completely healed. This time, I didn't double over in pain and cough up mess like I did last time. But I wasn't gonna let her bite me again.

"I'm hungry!" she yelled again.

"I know. And I'm sorry. I won't leave you here that long again, okay? Can you calm down for a second 'til we get to the woods?"

She spoke through her bared teeth. "Bring me your fishmonger friend, then."

"Simone, now we ain't goin' through that again, you hear me? Now, if you can't wait 'til I get the wagon hitched, I'm gonna have to tie you up. Is that what you want?"

"No." At least her voice had calmed.

"I'm gonna put this chair down, okay? If you pounce on me, I'mma beat the hell outta you with it, you hear?"

Simone nodded, pressing her pale lips closed. I lowered the chair slowly, but still held on to it, just in case. I put some space between me and Simone.

"You prefer those people instead of me," Simone said, her voice heavy. "You see? I said I wouldn't attack you—"

I thought my eyes were gonna roll outta their sockets at the audacity of her words. "Did you forget what jus' happened in there? You think I'm holdin' on to this here chair to redecorate the place?"

"Well, I'm not attacking you now," she said as if I was too stupid to realize the difference. "You can trust me. You can't trust them."

"You never have to interact with these folks 'cause you're always in your box durin' the day. And it ain't like you can go callin' on folks durin' the day anyway. You haven't really gotten to know anybody but me. If you trust me, then trust I wouldn't befriend someone who's gonna hurt you, let alone myself."

Simone stood there chewing on the inside of her mouth. "The wagon isn't going to hitch itself, you know."

I'd learned that winter in Northwest Indiana proved to be ideal for Simone. The snow made everything so eerily quiet. It gave unsuspecting humans a false sense of security and peace. Seeing a poor young woman, all alone in the cold, would give any man pause. He'd offer her a coat and escort her to a warm place. Might even strike up a conversation to find out if there was a beau somewhere waiting for her. Sounds nice, don't it? Well, if you were that guy and the poor young woman was a vamp returning your kindness with a gaping hole to your neck, you'd wouldn't think so. That's what our first winter in Indiana was like.

The Tolleston woods had lots of places for every kind of creeping thing—including a vamp—to hide. A river called the Little Calumet flowed a ways south of it. Drew hunters from all over. Why they chose to hunt in the middle of the night, I had no idea, because there were always reports in the papers about somebody getting shot. I mean, a long gun, traps, and lanterns and such was a lot to carry around. And if the light didn't give you away to the animals, all that clanging that went on was enough to tell on you. Folks gotta eat, I guess. But the noise only made finding Simone's meals that much easier.

It didn't take long to learn the habits of these hunters. Lots of them, it seemed, only came out for sport. They'd be puffing on their fat cigars, bragging about whose deer or fish was bigger, about who bagged the most rabbits or muskrats. Someone hunting for food to live wouldn't care. They'd be more worried about whether what they got was enough to feed the family and for how long. I'd hear them measuring out the portions aloud, debating if they should try to get a couple more or head back to the warmth of their homes. Those men I avoided. Killing them essentially meant killing a whole family, and I couldn't have that on my conscience.

But those fat cats outta Chicago were fair game and easily tricked. The last few times we were out here, I'd dug a hole in a frozen slough near where they usually hunted, and Simone jumped in. She screamed for help, acting like she'd fallen in. Some sucker heard her and came running to her rescue. Then, right as he pulled her from the hole, she'd clamp onto a piece of exposed skin, usually a hand or a cheek—a neck, if she was lucky. Then she tossed him down the hole. Less cleanup for me. Sometimes she'd act as though she'd been shot by a stray bullet. Simone wasn't too bright when it came to that. She'd actually get shot, except it might be a wound to her head or right in the gut that healed up after she fed and rested for a couple of days. You should've seen the look on those fellas' faces when she showed them a hole in her body that didn't bleed or should've killed her outright. They never had long to ponder it though because they'd be twitching and dying in no time.

Sure hate to think what that place is gonna look like when the weather breaks and all them bodies turn up. By then, me and Simone should be well on our way out of Tolleston and away from any suspicions.

But hunting wasn't the only thing we did in the woods. A few times, Simone and I simply stood in the middle of a clearing and let the flakes fall on our tongues. While the snow I caught instantly melted from my body heat, Simone's piled up until she could swallow a whole mouthful. Other times, we'd lace up our boots and get to sliding over the frozen sloughs. I was always surprised that our squeals and laughter didn't draw more attention.

This time, Simone got her foot caught in a bear trap, on purpose. She smiled and winked at me, then laid out in the snow, howling like a right fool. I took refuge behind a tree and waited. It had been a while since we'd come here, but I was certain someone would be along sooner or later.

Sure enough, a large man with a heavy duster and fur cap came slinking through the snow with a rifle in his hands. Couldn't see his face, but I followed the hunter through the woods, all while trying not to trip over fallen tree trunks or slip on frozen mud pits hidden beneath fresh white powder. I hoped he wouldn't venture too far from Simone.

Finally, Simone's screams caught the hunter's attention. His head perked up and turned in the direction of the fake plea for help. He lifted the lantern hanging on the end of his rifle. As the light flickered across his face, my breath caught in my throat.

King!

I rushed from my hiding place, losing my footing with each step.

At one point, I fell so hard, I thought King felt the ground quake. But I guess it was really my swearing out loud that caught his attention.

"Lavinia?" he said. "What're you doing out here? And without a coat!"

I tried laughing off my foolishness, acting like some silly woman who'd simply lost her way. I loved the concern crinkling his brow as he threw his own coat over my shoulders. Loved the sweet way he scolded me for coming out here, instead of coming to him if I needed food. Loved the smell of his neck against my nose as he gathered me up in his arms and carried me to his wagon. A tinge of guilt rattled my soul as I noticed he hadn't bagged a thing. His only thought seemed to be about my well-being, not about what he was gonna eat. I was being selfish, I know, especially since the frigid air didn't bother me at all, and here he was without a coat. The pain I'd felt in my butt from falling had long left. This moment was all about me, nobody else. Despite how close Simone and I were, she never once asked whether I needed a break from my ghoul duties, if there was something she could do for me.

I took every bit of King's scolding because every word out of his mouth made me as warm as any fire could. He cared. For me. As I sat beside him in the driver's seat of his wagon, he wrapped a blanket around both of us, keeping one hand on the reins and the other around me. I pressed my body closer to his. Is this what love felt like? The knots in my stomach and my heart, ready to burst from my chest, signaled that it was. I stumbled over my words whenever I tried to thank him for his kindness. My face hurt from smiling so much, even when he hadn't said a word.

He gave the horse a light slap on its back to urge it along. I snuggled in close, imagining him carrying me into his dugout and placing me on his bed before a roaring fire, or at least the lit stove. How nice it would be to snuggle up against him all night and then wake up to his beautiful face in the morning! I wonder what King would think of leaving here with me and settling in Chicago, or maybe going where his mama's people were. Someplace where there were no vampires, no threat of dozens of frozen corpses appearing with the spring thaw.

Then a pain exploded in my head like a bullet had gone through it. A shrill scream left my mouth. I shook the blanket and coat off, then jumped from the moving wagon, landing in a heap of snow. I couldn't hear a thing; didn't even know if King had stopped the wagon to see after me. I writhed on the frosty powder, screaming and crying, all the while holding my head as if the pressure from my hands would stop the pain. It didn't. Blinded by the torture, I finally stood and took to running in whatever direction my feet dictated. For a moment, the pain increased until I fell to my knees and crawled in another direction. Suddenly, it stopped. I wandered a bit to get my bearings until I saw that I was a few yards from Simone, who'd apparently found a different hunter to feed on in my absence. The two dark figures huddled in the snow. One of them was laid out, its arms and legs twitching while the other was bent over it, growling like a dog tearing a steak apart. All the slurping I heard was enough to turn my stomach. I left Simone to her business and turned to locate King.

But there he was, right behind me.

"Lavinia?"

He reached for me, and as I took a step toward him, trying to block his view, the pain gripped me again. King suddenly raised his weapon. His boots crunched against the frosty powder as he approached the feeding frenzy.

I angled the barrel of King's rifle toward the ground. "Shh," I said. "Let's get out of here!"

King squinted his eyes and craned his neck. "What is that? It looks like—"

"Nothin'!" I said, pushing him away from the scene. "A bear or somethin' feedin'."

"That ain't no bear!" King said a bit too loud.

I turned my head to see that Simone had lifted hers. The moonlight showed how sloppily she'd fed. A thick swath of blood trailed down from her mouth like it had been painted on with a leafy tree branch. She stood, head lowered, arms out to her sides. Palms flexing. Then she broke into a sprint toward us.

"King! Run!"

I never would've cast King for a dummy, but he stood there for a moment like he was waiting on his brain to register what was happening. I screamed for him to run several more times before he got the message. He dropped his rifle and turned right when Simone was about to pounce on him. Except he turned right into a tree, knocking him to the ground. I grabbed her from behind, spinning both of us around, and held fast to keep her from King, who was now spread eagle on the snow.

Simone shook me from her. "Why did you do that?"

"You already fed!"

"You're protecting him!"

"And?"

"And?" Simone stuck her finger in my face. "You're supposed to be helping me, not him!"

I slapped her finger away. "And I said he was off-limits! You're so stupid sometimes! He saw you like," I waved my hands up and down in front of her, "like . . . this."

"What if he goes back and tells people what he saw?"

I rolled my eyes. "He won't."

I mean really, who would he tell? From my time here, I learned that King and I were the only colored folks in the area. I couldn't imagine him gossiping like some old biddy as he hawked fish to the neighbors.

"Not if I have anything to do with it."

I'll fry you 'fore I let you hurt him!

We both gasped. The thought came to my mind before I knew it. And Simone had heard it. Her nostrils flared and her jaw clenched. I didn't mean what I thought . . . did I? Would I kill Simone if King was in danger? Could she even *be* killed?

"I didn't mean that!" I said, clasping a hand over my mouth as if to keep any more stupidity from falling out.

"No?" Simone said, with an eyebrow raised. "These people are all you've thought about lately. There used to be a time all you ever worried about was me and planning out the next feeding."

"What is this? Jealousy? I ain't never seen you so particular for anybody. Blood is blood, like you told me. Don't matter who it comes from."

"I've never seen *you* so particular for anybody either. And you're wrong. You were the first Negro I'd ever tasted." She threw her head back and smiled. "Like rum-infused sugar. Sweet and intoxicating." After what I guess was her reliving one of the three times she'd bitten me, she opened her eyes and frowned. "But since I need you . . ." Simone punctuated the pause with a wicked stare and then walked away.

I stood there in the silence of the darkened woods, trying to make sense of what Simone had said. She wants to eat me? Me, the one who'd saved her I don't know how many times? The one who had to bury all her victims? The one who had to drain any blood pooling in her dead body once a week so she could feed again? I hope she doesn't think all that flattery about my blood was supposed to make things better. It only made me wanna watch my back around her. She wouldn't do anything to me . . . would she? Could she?

I closed my eyes and started forward, using my connection with Simone to locate her. I was relieved to see that she had taken the horse and was returning to the dugout, but surprised that her sadness, tinged with a bit of her own fear, nearly matched mine.

Took a bit before King finally woke up.

"What happened?" he said as he rubbed the goose egg sprouting on his forehead.

"You ran into a tree." I helped him to his feet and wiped snow from his backside. "You alright?"

"I guess so." He squinted his eyes and then looked around. "Where's your mistress?"

I shot him a confused look. "My mistress? Why would she be out here?"

"I thought I . . ." He turned toward where Simone had been feeding. Luckily, I had time to dump the body before he woke up. Even the puddle of blood Simone had left behind got covered with a mound of snow.

I held him by the elbow and guided him to his wagon. "You sure you're alright?"

I helped him inside and then climbed in beside him, taking the reins in my hands. Now it was his turn to lean against me. I guided the horse toward his home, careful not to jostle him on the way. Once inside the dugout, I laid him carefully on his bed, stripped him down to his union suit, and tucked him in.

"Funniest thing," he said. "I thought I saw your mistress out there . . . eating a man!"

"Eatin' a man?" I said over my shoulder as I stirred the glowing embers in his stove back to life.

"Yeah, reminded me of the stories my mama used to tell me about wendigos, man-eating spirits."

Oh, Lord! He's starting to sound like the Raduts. I sat beside him on the bed. "You talkin' crazy now, King. Maybe I should stick around a while, jus' to make sure you're alright. Why don't you tell me a bit more 'bout your mama's spirit things."

I wanted to crawl in and hold him, but I watched him sleep instead, making sure his chest continued to rise and fall. Stayed all night sitting up in bed beside him. It was nice to see him roll over and smile at me the next morning. I made him breakfast and had him promise me to stay in for the day. Then I stopped at my dugout and stood at the hole where Simone's box lay and swept some snow over the lid. I wasn't sleepy, so I sat atop a ridge between my place and King's. I couldn't hear Simone at all. Wished I could hear King's thoughts. Sunrise brought my attention back to Simone's resting place and questions about where we would go from here.

NINETEEN

Martin stands at the door of the jailhouse with a woman who isn't his wife. I've seen his wife lots of times before—she and Mrs. Wiltshire did their quilting together—and this ain't her. This woman, a curvy young thing around Simone's age, hands him a tan-colored picnic basket. Dinner, I assume. The sun is still out, but not shining as brightly as it was when Martin and I started chatting about the whole Simone affair. Lots of folks have a servant girl working for them. I think nothing of this, until I see the girl's shy smile, the way she leans in with her chest packed into a too-small bodice, the light giggle as he whispers something in her ear.

The girl bites at her bottom lip and tilts her head toward me. "Is that her?"

Like I said, the jail ain't that big. I'm right here, feet away from her.

Martin smiles at her. "Yeah. She's been in here weaving a yarn about vampires."

"Vampires?" She giggles again. "What is that?"

"According to her, they're dead people who drink blood from living people, like this," and he starts nibbling at the girl's neck.

She squeals and slips outta his grasp. They chase each other around the desk making all sorts of racket until Martin catches her and they start moaning and pawing at each other. If this is what I gotta deal with all night, the posse can come hang me right now.

"How long will you be?" she asks as he herds her back to the door.

Martin leans against the doorframe. His free hand strokes her cheek. "She'll be here until the train to Hammond comes through. Gotta make sure no one tries to get a head start."

"But if somebody did," she says, "you wouldn't have to stay here all that time."

Martin shakes his head and looks down at his boots. He softens his voice. "Can't have a repeat of last time. You know what folks have been saying, Charlotte."

The lady friend runs her hand down his arm. "This one's different. Besides, you're not drunk now, are you?"

I chuckle. This girl must not know there ain't a ceiling to this man's tolerance. Been drinking with him all day and even I'm surprised we're still awake.

"And I'm gonna keep it that way. Constable's not gonna make a fool outta me this time."

"But," Charlotte draws out, "if you let the town take care of this little problem, you and I can . . ." She bites her bottom lip and starts fingering a button on his shirt.

They giggle-talk among themselves like I'm not here. I'm used to it. Saw lots of it back at Miss Tillie's. Her husband would cat around the slave shacks every week like it wasn't nothing. Miss Tillie didn't even seem to care about that, or the fact that five of the boys working in the big house were all brown versions of her husband while she was with not one baby of her own. But her catching him with a local widow? That's what sent her over the edge and put him on the cooling board.

I immediately wonder where Martin's people are from and if Simone had had a taste of them yet.

Sorry. Old habits.

"Be quick about it," he says as if confirming a plan I didn't hear. He checks his pocket watch. "Nightfall. He always takes supper with his wife, then he'll be by to relieve me. He can't stop all of them by himself."

Once Martin sends the girl on her way, he posts himself next to my jail cell, scooping the dinner she's brought him into his mouth. Root vegetables and salted pork. Martin gives a third of his meal to me. We both stand at the bars, wrestling through the tough meat.

"Sounds like an admission to me," Martin says after swallowing the leather.

"An admission of what?" If anything, that girl should be in jail for serving these undercooked turnips.

"Guilt. You wanted Miss Arceneau dead. Because of the fishmonger."

"That happened months before Simone for-real died. If she's even for-real dead, that is."

Martin's fork clangs against his tin plate. "But that's the exact way she died, right? According to you, it was the sun that killed her. You said that night you wanted her to fry."

"But that doesn't mean—"

Martin paces the jail, speaking to himself more than to me. "She was angered by your relationship with him; that you'd been hiding things from her. She must have caught you with him, then you killed her."

I tilt my head and raise an eyebrow. "Did any of your witnesses say we were fighting when they saw us?"

"They saw you slapping the hell out of her on the front lawn!"

"Only to rouse her."

"Then you must've fought in the house before you got outside."

"If I was mad enough to kill her, they would've heard the whole commotion before we got outside. And if I was that mad, you think a bunch of gawkin' neighbors was gonna stop us from fightin'?"

Martin shrugs. "Maybe."

I retreat to a far corner of the cell. "How 'bout maybe not. I was mad at her that night, but I didn't stay mad at her."

"You were plotting, waiting for the right time to kill her with sunlight."

I smile and return to the bars. "So, you believe me then? You believe she was a vampire. Sunlight wouldn't have killed a normal person. And if you believe she was a vampire, why's it so hard to believe I didn't kill her?"

He pats the air with the palm of his hand. "Calm down. I'm not there yet. Not completely sold on this wild tale of yours. What happened after that night she almost attacked the fishmonger?"

"Simone and I kept a cordial distance from each other. She stayed buried in her box 'til it was time to feed, which meant I only saw her once a week or so. Ain't like she knew time was passin' noway. If she did, she never let on. Guess neither one of us wanted to be in another situation where we said things we regretted. Everything was strictly business between us for a while. I'd wake her once a week as usual after I staked out a victim, clean up the mess, then return to the dugout before heading back out to the Wiltshires' the followin' mornin' . . . all without sayin' a word to each other, through our mouths or otherwise."

Martin rubs the stubble on his chin. "Weren't you afraid to leave her there in your dugout after that thing with the fishmonger?"

I sigh, thinking back to that argument. "We had an understandin'. She wanted to leave and knew we had to do it as soon as the spring thaw hit. The only way that could happen was with any money I saved from workin' at the Wiltshires'. I can't make money if I'm worryin' 'bout her eatin' King. So, she agreed to leave him alone."

"And you believed her?"

I shrug. "What choice did I have?"

"So, how long did this episode of not speaking to each other last?"

"Lasted a good while," I say. "I remember things not changin' 'til after the trees started buddin'."

Martin's eyes bulge. "That long?"

"Told you: vampires got no concept of time. She wouldn't know one way or the other if I stayed at the dugout or moved to the moon. 'Sides, I was enjoyin' myself. Had somethin' to do durin' the day. Had people to talk to. Was improvin' my readin' and figurin'. And gettin' distance between me and Simone had me feelin' less guilty about what we did at night. I had to keep all that stuff to myself. When I told her about the job at the Wiltshires', she had a fit. 'What if someone finds me, Lavinia?' she said. 'What if I wake up in the daytime?' 'What if the Raduts find me?'"

"What if the Raduts *had* found her?" Martin asks.

I wave off his comment. "They wasn't gon' find her. For all they knew I was stayin' at the Wiltshires' and there was a blizzard damn near every other week to keep them from sniffin' 'round my dugout anyhow."

Martin joins me at the bars, his plate clean. Mine still held those hard-ass turnips. I hand him my unfinished plate and he finishes the vegetables in three bites. "So, what broke the ice between you two?"

I rub my throat, as if trying to coax the right words outta my mouth. Some things about Simone ain't easy to explain. Using words like "life" and "death" means something different when I'm talking about her.

"She almost died."

TWENTY

These folks couldn't wait for the weather to let up. Soon as the snow melted and the sun got to shining, them folks were out in droves. Mrs. Wiltshire constantly had company over to the house. By then, my reading had improved so much, that during afternoon tea, she'd invite me to read those crazy fairy tales to her guests. They'd clap when I was done, and then Mrs. Wiltshire would ask my opinion about parts of the story. I'd sit there for a couple of hours with her guests discussing the story like I was the one calling on them. I wasn't the maid, the cook, the help. To them, I was plain old Lavinia.

Mother Nature couldn't make up her mind. One minute it would feel like spring was on the horizon. The next minute, two inches of snow was on the ground. What did stay constant was old Mr. Wiltshire's absence from the house. I could count on one hand the number of times this man came home at a decent hour and broke bread with his poor wife. When he did tiptoe home, it was well after Mrs. Wiltshire had retired for the evening. I think he got up too early for breakfast even, simply to avoid seeing her in the morning. Never said two words to me, not that I was itching to have a conversation with him nohow.

But the warmer weather brought out the crazies, too. One afternoon, the Raduts called on Mrs. Wiltshire. I was seeing them for the first time in months and when the visit was over, the Raduts insisted that I see them to the door.

"You like job?" Valerica asked, motioning for me to join them on the porch.

"Love it," I said with a smile.

"You have nice place to live, yes?" Victor chimed in. He closed the front door. "Not like hovel on beach, like Valerica tell me."

I raised an eyebrow. They called me out here to ask this?

"Has been a long time," Victor said. "Vamp is still on the loose. We must find her."

Should've known this was too good to be true. No wonder they wanted to get me alone: didn't want Mrs. Wiltshire to know how crazy they were. Mrs. Wiltshire never said nothing about vampires. Maybe they didn't have them in England. Or maybe Mrs. Wiltshire had enough sense to keep her crazy to herself.

I folded my arms across my chest. "All this time, that vamp ain't done nothin'. Why go back wastin' all your time lookin' for her? She's prob'ly gone by now."

Victor pointed to the woods behind the house. "The hunters. They pop up all over the place over there. Bites on them." He pointed to his neck.

I bristled at the reference. I'd been following the stories in the papers, how bodies were starting to turn up in the thawed-out sloughs in the hunting grounds. I kept that fact from Simone since the first words outta her mouth would've been moving away. The only thing connecting me and Simone to the hunting grounds was King, but he never brought up that night in the woods, apparently convinced that he hadn't seen what he thought he saw. I'd been meaning to go by there, gauge his thoughts, and see if he'd put two and two together yet. Maybe the Raduts were the push I needed to get over there and cover my butt, if needed.

I relaxed against the doorframe. "What makes you think it's the vamp? How you know an animal didn't get 'em? Them dumb hunters over there gettin' themselves shot all the time."

"I hear of story from cousin," Victor said. "A young girl killed by a woman who fell dead. They bury but body disappear. She is here!"

"Why don't y'all jus' move if you're that scared of her?" I asked.

"Because they will follow us," Victor said, his eyes all narrowed like the sun had gotten in his eyes. "Like they follow us here!"

I groaned, irritated by the interruption and anxious to get them out of earshot of Mrs. Wiltshire. "Ain't nobody followed you!" I pointed at Valerica. "She said they can't cross water. And if she could, why would she go after the hunters instead of you? She came to your place that night. Don'tcha think she'd have got you by now if she really wanted you?"

The pair looked at each other as if the answer to my questions were on their foreheads or something.

"Well?" I asked.

"You search with us, tonight!"

I lowered my arms. "Excuse me?" Wasn't sure if I was shocked by him having the nerve to order me around or that he'd gotten wind of that little girl Simone got ahold of before we got here. Guess all the Romanians up here must know each other. But that happened a while ago. How long had he been holding on to that little nugget of information?

Valerica slid her hand down my arm. "Please. We cannot go without you."

"You forget I got a job over here," I said. "What makes you think I got time to be messin' 'round with you?"

"But we got you job," Valerica said.

"And what does that mean?" I asked.

"It means you owe," Victor said, pointing a finger at me.

"I owe you for what? Gettin' me this job? Ain't nobody told you to get it for me."

"But you took," Victor said.

"Well, I wouldn't've if I knew you was gonna come back at me for it!"

"Lavinia, please." Valerica was talking to me but staring at her crazy husband. "Help us get rid of vampire."

"Valerica . . ." I sighed. Though I had fun with them, a lot had happened to me since the last time I saw them. They'd been my only friends at the time, the only people I'd interacted with other than King. With them, I could be semi-normal. I could even talk about vamps with them without sounding like a nut. But I'd turned a corner. I didn't just see myself as a ghoul anymore. After months of working for the Wiltshires and tending to Simone when needed, I'd found a nice balance between my two lives. If I didn't want Simone messing it up, what made these two think I was gonna do it for them?

"Maybe you would not have problem hunting," Victor said, "if you have no job."

I looked at him and Valerica. "Meanin' what?"

Valerica tugged at her husband's arm, urging him down the steps. "We go. You think. Maybe hunt another day."

Then they got to trilling at each other, each sentence louder than the one before. Whatever Valerica said got him all sorts of mad. He pointed to the house and Valerica sheepishly walked back inside.

"Where you goin'?" I asked Valerica as she breezed past me.

She kept her eyes forward. "Forgot something."

My body stayed against the front door, keeping it open with the expectation of Valerica leaving and taking her crazy husband with her. Victor didn't budge either. He stood in the yard, eyeballing me, as if he could will me to go vamp hunting with them. I mean, even if I did go with them, I sure as heck wasn't gonna go at night. How much sense did that make? Vamps hunt at night, so if Simone was actually gunning for Victor, wouldn't she have a better chance when the sun went down?

I wanted to tell him that, but Valerica was taking too long. I don't know what she could have forgotten; they came calling with empty hands. I suspect that was because they'd planned all along to corner me, not really sit with Mrs. Wiltshire. Anyway, I walked back into the house and found Valerica talking to Mrs. Wiltshire in the kitchen. I don't think they heard me coming because I heard Valerica say:

"And she not taken anything from you?"

"Heavens, no!" Mrs. Wiltshire said with a hand to her heart. "She's been positively delightful. Why would you think such a thing?"

"She was slave, yes?" Valerica said. "These people, they do not know of having nice things like you have. She comes to our store with things to sell. Where does she get them from? You? Other people she steals from? Woman came to the store and said pipe Lavinia sold to us belonged to her husband."

Mrs. Wiltshire clutched the brooch around her neck. "You don't think she's taking things from me, do you? John still isn't pleased with a Negro in the house, even if it is a woman. Oh, dear. If he finds out . . ."

"And there was story of young girl killed in town not far from here."

"What has that to do with Lavinia?"

"Newspaper said killer travel with Negro woman. How many Negro women here?"

Right then, Valerica looked up at me peeking around the corner into the kitchen. "You check, Jane," she said, patting the old woman on her arm. "Maybe I'm wrong, I do not know. I'm sure everything is fine." She smiled, then walked past me to the front door like I didn't hear her bad-mouthing me a few seconds ago. If daggers could come outta my eyes, they would've got her right in the back.

That night, after the Wiltshires were tucked in their bed, I hightailed it over to my dugout. My plan: get rid of all my pilfered stuff.

"Good idea," Simone said. She was sitting up on my bed, back to me, with her hands out toward the fire she'd lit in our little stove.

I snickered at the sight of her acting human, as if she needed the warmth. "What you doin' with the stove lit? You want somebody to come over here to find you?" When she didn't answer, I asked, "You speakin' to me now?" I raised an eyebrow to disguise the fact that I was glad she was there.

"After your day today, I figured you'd need someone to talk to about your Radut problem." She hadn't turned around yet. I counted the days since she last fed to make sure she wasn't gonna pounce on me again.

"At least it's only been three days since you've been gone this time," she said, hearing my thoughts.

I sighed and took a seat beside her. "So, what'd you hear?"

"According to the Raduts, you're a thief. And they know about the little girl I sampled on the way up here. If the Raduts weren't so distasteful, I'd probably thank them for trying to get you released from your job."

"You heard all of that sleepin' in your box?"

Simone pulled a string from the waistline of her dress. "It appears you've been taking advantage of the fact I can't hear or do anything in that box. So, I didn't go to sleep the last time you left."

I turned to her. "And you've been sittin' here the whole time with the stove goin'? What if somebody came in and saw you?"

Finally, she looked at me and flashed her wolf teeth. "Then we'd have the week off from hunting."

We laughed, the tension of the last couple of months melting like the winter's snow. It was good to hear her voice.

"I'm glad we're speakin' again," I said as she hooked her arm around mine and laid her head on my shoulder.

"I'm glad you finally learned you can't trust everybody."

"This again."

"It's true!" Simone whined. "I know you're the one who's usually taking care of things, but you have to admit: I was right about this one."

"If it'll make you feel better. But I think Victor made Valerica say all that stuff about me."

"They're a package deal, like us. Don't forget that. Now, if we can get rid of these other humans in your life—"

"Here we go!" I stood up and grabbed my carpetbag. "It's more than jus' bein' 'round other humans, Simone. Other than King, I ain't seen another Negro in this area. All these folks probably know 'bout me is bein' an uneducated slave and that's it. I'd like to think I'm showin' 'em I'm no different than them. That I can contribute to society jus' like everybody else. I don't want 'em to see my skin color; I want them to see me. Plus, I like it, understand? I like bein' around people, talkin' with people, bein' in the sun—"

"Unlike me."

"We done had this talk, Simone," I said, shoving my odds and ends in the bag. Since we hadn't been hunting much these last few months, there wasn't much left. "I ain't like you. You got needs jus' like I do. They're jus' different, is all."

"You mark my words," Simone said, finally rising from the bed to help pack my carpetbag. "The sooner you get rid of these people in your life, the better off we'll be, and the sooner we can start over in Chicago."

TWENTY-ONE

Mrs. Wiltshire never said anything about what Valerica had accused me of. I guess that was a good thing. Whether she was waiting for me to steal something or didn't believe Valerica at all, I don't know. But nothing changed between us. I cooked and cleaned. She still trotted me out to her guests to practice my reading. I even started talking to Simone during the day in case she decided to come out of her box and listen to me. I wanted her to know she could trust Mrs. Wiltshire. I did go hunting with the Raduts a few times, but it wasn't the same. Part of me wondered if they wanted me to hear that conversation with Mrs. Wiltshire. But that didn't make them clever. If they only knew I was the one keeping the vampire they hunted from making a meal outta them. Wonder how they'd feel about that.

With me and Simone back on speaking terms and my dugout clear of evidence of theft, I took a day from work to bury my goods deep in a sand dune somewhere. As I left the dugout with my stuff, I got a glimpse of King's place. I'd barely seen him at all since that incident in the woods. Part of it was because the weather up here couldn't make up its mind about what it wanted to do. Mostly because I didn't wanna give Simone any reason to go back on our deal. I even tried not thinking about him during the day. Besides, Simone and I needed to get outta here soon, especially since we were so close to finally being able to afford a move to Chicago and put the Raduts and dead hunters behind us.

As I trudged along the beach with my carpetbag looking for the perfect dune, a swift early spring gust off Lake Michigan slowed my pace, pushing me toward the water. Pushing me right to King's door. Puffs of white smoke from his dugout and his boat tethered to a pole stuck in the sand told me he was home. I exhaled, closed my eyes, and knocked.

King opened the door and my breath left me. As if I hadn't seen this perfect man every day in my thoughts. He didn't smile or say anything. He was probably wondering where I'd been all this time. I smiled as King stared at me with the same blank look that had greeted me when he opened the door. I couldn't think of anything to say. Couldn't even muster a "Hello." So, I turned on my heel and started to walk away before I embarrassed myself any further.

"What's wrong with her?" King said, the sound of his voice shocking me to a stop. "Your mistress, Miss Arceneau. What's wrong with her?"

I closed my eyes and swore under my breath. "What do you mean?"

"I've seen her some nights out here, not far from my dugout, standing there looking at me."

So, this wasn't about that night in the woods. "She was here? When?"

"At dusk a couple of times. I thought she might have been looking for you. But she'd just stand there staring, like she was waiting for me or something."

I'd deal with that damn fool later. At least she kept her word by not eating him. I turned my back to him and silently swore. "Told you. She's sick."

"What kind of sick?"

I shrugged. "Jus' sick."

"No kind of sick I've ever seen. Those dead hunters they found over in the Tolleston woods with their throats all torn out. You sure she doesn't have something to do with that? I can't get that night I saw you in the woods out of my head."

"You still thinkin' 'bout that? Who knows what sorta ride your brain took while you were laid out, but I can tell you, my mistress wasn't there that night."

"Can't help it. I guess seeing her so many times during the winter kept it on my mind. Made it seem awfully real."

I pursed my lips. *Thanks, Simone!* "What exactly do you think you saw that night in the woods?"

"I saw her coming at me with blood streaming down the front of her dress. I saw you trying to keep her from me."

Good. At least he remembered that part.

I stared out toward the lake, hoping something would come to me. Maybe I should just come clean. There was a chance he'd understand.

Ha! Tell him the truth? See where that gets you! Guess Simone figured she'd give a little unsolicited advice. Last thing I needed was her voice in my head.

I turned to King and said, "Blood. She needs blood or she gets sick."
Idiot!

"You mean like a transfusion?"

"A what?"

King smiled, the tension in his jaw relaxing a bit. "One of my customers is the town doctor. Overheard him talking about taking blood from a healthy person and giving it to a sickly person. Guess they did it during the war. Is she that kind of sick?"

I raised my eyebrow. "Yes. That is exactly what it is. I didn't know there was a name for it. But you couldn't have seen her out here. She's all the way in Tolleston, remember? She really doesn't get out much."

"Right. Tolleston . . . Well, I knew it had to be something." His face relaxed, and he pulled his fingers through his hair before looking back up. "Or maybe seeing her was me missing you."

I lowered my eyes and pressed my lips together to keep my own smile from sprouting. "I missed you, too." I backed away toward my dugout. "I best let you get back to whatever you were doin' in there. I'm sure you got a lotta fishin' to do after that long winter off the water."

"Lavinia?"

God, I loved it when he said my name! Sounded even better than the first time I heard Simone say it. A flicker of hope lit within me as he jogged toward me. Maybe it wouldn't be so hard to come clean to him about what me and Simone really were.

"Maybe I can thank you with a boat ride? I remember how excited you were when you first arrived at the lake."

I touched my chest. "You remember that?"

There he was with that boyish shyness again, eyes tracing the path his toe was making through the sand. The hint of a dimple teasing on his right cheek. If I ever wanted to fight off a chill, this scene would warm me to my toes.

Wading through the water to the boat was scarier than I thought. I'd never learned to swim. Where I was from, all we had were still creeks capped with floating islands of moss and green snot. Nothing this big and wide and active like Lake Michigan: churning all about, fighting against the wind. In ankle-high water, I slipped on a bed of pebbles that gave way to tiny hills of sand. Gave me a reason to fall against King. With a chuckle, he took my hand and led me into deeper water that sent my body rocking with the waves rolling past. I brought the back of my skirts forward between my legs and tucked the hem into my waist-band, creating a pair of makeshift britches. Ribbons of cold water and coarse plant life swirled around my legs.

Getting inside the boat wasn't that easy, either. King held my hand while I stepped aboard, all the while thinking the thing was gonna roll over with it sitting so close to the water. Then he pushed it into the lake and hopped in like it was nothing. It was a wide thing with two wooden slats at the front and back for us to sit on. The middle section held rope, some pointy metal sticks, and a neatly folded pile of mesh netting. With an oar in each hand, King pushed us further from the shore.

We talked about nothing in particular. Favorite colors. Funny shapes we saw in the clouds above. Recollecting what we were doing when we heard Lincoln got shot. Then we said nothing at all, and that was fine with me. King let me enjoy watching the shore get away from us and the endless horizon ahead. Every time I looked back at King, he smiled.

The oars slapped against the water in time to the swaying of the boat.

King didn't bother me as I threw my head back, eyes closed against the bright sunshine, letting the lake lull me into a lazy calm. I daydreamed of the last memory of my mama's face before I got sold off to Georgia. Nothing more than a fuzzy ebony blob. But I remember her voice. The way she said my name, even when she was cross with me. I imagined myself in Simone's Montreal, walking down gaslit cobbled streets in some fancy silk gown on my way to a cotillion. King's name, the only one on my dance card. He'd take me in his arms and twirl me about the candlelit room while a string quartet made love to their instruments. All colored folks dressed as fancy as me, clapping at how gracefully we danced. I was free in my dreams and, out here, comfortable as a babe in a cradle. King had given them back to me.

What if we simply drifted away? Found a little island or something where it was only the two of us together forever?

Then my head exploded in pain. I took to screaming like a right fool, probably scaring King half to death—again. I pressed my hands against my temples. Pain weighed on my eyelids. Through the haze, I saw the shore was a ways off, too far for me to swim . . . if I knew how. But I was drowning in pain, and before I knew it, I threw myself from the boat. Submerged, the pounding in my head got louder, stronger like I was about to give birth to my brain right out of my eyes. I kicked and writhed in the darkness. I opened my mouth to scream, to die.

But my head broke through the water and air entered, burning a trail down my throat to empty lungs. King had jumped in and grabbed me. He tried directing me to get back in the boat, but I screamed for the shore, choosing to hold on to my head rather than him. After splashing and fighting for what seemed like forever, the pain subsided enough for me to open my eyes and see that I could stand and walk to the shore.

The whole ordeal wore me out. I collapsed on the sand and tried catching my breath. King lay beside me, panting too, watching his boat drift away. First time I heard him swear.

"What was that?" he asked, eyes still on the boat, now barely visible on the water. "That's the second fit you had."

"I'm sorry—"

He swore again and ran his hand over his wet face. "Where the hell am I gonna get another boat?"

"I'm sorry!" I said, on the verge of tears. Everything on my body hurt. Wouldn't last long. But wasn't nothing being a ghoul could do about the pain in my heart. "I get these pains in my head . . ."

"What pains?"

"I can't . . . I'll make it up to you. I'll get you another boat."

"How the hell do you plan on doing that? Is your crazy-ass mistress gonna buy me another one?"

I flinched at his words. Who was he to say that about her? He didn't know her. Yeah, Simone was crazy, and had tried to eat him and had probably stalked him all winter. But she was mine, and the only one with the right to call her that was me. "You think I did this on purpose?"

"I didn't say that."

"Then what are you sayin'? Ain't my fault I can't control my head pains!"

"I know that!" King sighed, scooped up a handful of wet sand, and lobbed it toward the lake. "It's just . . . my boat."

He wasn't listening. Truth was, I wouldn't either if somebody lost my livelihood. I shook my head and stood. Here I was, trying to be normal and do normal *human* things as if I had a life without a vampire. Couldn't even dream about it. Who was I fooling? All the mess I'd done for a creature that shouldn't even be living . . . Simone was right. I was far from being human anymore.

I walked away, letting silent tears roll down my face. A part of me hoped to hear King call my name again. But of course, he didn't. Was too busy watching his boat float away. I could easily get another one for him. All it would take was another trip out to the Tolleston woods with Simone and find someone fishing out on the Little Calumet River. Most of them had little skiffs they pushed around with a long wooden pole. But them fat cats out of Chicago; now they had real boats.

Listen to me. Who plots to get folks killed for a boat? Whether or not King would even accept a new boat from me, I didn't know. He'd always think it came from Simone and wasn't nothing I could say or do to change his opinion of her, especially since I kept making him think he didn't really see what we both knew he saw. I didn't even know why I cared. All he did was give me a few moments of normal, of feeling like a woman—a real woman. Like that was too much to ask.

Hell, I didn't need a man getting up in my head. Maybe Simone and I should just cut our losses and move on. Find some other place to settle that didn't have crazy Raduts or a man who looked at me like *I* was the crazy one.

As I got closer to my dugout, I saw a large piece of smoldering brown cloth piled in the grass. Who would be burning something way out here? Didn't remember seeing no camp or nothing when I left this morning, but no telling who was doing what in these dunes. I inched toward the cloth and saw it was burlap burning. An outstretched charred claw slowly opened and closed, clutching the dirt. Not thinking, I snatched the burlap away, and there was Simone, lying on her stomach. Patches of her arms and face were blacker than mine. No sound came from her when her clothes started sparking up again.

"Lavinia! What on earth?"

King stood behind me, a hand over his mouth blocking the stench of burnt flesh. He took off his shirt and tossed it over Simone's head. His hands batted down flames.

"You stupid vamp!" I said through my sobbing. "How could you be so stupid!" I stripped down to my underthings and wrapped my skirt and shirtwaist around Simone's exposed arms and legs. Then it struck me, I'd been so caught up with King that I hadn't seen a thing Simone was up to.

"Who would do something like this?"

"The sun," I said. "She ain't s'posed to be in the sun!"

When I couldn't lift her, King nudged me aside and hoisted her up. It took no time to get to my dugout. King laid her on my bed and peeled our clothes from her wet, sticky skin. The stench of her burnt flesh caused both of us to gag. King even ran outside a couple of times to vomit.

I paced, wondering what to do next. "What the hell . . . Why the hell were you out there!"

"Drowning," she rasped. "We . . . were . . . drowning."

"You dummy! We weren't—"

Oh. My. God. She saw, *felt* all of that? Had come out of her box . . . for me? Here I was, thinking of a life without her and she's out here burning to death, risking herself for me.

King covered his mouth again and bent over Simone. "There's no breath in her, Lavinia. She's gone."

"No!"

"Lavinia!"

"Either help me or get out!" I screeched.

King held me by my shoulders and shook me. "Stop it! Look at her! She's dead! You can't help her."

"Her box. I need her box."

I snatched myself away from King and headed to Simone's little grave. The lid was already off, but I had a hard time grabbing hold of the sides of the smooth wood to lift it from the ground. King got the other end of it, and together, we got it out. With my bedsheets beneath her, King and I placed her in the box.

"That box was a coffin? I'm not gonna ask why you have a ready-made coffin right outside your door."

"Then don't."

I lit my kerosene lamp and used the light to find a knife. I inhaled slowly.

"Stop! What are you doing?" King yelled as I cut a swath across my palm. I squeezed my fist, letting the blood stream between her blackened, chapped lips. Then I placed my bleeding hand right on her mouth. I braced myself for a bite that didn't come. When the wound healed, I'd cut it again.

From the corner of my eye, I saw King's confused face in the shadows. "I told you. She needs blood. Don't expect this little bit'll do anything, though."

"That's not how transfusions work." He turned toward me as his sorrowful eyes traced my face. "Lavinia, she's gone."

I studied King. Such a big man. Half of what he had might do the trick. If I jabbed him good in the gut, he'd double over enough for me to slide the blade across his neck . . .

I dropped the knife.

"Get outta here, King. Get out 'fore I do somethin' I'm gonna regret."

"You can't bury her on your own."

"I'm not gonna bury her."

I got down on my knees and pushed the box under my bed. All that mess under there clattered and crunched until I got the wooden coffin all the way under.

King wrinkled his face in disgust. "You're leaving her under the bed?!"

"I can't put her back in the ground, all alone, buried in the earth."

"Put her back?" King took my arm and dragged me out of the dugout. Took a minute for both of our eyes to adjust to the sunlight. "Look. I'm sorry your mistress is dead," he said, rubbing the darkness from his eyes. "I had a hard time letting family go, too. But keeping her under your bed? That's not normal."

"Ain't nothin' 'bout me and Simone is normal. I owe her." I sat cross-legged on the ground and began picking off the yellow heads of brown-eyed Susans polka-dotting the green prairie grass. "You don't know what all she's done for me. She was there in Georgia with me. You didn't know what it was like there." I squinted as I looked up at King.

He stood there, mouth open, like he was processing what he'd heard. "You're right, I don't know what your life was like before you got here. But I promise, letting her rot under your bed won't bring her back and it won't make you feel better. Maybe you owe it to her to move on."

"You been free your whole life, King, so I don't expect you to understand. But she gave me my name back. She gave me . . . me again. I'd still be on that same Georgia plantation I slaved on if it wasn't for Simone. And like you said, what was I gonna do out here on my own without a man? Without her? For her to come out in the sun for me . . . That's why I need you to leave, King. Don't make me choose between savin' your life or hers."

King set his hands on his waist and sighed. A look of pity—or maybe disgust—peeked through his beautiful features. "At least let me bury her for you."

"Get on out of here, King," I said, rising to my feet, eyes on the dugout. "I'll get your boat back." I reckon he wouldn't follow me. At this point, I didn't care. I'd told him all I could muster about my lifestyle. Wasn't nearly enough for him to understand that I didn't need his pity. Between thoughts of Simone, I vowed to get him a boat, and then pack up Simone and get the hell outta here.

The smell of burnt skin still filled the air and I needed time alone to wait. And wait I did. For days. Came back every night after work hoping to find her healed and sitting up on my bed. Waited to hear her scratching against the wooden lid to be let out. Waited for her to say my name. Waited for any sign of life.

In truth, I was afraid to look in the box. Wasn't ready to think about what I was gonna do without her. There was only a bright, pulsing light in my mind, but I couldn't see any of Simone's thoughts or memories. But I dared not take her from the box. I wondered, if she were dead-dead, what would that mean? A second freedom? In this post-slavery world, what did *that* even mean? Most of what I'd been able to do was because of Simone. Could I still go where I pleased, say what I pleased, and not worry about swinging from a tree with her gone? Would King give me that same protection Simone had? Wasn't sure I wanted to shackle myself to a man, cooking and cleaning up after him. Look at poor Mrs. Wiltshire's situation!

By week's end, I had to know. I slid the box out from under the bed and stared at it for a good long while. I knocked softly on the lid. Nothing. It creaked when I opened it with a shaky hand. Simone lay there, looking worse than dead, but better than when I found her outside. The charred skin had dried and started cracking. Some of it had flaked off, leaving behind skin as fresh as a baby's butt. When I tried to rouse her, she moaned in pain. Didn't usually take this long for her to heal. What she needed was more blood, a full feeding to get her back on her feet. But she wasn't in no condition to go nowhere. It's not like I could serve someone up on a silver platter for her now, could I?

I shut my eyes. A pain, worse than any of my headaches, bled through my heart. It hurt to leave her like this. That ain't what I do. My job was to protect her, make sure she was safe. Not let her rot in that box unable to move or feed. Not being so selfish with my own wants to keep her from doing stupid stuff. I couldn't even imagine what life would be like without her. We'd only been together less than a year, but me before her . . . who was that? Some freed slave too scared to leave a plantation of bad memories? What would I do out here on my own? Smart as I liked to think I was, I wouldn't be strutting around as proud as any white person without Simone.

Simone. The first one to give me my name back. I owed her my life.

She was dying and there was only one thing I could do for her now. Find a way to end her misery.

TWENTY-TWO

I wipe a tear from my eye after recalling that whole episode.

"So, you did kill her," Martin says.

"Are you even listenin' to this story?" I ask him.

"Of course, I am," Martin says, checking his pocket watch. "She got all burnt up from the sun, so you decided to kill her to put her out of her misery."

"That don't necessarily mean I killed her. Putting her outta her misery could mean makin' her feel better."

Martin snorts. "That's not what the phrase means. Anyway, that's the first time I heard you claim it was a mercy killing. Why didn't you say that before?"

"Would that have changed anything?"

"You killed a white person!"

"And you're killin' a Black one! Is her life more valuable than mine?"

"Nobody found her guilty of anything."

I laugh. Hard. After everything I've told him, he doesn't think murdering to survive is a crime because it was committed by a white woman. I return to my cot.

Martin doesn't seem to register my irritation. "Wait, Lavinia. One thing I've been wondering—if ghouls heal whenever they get hurt, then what are you so worried about anyway?"

"Have you not been listenin'? I'm not a ghoul anymore." I throw my bloody, bandaged arm up in front of his face. "Does this gash look like I'm all healed up?"

I hate thinking about what happened to make me go back to being human. If that's even what I am now. All I know is that I can no longer hear what Simone is thinking. I can't check in to see if she's about to pop up once it's dark and come rescue me—like her butt didn't land me in jail in the first place—or if she's finally on the other side. That, and I bleed like everyone else now.

"I don't know why I'm even bothering tellin' you all this." I drop my arm into my lap.

"Don't stop," he says with a chuckle. "It's entertaining. What else are you going to do? Sit there on that cot counting the seconds until the train comes? Think of this as your confession of sorts. The law dispenses its justice, but the good Lord will pour out his mercy."

Maybe you oughta be asking the good Lord to forgive you for stepping out on your wife.

"Go ahead," Martin says. "Tell me how you put Miss Arceneau out of her misery."

I asked Mrs. Wiltshire for a day to myself. A week had passed since Simone got all burnt up, and my daily vigil was taking its toll. I hadn't slept in a week, because of how busy I was trying to keep my job and wait for Simone to wake. Every night, I'd bleed some part of my body, but it wasn't enough. Guilt swallowed me as I watched my self-inflicted wounds heal in seconds while the blood I shed only inched Simone toward healing. I thought back to when I first met her, how sick I was and how easily I could walk to the forest and find me some monkey balls or sweet gum leaves. None of that would work for her. But if I didn't get some rest, somebody was bound to find two corpses in this dugout. So, I took my day and collapsed in the dugout, withdrawing to my thoughts and willing Simone to rise from her box.

Except that's not how my day went.

In the middle of the afternoon, right when I was getting a good sleep in, the Raduts appeared at my door. Irritable and half asleep, I was cordial enough to acknowledge their presence, making sure to keep the door slightly ajar so they wouldn't see their vampire laying in a coffin in the middle of my dugout.

"Not this vamp mess again," I drawled out as I shielded my eyes from the sunlight. Was in the middle of a nice dream of a mighty wind gusting off the lake, robbing King of his clothes. Ain't gotta tell you how sour I was at having to replace that image with those two. "You lasted a whole winter with nothin' happenin' to you. Let it go."

Victor pushed his wife from the door. "Who are you to tell us what to do? You want to keep job with Jane?" He pressed his stank-breath face into the door crack and lowered his voice. "Maybe we tell Jane you cause dead men in woods. That you brought nosferatu. That you killed little girl in Crown Point. Or better, we tell husband. He not like your kind anyway."

I reeled my head back so I could get a whiff of onion-free air. "First, she don't believe in vamps. Second—"

"But who will husband believe?" Victor asked, his brow raised in smugness. "Me, or someone like you? Who will constable believe when I tell you killed little girl!"

I closed my eyes and counted to ten to calm my nerves. All this time since leaving Miss Tillie's, I'd had a taste of what it meant to be a free person able to make my own decisions and truly do as I pleased . . . to the extent I could, given my current circumstances. In an instant, Victor reminded me that no matter how educated, wealthy, or needed I was, my skin color masked it all. All because I wouldn't do what they wanted.

In my heart, I knew he was right. Mr. Wiltshire ain't said two words to me the whole time I'd worked there. At least he was gone most of the day in that saloon of his. But all it would take was a broken-English word from Victor and that man might believe him. And that little girl

Simone ate? What else could I do? I glanced over my shoulder at the open coffin.

"I know where your nosferatu is." I nodded toward the coffin inside.

The Raduts stood wide-eyed at the door. This time Valerica pushed Victor aside and asked, "You have her? In your home? How?"

"Rice," I said, remembering the Raduts' belief of vamps compulsively counting stuff. Victor had been walking around with a pocketful ever since the vamp hunt started. The only thing I ever saw Simone count was the different nationalities she'd tasted. "Left a trail all the way to my place. She's in here, right now. But no loppin' off heads." Simone had suffered enough. She didn't need to see these fools waving knives and such all over the place.

The late afternoon sun made it easy to open the door without letting in a whole lotta light. As small as my place was, the rays stretched only a foot or two past the threshold. My bed and Simone's open coffin took up most of the space I had. She lay in there, still horribly burnt, with charred hands placed over her stomach. Should have brought in some of them blazing star flowers to place on her, make the whole affair more dignified. Funeral-like. The pair inched inside the dugout, as if they were waiting for Simone to pounce on them right there.

"We drag in sunlight," Valerica suggested. "She's already burned. We finish."

"No," her husband countered. "Box looks heavy. She will rise before we get it out."

"But Lavinia got it in," Valerica pointed out.

"What y'all think," I quickly added, "that I had this thing buried outside my dugout? Had a fisherman help bring it in when I got here."

Victor scratched one of his chins and hummed through his nose. Then his eyes brightened. "Stake. We stake her. I get wood and make stake." He returned in no time with one of the many pieces of driftwood laying all over the beach several yards from the dugout. Once we were armed with stakes, Valerica and I hopped on the bed, perched on our knees, while Victor straddled the coffin, stake raised in the air.

"You sure you know what you're doin'?" I asked.

"Yes," Victor said. "Hit heart. Nosferatu die. Easy."

"How you know if you're hittin' the heart with the stick all raised up like that?"

Victor turned to me. "What you mean?"

"Well, you don't wanna miss, do ya?" I didn't want to think about Simone being treated like a pin cushion while the idiot bumbled about.

Victor's brow knitted together, then he nodded. He squatted, almost sitting on Simone's stomach. With both hands wrapped around the stake, he pressed the pointy end on Simone's chest. I didn't understand how the stake was gonna kill her if her heart didn't even beat. Wonder if they knew that. Most of what they told me about vamps was nonsense anyway. Maybe that's why they cut off the heads. To be sure the vamp was dead-dead.

Victor lifted the stake a couple of times, testing to see if he'd hit the same spot. His hands shook. He raised the wooden weapon higher, then looked at Valerica. She nodded.

"What's takin' so long?" I asked. "Thought you did this before."

"Shh!" Victor said over his shoulder. "I've seen done."

"You *seen* it?! I thought you knew what you was doin'!"

Valerica nudged my shoulder. "Quiet, or he miss." Then she said something to him in their language.

Victor licked his lips and took one big breath.

Clean, I thought. *Make it clean.*

In an instant, Simone had Victor by the neck with one hand and the stake in the other. Her fingers bore into his flesh as she used his body weight to lift herself from the coffin. As his blood dripped down her outstretched arm, her eyes opened, eyeing the crimson flood inching so close to her open mouth. But that took too long. Victor's scream—never heard a man scream like a woman before—stopped when the sound of her teeth crunching against his neck took over. Simone held the back of his head like they were two lovers necking.

Valerica didn't seem to get what was happening. She straightened her back and stared for a few seconds at her husband twitching like he'd been hit by lightning. Then she screamed. Valerica hopped from the bed, yelling, "Nosferatu!" and ran outta the dugout with me trailing behind her. Though there was nary a soul in sight, I was still scared that some-one—like King—would hear her, then come running to the dugout to find Simone snacking on Victor.

Valerica only got as far as the Grand Calumet River behind my house before I tackled her to the ground. We fought, almost rolling into the river. I slapped her. Didn't need another repeat of my last water experience.

"Shut up!" I said, my hand over her mouth. Her hair and clothes had collected dozens of the tiny, sharp sticker bugs growing all over the place. Could feel them stabbing my own skin. I let her wear herself out trying to get away before moving my hand. "Victor's gone. Can't do nothin' to help him now."

"The nosferatu. She can't come into sunlight. We kill her. For my Victor."

"We ain't killin' her."

"We kill her!" Valerica raged, squirming beneath me again. "We kill her, or she kill us too!"

"She ain't killin' nobody else."

"She will, and Victor will come for me now!"

"That ain't how it works. Ain't none of that stuff you heard about vamps is true. Victor ain't coming back. She won't hurt you. Trust me!"

"Why?"

"Because!"

I had to tell her the truth. She knew too much. Had seen too much. I tried to find the right words to tell her why I did what I did.

"I . . . know her. Simone, the vamp, is my friend. She'd never hurt you if I told her not to. I'm sorry about Victor, I really am. But Simone . . ."

I rolled off her and knelt by her side. I took her hand in mine. "I'll help you get back to the old country where no one can hurt you. You can start over. You're free now. Same as me."

"You . . . *know* her? She is friend?" A look of disgust rolled over her face.

"Don't look at me like that, Valerica. Yes, Simone is my friend. And even though you tried to turn Mrs. Wiltshire against me, I didn't let Simone do anything to you. She ain't like none of them stories you've heard about vamps. She ain't after you or Victor. She don't even feed—"

I felt Simone's strength returning. Could see the damaged pieces of her skin flaking off in sheets as she drained the life out of Victor.

I shot to my feet. With my skirts lifted, I raced back to the dugout, all the while willing Simone to stop. My whole body felt heavy and full as she lapped up every drop of Victor's blood. I should've stayed. Should've gone after Valerica later, after Victor died on his own. No one outside of Miller Station would've believed the woman's ranting about some nosferatu. This wasn't Romania, where folks believed in vamps and man-wolves. Folks here were God-religious. I'd seen the preacher men in their wagons riding back and forth between towns. Simone told me she was Catholic and answered to some man named Pope who lived an ocean away. Even she had never heard of vamps until she got bit by one.

I got to the dugout right when Simone lifted her head from Victor's throat. Her eyes rolled to the back of her head as she tossed his body aside like a discarded toy. She licked her lips and wiped a thin stream of blood from her chin. Simone looked as fresh as rain. And she didn't waste a drop.

"You didn't!"

Simone stood, stepped from the coffin, and then perched herself on my bed. "How could I not? I needed it."

"But . . . He's gonna turn!"

Simone looked down at the man lying face down on the floor. "You think?"

"Simone!"

"I've never turned anyone. We don't even know if it's going to happen."

"You ain't never turned nobody 'cause I never let you. Now what we gon' do?!"

Simone shrugged. "Do what we always do: get rid of the body."

"Get rid of the body?" I snapped, pacing a tiny, clear section of floor in the dugout. "It's always 'get rid of the body' with you. It ain't that simple, Simone. Valerica knows what happened. Wouldn't be surprised if she don't bring a posse of her crazies back with her."

"Well, what did you think was going to happen when you brought them here?"

"What I expected was for them to be forever-dead, not one coming back from the grave and the other on the loose! Why can't you ever think more'n two seconds ahead?"

This was bad. If he did turn, we couldn't let him live. Didn't matter how I felt about the man. We'd already done enough damage taking his life and giving him one he feared more than anything. And I wasn't watching over two vamps. The one I had was work enough.

"Well, he's goin' in your box," I said.

"My box?" Simone said all wide-eyed. "Why not leave him outside and let the sun take care of him?"

I crinkled my brow. "He ain't gon' burn if he ain't turned."

Simone hopped down from the bed. "Fine. Stake him."

"I ain't doin' that!"

"Why? He's dead, isn't he?"

"Then you do it."

"I'm not touching him."

An exasperated groan left me as I stared at the ceiling. "Well, he ain't stayin' in here, that's for sure."

"So, now it's back to the sun. Grab his legs."

"Wait a minute!" I said, my arm blocking her from Victor's body. "You see how big this man is? Ain't like you can help me drag him out there. We gotta leave him here 'til nightfall."

"And if he turns before then?"

I set my fists on my hips and glared at her. "If we put him in the box and he doesn't turn, then we leave him there. But if he does turn . . ."

Simone smiled. She pressed her palms together and softly clapped with her fingertips. "A nice big bonfire at dawn. Grab his legs."

"Wait a minute!" Martin nearly knocks his chair over jumping to his feet. Night has long since fallen and Simone has yet to bust me out, but he's remained focused on my story like I am gonna reveal the whereabouts of a treasure at the end of it. "Do you hear yourself? You just admitted to plotting against and killing Victor Radut!"

I nod my head. "That I did."

"And you think that helps you . . . how?"

"And how do you think it don't?" I ask. "If I wanted Simone dead, I would've let them idiots kill her, 'specially since she couldn't fend for herself."

He removes a pocket watch from his vest, clicks it open, and then checks the time. "Night air must be getting to you. Either way, it means you're capable of murder." He points at me. "Might wanna change that bandage."

All that drinking has me forgetting about my arm and the pain. It's still there, murmuring under the strips of dirty, reddish-brown cloth. A reminder of the power I once had. I lift a corner of the bandage and see the entire underside is caked in blood, but the wound appears to have stopped bleeding. I peel off all the cloth to reveal the jagged wound. I wasn't about to admit to Martin that I'd carved it into myself. A test to see if it would heal. Sure as hell failed that one.

Martin is at my cell with fresh bandages. He whistles. "Now, that looks right nasty."

He unlocks the cell and walks inside. Gently, he takes my arm in his large, sandpaper hands and stares at the wound. His thumb scrapes the curve of my elbow. Now his whole hand is running up and down my exposed skin. This action and the expression on his face isn't new to me. From his raised eyebrows and the rubbing of his fingers together, I can tell he's surprised my coloring is a part of me and not some celestial dye the good Lord painted on. Which doesn't make a bit of sense if you think about it. After everything I've gone through, don't you think if my skin color could come off, I would have washed it right out and walked off Miss Tillie's plantation long before now? Now, I'm waiting for him to start fingering my hair.

I purse my lips together and shake my head as Martin continues his examination. As much as he's rubbing on me, I'm not panicked. From what I know about Martin, he ain't that kind of man despite what he's doing behind his wife's back. This feels different. Something approaching genuine concern and curiosity. He even gazes at me like he's noticing me for the first time. I smile, and he smiles back.

My wound is cleaned and dressed in no time.

"Charlotte's coming back," Martin quietly offers as he tosses my soiled bandages in a wastebasket.

"Okay." Not my business where he sticks it.

"Lavinia," he lowers his head and pats the air. "She's bringing her uncles and a few other men."

"But the constable said—"

"I know what the constable said." He checks his watch again. "But you did just admit to killing that Radut fella. And you're gonna hang either way, whether it's tonight or down the road—"

"I didn't kill nobody, Martin. The last guy you let swing was innocent too, just like me. What do you think, Martin? The constable and them fellas that was here earlier make it seem like you ain't got a bit of sense between your ears. But I know you're smarter than that. Smart enough to sit here and parse through my story. You gonna let your lady friend's uncles come and make a fool outta you again? And as far as Victor Radut is concerned, did you even know him?"

Martin sighs. "Can't say that I did. He sounds right awful, according to you." Then he perks up. "Wait. Was that the couple over in Miller Station whose store burned to the ground?"

I nod yes, remembering the disaster.

"Didn't they die in that fire?"

"Did they?"

Twenty-Three

Vamps got no patience. Since they only come out at night and can go so long without feeding, they got no concept of time. Everything is a rush to them.

"I'm bored," Simone whined on our fifth night of waiting for Victor to turn.

"Not my problem," I said. We stood on both sides of the grave right outside my dugout door. For the whole night that's all I did: stare into a hole in the ground, waiting for something to happen. Made Simone stay awake in the dugout the next day while I worked at the Wiltshires'. I didn't expect he'd wake up with the sun shining on him. But since Simone swore she'd never turned nobody and neither one of us knew if all vamps woke up at night, I took no chances. Spent the whole afternoon talking to myself to keep the restless vamp focused on her job.

"And hungry."

"That, I know, ain't true. You jus' drank a whole man. You oughta be good and full for a couple more days."

"You don't know that I drained him," Simone said, picking at her fingernails. "It's been five days. If he were going to turn, he would have by now."

"How long it take you?"

Simone shrugged. "All I remember is getting attacked, then waking up in a morgue. I don't know how long I was dead."

"Then we wait."

"But I'm bored!"

I looked over at Simone. "I heard you the first time." I was tired of waiting, too. I had things to do, like finding Valerica and getting a boat for King. Waiting for Victor had one advantage: I got to stand outside and watch for anybody coming this way. No telling what Valerica had said or what she was gonna do now that her Victor was gone. Was kind of surprised neither she nor the constable had shown up yet. Might still be in shock from what she saw. Maybe she had told the town and nobody believed her. I wasn't taking any chances.

King had stopped by on the second day of my vigil, relieved I had buried Simone. I let him believe that. Simone was really under my bed since Victor was still in the ground. King said nothing about the boat. I didn't mention it either. We stood silently, looking down at the closed coffin in that hole. I wondered what he thought about all the things I'd told him about Simone needing blood. I reckon he wouldn't have called on me if he thought I was crazy.

"When you're ready," he'd said, "come on by and bend my ear, cry, whatever you want. I'm here for you." He held my hand for a good ten seconds, then squeezed it before he left with a look of sympathy on his face.

"I still think he would have turned by now," Simone said. Now she was swaying side to side, braiding a long lock of her black hair over her shoulder.

"You might be right," I said. "But we gotta be sure. Can't have him wakin' up, not knowin' what's goin' on. And with all his blood gone, he gon' be one hungry vamp."

"*If* he turns."

"If he turns."

Simone knelt and rapped on the coffin lid with her knuckles. She looked up at me. "See. Nothing. Can we at least stretch our legs?"

I sighed. Simone was probably right. If he was gonna turn, he would have by now. I scanned the dark landscape. If not for the whitecaps on the tiny waves rolling to the shore, I wouldn't have been able to tell the difference between the lake and the midnight sky. "I guess I do need a boat."

Simone jumped up to her feet and clapped her hands. "Goodie! We're going back to Tolleston!"

"Not this time." I linked arms with Simone and steered her east. "I need somethin' bigger than them skiffs they use. Should be easy enough. Gotta be more'n jus' King out here fishin' on this lake."

"I would think you'd avoid the lake after your . . . incident."

"King lost his boat that day 'cause of me," I told her. "The least I can do is get him another one." I was slightly terrified that we might have to put the thing in the water and row it back over here. But I couldn't let the dawn catch Simone if dragging it across the beach took too long.

It was nice getting away from our vigil. We followed the shoreline, chasing each other and squealing in delight for no reason other than hearing our voices being carried away by the wind. We passed by a smattering of cabins tucked neatly into the dunes, all lit up from the inside by kerosene lamps. We made up stories about the people within those walls, guessing who they were, what they did for a living. Simone even took the scent from their suppers and speculated what the folks might taste like.

"What d'you do," I ventured to ask, "when you woke up a vamp?" I already knew the answer, figuring the night her father beat her and the night she woke up were one and the same. But I needed to know what to expect if Victor woke up. Needed to know if she'd tell the truth.

Simone shrugged. "I went home."

"Guess you gave them a start," I said with a chuckle.

"No. She was happy to see me. Apparently, I'd been missing for a few days."

"She?"

"My mother. She was the first person, first familiar person, I ran into."

Darkness fell over Simone's face like a pall. I pressed further. "How'd you know what to do?"

She shrugged again. "I didn't know. My body, my hunger, just told me. End of story."

That wasn't the end. Simone looked at me with them big ole doe eyes of hers. Did that whenever I asked a question that she didn't wanna answer out loud. Simone never minded telling me about the dumb stuff she'd done. Mostly because she didn't know it was dumb. But she'd done some right awful things in the months before we met. Like feeding on children because she wasn't all that confident about taking down grown folks yet. Or getting what she could from the amputated limbs of fallen soldiers during the war, spitting out Minié balls and avoiding all the blackened, gangrenous parts. That stuff she put out of her mind, so they never came up until I asked her about them.

The poor child was so hungry, she did what came naturally—or unnaturally. I'd seen folks doing that after the War Between the States. Bunch of starving ragamuffins who ate any and everything they could find. Like them Rebs digging out corn kernels from horseshit to survive. I knew Simone had smelled the blood pumping in her mother's neck and, had her father not awakened to the commotion, there might've been two vamps run out of Montreal. Not that she'd come clean about that, though. I guess I had my secrets, too.

Simone stopped in her tracks. She raised her eyes to the starlit sky. "He's awake."

"Who?"

"Victor." She smiled. "I can hear his thoughts. It's . . . too dark for him to see . . ." Then worry spread over her face. "He's panicking."

I closed my eyes to see if I could hear his thoughts or see what Simone was seeing. But there was nothing. A blank wall. Like her mind was so focused on Victor's, hers was completely blocked from mine.

"He's opening the lid."

I tugged Simone's arm. "We gotta go back."

"Why? He's just sitting there, looking around."

He wouldn't stay there long, I reckoned. The man's been dead for five days. And there wasn't a drop of blood in him. Probably woke up thinking his fight with Simone happened a couple of minutes ago. He'd be wondering where his wife was and go looking for her. And if he was as hungry as I imagined he'd be, he'd waste no time satisfying his appetite.

"Shh!" Simone commanded. "I can't hear with all your thinking!"

Her arms were spread out to her sides like she was trying to gain her own bearings.

I was a mite miffed that she could hear Victor and I couldn't. A twang of jealousy hit me. Not that I wanted Victor tied to me in any kinda way, but she'd have another like her, with a special connection that didn't include me.

"Well?" I asked. "What's he doin' now?"

"He's in our cave, calling for Valerica. He can't see anything. He's leaving."

"Where's he goin'?"

Simone snapped out of her trance. She made an uninterested tilt of her head. "Home, I guess."

"You guess?"

"He's thinking in Romanian. I don't speak Romanian. Do you?"

"Then what're we waitin' for? C'mon!" I reached for Simone's arm, but she jerked away.

"We're not chasing after him!"

"We can't leave him on his own. No tellin' what's gon' happen when he runs into somebody."

Simone waved me off. "He'll be fine."

This time I grabbed her by the wrist. "Girl, bring yo' butt! You want him out here killin' folks and tyin' that to us?"

"You still want to kill him?"

"That was the plan," I said, searching the beach for a piece of driftwood I could use for a stake.

Simone snatched her arm away from me again. "He's simply confused, that's all. We can help him—"

"Help him? Help him do what? He was huntin' you down, remember? It was your idea to burn him up in the first place."

"That was when he was human. He might be different, now that he's like me."

I scoffed. "Are you serious? He ain't a puppy! You can't keep him like a pet or somethin'."

"Well, we can't kill him!"

"And why the hell not?"

"Because."

I stared at her. I don't know why this girl always thought "because" was an acceptable answer to my questions. "Because what, Simone?"

She shrank within herself and stared at the ground, the toe of her boot making random marks in the sand. "You have your humans," she said quietly.

I raised my arms then slapped them back against my thighs. "Not this again! Lord, chile, we ain't got time for this." I pointed toward the dugout. "That thing is gonna eat somebody, you understand? I don't think he's gonna take the time to see if they're alone or innocent or won't be missed. He's jus' gonna pounce. Is that what you want?"

"You were thinking about King this whole time," she whined with a stomp of her foot. "You're always thinking about him! What am I supposed to have when you leave me?"

"Leave you how? I can't leave even if I wanted to."

"What does that mean?" she said, a tempest brewing in her eyes and fists balled up at her sides. "You're gone all day. Longer even, sometimes. You figured out how to block your thoughts from me. What's to say you don't figure out how to leave me for good?"

"Simone." I took her hand in mine and gazed into her baby blues. I suspect they would've been full of tears had she been able to cry. "It's because I can't. The head pains I get are . . ." I searched the beach for something else to focus my eyes on so I could get it out. "They happen when I think about what my freedom might've looked like had we not met."

"Oh," she said flatly. "You never told me that."

"Please, let's jus' go find him, okay? I promise I won't do anything to him, alright?"

She was far too eager about helping Victor after my confession, reassuring me the whole way to the Raduts' place. Kept explaining how she'd teach him everything he needed to know, that he wouldn't have to struggle like she did. It'll be fun, she proclaimed. But I had other troubles on my mind. What was I supposed to do with another vamp? What if he turned somebody else? And why wasn't Simone angrier about the fact she can count the times I'd wanted to leave her just from my head attacks?

Victor never seemed too right in the head to me. Too emotional and angry. Don't figure he'd be happy now. He'd become the very thing he feared back home. I hoped he was more like Simone than the crazy vamps he'd described in Romania.

What concerned me more was caring for the two of them. Feeding Simone took effort. Days of hunting for the right location, the right victim. But now there'd be two of them. And if Simone could drain a whole man in one sitting, imagine how much blood a full-grown vamp-man was gonna need. There'd be more bodies that I'd have to get rid of, all by myself.

Victor hadn't made it to Miller Station yet, so we could cut across the dunes to get further inland and catch him on the old Chicago–Detroit stagecoach trail. I kept my eyes to the east. It was still dark, but the slightest hint of orange on the horizon meant I'd only have an hour to get Simone to safety. As we ran to catch him, I made note of over-grown brush or hollowed-out tree trunks I could stuff her in.

I ain't gotta tell you that Victor wasn't happy to see us. He tried running away but was too weak to get anywhere. Simply hobbled a few steps then collapsed on the ground. Between all the craziness he was yelling, we managed to calm him down once we mentioned Valerica.

"You want to go home to her, don't you?" Simone asked. "We'll take you there, but first you need to eat."

Victor held his stomach and nodded with a look of pain on his face. "Eat. But not food. Want . . ."

He reached toward me with his mouth open. Gums pale and drawn back, making his eyeteeth longer and sharper than they'd been before. I caught whiffs of more beach than decay from his skin. Moans of hunger pains deepened to a low growl. Simone stood between us.

"Not her," she said as if Victor had lost his hearing and his mind in death. "She helps us find food. She . . ." Simone pointed at me, ". . . will help you."

I had to think. I needed to get them underground somewhere before dawn, but Victor didn't look like he was going anywhere without food. Where the hell was I gonna find people at this time of night out here? The only cabins I'd seen were on the beach. Not like I could go knocking on somebody's door asking to borrow a cup of blood.

"What about animals?" I asked. "Can't he jus' suck down a rabbit or somethin'?"

Simone turned up her nose. "That's disgusting."

"It's blood, ain't it? And we're runnin' outta time. Ain't like animal blood's gon' kill him. He can have a real feedin' tomorrow."

Simone turned to Victor. "Rabbit," she said slowly. She made rabbit ears with her index fingers and hopped around. "Rabbit. You find rabbit. Eat it."

I tried not to laugh as Victor made an "O" with his mouth and nodded as if Simone's way of communicating had finally gotten through to him. I watched as the fool hunted for his food. Whistling and calling for it like he'd lost his cat. He and Simone were foraging around the bushes all hunched over because they could see better than I could in the dark. Then a coyote showed up. Victor had no qualms about pouncing on the animal. Couldn't tell if his vamp brain had taken over or if he was that hungry, but he acted like he knew exactly what he wanted and how to get it. And he fed even more sloppily than Simone did when she'd gone too long without a meal. Made me wanna retch. When no more blood came from the first bite, Victor started gnawing all over the animal looking for more. He had a lot to learn. I could only imagine him going after anything with a pulse and getting us all lynched.

"Sun's risin'," I warned, pointing to the orange tint in the east. "We ain't gon' make it back home."

Simone held on to me like a frightened child, her face buried in my chest. Ole crazy had the dead coyote by the neck, squeezing it like a lemon. We were too far from the lake and the sand dunes. Would've been easy to dig a hole in one of those and wait the day out. The cabins we'd passed would've been raised off the ground to minimize sand from blowing up through the floor slats. Could slide them underneath. But fishermen rose early to get a jump on the day, so I couldn't risk getting caught by one of them, especially if I planned to come back for a boat. The closest spot I could think of was where Victor had been heading in the first place.

Seemed to take forever to get to Victor's house. He wouldn't let the damn coyote go, and Simone acted like she was too scared to move thinking the sun was gonna burn her alive. I snatched the dead animal away, slapped them both, then ordered them to get moving.

The Raduts' place was in a populated area and sandwiched between a smithy and a feed store. Furniture piled up against all the downstairs windows gave the establishment an out of place, abandoned feel. A wide dirt road split the desolated business district in half. A raised wooden sidewalk ran along both sides of the street. Too low for Victor and Simone to slide under. Above a few of the businesses, the curtained windows remained still. Victor and Simone weren't used to skulking around like I was. Every rustle from the trees or the distant clop of horse hooves sent them scrambling behind me. We ducked in the narrow passage across the street that separated two buildings and looked for any signs of life in the Raduts' upstairs residence.

"Wait here," I ordered the pair in a hushed tone.

"Why do I have to stay here with him?" Simone pouted.

"'Cause I don't want him goin' in there, scarin' the bejesus outta her. She saw you eatin' him."

"'Eating him'? Such a flair for the dramatic."

"You know what I mean!"

"So? He still looks normal."

"And he still looks hungry to me," I countered. "Either he's gonna pounce on her or the next livin' thing walkin' by."

"Pounce on his wife?"

"You pounced on your mama!"

Thought Simone's eyes were gonna bounce right out of her head. "How do you know about that!"

I groaned at the irony. As if she ain't spent the last year all up in my brain without permission. "Will you jus' mind me! If Valerica ain't there, Victor can let us in. Victor . . . Where the hell is he?"

Glass splintering and screaming answered my question. I don't know how he got inside. The store was still dark, but a dim light, probably from a candle, lit up one upstairs window after another. Simone and I ran across the road, all the while checking for the movement of curtains from the neighbors. Victor had knocked out a window at the back of the store. The board that was supposed to be covering it had been splintered in half. Either Victor was stronger than I thought, or he had a real hankering to see his wife. Through the hole, I heard both of them yelling and screaming at the top of their lungs.

Victor had managed to corner Valerica in a bedroom closet. She threw any and everything at him. Even a pillow, like that was gonna do anything. Chaos filled the room. Victor had a crazed look in his eye: hunger, anger, and fear competing for attention on his face. I was behind him in the doorway, begging for Valerica to listen to me. Simone? Well, she wasn't much help. She stood in the hallway, picking at her nails again.

"Nosferatu!" Valerica screamed before grabbing a lit kerosene lamp and hurling it at us.

The lamp burst against the wall. White-hot fire flowed down to the floor, following the trail of spilled fuel. A wall of fire trapped me and Victor inside the room with Valerica. The Raduts pleaded with each other in their language. Whatever they said, it didn't sway either one of them. I snatched bedsheets, curtains, anything to beat down the flames. Thick dark smoke blocked out the brightness of the fire. Valerica was hunched over, coughing up a lung. None of it bothered me.

With everything going on, the woman refused to budge from that closet. I never understood that. How people froze in fear, even though help was standing right in front of them. I kept trying to coax her out, all the while, she was clinging to the doorframe, shaking her head at me. Soon, all she could do was fall to her knees, coughing. Flames swallowed the room. Even I could feel the heat on my back, pushing me closer to the door. Through the smoke, I saw Valerica spread eagle on the floor. The hem of her frock ignited.

Victor pounced on his wife. I couldn't tell if he was trying to keep her from burning or if he was having his last meal, but I couldn't be concerned about them. I doused a blanket with water from a washbasin and tossed the heavy, wet covering over myself. Through the wall of fire, I jumped out of the room to find Simone gone. I ran downstairs and into the store. Empty. Through the window, muted sunlight greeted me, and I saw a handful of neighbors approaching the building and pointing up at the flames. Simone wouldn't be out here, but where could she have gone? I stopped my frantic pacing and closed my eyes, hoping to find Simone with my mind. She'd slid beneath the crawl space of a neighboring house. Glad she wasn't upstairs burning to death. But how was I gonna get outta the store without these people thinking I had something to do with it?

I emerged from the front door, my fake hacking and coughing converting the crowd's look of confusion at the sight of me into concern. I stumbled, bracing myself against one of the posts holding up the awning.

"Look! It is her!" I heard a woman say. "It is Lavinia!" She waved to several more women who rushed to me. Though I didn't know their names, I recognized a handful of them as the ones who'd brought food after that night I'd supposedly kept them safe from Simone.

"What is this?" another woman asked me, while another nearly knocked me over, beating at my back to get the phantom smoke out of my lungs. My head swam as a mixture of English and Romanian questions deafened my ears.

"It was awful!" I said loudly to shut them up. "The Raduts! The vampire!"

The women all crossed themselves. I did the same, lowering and shaking my head.

"You tell us," said a woman still in her nightdress. Wisps of long, blond hair had escaped her sleep bonnet.

I let them lead me away from the store, the upstairs portion nearly invisible from the roaring flames. I continued to cough and fan myself.

Then I took a deep breath and recounted my tale: "We'd jus' come from lookin' for that vampire. Thought we'd find it out in Clarke Station, but there wasn't a trace of it anywhere. But when we got back, there the vampire was! Sittin' up there in the parlor like she'd been waitin' on 'em all night. Her white skin glowing in the night. Her teeth drippin' with spit and blood!"

They crossed themselves again and then kissed their thumbnails.

"That old vamp went after Mr. Victor." I drew my hands into claws and jumped at one of the women causing a collective "Oh!" from the group. "But then Miss Valerica, she picked up a . . . a . . . a pair of wooden knitting needles and stabbed that vamp." I raised one fist in the air and brought it smack down onto the palm of the other.

The women nodded and whispered among themselves.

"How did fire start?"

"Oh, yes! The fire. Well, Miss Valerica must not have gotten her right in the heart 'cause that vamp got to stumblin' and fell back on a lamp. Whole place went up like that." I snapped my fingers.

"They are dead?" The same woman who'd been talking must have been the only one who spoke English. Every time I said something, she relayed it back to the group in Romanian.

I glanced back at the fire again, certain it would take a miracle for the Raduts to survive. The men with the fire brigade had started a line, passing buckets of water from a wagon to douse the store to keep it from going up. Glass popped and crashed as pieces of the upstairs windows fell to the earth. Fire crackled and licked at the sky as it broke free of the roof.

"They gone," I said, wiping my tear-free eyes. "They all gone."

And with that, the women started wailing and beating their chests. I joined in, too. Not because I was feeling any sympathy toward the Raduts. I did, at least, try to let Valerica go out with some dignity, even though she'd lied about me to Mrs. Wiltshire. But that was all Victor's doing. I could care less about him. It was the rhythm of passing buckets, the camaraderie of being among . . . people, that consumed me. Joined together by the common thread of shock and grief, no one thought to question my presence. No one ordered me to leave or accused me of anything. Here, in front of the Raduts' burning house, I was part of something again, a community working to keep their little town safe. And nobody seemed to care that I was a Negro.

Once the flames were extinguished, I slipped inside the outhouse before the celebration died down and folks started carting those bodies out and realized there were only two. Once my nerves calmed, I let my mind wander to the Raduts. Such a sad ending! But it was for the best. Look at all the havoc Victor caused in his short rebirth! No way I could've contained him. And though Simone seemed slightly interested in helping him transition, I knew that wouldn't have lasted long. Simone's allergy to responsibility and common sense meant I would have been the one taking care of the fool. Now that I'd seen it myself, I knew Simone wouldn't be making another vamp on my watch.

Well, that was the plan. What I didn't bank on, what I never banked on, was Simone's level of cooperation in all of this.

TWENTY-FOUR

How many times does one experience freedom in their life? Based on what I've been through, I'd say at least three. With this latest one, freedom from the Raduts' blackmail, one more link from the shackles of simply being a Black woman in America crumbled away. I didn't need to fear anyone stopping by the dugout unexpectedly or screwing up my job with the Wiltshires. Did I feel sorry for the Raduts? Not a bit. Sure, I'd claimed Valerica as a friend once, despite her showing her true colors in the end. But Simone was my priority. Maybe the only friend I needed. I would've given anything to bring her back to life . . . or death . . . or living death . . . whatever you wanna call it; still haven't found the right word for it. Anyway, I would've done anything, even sacrifice my two human friends.

Speaking of which, not long after the fire, I found the perfect boat to replace the one I'd lost for King. It was a mite small, because I couldn't manage dragging anything as big as his old boat across the beach. Ghouls may be semi-indestructible, but we ain't superhuman. And my getting back in the water sure as hell wasn't happening. To Simone's dismay, I didn't tell King about the boat until the next day. She concluded that since she helped me steal and deliver it, she should be there to see his face when I presented it to him.

Yeah, right. And waste no time knocking me over to get at his throat, too.

He was nice enough about the boat. Didn't ask where I got it. Even tried easing my fear about getting back in the water. I wore my best frock, a yellow piece dotted with white flowers. Though I didn't need it, I wrapped a white shawl around my shoulders that I'd been knitting on my slow days. To look demure, as Simone put it. Had worked for her when she tricked her victims into thinking she was some shy little thing needing help.

With me sitting inside the vessel, holding onto the sides for dear life, he walked the boat out into the water until the lake was up to his bare chest . . . his dark and ripe-blackberry-ready-to-pop chest . . . How I wish I was Lake Michigan; my tongue, the waves kissing him over and over again. To have him in me. If he only knew the real reason why I was showing all my teeth to him.

Okay, yeah, I let him believe Simone was dead. I simply smiled and nodded when he mentioned her and how I might be feeling. Sure, I felt a little guilty as he stood in waist-high water beside the boat to keep my fear of drowning at bay, but Simone going on and on about trusting folks niggled at the back of my mind. Especially after Valerica turned on me like she did. Believing King couldn't do the same to me, I needed to know if he could keep Simone a secret or if he'd judge me poorly for the things I'd done for her. If so, there would never be nothing between us. Couldn't be. So, I asked him the one question that might ease my doubts.

"What's the worst thing you ever done?"

Simple enough question to vet a person's trustworthiness. Learned it from an old field hand back at Miss Tillie's who'd been sold to five different plantations across the South before ending up in Georgia. You see, if the person you're asking reveals something contrary to what you know about them, that tells you how much they're willing to trust you. And complete trust was needed if King was gonna be a major part of my life. Factor in an understanding of body language and you'll never go wrong. Never choose a person who reveals a sex secret; they're just bragging and selfish . . . and kind of nasty. And never choose someone with an answer that's predictable, like a preacher who pinches from the collection plate or a rich man cheating on his wife.

I often wondered, if someone asked me that question, what my answer would be.

King stood there with his hand on the boat, his arm bobbing up and down in time with the waves. He smiled quickly, then raised his head to the clear blue sky above. Bottom lip between his teeth and a dimple announcing itself on both sides of his face, he told me:

"Killed my daddy."

Wasn't expecting that.

He stared off toward the horizon, his face blank. I hope he didn't think he was just gonna drop that little nugget and leave it there without comment. How was I supposed to process that? This man I can't stop thinking about, this man I'd been alone with was . . . a killer? Couldn't be. I mean, my losing his boat struck quite a nerve. But he still followed me home and helped me with Simone when we found her frying in the sunlight. I'd ponder many a day whether to come clean with King, to tell him the truth about me and Simone. About why I brush off his many invitations to stay. Before I could do that, I needed to know what I was dealing with.

"By accident," I added as if he'd forgotten to.

"Heat of the moment," he said. "I couldn't take him beating on my mama."

He must have noticed the frown on my face, my eyes asking, *A preacher man?* For he continued: "My mother still practiced the natural healing ways of her people. He didn't like it, so he tried beating it out of her. Then one day," he pressed his lips together and looked down at the water rolling over him. "I hit him. Hit him until . . . Anyway," he looked up and smiled reassuringly. "That was a long time ago. I was just a boy then. Been living here ever since."

"That sounds right awful," I said. I flexed my fingers, not realizing I'd been clutching the side of the rocking vessel as he told his tale. "To love somebody who can turn on you in an instant."

"And here she thought marrying him would save her from when the government removed her people to the western territories. Traded one bad situation for another."

I turned my eyes west toward my dugout. "You saved her. Like you saved me."

"I can't see you as the type that needs saving." He leaned over and kissed the back of my hand that was still clutching the side of the boat.

"Guess we're even with secrets now," he continued. "At least I don't have a dead body buried beside my place." He chuckled as if he didn't believe my tale. Or maybe it was to lighten the impact of his confession. I forced a smile.

"What if I told you she ain't dead," I said, counting the number of knits and purls on one row of my shawl. I stayed focused on one set of stitches as the words left my mouth. "She jus' ain't alive durin' the day."

"You're pretty good at spinning tales, I'll give you that," he said, the smile never leaving his face.

I leaned back in the boat and crossed my arms. "And I'm s'posed to believe you killed your own daddy?"

"Now, why would I lie about that?" He waded closer to my side of the boat.

"Question is, why would you tell me somethin' like that? Ain't you afraid I'd run off or go to the law?"

"Go to the law?" He laughed, then looked me square in the eye and said, "I trust you."

I wondered how long he'd been wanting to tell me that. How many times had he been sitting in that dugout of his, contemplating whether today was the day? How many times had I done the same thing? I'd been near to bursting, carrying around all my baggage. Never thought I'd have somebody—other than Simone—to dump it all on. But here was King, handing me the key to the darkest part of his soul.

Could I trust him with the keys to mine?

King flicked water in my face. "Well? What about you?"

I smiled and steeled my spine. "Make me dinner tonight and I'll tell you more."

I took my time eating the fried rabbit and dandelion greens he'd served. The man could cook. If I had any appetite at all, I'd be three hundred pounds living with him! King hadn't reacted all that funny when I said Simone was still walking the earth. Guess that's a plus. But I had no idea what he'd think of me once he realized I wasn't joking. Each bite of food gave me time to test out different ways to tell him the truth—the whole truth. I even contemplated summoning Simone to prove to him I wasn't crazy. You see, folks say "seeing is believing," but getting an eyeful of an upright dead person, walking and talking, is still hard to swallow. Always is. Even Thomas doubted Jesus when He came back. Probably why Simone didn't wanna take full humans into our confidence. Better to keep them in the dark instead of learning all that work we put into trusting them was for naught.

King had been going on about his mother the whole time. I couldn't tell you exactly what he said, I was so busy telling myself that as soon as I finished this meal, I was gonna spill it all. But a knock at his door messed that up. There Simone was, staring at the ground, both hands on either side of the doorframe as if she were ready to sprint inside. She lifted her head right as the firelight cast a glow on her white skin.

"Why King," Simone said, with that syrupy-sweet voice of hers. "Surprised to see me?"

I sure was. I was so caught up with coming clean, I'd forgotten all about her hearing my thoughts. And now here she was, coming over to prove me right.

"What? How . . . ?" His voice shook with fear. "You died. I saw you. Burnt to a crisp."

"Oh, don't look so shocked," Simone continued. "Lavinia told you I wasn't dead."

"But you look—" Confusion etched King's face.

"Alive? It's amazing what a few pints of blood can do for a girl. And as usual," she shook her head and sighed, "you are looking rather delicious tonight."

I rushed between them. "See, King? I told you she wasn't dead."

Simone kissed me on the cheek before sashaying toward King in a way that would've made me jealous had I not known her. The poor man backed away from the door until he cornered himself against a wall. Simone sat in his seat with her legs crossed, arm draped over the back of the lopsided chair—showing more ankle than was acceptable—and started picking at the leftover bits of food he had on his tin plate. Hated when she did that. She didn't have working plumbing to properly digest any real food, so it ran right through her nether parts while she rested. After making her clean up the mess once, she stopped finding shitting up her coffin funny.

King stood there for a minute, mouth hanging open like his brain was trying to reconcile what his eyes saw.

"Say somethin', King," I said, my voice shaking from what came next.

"It was true . . . The newspaper story about the woman eating that poor child. That was true."

The expression of disgust on his face, either at me or what his mind finally pieced together rendered me mute. All I could do was nod to acknowledge the truth of it all.

"What kind of demon is she?" he asked.

"She ain't a demon. She's a—"

"Demon!" He glared at me like I was the crazy one. He fumbled with something behind him. "No other reason for her to be standing here!"

"King—"

"Get out!" he growled, raising the rifle he'd managed to wrangle from behind him. Despite the fear and anger on his face, the weapon pointed in our direction was as steady as a branch in dead air. "Take your demon and get the hell out of here!"

King shooting me in the head would have hurt less than how I felt in that moment.

"Pity," Simone said, rising to her feet. She narrowed her eyes and approached King with slow, calculated steps. She moved the barrel of the gun away with the side of her hand as if it were a minor nuisance blocking her path. "I spared you, for Lavinia's sake. All bets are off now." Simone jutted her head toward King and bit at the air like a bear trap snapping shut, sending the gun clattering to the ground and the man further against the wall.

"I'd been tryin' to find the right words to tell you." I reached toward him, but he swatted at my hand like it was a snake about to bite him. If he could've melted into the wall to get away from me, he would've. "She ain't gon' do nothin' to you, King. Honest!"

"Honest? You haven't been honest about a damn thing. All this time and you never bothered to tell me this?" The disgust on his face broke my heart. He was trembling like a chill had gotten ahold of him. "Just leave. Both of you."

"Come, Lavinia," Simone said. She took my hand and led me to the door. "Guess he's not as sweet as either of us thought."

I tried not to cry as we walked home. Simone never let go of my hand, probably sensing my misery. We'd been sharing so much about each other. But I got comfortable, let my guard down. Big mistake. One I'd never make again. I knew then that I either had to keep Simone a secret or give up on ever having a normal relationship with anybody.

"But you won't be alone," Simone said, squeezing my hand tighter. "You have me."

"I know," I said with a sniff. "I jus'—"

"Need human contact once in a while? Why? What makes you think the next one is going to be any different? We live in our own special little world even your crazy Romanian couple didn't understand. You are trying to hold onto a life that doesn't exist for you anymore. You can pretend at being normal, but you can't deny what you are. That side of you will always win. Trust me, I know. Trying to be both will only bring heartache . . . or death."

She was right, for once. I'd never have both. Simone was literally in my blood. I couldn't abandon her if I wanted to. No telling what turn my life would've taken had I stayed in Georgia. Doing the same ole thing, day in and day out. Being nothing more than an ex-slave who nobody gave a hoot about. Who couldn't even have the name her mama had given to her. I wanted King, true. But the way he reacted . . . the sheer revulsion on his face. He didn't even look like the same man who'd once held me so close I felt his heart beating through his clothes. How stupid I was to think a human would understand anything about my life! Whatever connection we had was not enough to overlook the dead body I lived with.

I sat upon the thinking dune for the rest of the night. Simone let me be as she sat at my side, staring into the darkness toward the lake. My whole soul ached as King's rejection looped in my brain. I vowed to never feel this way again. If this was to be my life, I'd be the one in charge of the happiness no human could ever give me.

TWENTY-FIVE

In short order, I returned to a normal rhythm of life: using my time working for the Wiltshires to stalk out victims for Simone's weekly feeding. And to forget about King. I lived for running errands for Mrs. Wiltshire because it gave me an excuse to watch and follow folks. I didn't need to do any of the skulking or peeking around corners. Too obvious, especially coming from the only Negro woman in town. Instead, I always carried a covered basket with me like I was either going to or coming from the store. Really, any old prop would do, so long as I had a story to go along with it. But most of my reconnoitering came from listening to Mrs. Wiltshire gossip with her friends. From them, I learned all the sordid details about folks in Tolleston and the neighboring towns who deserved to be on the end of Simone's fangs.

I couldn't leave Simone for days at a time like I used to. She'd gotten wise to it and started sleeping under my bed instead of in her box, sometimes not going to sleep at all. Complaints about my working never stopped. But I could deal with that. Wasn't much Simone could do during the day. So long as I returned to the dugout every night—or every other night—even if it was only to spend the evening talking to her, she tolerated the arrangement.

I was so depressed with the way things turned out with King, I even agreed to take Mr. Wiltshire's supper to the saloon one night, as much as I hated doing it. I wasn't surprised or bothered by his regular snide comments toward me. None of that was new. What I hated was seeing how hard Mrs. Wiltshire worked to get her husband's attention whenever he felt like gracing her with his presence. All he cared about was clean clothes and food on the table. His wife and Simone must've been bitten by the same bug: complaining about the amount of time their partner spent away from home.

"He's much too old to work so much," Mrs. Wiltshire told me that afternoon. "Why, even the bartender has a day free from work! I can't even remember the last time we had supper together."

She was right. Even though the tavern wasn't open on Sundays, that was his day to calculate the week's take. I think he wanted to get out of the house.

"I ran my old mistress's tavern back in Georgia," I said with a bit of pride. Looking back, if Miss Tillie never had the saloon, I might have never met Simone. "Maybe I could help clean and close the place, so he can have supper with you a few times a week."

"That would be wonderful!" Mrs. Wiltshire sang, clapping her hands. "Why not start tonight?"

She prepared the meal herself, believing that if he tasted the love she put into it, he'd come home to her. She also thought that if he saw how hard I worked while he ate, he might be more inclined to leave earlier. No one would turn down free help, and Mrs. Wiltshire had been so nice to me that I couldn't say no. Plus, the saloon could become a new hunting ground for Simone. I'd never been there, but with it situated at the northern edge of town, next to the Tolleston depot right on the Michigan Central rail line, its patrons were folks wanting to either keep to themselves or maybe just traveling through.

With the basket of food swinging from my arm, I lifted my chin and walked through town. By this time of day, the sun had started to set, so there were still people strolling along the road. Several even stopped to pass along a message for Mrs. Wiltshire. By the time I got there, it was completely dark. If not for the raucous laughter and the yellow glow lighting the windows surrounding the clapboard tavern, I would've missed it.

Soon as I walked in, the world stopped. I stood in the open doorway, all eyes on me. Twenty-odd stone statues gaping at me like they'd never seen a . . . Oh, I forgot. With me being the only one here, they probably never had.

"What the hell are you doing in here?" Wiltshire, the burly white-haired owner, said. He stood by a table of drinkers with two glasses of beer clutched in one hand. He lumbered toward me like a bear sizing up his dinner, with splashes of brown liquid sloshing onto the floor. "Get your Black ass out of here, you gibfaced darky!"

"I'm . . . I'm here . . ." I held up the basket of food, hoping it made up for my lack of words.

"What the fuck did I say?" he roared, causing me to nearly leap outta my shoes like a frightened cat. Then he tossed the beer, soaking me and the basket.

I didn't have time to explain to the fool that his wife had sent me there to feed his nasty behind. Why the hell else would I be there but for him? I could've been there to tell him his wife was dead, he didn't know. But I wasted no time leaving. Once outside, I shook the excess beer off and wiped away the liquid stinging my eyes with a dry spot on my blouse. In the darkness, I listened to the whistle of an approaching train, recovered from the sting of the encounter, and wondered what to tell Mrs. Wiltshire.

Then I heard the squeal of a door opening on its hinges. I hid and braced myself for round two with a lynch mob. Instead, it was Nate, the mute, woolly-haired bartender. I almost didn't see him when he stepped outside, even with the lantern he held. He'd been standing behind the bar during the whole episode, wiping the rim of a glass. I only noticed him because he set down that glass he'd been polishing to pull out a thick piece of wood about as long as my arm. When he slapped it on the bar, the place went quiet. Even Wiltshire stopped his hollering. I don't know what happened after I skulked outta there. Guess he was ready to have his say now, too.

"You work for Mrs. Wiltshire, right?" he said after locating me behind a water barrel. "Miss Lavinia, is it? What did you want?"

The hair on the back of my neck stood on end. Miss Lavinia? Now, that I ain't heard before. Here I was, out in the middle of nowhere behind a saloon with some strange man giving me propers with my name. It was so dark, I couldn't tell if he'd come out with the two-by-four or a glass of beer, even with my ghoul eyes. But he did remember my name.

He wiped his hands on the stained apron tied around his waist and approached me. He untied the apron and handed it to me. When I stared at it, and then him, he motioned with his finger to wipe my face.

"Probably need a drink after all that," he said. I thought he cracked a smile, but I couldn't tell with all that hair on his face. "I'll give you one, if you want."

My shoulders relaxed. "Miss Wiltshire sent me with her husband's supper." I held the wet basket out in front of me as proof.

The bartender's cheek twitched. "Poor old girl's wasting her time with his ass. Gimme the basket. I'll let Wiltshire know about the supper."

"She wanted me to help out here so her husband can come home at a decent hour." The words shot outta my mouth so quickly, it didn't even sound like me speaking.

He turned up his nose. "You want to work here?"

"Ain't about wantin' to work," I replied. "Miss Wiltshire jus' wants her husband home from time to time. Thought I'd oblige her if I could. I used to work at a saloon in Georgia. After the war."

Through all that hair, I couldn't tell if he was smiling or sticking his tongue out at me. But I did see him nod. "Gimme an hour. After he eats, I'll send him on his way."

I pursed my lips. "I gotta stay out here?"

"Nowhere to hide you in there. Won't be long. But I can bring out a drink to tide you over. I usually need one after dealing with him all night. What's your pleasure?"

I handed him the basket. "No, thanks. Don't think I'd want nothin' comin' outta that place nohow."

The bartender shrugged. "Suit yourself." He started back to the tavern then looked over his shoulder and said, "You should be fine if you stay by that barrel. But if something should happen, just bunch the apron up against this side window." He pointed to the one closest to the door he'd exited. From there, I had a clear view of the bar. "I'll come get you when he's gone." Then he went inside, the wooden door slamming shut against the jamb.

"Well, that went better than I expected," I heard Simone say. It sounded so clear that I turned around, expecting to find her beside me.

And there she was.

"What're you doin' here, girl?" My voice sounded scolding, but I was sure glad to see her, what with all the coyote racket getting louder by the second.

"How'd you get here so fast?"

"I turned into a bat and flew," Simone said with a dismissive roll of her eyes. "You're supposed to come home after work."

"I jus' saw you last night," I said, motioning for her to join me by the tavern's back door.

Simone set the lantern on the barrel and started in with me. "We agreed you would spend less time with these people."

"Did I miss a conversation? 'Cause I don't remember sayin' that."

"I didn't think it needed to be said after King. Now you're all into these Wiltshire people. Did you plan on coming back to the dugout at all tonight?"

"Depended on what was gonna happen here," I said. "Could be all kinds of goodies in there for you to snack on. If I helped out here from time to time, we wouldn't have to traipse through the woods every week."

Simone's doubtful expression didn't change. "So, what are we waiting on?" She went to open the door, but I stopped her.

"I ain't been in there yet. Gotta see who's there first and then figure out the right one."

"The right one is that nasty owner," Simone said, running her tongue along her upper teeth.

I shook my head. "You can't kill him. Mrs. Wiltshire—"

"Should I remind you of Miss Tillie? That Radut woman? King? Did any of those relationships end well for you?"

I stroked Simone's cold cheek then placed my hand on her shoulder.

My only constant in the last year. Wiltshire was a son of a bitch, but I couldn't stand to think of his wife crying over a man who obviously didn't want to be around her, but I at least wanted to give him half a chance.

"You know what, Simone? You're right. I put too much trust into people who haven't earned it. Can I trust you?"

She rolled her baby blues. "Of course you can, silly!"

"We'll see 'bout that." The wheels in my brain churned with a plan. I grabbed Simone's hand and dragged her behind a cluster of bushes on the other side of the train tracks. "Now, we wait."

"For what?"

I pointed to the saloon. "For Wiltshire."

An hour later, the bartender was good to his word, as Wiltshire left the saloon. Surprisingly, he didn't take his horse. I crossed my fingers as Simone rose to follow him. Once they were gone, the bartender let me in through the back door.

"Thank you, Mr. Nate," I said as he closed the door.

He chuckled. "Nate's fine. You don't have to work here, you know. I can handle this place on my own."

"I don't mind," I said, tying his apron around my waist. I needed to wait for Simone to get back anyway.

"Follow my lead, and you'll be fine," he advised. "Gotta get 'em drunk enough to forget you were here." He winked, then held the door open for me which led from the back room into the bar.

Nate handled the drinks and the drunks, while I cleaned tables and swept the floor. He didn't say much to anybody, kept his head down, and spoke only when spoken to. I followed suit. None of the men seemed to remember the episode with Wiltshire earlier. I hesitated at first to ask Nate anything, but when I finally had to because I needed another rag to wipe the tables, he politely offered to get it for me. Even brought out that plank of wood a couple of times when somebody got too mouthy with me.

As I worked, I checked in with Simone as she followed Wiltshire home. Having never gone stalking with me, she only saw the results of days of watching and waiting. This, at least, gave her an opportunity to see all the work I put into her meals and prove how much I could trust her. Through her mind, I saw Wiltshire walk fifteen minutes to a home I didn't recognize.

That's not his house, I told Simone. *And that woman he's kissing ain't his wife.*

She looks juicy. I could only imagine Simone licking her chops.

Patience, I cautioned.

Through Simone's mind, I saw him drawing each curtain closed, extinguishing each lamp. That dog. I summoned Simone back to the saloon, expressed my pride in her ability to control herself, and put my next feeding plan into place.

"We're going home?" Simone whined after she met me behind the saloon. "What about the man?"

"Patience," I repeated. "You'll have your chance . . . when I say."

"Miss Lavinia?"

I pushed Simone behind the water barrel as Nate emerged from the back door of the bar.

"Closing up the place. Need me to carry you home?"

"I can manage on my own," I said with a smile.

"I'd feel better knowing you got there in one piece." His voice was firm, in a parental sort of way, like an older brother pulling rank.

"Not going back to the Wiltshires' tonight," I said, hearing Simone's reminder that I was to be with her that evening. "Was gonna pay a call to a friend over on the beach."

"And you were gonna walk there in the dark?" He placed his hands on his hips and looked east toward the lake. "I'm not going in that di-rection—"

"No matter," I said, anxious to get going and Simone outta my brain. Five more minutes, her thoughts said to me, and this saloon would be down one bartender. I turned to leave, but he caught my arm.

"Sorry, Miss Lavinia," he said, quickly releasing me when I turned back to him like he'd just smacked my rear end. "It wouldn't be proper letting you go off on your own and not knowing if you made it to your destination. Haven't you heard about the attacks?"

I shook my head, knowing he was probably referencing those hunters.

"Some town out east," he continued. "Miller Station, I think. Read it in the papers."

Miller Station? Probably one of those men out there trying to pin their abuse on some phantom stalker. I waved it off.

Lavinia, Simone warned.

"I couldn't put you out like that, Mr. Nate . . . Nate." And as cordial as you were to me tonight, I couldn't let you get eaten. Don't know you well enough, yet.

"I insist," he said, with a hand upon his heart and his drawl heavier than what I'd heard tonight. "My mama would skin me if I did otherwise."

"She here?" I asked, following him to the horse he had tied up in front of the saloon.

"Tennessee. I hear the South in you, too. Whereabouts are you from?"

"Georgia. Been here only a little while."

"Me, too." This time, I think he actually smiled, for his cheek shifted and his brown eyes twinkled a bit in the moonlight.

Despite Simone's warnings, I had no qualms as Nate mounted his horse and then with an extended arm, helped lift me so I was seated on the saddle right behind him. As we rode in silence toward my dugout, I almost wished King could see me with him. I don't know why. Nate wasn't treating me any differently than King would have . . . if he wasn't so disgusted with me. I imagined Nate doing the same, if I ever had a reason to trust him for anything. I could have introduced him to Simone, told him she was the friend I was going to visit. But why bother? He was merely the bartender, after all. How often would I be running into the man anyway?

"What are we waiting on?" Simone asked as she greeted me at Wiltshire's saloon a few days later.

Remember when I said vamps had no patience? Well, Simone didn't understand the word "wait." It had been only three days since she followed Wiltshire to that woman's house, and she had a hankering for him. She'd met me at the saloon every night with the same greeting. And as always, I ignored her. This night, I leaned against the water barrel, waiting for Nate to let me in the back door after Wiltshire took his leave. I was grateful for him helping me, but something about him niggled at the back of my mind. Could feel his eyes on me as I worked, only to act like he hadn't been eyeing me when I caught him.

All the while, Simone knew I was stalling. I was hoping Wiltshire had a change of heart regarding his nightly activities. I never selected a victim and then immediately fed them to her. I had to learn their routine to find the best spot for the kill. Determine if they deserved to be Simone's next meal. No witnesses. Limit the disposal work. But of course, she didn't appreciate none of that.

"What are we waiting on?" Simone repeated. "You're protecting him, aren't you? To keep that wife of his happy."

I shushed her, as if her voice would cut through the music, laughter, cussing, and glass clinking in that loud tavern. "I'm doin' no such thing," I said. Except I was. I'd spent those same three days stalking the woman Wiltshire was courting. I reckon if I got rid of her, then he'd have no choice but to return to Mrs. Wiltshire. "His plaything is fair game."

Simone stomped her foot. "I don't want her!"

"Why the hell not? Blood is blood, remember? Plus, she's some old widow with no kids and she's messin' around with a married man. Ain't nobody gon' miss her."

"She's German," Simone countered. "I'm tired of Germans!"

"How you know she's German?"

"Isn't everybody in this town?"

I rested my fist on my hip, pursed my lips, and cocked my head to the side. "Now, that don't make no kinda sense, Simone. The Wiltshires ain't German and they live here." I had no idea what the woman was. Not like I interviewed the folks I stalked before deciding whether they'd wind up being Simone's supper. All I cared about was making sure that I wasn't feeding some innocent to her, not where they were from. But I didn't blame her for thinking that. Hardly anybody spoke English in Tolleston unless they had to, but Wiltshire's mistress didn't have a strange accent, so I wasn't sure.

"Why don't you give me one more day to find out what the woman is," I told Simone with my hand placed firmly on her shoulder, guiding her from the saloon. "If she's somethin' new, you can have her. If you still don't want her—"

Simone spun around, wide-eyed. "Then Wiltshire?"

"Maybe," I pushed her forward again. "Go home."

She dug her heels in and elbowed me. "Not good enough. Tell me why I shouldn't march in there and take him now?"

"'Cause I said so."

"Are you going to stop me?"

I squeezed the bridge of my nose with my fingers. "Simone—"

"I know what you're doing, Lavinia."

"Do you? Really? I'm doin' my job. Makin' sure we don't get caught. Tryin' to provide for us."

"As if cleaning someone's house is going to pay enough to provide for us."

The back door cracked open, and the bartender stuck his head out. Not a word was uttered. I pushed Simone to the ground out of sight and growled under my breath an order for her to go home. She didn't. As I worked cleaning the tables and fetching drink orders, I saw her peeking through the windows. Sometimes I'd catch her pacing. Other times, she'd stand there with her mouth wide open, baring her fangs at me. Nobody seemed to notice her, especially after a brawl broke out. The whole place erupted when one fella accused another of cheating at a card game. As much liquor as Nate served them, I'm surprised any of them were keeping track. But even he and his two-by-four named Betty had a tough time getting control over the situation. With chairs and fists flying around, Nate managed to grab me around the waist and push me behind the bar out of harm's way. Eventually, he kicked everyone out and closed the place down early. I reasoned Simone would be happy about that. But she was nowhere to be found. Guess she got tired of waiting and slunk off to the dugout.

Except she didn't.

"Welcome home, Lavinia," Simone said when I finally arrived back at the Wiltshires'. She stood at the fireplace holding a knife to the old woman's neck. Fangs bared, there was no mistaking what was about to happen.

"The hell you doin'?!" I stepped toward her but stopped when she poked the tip of the knife into the old woman's throat, drawing blood. With all the commotion at the bar, my occupied mind missed this plan.

Mrs. Wiltshire released a muted squeal of pain. All the blood had hightailed it from her face. Poor woman was as white as the hair on her head.

Simone licked her lips. "Given our earlier discussion, I have a different proposition. You quit your job and I won't eat her."

"Are you insane?" I asked. "You gon' mess up everything!"

"Quit your job!"

"And if I quit, then what? What you think gon' happen when we walk outta here? She done seen you now. You gonna get us both lynched."

Simone shrugged. "Well, I guess I'll have to eat her then."

I narrowed my eyes at her. "You wouldn't!"

She returned my glare. On cue, she held Mrs. Wiltshire's arm out, thrust back the sleeve of the woman's blouse, and drew a long gash across her flesh. A swath of red erupted, along with a scream from Mrs. Wiltshire. Simone hissed at the woman like some rattler about to strike, then dragged her finger over the wound. Finger red with blood, she wiped it clean against her tongue. Her lip curled in disappointment. "English. As bland as your name, Janey."

The woman passed out in Simone's arms. If I wasn't so mad, the sight of Simone trying, and failing, to keep Mrs. Wiltshire upright would have tickled me to my toes. Eventually, Simone let the dead weight drop to the floor.

I walked over and slapped the knife from her hand. "You idiot!" I paced across the rug, cussing under my breath. Simone never, ever interfered with her meal prep. She might have complained about the choices from time to time, but lately with my work at the Wiltshires', Simone was so hungry by the time we went hunting, she didn't care what I gave her.

"That's right," Simone said, hearing my thoughts. "Your negligence caused this. If you simply paid attention to me—"

"Good Lord, girl! You are such a baby! When have I not provided for you? Jus' 'cause you had to wait a few extra days to feed?"

"You left me on purpose to be with these people!"

"You didn't even know that 'til I told you. Now, we're gon' have another Radut situation on our hands."

Simone got down on her hands and knees beside Mrs. Wiltshire. "Let me feed first before you burn the house."

"No! That ain't what I meant." I yanked her up. "We ain't burnin' nothin'. Jesus! Let me think."

"What is there to think about?" Simone shook her head as if the answer were obvious.

What was there to think about? I'd long since given up on thinking any of these human relationships were real or lasting. How soon would it be before Wiltshire said or did something that turned his weak wife against me? Or when Nate realized he was getting too familiar with me? But killing them wouldn't be like the reckless hunters out in the Tolleston woods. We'd learned that Simone simply biting, rather than tearing at her victims, made the wounds less suspicious. Simple, right? Disposing of the Wiltshires in a place where the neighbors knew each other's comings and goings complicated things. And Mrs. Wiltshire was no dainty flower. No way I would've been able to get her outta the house without Simone's help, which I knew wasn't happening, and with a dozen pairs of eyes watching?

But what else could I do?

"What if we could both pass as humans right here in this house?" I asked Simone.

Simone raised an eyebrow. "Why would I want to do that?"

"'Cause you owe me. Now jus' do what I say, and we can both get what we want."

Later that night, Wiltshire returned to find Simone and me in his parlor. We'd dragged Mrs. Wiltshire into the kitchen when we heard Mr. Wiltshire's horse neighing outside, signaling his return. I sat in a plush high-back chair, sipping on a smooth brandy I could actually taste. But I don't think Wiltshire's crinkled brow had anything to do with him seeing the maid sitting in his chair, sucking on one of his cigars. Not with the vampire at his neck. Simone sliced his arm, squeezing it to release the blood into her mouth without turning him into anything. This time she obeyed me, taking only enough blood to weaken him so he couldn't go anywhere or do anything. He deserved it.

But when it was Mrs. Wiltshire's turn?

"Why not?" Simone asked.

"'Cause she ain't done nothin' to me or you."

"Not yet. Honestly, Lavinia, have you learned nothing? The Raduts turned on you when it was convenient for them. King tossed you aside when the truth about me wasn't convenient for him. What do you think this weak creature's going to do? It will only be a matter of time before she shows her true colors. They all do." She sidled up to me and whispered, "You know it, and I know it. Think, Lavinia. This old lady doesn't see you as a person. You're merely the help to her. Nothing more. Why delay the inevitable disappointment? You don't need her. *We* don't need her."

Had it been up to me, I would have spared her. Though Mrs. Wiltshire had something I wanted—the house—she didn't deserve what happened to her. She was another unfortunate casualty. Once again, I was faced with choosing between Simone and a human. And once again, my unbreakable connection to Simone won out. Had no choice but to let her make the old woman as docile and weak as her nasty husband for my plan of keeping a foot in both worlds to work.

Just like Etienne, Simone slowly bled them every day. I made sure she used her fingers, and not her mouth. When the old couple walked, they shuffled along like two lost souls. Physical weakness made them practically useless. They'd stand there sometimes until me or Simone goaded them along. Despite his pitiful state, I made Wiltshire accompany me to the tavern, forcing him to work. I'd hold onto his arm and escort him inside; gingerly walking as if his bones pained him. He'd stand at the tables like a zombie, his sunken eyes drifting over confused patrons like he was watching clouds in the sky. They'd question him, and then he'd snap out of his trance, only to forget why he was standing there in the first place. Then he'd shuffle back to the bar and lay his head down. I'd give him a few moments of peace, then nudge him to start the show all over again.

While working at the saloon, I studied Wiltshire's business: learning his books, where he got his booze, how he managed the place. Nate was nice enough to answer any questions I might have. He seemed to bristle whenever Simone—whom I introduced as the Wiltshires' niece from Montreal—got bored and decided to tag along. Whatever he thought he knew, he never let on. Always quiet, never uttering a word to the patrons unless asked. Maybe it was the two-by-four he kept beneath the bar, but something told me that there was another reason he preferred to blend into the woodwork around these folks.

"Poor Mr. Wiltshire," I'd say with a shake of my head to anyone within earshot. "Jus' as sickly as he can be."

"You his nurse now, too?" Nate asked me one night at the saloon. As usual, he'd been staring at me and wiping around the rim of a glass for a good while. Seemed like he was working up the nerve to ask me that question.

"Somethin' like that. His wife's jus' as sick."

He raised an eyebrow. "Funny how that happened, huh?"

I met his gaze. "Yeah, funny."

"What's wrong with him?"

I shrugged. Just deserts? "They up and took sick. Good thing I was there to take care of 'em. Guess everything happens for a reason. I reckon Mr. Wiltshire ain't gon' be on this earth for long if he keeps comin' in here every night."

Nate gave an "Oh, well" tilt of his head, and went back to his silent glass polishing.

Simone kept the Wiltshires barely alive and locked in the root cellar of the house we now claimed. She trotted the half-dead couple out when the bartender brought by the weekly take, or when church folks stopped by after Sunday services. We purchased thick, heavy curtains for the windows so she could entertain callers with her dear old aunt and uncle during the daytime. Visitors soon got used to the odd arrangement and the perpetually-dim house. And with the ever-present fear of death, the Wiltshires had no choice but to play along.

"These people are boring me," Simone said one day as we lounged in the Wiltshires' parlor, enjoying the crackling of burning wood in the fireplace. The couple was in the root cellar sleeping off another night of terror. "And I'm tired of nibbling on leftovers. He's already signed over the deed to the tavern and the house. Besides, Jane's wounds are start-ing to smell. Let's finish this already."

"I know. I'm jus' worried folks might not take well to two women runnin' a tavern. I wonder if Nate is someone we can trust. You know, to be the face of the place."

Simone draped a lazy arm over my shoulder. "Au contraire, you don't need these humans to do anything. All we need is each other. And look at you! The mistress of your own house. Did you think that would ever happen in your lifetime?"

I hate to think of it now, but the control we had over the Wiltshires, the control I had, made my skin tingle with excitement. This new feeling was almost as intoxicating as Wiltshire's brandy. Here I was, a former slave, giving orders to white folks! I decided I was doing this not only for me and Simone, but for every Negro who'd ever been in bondage. Every woman who'd lost herself in some man's shadow.

At least that's what I told myself to stay sane.

Truth was, Mrs. Wiltshire pulled on my heartstrings. Though she had encouraged me to practice my reading and writing skills and spoke to me every day like we were old friends, I couldn't help but think it was because she had no one else. She might've been a whole 'nother person had her husband treated her better. My presence simply filled the hole. Poor woman was whiter than a sheet and slower than a slug in molasses. I'd thought my humanity died that day Simone kissed me in the jail. In reality, it died with Mrs. Wiltshire.

I try not to dwell on it too much nowadays.

TWENTY-SIX

I don't care how beautiful a vamp might've been in life, when they turn, they turn. You couldn't miss how pale they were, how their skin clung to the bones in their faces, how sunken and lifeless their eyes were. And then the long eyeteeth! If nothing else about their features bothered you, seeing them sharp daggers coming at you like a panther would be enough to send you packing. Since Wiltshire's tavern sat out in the middle of nowhere, there were no gas connections to light the place. Only kerosene lamps drowning everything in a dull yellow haze. Bright enough for you to see the cards or booze in front of you. Dark enough not to notice the pockmarks on the face of some hussy trying to coax you outside for a midnight romp in an empty railcar.

Simone's contribution to working the saloon was giving the unruly crowd a glimpse of her true self. She'd sit at the end of the bar with a frilly fan concealing her face. A brass candelabra with five lit tapers beside her. If someone's tongue got a little too loose or a card game started taking a turn, Simone simply called the offender over to her, lowered the fan, and placed her pale face right up to the candlelight. All the hissing and fang-bearing would take but a second before the offender would high-tail it out of there so fast, smoke was coming from his shoes! Funny thing was, they must've chalked the experience up to drunkenness or bad lighting, anything other than a monster in their midst, because they always came back.

Same was true of the folks who came calling to the house. I think they were more intrigued by Simone's odd appearance than the welfare of the Wiltshires. After a while, men and women alike were stopping by to visit with the Wiltshires' French-speaking niece, with only a brief inquiry as to their sickly neighbors. Even cornered me at the kitchen's back door from time to time to ask after Simone. I could tell she liked all the attention. Took her back to her debutante days in Montreal. Made her feel human, she said once, which really pissed me off because here I was—a sorta real human—who couldn't get one lousy man to pay attention to me. And yet here was Simone with all eyes on her, holding court with the same humans she'd constantly chided me for spending time with. All these folks parading in and out of the house for Simone, I felt lonelier than I ever did before.

Mrs. Wiltshire's pastor, Reverend Karl Norquist, sure called a lot. Every Sunday afternoon he stopped by to take tea with Simone. Never recalled seeing him this much before. The first time I introduced them he started speaking French to her. I'd learned some words, but not enough to follow a whole conversation. Apparently, neither did Simone. She stood there and smiled like poor old Mrs. Wiltshire did, when she could. I let them be, figuring she was a mite nervous remembering how to be human. So, I stayed in the kitchen, the only room in the house where daylight poured through the windows like nectar from heaven.

Posing like I was the help didn't bother me. I didn't really do nothing except ask the company if they needed anything. They were usually too taken by Simone and the exaggerated French accent she used with them to want anything else. I'd sit in the kitchen, reading a book with my feet propped up on a chair. Or be outside tending to the vegetable garden Mrs. Wiltshire had started. I often wondered if her power of attraction was something all vamps had that didn't work on ghouls. She swore it wasn't, but then again, the ins and outs of vampirism was something we were both still learning.

Then I heard the craziest thing come outta her mouth.

"I'm not used to houses being this close together," Simone said, her voice traveling the short distance to the kitchen. "I could put two Tollestons on our plantation back in New Orleans."

New Orleans? That's the second time she'd said that. She claimed the first was a slip of the tongue. But twice?

"New Orleans," Norquist said. "A world away from Indiana. I take it your family fought for the Confederacy?"

Mrs. Wiltshire had fallen asleep on the sofa, her head lolling off to the side with a bit of spittle dangling from her chin. Norquist and Simone didn't notice her, or me come into the parlor for that matter. I set the tea down on a serving table near the sofa.

"Y'all want some tea?" I said loudly.

Mrs. Wiltshire woke with a start. Didn't even bother wiping her mouth. She smacked her lips a few times, looked around the room, and sank back into the sofa. I poured her a cup anyway. By the time I gave it to her, her eyelids had lowered and her jaw hung open. I shook her, but it did no good. I handed the cup to Norquist instead.

"You owned slaves, I assume," he said to Simone.

"About a hundred, if I remember correctly."

I almost spilled Simone's tea on her.

She glared at me and slowly took the teacup by the saucer underneath it. Their conversation turned to her life in New Orleans. The descriptions rolled off her tongue like she'd rehearsed this already . . . or had lived it. Nothing like the Montreal stories she'd told me. Her father had been a chef, not a landowner like the ones she claimed to despise. And slaves? She never mentioned slaves before. Why she changed it, I don't know. What I did know was that I looked at Norquist a bit differently after the keen interest he took in Simone's slave-owning family.

"I've never had a Swede before," Simone mused after Norquist's visit. She'd found her way into the kitchen, remaining in the doorway of the adjoining room to avoid the sunlight. She went on to mention all kinds of stuff I hadn't asked about the man: the curl of his blond hair, some funny tale he'd told her, the way he bit at his pinky fingernail like a nervous boy courting for the first time.

I tossed the rag I'd been using to dry dishes into the washbasin and laughed. "You can't eat a preacher!"

"Says who?"

"Don't think God'll take too kindly to you eatin' one of His. 'Sides, you seem to like the reverend's company well enough."

I never minded Reverend Norquist coming by when he was calling on Mrs. Wiltshire. He spoke in English when he did his God-talk, loud enough so I heard him all the way in the kitchen. Must've been trying to save my heathen soul, too. Simone had told him some part-truth about her sun condition; that she blistered and boiled whenever the slightest bit touched her, so he didn't seem to mind sitting in that stuffy parlor with the windows closed and the curtains drawn. Don't think he would've cared either way. At the end of his marathon visit, Norquist had taken her hand—guess he didn't notice how cold it was—and prayed that one day, God would heal her.

Simone shrugged. "He's nice. Our conversations aren't always about God, though some things he says about blood and forgiveness intrigue me. Different than what I was taught. He seems genuinely interested in me as a person."

I rolled my eyes. Where have I heard that line before? Up until that point, I thought vamps couldn't feel with their dead hearts. Simone didn't even shed a tear when she thought I was gonna die in that jail. Then again, something drove her outta that box that day I almost drowned. Something more than losing the hand that fed her.

"Uh-huh. Guess a man's still a man, no matter what he's wearin' 'round his collar."

"I guess."

"Guess you really ain't serious 'bout eatin' him either, huh?"

Simone smiled and, if she could, would probably be blushing too.

I trotted down the narrow hallway behind her. "What was all that stuff about you livin' in New Orleans?"

"What?" Simone walked past a sleeping Mrs. Wiltshire. She poked the old woman on the shoulder and giggled as she slid onto the sofa.

"New Orleans," I said, patting Mrs. Wiltshire's hand to rouse her. "You told the reverend you were from New Orleans instead of Montreal."

"Did I?"

"You did." I pulled Mrs. Wiltshire to her feet. She wobbled on her heels like a top before falling into my arms. It was too early to put her back in the root cellar, somebody might still come calling. So, I walked her around the parlor, her thick and heavy arm slung over my shoulder.

"And you owned slaves? Who you lyin' to, Simone? Me or the reverend?"

"You've never told a fib to impress someone?"

"Depends on who you're tryin' to impress and why you're doin' it."

She stared at me for a second before sauntering up the stairs, humming softly, her thoughts coming to me clear as day: *Mrs. Karl Norquist. Mrs. Reverend Norquist. Simone Norquist.* Even saw flashes of her with a couple of kids in tow and the reverend on her arm. The whole family strolling down Main Street in broad daylight. First time I knew her to consider being normal, as if all Norquist's talk of Christ's blood healing her would really help. She'd talked a bit about some guy named Henri, another preacher man she'd been sweet on when she was a girl.

In a way I felt bad for her. Simone's chances at love with a human were worse than mine. What'd she think, they'd get married and make a coffin their marriage bed? Could she even do what wives were supposed to do behind closed doors? If she could, Norquist would be essentially doing it with a dead body. I cringed at the thought.

I left Mrs. Wiltshire standing by the fireplace with her hand clutching the mantel for balance. I followed Simone up the creaking stairs into the master bedroom I now claimed. I caught Simone sliding under the four-poster bed, holding that singed burlap against her body.

"We gon' have to keep our stories straight, Simone," I said, leaning against the doorframe. "I been tellin' folks you're from Montreal and now you come messin' it up talkin' 'bout how you're from New Orleans."

"Slip of the tongue," Simone said from beneath the bed. "I don't think Karl cares either way."

"And why you all sweet on another preacher man anyway? Thought you said things went sour with that other one in Montreal or wherever you claim you lived."

"Ugh," she said with a bit of disgust. She poked her head out from beneath the bed. "Can we not talk about him, please?"

I leaned my head down toward her. "Fine. But you gotta start bein' honest with me."

Simone slid all the way out from the bed, the burlap still in her hands. "Fine! My family did, yes. That doesn't mean *I* owned them."

"What you call it, then?"

Simone sighed. "What do you want me to say, Lavinia?"

"Nothin'." I straightened my stance. I couldn't tell if Simone was lying to me on purpose or if her vamp brain had mixed up her memories. I'd hate to think she chided me about trusting folks when she might be the one I gotta look out for.

A loud thump downstairs brought my attention back to Mrs. Wiltshire. "I'd hate to see the look on Norquist's face when he meets the real you."

"Huh," Martin says. "So, she wasn't really their niece?" He's back to chawing on that tobacco again—an after-supper treat, I suppose.

I crinkle my forehead at his revelation. "You jus' now figurin' that out?"

"I mean, I never thought about it until now."

"With everything I jus' told you?"

Martin nods his head.

"So, you believe me?"

He sighs, removes his hat, and runs his hand over his graying hair. "That's how you two ended up with the Wiltshire house," he says, ignoring the question. "Had us all fooled, you did."

"Not my fault none of you looked close enough or asked any questions. Had y'all been payin' attention, you'd've probably figured it out."

"It *was* strange," Martin continues as if he is here talking to himself, "that they took ill all of a sudden like that." He finally remembers I'm here and turns to me. "They never screamed or tried to run?"

I shake my head. "Too weak. The blood they needed to function right was what was keepin' Simone upright. 'Cause she was pickin' at 'em every day, they never had time to heal and strengthen up."

"I remember their funeral," Martin says with a chuckle. "First one in a while here that I could follow because it was all in English. She ate them too, huh?"

"Actually, no."

Martin's eyes bulge out. His hand clutches his throat. "She turned them into . . . whatever you said she was?"

"A vampire?"

"A vampire. They turned into vampires?"

"Naw," I say. "They jus' died. Simone had stopped bleedin' 'em a couple of weeks later. Wound up with some sickness in their blood she couldn't stomach. Mr. Wiltshire went first. Guess his wife didn't wanna live without him. When we found him keeled over in the root cellar, Mrs. Wiltshire . . . poor thing didn't even have the strength to cry."

"Sounds like you regret what happened to the Wiltshires."

"Miss Jane, yes. I should've only let Simone bleed Mr. Wiltshire; he was the one I wanted to punish, the one who deserved it. Thinkin' back, I was jus' as weak as Mrs. Wiltshire when it came to Simone."

TWENTY-SEVEN

After Mrs. Wiltshire's funeral, Nate stopped by one afternoon. I'd completely forgotten about the saloon in the week since the old couple died. I was so busy dyeing mourning dresses, draping the house in black, and tending to callers paying their respects to the bereaved niece. And there was a strong stink of rot I couldn't find. I didn't ask Simone about it, thinking it was just guilt manifesting. The callers to the house either couldn't smell it or were too polite to mention it.

"Nate," I said when I opened the door.

"Lavinia," he said, his eyes trained on the porch. He held out a brown leather pouch. "This week's take."

I took the pouch and gaped at the wad of bills and coins inside. "You kept the place open?"

Nate glanced to the left where the neighbor woman was out tending to her rosebushes. He lowered his voice and his head. "I wasn't sure what you planned on doing with the place. Assumed I'd keep it going until you told me otherwise."

Until *I* told him otherwise? "Why don't you come on in for some coffee and we can talk?"

Nate glanced over his shoulder again before stepping inside. I poked my head out the door, wondering who he was looking for. For a second,

I thought maybe this was a setup, that he was here to try and take the place from me and bringing by the weekly take was only a ruse. If that was his plan, he had another thing coming, like the vampire resting upstairs under the bed.

He said nothing as I poured both of us a cup of coffee and stared at me as we sipped in tandem. I didn't expect Nate to say too much to me, and he seemed fine sitting there with his back all straight in the quiet, eyeing me like he always did. Was surprised he even came in for coffee. I used the silence to think of what to say in case his next words questioned the saloon's ownership.

After several seconds of the uncomfortable silence, I finally said, "Somethin' you wanna say to me, Nate?"

My question seemed to catch him off guard. "What do you mean?"

"You always eyein' me like I got two heads."

"Sorry." He put his cup down and lowered his eyes. "You remind me of someone."

"That a good thing or a bad thing?"

Taut lines appeared around his eyes. With all that hair, I guessed he was smiling. "A good thing."

I didn't know what that meant. Could be I reminded him of his wet nurse. Could be I reminded him of the poor woman who had no choice in what he did with her. Either way, I needed to know what his intentions were with the bar, and whether I would remain in charge. I set my cup down on its saucer and held it with both hands to keep my nerves in check. Glad only I could see the black coffee ripple from my anxiety. Only one way to find out.

"What's the worst thing you've ever done, Nate?"

He froze and straightened his back. Brow furrowed, he looked around the kitchen and lowered his voice. "Why?"

I traced the rim of my cup with my finger. "Somethin' I ask folks to get to know 'em."

"What's the worst thing you've ever done?"

I chuckled. "Ain't enough time in the world to tell you all that. I jus' wanna know if I can trust you, is all."

"Do you?"

"Can I?"

Nate studied his coffee, his shoulders rising and falling with each contemplative breath. Then he looked up at me and said, "Lied. A lot. Followed an immoral order from my commanding officer in the war and didn't speak up when it mattered."

My heart sank. Can't ever trust a liar, even an admitted one. You knew what to expect from a thief, but a liar is as unpredictable as a mischievous toddler.

"I'm sure you had no choice in the matter," I said flatly.

Nate shook his head. "No, I had a choice. But I was too scared of somebody finding out who I really was. So, I stood by and said nothing when my regiment killed those men at Fort Pillow."

I didn't know what a Fort Pillow was. But Nate quickly added that he was only fighting for the Confederacy because his daddy wanted him to take his brother's place.

"If I survived the war," he said, "he'd give me his name and give my mother her free papers."

I tried not to look like I'd been caught with my britches down, but you could've knocked me over with a feather. No wonder Nate never looked nobody in the eye. He'd been passing all this time and didn't want nobody to take a hard enough study to figure out he wasn't all white. He sure fooled me! I mean, his features were dark: brown eyes, a head full of curly brown locks that hung loosely over his ears and the back of his neck, sideburns, and facial hair that covered the whole bottom of his face. Another way to hide himself from the world. But aside from all the hair, nothing about him really stood out. Miss Tillie had some high-yellow Negroes on her plantation, but I didn't think twice about them because we all knew they were colored. Never would've thought of them as half-anything because no matter how light they were, colored was the only half anybody ever saw. Wasn't none of them as light as Nate, though. Almost like the sun never kissed any part of his body.

But I understood about wanting his daddy's name, the need to belong to somebody, even if that somebody was his mother's rapist.

"Looks like your mama got her free papers and you got your daddy's name."

Nate stared past me, probably replaying in his mind all that he'd told me. He snorted out a soft chuckle. "Who said Nate Efron is my real name?"

"Well, look, whatever your name is, you're more'n welcome to stay on at the saloon," I said.

"Would think you might say that," he said. "A colored woman running a saloon up here? Town would probably burn the place down with you in it. You need a man there."

"Ain't like they've never seen me before."

"Seen you working," Nate pointed out. "That, they're used to. And we might need to bring on more help. You've seen how busy it gets in the evenings."

The coffee ripples calmed, and I looked at him. For the first time, I didn't notice any tension in him. He'd sat back in the chair, his boot lightly touching my own beneath the table.

"It was jus' you and old Wiltshire all this time, wasn't it?"

"Yeah, but—"

"Me and you should be able to handle it."

"I don't doubt that," he said. "But you've seen that crowd."

"I've seen worse," I said, mimicking his posture. "This ain't the first saloon I've worked at. Matter of fact," I stood and took our empty cups to the washbasin, "why don't we go by there now and see what's what?"

As we walked to the front door, I copied Nate, scanning for eavesdroppers, before I asked him quietly, "You don't mind lettin' folks think you're white?"

"I'm not making them think anything," he said as he held the door open for me. "Just not offering any information nobody asked for. Like you two, not correcting folks about Miss Simone being the Wiltshires' niece." He stood there, his body holding the door ajar. Those lines around his eyes appeared again.

I got prickly all over. "Now, look, Nate—"

"Come on, now," he said, looking just as content as he wanted to be, having figured out my secret. "You're gonna lie about it? To me? We just went through this whole thing about trust."

I folded my arms across my chest and set my jaw. I acknowledged the truth with a nod. "That we did. Just didn't think you'd try testin' it out so soon." I huffed and threw my hands in the air, certain this was the real reason for his call. "So, now what?"

"Nothing," he said with a shake of his head. He released the door then sidled up to me. My nose welcomed his clean scent of soap and rainwater as he stroked his beard. "Two women living here alone. Me, living alone. We do what we have to do. I think we both know this con-versation isn't leaving this porch."

"What you want, Nate?"

"My job. That's all I want. You need a man to run the place anyway, don'tcha? No need to mess up what we got going on here, right?"

Well, aren't we a pair! Two colored folks playacting like we're the same as everybody else. I wondered if he'd come clean if somebody did ask. Or was he smarter than me, realizing that letting people believe you are who they think you are was safer than being honest. Wish I'd learned that lesson sooner.

"Folks are gonna ask about the place," Nate continued, as we strolled down the road toward a wider road, which led directly to the saloon about two miles away. Even though the men were away and the women were inside tending to their houses, he kept a respectable distance as we walked side by side a good arm's length apart. "Long as they know it'll stay open, there shouldn't be a problem."

"She does own the place," I added, keeping my eyes on the hem of my skirts swishing up dust from the ground. "Miss Simone. Wiltshire signed it over to her before he passed."

"Might work best if they think he left it to me."

I opened my mouth to protest, but knew he was right. If they thought Simone owned it, they'd probably fall over themselves trying to marry her and take it.

"That's what you're gonna tell them?"

"Only if they ask. They'll assume it anyway if I look like I'm running the place."

We rounded the corner and wound up on Main Street with a whole lot more people milling around. Without saying a word, both of our eyes went to the ground, and our conversation ceased. We continued walking on the dirt road, dodging the horse dung and passersby too engrossed in their own conversations to pay any attention to us. A few of the men nodded a greeting to Nate, who replied in the same silent manner. I wasn't certain if Nate kept quiet so people didn't think we were together, or if he was simply practicing the safety of silence. I made a note to increase his pay by a whole dollar.

There were fellas waiting for their refreshments by the time we arrived. Made them stay outside while I took stock of the place. Together, we made a list of everything we needed. Nate took his usual post behind the bar while I grabbed an apron and broom and got to cleaning while the patrons started spilling in. When one drunk got a bit mouthy at me during the early evening rush, Nate slapped that two-by-four on the bar, which shut him up quickly and sobered up everybody else for the rest of the evening.

As Nate pushed the last patron out of the place, I took a moment to ponder where I was. This place was mine. The decisions made were mine. And that money Nate had given me? All mine. For the first time since that fire at the Raduts', I was around people without wondering which one I should feed to Simone. How normal it all was!

I savored my days working there because once I got home after the place closed, I practically disappeared when Reverend Norquist came to call on Simone. The day after he presided over the Wiltshire funeral, he was there. And the day after that. You'd think Simone was the only parishioner he had. Though he called himself comforting Simone in her fake grief, neither one of them seemed to remember that was the case. He'd simply ask how she was feeling, then they'd get to talking about everything else but the Wiltshires. Since it was so late when he called— nearly dinnertime—I went into the kitchen and started preparing a meal from our sparse supply, given that I rarely ate, and Simone didn't need it.

About a week after my arrangement with Nate, a knock at the kitchen door brought me out of the root cellar with three white potatoes in my hand. I prayed it wasn't another caller because I wasn't in the mood to feed no army. Wonder why whoever it was chose to come to the back door.

When I opened it, the last person I thought I'd ever see again stood there looking worse than I did when I had the pneumonia.

Valerica appeared as some half-dead scarecrow who'd fallen off her perch. The blond hair she'd worn in a thick bun at the nape of her neck had thinned, sticking out from her head like it was starving for moisture. Sunken eyes sat atop dark half-moons crowning her cheeks. A dirty shawl was wrapped around that same singed frock I'd last seen her in. Burn holes all over it like she'd been hit with buckshot. Even though it was still light out, I looked past her into the backyard, half expecting to see Victor behind her.

From her came that familiar, faint stench of death.

Now, normally I ain't one to do stupid stuff. But slamming the door shut didn't even register. I took a step back and said nothing as she entered the kitchen and closed the door behind her. Didn't do nothing as she pulled a knife from inside her frayed sleeve, raised it over her head, and then stabbed me right in the shoulder.

A shocked breath left me as I stared at the knife sticking outta me. Waited for pain that only pulsed like a playful pinch. Don't know if I was madder at being stabbed or that I'd have to spend an afternoon stitching up and washing blood from my blouse. I glared at the knife, then at Valerica.

"Guess you was aimin' for my heart," I said, snatching the knife from my shoulder. "You missed." I widened the hole in my blouse and watched the wound slowly close, then disappear. Then I returned the favor, slinging the knife into her shoulder like one of those traveling circus performers. She wasn't expecting that. Valerica stumbled back against the open kitchen door. When all she did was gasp and look at me like I'd stolen her last cookie, I said, "Figures."

"You are ghoul? Like me?"

"Ghoul?"

That was the first time I'd heard the word used to describe what I was.

Not like I needed one before. Nobody was ever gonna ask, "So, what do you do for a living?" What was I gonna say, chef de cuisine for vamps?

"Ghoul," Valerica repeated, her turn to remove the knife from her shoulder. She wiped the stained blade on the sleeve of her blouse, adding to the layers of dirt and grime. "Those who help the undead. That is why you killed my Victor. For your undead mistress."

"I tried to tell you—"

"In old country, ghouls eat the dead." Valerica shook her head. "But that is not true."

I pursed my lips. "I could've told you that. Lots about your country's beliefs ain't true."

"But," she lowered her head. "We do ghoulish things. You for your mistress. Me for Victor."

"You mean he's . . . around?"

She pointed toward the floor. "Sleeping now. Under house."

I immediately ran outside and searched behind the wooden lattice covering the part of the house that was raised from the ground. I didn't have to search for long. The smell of rot and earth led me right to his resting spot. So, it wasn't my nose playing tricks. From the shadow under the house, I could tell he was no longer that fat, bloated thing who I'd done business with a few months ago. He lay there, stiff and still, stanking like all get out.

The attacks Nate heard about were these two? And how did Simone not see this?

"How long he been under there?" I asked Valerica, who'd followed me outside.

"Week," she said.

I fanned the air in front of me and stood up. "A week? And where you been?" She pointed to the woods directly behind the house. I wanted to scream for Simone and ask her how she missed these two fools right here under our noses. When I shot her the thought, I got nothing back, probably because she was so engrossed in whatever line Norquist was feeding her at the moment.

"You can't wait that long to feed him," I told Valerica. "That's why he smell so bad."

"But I cannot give him anymore." She adjusted her clothes to reveal faded bite marks on her arms, legs, and neck. According to her, when animal blood couldn't satisfy Victor and hunting people got them nearly killed, she let him nibble on her. No wonder she looked so bad. As weak as she was, he wasn't giving her time to heal. Even her stab wound still bled. The crimson sphere on her blouse continued to grow, sending a blood trail down to her waist.

"That's why you came here? You were gonna feed me to him?" I asked.

"You owe us!"

"You're right," I said, causing Valerica's brow to crinkle in confusion. "We did you wrong. I was only lookin' to feed Victor to Simone so you wouldn't have to be so scared of him all the time. But that ain't how it went, and I'm sorry. Took both your lives from you, knowin' how you felt about vamps. Simone should've told me you two were still alive. I would've helped you. But you're here now. So, we gotta make things right."

Valerica studied the ground as if searching for her words . . . or was shocked that I agreed with her. Her lips moved, but nothing came out, like she was rehearsing what to say next.

Then her head popped up. With her finger pointed at my face, she said, "You ruin our lives!"

"I jus' said so, Valerica." I swatted her hand away. "Look, if you wanna be honest, you and Victor were tryin' to ruin our lives first. You wanted to stake Simone and had the nerve to tell Mrs. Wiltshire I was stealin' from her."

"Did you not? Jane and John are dead, yes? And now this is all yours. The Wiltshires. Nosferatu eat them, too?"

"They died." Though I didn't think I owed her an explanation, I was glad I could say that with a straight face.

Valerica folded her arms. "They are nosferatu now!"

"They ain't nothin' but dead, Valerica."

"You will make this right, Lavinia!"

"I already said I would. I can teach you how to hunt for Victor so he can stop feedin' off you."

Valerica seemed to shrink into herself as her eyes and voice softened. "You will help?"

I wasn't lying about helping them. I'd done what I had to do to save Simone. Valerica was only doing the same for her husband. All they needed was some training. Since her predicament now matched mine, I didn't have to worry about her going to anybody about me.

I placed an arm on her shoulder and guided her back to the house. "You can stay here with us—"

Valerica stopped in her tracks and shook her head. "Stay in house with vamp? Victor would never—"

"He can keep his stankin' butt out here if that'll make him feel better."

"You want to make me feel better? Kill your nosferatu."

"The Wiltshires ain't vamps," I reminded her.

"Not Wiltshires. Your vamp-girl."

"That ain't happenin' Valerica. You know that."

"In old country, when nosferatu dies, all goes back to normal. You kill vamp-girl," she ran her finger across her throat, "and everything fine."

I cocked my mouth to the side. "That makes no sense. What do you mean by 'back to normal'? Normal for them is dead. You sayin' you want Victor dead?"

She winced and rubbed her temple.

"Yeah," I said with a snort. "You want him dead. You thinkin' 'bout it right now."

Valerica stomped her foot, but the silence of it against the grass killed the effect. "You said you'd help me!"

"I will," I said calmly. "I jus' ain't doin' that. What else you want?"

Her face hardened. Jaws set and eyes narrowed, she said, "One day. You have one day to kill vamp."

Got her nerve! Valerica was barely a whisper of her old self, standing here, yet she was threatening me? If a knife to the shoulder didn't cause me to pause, what did she think she could do?

"Or what?" I ventured to ask. "You gonna get your friends to come after us? How you gon' explain where you been since the fire? What about Victor? You gonna introduce them to the new him?" I extended my arm toward the kitchen door. "Better yet, why don't you g'on in there and stake her yourself? She sittin' up there in the parlor with a preacher man. Tell him why you're stabbin' her in the heart."

Poor woman looked like she was about to come outta her skin. Her fists were balled up at her side. And with what little blood she had left crimsoning her cheeks, she almost looked healthy. An exasperated sigh rumbled out of her mouth. "No! She's your vamp. She did this and you owe! No one knows me here. I tell town you kill Wiltshires and steal their house. I tell who vamp-girl really is. You know they believe whatever I tell them."

This again. And with those words, she knew she had me over a barrel.

"And what about Victor? Why I gotta kill my vamp when yours is out here doin' the same thing? What's to stop me from goin' back out to Miller Station and tellin' those nuts about you?"

As if she were in my brain, Valerica said, "They will not listen to you."

Facing me, she walked toward the thick greenery. The shadows from the overhanging canopies of maple, cottonwood, and catalpa trees darkened her retreating frame. "One day, Lavinia. Either vamp-girl dies, or you will."

Martin stands at the open door of the jail. Charlotte has returned without her uncles, for now. Either she doesn't want to come inside the jail, or Martin is preventing her. I'm hoping for the latter. A cool evening breeze blows in, shooting past the bars of my cell and rushing out the little barred window. I smell rain in the air. I wonder, will the uncles come for me in a rainstorm?

"You're not very bright, are you?" he asks, looking out into the night. "The longer you tell this story, the more you incriminate yourself. Seems like you had plenty of reasons to kill Miss Arceneau. Protecting the fishmonger. Protecting the house and tavern you stole."

"I didn't steal the tavern," I remind him. "Check the deed. Wiltshire signed it over to Simone."

"After you bled him to death!"

"Do you hear yourself?" I ask. I wrap my hands around the bars and press my face between the gaps. "You can't be convinced I'm guilty without acceptin' everything about my story. If you believe I killed Simone to keep the house and saloon, then you gotta believe I had that conversation with Valerica, a woman who supposedly died in a fire."

"That doesn't mean—"

"And," I say louder, "you gotta believe that Simone was really a vamp. Otherwise, what reason would I have to do what Valerica wanted me to do? So, which is it? You believe me or not?"

Martin sighs. "It doesn't matter if I believe you or not."

"And you'd let an innocent woman hang?"

He says nothing for a moment. Only stares ahead for a good while. I leave him be. Maybe he is finally putting the pieces together. Maybe he does believe I don't deserve to die because I didn't kill Simone and is just too weak to do anything about it. Doubt he's ready to admit that it's not Simone who has the strongest thirst for blood in these parts.

Charlotte whispers something in his ear that causes him to nod. One last look out into the darkness and he follows the girl to the desk. Pulls the chair out for her and they whisper again as she sits. Wonder how long she plans on staying this time? Until her uncles come?

He turns and paces around his desk. "Let's say I believe your story. All of it. That would mean you're still not as innocent as you'd like for me to believe. You may not have wielded the weapon—the fangs or whatever. But you were an accomplice. If not for you, Miss Arceneau would have never killed all those people."

Charlotte frowns. "Miss Arceneau killed somebody?"

"She would've killed whether I helped her or not. At least with me, she was more discriminatin', and not jus' feedin' on the first thing her eyes fell on. This jail would've been stock full of crooks, abusers, and the like if it wasn't for us. Culled the herd, so to speak, to give upstandin' folks like you space to live in peace."

Martin continues to pace. "Why choose you then? She told you she was tired of living when you met in that saloon."

"I don't know, but I can tell you what I was tired of: them damn Raduts. If they only left us alone, none of the rest of this story would've happened."

"You mean you wouldn't have killed Miss Arceneau?"

He must think if he says I killed Simone enough times that I'll slip up and confess. Won't happen. Her death wasn't by my hands.

"Think what you want," I finally say. My mouth is dry. And I'm tired. Not sleepy tired. Weary from being disappointed in folks. Simone, the Raduts, Martin. Even thinking about them wears me down. Maybe dawn will be my time to finally go.

"You got nothing to say now?" Martin asks. He turns to his lady friend. "Been yapping all night and now she's got nothing to say."

I plop down on the cot and stretch out. Lay my hands on my stomach like a corpse. "I'm tired. And besides, your little girlfriend is here. Don't wanna interrupt your romp."

"Thought ghouls didn't get tired."

"You got selective memory, Martin? Doesn't matter. I'm tired of tellin' this story. Whatever I say, you jus' gon' keep sayin' I killed her. What difference does it make?"

Martin settles himself at my cell. "Well . . . What happened to the Wiltshires?"

"They dead. You know that already."

"And the Raduts?"

"They dead, too."

He lowers his voice. "You didn't tell me that part."

I hear liquid sloshing around in a container he's taken from the picnic basket Charlotte brought earlier. I look over and see Martin shaking half a bottle of some brown liquor.

"Split it with you," he says.

"You bribin' me?"

"Maybe?"

I stand and take the offering. "You'll be three sheets to the wind 'fore I get to the end of this story."

"Well, damn! How much more is there to it?"

"Oh, there's more."

TWENTY-EIGHT

I half expected to see Simone standing in the kitchen once Valerica left. But she'd been so busy with Norquist to hear anything we talked about. Probably why she didn't know Victor had come back. I guess it's a good thing Simone missed that part. She couldn't stand the Raduts and learning that they weren't dead and were threatening to take everything away from us, again, might've led to a bloodbath right then and there. Plus, I didn't want her throwing this back in my face. The less she knew, the better.

The situation kept rushing through my mind. Valerica's threat ringing in my ears caused a headache almost as bad as my ghoul head pains. I paced in the kitchen and wrung my hands. The scent of Victor's rotting corpse stuck in my nose. If I could smell him in the house, could Norquist? Would anybody else coming by? What if that thing woke up and attacked us in the night? I could drag him out in the sunlight and get this over with right now. But how was I gonna explain a body burning in the backyard? And that still wouldn't stop Valerica from blaming me for the Wiltshires' deaths.

Gotta think. I walked out the front door so Simone would see me leave—not that she was paying attention anyway. Slammed the door just to make a point. As soon as I stepped onto the porch, I heard lively band music in the distance. My ears led me to a grove near the town's Lutheran church. Red, white, and blue banners were tied around every tree trunk. The place was awash with American flag–inspired frocks and touring hats. Tricolor bands adorned cream-colored straw boaters atop the heads of every male in attendance. Had it not been for the fashion show, I would've never known that it had been almost a hundred years since America got its freedom from England. Not that it made much difference to me. Funny that the only born-and-bred American in the house—including the creature underneath it—was me. Yet even they had way more rights in this country than I did. But on this day, everybody in Tolleston was out celebrating. Good thing, too. Gave me a chance to work through my problems and eyeball potential victims all at once.

I decided to blend into the crowd, as much as I could, that is. Found a catalpa tree with its large fanlike leaves and long, green, cigar-shaped hanging pods to lean against near where the five-piece brass band played. Flashes of sunlight popped against their gleaming instruments as they moved. People-watching had become a hobby, whether I was searching for Simone's next meal or not. Since my own life was less than normal, I enjoyed imagining the lives of others.

You'd think with there being so few Negroes in town, that my eye-balling would draw attention. It never did. I wondered if these folks chose to ignore me or didn't even see me. In the old South, folks seemed to go out of their way to point out I was a Negro, as if I didn't know that. Up here, their indifference was almost as bad. Either way, it worked to my advantage. On this day, folks flocked to me like kids to a creek on a summer afternoon. Regulars to the saloon touched the brim of their hats and nodded as they walked past. Women stopped to ask after Simone. I wasn't used to all this attention. When folks start recognizing you—and the vamp about to eat them—it's probably time to move on.

I thought the July heat was getting to me when I spied King in the distance. A small, slender woman with straight, jet-black hair almost down to her waist stood next to him. One of his mama's people no doubt. Though it had been more than a few months since I'd seen him last, jealousy struck me like a thunderbolt. But only for a second. He stopped and stared in my direction as I had brief conversations with five people. Granted, we were talking about Simone, but King wouldn't know that. The fact that I appeared important was all that mattered. Finally, I got my pride back. Didn't have to wallow in the memory of him kicking me out, of the look of fear and disgust on his face when I last saw him. It would be his curious expression of "How does she know all these people" that I'll take with me to bed every night.

Then he nodded, touched the brim of his newsboy cap, and smiled. At me.

Next thing I know, his beautiful face was only feet from mine.

"Evening, Lavinia," he said.

My lips could only return the smile.

"Looking mighty fine, I should say."

Yes, you should, I thought to myself. Mrs. Wiltshire had tossed out the two tattered dresses I owned and insisted on clothing me in what she'd deemed "appropriate attire." What she probably thought was plain fare were like ball gowns to me. With her gone, I had a closetful of nice frocks at my fingertips that only needed some taking in.

He stepped closer, removed his cap, and tilted his head downward. "You probably don't want to hear this . . . wouldn't blame you if you didn't . . . but . . . I want to apologize for the way I acted when, uh . . ."

"Simone," I finally said. "When she came to your place, and you told me to get the hell out."

"Right." He rubbed the back of his neck. "I came by . . . but you were no longer in the dugout."

"Got a job here in Tolleston," I told him with my chin lifted. "Givin' me room and board."

"So I heard." He must have seen my face because he quickly added, "I asked around." He smiled again. "I never come to these celebrations, for obvious reasons. But I was hoping you might."

Really? "Why is that?" I asked, faking disinterest.

His eyes fluttered as if my question had caught him off guard. "Like I said, I wanted to apologize."

"And now you have."

My shoulders relaxed. Guess that was the closure I needed. I started to turn around and go back home, but King was still standing there looking at me and fiddling with the brim of his hat.

"Lavinia, wait."

Since I really had nowhere to be at the moment and the thought of watching Simone's courting session turned my stomach, I let curiosity get the best of me.

"That's not the only reason why I wanted to see you. I didn't realize how lonely it was out there until you left."

I turned my head away and smiled. Couldn't help it. I nodded toward the woman he'd been standing with. "Looks like you cured your loneliness."

King turned and waved to the woman. "My mother's been visiting for a spell. She wasn't excited about coming out here either. I might have mentioned you to her."

"Did you, now?" I leaned in closer. "You include Simone in that description?"

He cleared his throat. "About that. My brain couldn't process what my eyes were seeing. But you've never lied to me. Never said anything that wasn't true. I'm sorry I didn't give you the chance to explain."

I raised an eyebrow. "So, you're fine with . . . that Simone is . . . different."

"I saw what I saw. Nothing's going to change that. But maybe, I could call on you one day and you could explain it a bit more."

Call on me? Our last exchange still stung, but I'd been so caught up in the Wiltshire drama that I rarely had time to think about it. When I did, the wound reopened. Wasn't no amount of sweet gum tincture that could ease that pain. Diving into work was my salve. But now he knows. Had seen with his own eyes what Simone was. What more was there for him to know?

"I'd like that," I finally said. Hell, if Simone can go courting, why can't I?

He stepped even closer. I closed my eyes and inhaled the calming scent of the beach wafting from him. I wanted to wrap my arms around him and hold him close to me. He took my hand and smiled again; one deep dimple sunk into his cheek. I held my breath as I bit the corner of my bottom lip.

"I best get on home," I said, wanting to end this moment on a high note.

King's face registered disappointment. "So soon?"

"I was jus' comin' to clear my head. I got no interest in what they're doin' here either. They celebratin' a hundred years of freedom, but had us in chains for more than that. Looks like I got a special treat runnin' into you."

"Can I see you home?"

He could see me to the moon and back if he liked. I leaned to the side, glancing at the woman he'd left beside a tree. "What about your mama?"

He tucked my arm in the crook of his. "How about I introduce you to her?"

The three of us strolled leisurely to my house. King's mama was a little thing, about the same size as Simone. I first thought she looked much too young to be King's mother. Though her skin was as smooth as caramel, strings of wisdom and age had settled at the corners of her eyes. I told them all about working at the Wiltshires', about their death, and how their niece had come to live in the house and take over the saloon.

"This sounds like a much better setup for you. You know, than before." King mused. I pressed my lips into a tight smile and nodded yes. Been lying so much lately, it almost came as naturally as breathing. I knew when King came calling he'd see that Simone was still in the picture, but heck, this moment ain't about her. Let me enjoy it while it lasts. I'd figure out the rest later.

By the time we reached my house, fireflies were dancing up a storm in my front yard. Dusk had settled, signaling a chorus of crickets to join the band music I could still hear in the distance. I stood on the back porch, waving goodbye to King and his mama. He'd promised to bring over a fresh piece of fish tomorrow afternoon. That would give me enough time to figure out what to do with Simone when he came to call. She hadn't rested in days, thanks to Norquist. I wouldn't be surprised if he came by again tomorrow. But that would be a plus. When I come clean about her—I mean *really* come clean this time—King would see that she could act normal, that he wasn't in any danger around her.

And I'm sure Simone would care less about him now that Norquist got her nose open.

Soon as I walked through the back door, I noticed the whole house was dark and quiet. The weak evening sun cast an ochre shade over the kitchen, not even a lamp or candle had been lit in the whole place. A hint of rot bit the air. I closed the back door slowly, listening for the locking mechanism to latch. Couldn't do nothing about the floorboards creaking beneath my feet.

As dark as it was in the house, I was certain Norquist had long since left. But Simone and I hadn't been hunting in a week. I closed my eyes and braced myself as I inched down the narrow hallway toward the parlor. For a second, I was pissed, thinking that if Simone was in there feasting on the reverend, I'd have to spend the whole night and the next day cleaning up the mess instead of readying myself for King's visit.

Or worse. What if the Raduts had gotten ahold of her?

In the hallway right outside the kitchen, I found some matches in a side table drawer and lit the hurricane lamp I'd been carrying. Shadows on the walls scurried from the lamp's low flame. I should have gone to see if Victor was still under the house, but I went to the parlor first to check for a dead preacher. Simone stood in the middle of the parlor. With the drapes drawn, she was barely visible in the lamplight.

"Are we really doing this again, Lavinia?"

I extended the lamp out in front of me and swept the room for a body. "Where's Norquist?"

"He left a few minutes ago."

Relief. The tension in my shoulders melted as I set the hurricane lamp on a nearby side table. Then I went to the front door and secured the lock.

Simone didn't move. "You didn't answer my question."

"Are we really doing what?" I walked around the parlor, checking the corners. But I hesitated going near Simone. Her odd demeanor had me on edge. Was Norquist under the sofa? Had she thrown him down into the root cellar? Did she know about the Raduts?

"You were with him. I saw you."

"You talkin' 'bout King?" An incredulous snort left my nose. "You got your hackles up over him? That's it?"

"Why were you with him?" Her voice was loud and heavy.

"Saw him at the Fourth of July picnic in the grove by the church. He was out there with his mama."

"And you brought him here? You're going to allow him to call on you here? Does he know I'm still around?"

"He didn't ask after you. 'Sides, Norquist calls on you," I pointed out, fists balled up on my hips. "You don't see me raisin' sand over it."

Simone took a step closer to me. Whispers of rot coming from her told me she really hadn't eaten Norquist. Can't imagine somebody itching to sit up in this hot box for hours smelling that.

"He never sent me running with my tail between my legs. You're willing to lose all of this over a man who dropped you quicker than a hot potato?"

"That was you! You messed up what we had goin' on in the dunes. Nobody told you to come over to his place that night. If you'd've kept your behind in your box—"

"You always do this!" Simone stomped her foot against the floor. "You run after these humans and forget all about me. I'm not going to let this happen again!"

"I forget about you? You don't say two words to me when Norquist comes by here! How you gon' tell me I can't be with humans when you spend all your waking hours with one?" I paced the room, my breaths coming out in pants. Something welled up in my chest. "You never want me to be happy, Simone. All my time is spent lookin' for your food and cleanin' up after you. The few times I get to myself, you start bitchin'."

"You get the whole day to yourself!" Simone spat out. "No telling what you're doing while I sleep. You think I stay awake for Norquist? It's because I don't trust that you won't leave me to rot in this place!"

My eyes widened. "You so big on trust, I don't see you tellin' Norquist what you really are. Sittin' up here every day actin' like you're human when you won't even let me be one!"

"You want to talk about trust?" Simone asked. "Did you tell King about the Wiltshires? About me? That I'm still around? That if he wants you, he'll have to take me as well?"

"That ain't the point, Simone."

"That *is* the point. He went sour on you then, he'll go sour on you again. They all do. They could care less about whether the things they say or do will hurt you in the end. Don't be stupid like I was."

I waved her off. "Pfff. This about that priest again, that Henri fella? Girl, he's probably long dead by now. Why you lettin' what he did to you live so long?"

"Because he hurt me!"

"How you expect me to see things your way when you holdin' all this stuff so close? Now, I ain't gonna do a damn thing 'bout King unless you tell me what happened with you and the priest."

Simone huffed and plopped herself down on the sofa. Was kinda glad because she looked about near to bursting, standing there, fuming. I don't know why I asked. I had no idea if the story she would tell would be the truth, a piece of the truth, or what she wanted to be the truth. With her being awake most days, I could take a gander into her memories and see for myself. But I guessed whatever it was had to be something so awful, she'd buried it under a bunch of lies. Each concocted story giving her more distance from the truth. I'd hear her out tonight then go fishing later.

Simone lowered her head. "Okay, okay. I haven't been as forthright with you as I should have been."

"You don't say," I said, rolling my eyes. I walked over to the fireplace and rested my arm on the stone mantel.

"I'm sorry about the other day. I'm not from Montreal. I'm from New Orleans. My family did own a plantation there with about a hundred slaves. I had three of my own. Lucy had been with me since I was a little girl." Simone chuckled at the memory. "Were practically sisters, like you and me."

She looked up at me and said, "You remind me a lot of her. Anyway. Father Henri was really our parish priest, and I did fall in love with him. Everyone did. I went to confession every single day, thinking of more outrageous lies to tell so I could have him to myself for a moment."

Well, that explained why she was so good at switching up her stories. No wonder we were such a good match.

"One day I confessed my feelings for him. He told me that our being together could never be. He was a priest after all. His vow of celibacy prevented him from being with any woman. And I respected that. He wasn't really rejecting me. It was the Church's fault. So, I prayed to God that He would release Father Henri from his vow."

She gave a pained smile and swallowed hard. "And would you believe that God answered my prayer?"

I leaned forward. "He did? That's a good thing, right?"

Simone slowly shook her head. "Not if releasing him meant I would catch him having his way with Lucy . . ." She turned her head away, shoulders slumped. "Father Henri came by a few days later saying he wanted to buy Lucy. I never told Papa the real reason why. I . . . The look on Lucy's face when she was carted away. Like I was sending her to the guillotine, but it was too late."

"Too late?" The heaviness of her confession weighed on my furrowed brow. I didn't have to probe Simone's mind to recognize the fear and despair on poor Lucy's face. Had seen it when they carted away my mama and everyone else I'd grown to love. "You could've said somethin'." My fingernails dug into clenched fists at my side. "Could've stopped him if you wanted to."

Simone's lip curled in disgust. "And do what, live with the knowledge of him going after her every time he came to call, that he preferred her over me?"

"Jus' 'cause you was mad at him didn't mean Lucy deserved to never see her family again."

"I realize that. My life wasn't the same without Lucy." Simone's distant gaze settled on the floor. "I trusted her with everything, even my feelings about Father Henri. He destroyed us both."

She turned to me and said, "So, you see why I cannot allow you and King to be together. I'm not that young girl anymore, Lavinia. I won't see King condemn you to a life of unhappiness like Father Henri did to me, piquing your interest when it suits him."

"Still . . ."

"I did try to make it right," Simone added quietly. "After I was turned, I set Lucy free. King will meet Father Henri's fate if he darkens the door of this house." She stood and whispered in my ear. "Try me, Lavinia. I haven't eaten in a week. Try me and see what happens."

I let her walk away. Listened to the steps whine beneath her feet as she ascended the stairs. Three bedrooms in this house and she insisted on sleeping beneath my bed with that singed burlap sack. Why would I think she'd sleep anywhere else after all that? Was it love for me or flexing her vamp muscles? I sat on the sofa. I didn't believe this had anything to do with King. Simone didn't want me with anybody. Had killed the Wiltshires because I wasn't spending enough time with her. This girl was impossible. I wonder if she purposely didn't tell me about the Raduts as some kind of test, to see if I would choose them again over her.

The memory of Valerica's ultimatum straightened my back. With a lit candle in my hand, I dashed out of the kitchen door. I located the space under the house where Victor still lay, unmoved since I saw him last. My ears trained for movement in the night air. The crack of a twig, a rustle of branches from the wind—or a body moving through them— sent my head swiveling in all directions. Evening had long since settled, and I half expected to see Valerica strolling through the woods to wake her husband and have her revenge. But she never did. For most of the night I kept watch over the corpse, mulling over two ultimatums, neither of which had a good ending for me.

TWENTY-NINE

With so much on my mind that night, I walked out onto the porch, praying a Radut wouldn't greet me there.

My feet took me down the steps, into the yard. Before I knew it, I was at the saloon. A lone patron nursed a glass at one of the tables as Nate swept around him. I sat at the bar, head in my hands. I hadn't stopped thinking of my dilemma, which caused another dilemma of Simone hearing me if she wasn't asleep. At this point, I didn't care. Maybe she'd take pity on my predicament and offer a solution. I snorted out a laugh. Troubleshooting wasn't in Simone's wheelhouse, far as I knew.

Glass setting down on wood brought me out of my misery. Nate poured us both a drink. We stood there looking at each other for the longest time. Eyes narrowed like two gunslingers waiting for the other to draw first. We swallowed down that whiskey at the same time, our gaze trained on each other.

"You wanna talk?" he asked, setting up our next round. "Seems like you got some weight on you."

I shook my head. "You wouldn't understand."

Nate slung his wiping rag over his shoulder and leaned on the bar. "Try me."

I shrugged. "Why the hell not." I raised my glass and polished that one off. Unfortunately, I'd learned that being a ghoul meant it'd take more than a couple of drinks to get me to any happy place. And I wasn't ready to go back to that house and my problems anytime soon. I tapped the glass with my finger. "I got folks blackmailin' me."

After he filled it again, he wiped the few stray drops of whiskey from the bar with his ever-present cloth. "I know the feeling."

"Oh, yeah," I held my glass in midair. "Your daddy." Trust. Always with the trust. Seems like everybody I try to give it to takes it and stomps on it. I swallowed my drink and placed the glass back on the bar. I tapped the rim again. He angled the bottle down toward my glass but was stingy with letting the amber liquid fall.

After he downed his, he suddenly stood straight and looked at the door. I followed his frown and saw Valerica entering the saloon. I closed my eyes and knocked my glass against the bar for another refill as she took a seat next to me.

"You drink here?" Valerica asked.

"I ain't in the mood for your shit tonight, Valerica." I avoided Nate's glare, not wanting to hear how unladylike I was with the language. "It ain't been a day yet."

"This I know," Valerica said. She pointed to the glass in my hand. "I want what she has."

Nate looked at me and raised an eyebrow. I nodded and he poured her a drink as I swallowed mine. Valerica sat there staring at hers for a good while.

"You gon' drink that or what?" I asked.

"This is your place, right?"

"Simone's place," I corrected her while watching Nate wipe the spotless bar.

"And you have no problems, yes?"

"Not 'til you walked in here. What you want? Where's Victor?"

She cupped the drink between her hands and lowered her head. "I tell you already. Under house. I not wake him."

I huffed and turned to her. "And I told you," I said under my breath, "you can't jus' leave him like that. What if he wakes up on his own?" I leaned closer to her. "He'll eat half the town like that."

"Him I cannot control," Valerica said, her eyes still on the drink she hadn't touched. "You said you will help me, yes? You will help . . . get rid of Victor?" She winced like somebody had stabbed the right side of her head.

"Shh!" I hissed. I leapt from the barstool and dragged Valerica to the far side of the bar where Nate and the lone patron wouldn't hear. "What's wrong with you? I know you want me lynched, but damn! You want Victor hearin' you talk like that?"

Valerica frowned. "How will he hear?" She glanced around the saloon. "He's not here."

"Can't he hear you?"

"I don't understand."

"Never mind."

I guess it's a good thing they couldn't tap into each other's minds. They had enough stupid ideas on their own. Didn't need them putting two stupid ideas together. Though Simone and I had discovered the mental connection by accident, the Raduts were so self-centered that I was sure they'd never stumble on it themselves. I felt a little sorry for Valerica; bound to that disagreeable fool forever. Well, she picked him.

She must've read my mind.

"You say you will help." She was clutching my hands in hers. "That you owe. Help me get rid of him!" Valerica punctuated her words with her hands by yanking at mine, but stopped and winced again. This time an audible groan left her mouth.

"I told you I could teach you how to feed him. We could work together; kill two birds with one stone, so to speak. We ain't gotta be enemies, Valerica. We can make this work for both of us."

"I want to go home," Valerica said. "Home to Marotinu. This, all this, is Victor's fault." Then she seemed to shrink into herself. "I only want to go home."

She started to sob. Only thing I could think to do was hold her. She fell into my arms and wept on my shoulder. Poor woman. If only I hadn't run after her that day. I could've stopped Simone before she drained him, let the man die, and then go after Valerica later. I could've explained everything when she was calmer, when she could process her freedom. I messed that up. This wasn't Victor's fault. It was mine.

I patted her back. "You sure that's what you want, Valerica?"

She sniffed and raised her head. "Yes." She squeezed her eyes closed and pressed her palm against her forehead. "And the headaches. They make me want to die."

Right then, Victor burst into the saloon looking like a chewed-up piece of graying meat. For a moment, I thought Valerica had set me up with that little display of hers. The vamp snarled and growled. Before I knew what was happening, he pounced on the half-drunk patron faster than you could say "Jumping Jehoshaphat," and tore his throat out. Blood spurted everywhere. Victor slipped and slid on the mess with his fangs cemented in his prey.

Valerica grabbed my arm and shouted, "Victor! No!"

Nate remained behind the bar, a look of puzzlement on his face. He didn't say nothing as he paused in the middle of wiping the bar down. If Nate had any suspicions about us, old stupid ass Victor proved them.

I ain't never been so scared in my life.

What could I do?

Didn't matter, because before I could gather my thoughts, Nate emerged from behind the bar with that two-by-four of his and cracked Victor upside his head with a swing that whistled as it split the air. That stunned the vamp for a minute. Then Victor turned his sights on Nate. Even confronted with blood dripping from a pair of unnaturally long eyeteeth and a growl that didn't sound human at all, the bartender didn't budge. He planted his feet, raised that board behind his head, and swung so hard that Victor went sailing over to the other side of the saloon. His fat behind landed on a chair, shattering it to pieces.

Nate tossed the two-by-four on the floor like a spent rifle. "Get your man," he said evenly to Valerica like he was telling her to fetch a bucket of water. He stomped over to the splintered chair and grabbed two of the legs that had snapped into short, jagged spears. With a leg in each hand, he added, "Or I'm staking his ass to the floor."

I didn't know what was crazier: Victor's attack or Nate's reaction to it. I mean, the man wasn't even breathing hard after all of that.

Victor got his bearings and located his wife cowering behind me. The creature seemed surprised she was even there. They got to fussing in their language, their voices rising with each trilled phrase. Not once did Valerica try to leave her safe space. As their argument progressed, Victor stepped closer and closer, his arms waving in the air like he was beating away flies. He got close enough to reach behind me for his wife.

But his fangs found my neck instead.

The whole place went silent. Time slowed as Valerica raged behind Victor; her hands covering her mouth in horror. My head cracked against something hard. The tin corrugated roof in my view, I realized Victor had knocked me down. I couldn't feel anything; not my arms, what should be pain in my neck. Nothing. Then he was off me. Had he fed? Gotten his fill after feeding on the patron? Did Valerica finally gain control of him?

I rolled onto my side and wrapped my hand around the wound on my neck. Hot liquid poured through my fingers. I gasped, attempting to get back up. When I managed to get on my knees, I saw Nate pounding the life outta Victor with his two-by-four. The two stakes he had in his hand were embedded in Victor's back. Then my stomach wrenched and thick, green snot poured from my mouth. When it was all out of me, only the patron and Nate, on his knees at my side, remained.

With Nate's help, I stood and caught my breath. "Where is he?"

"Hightailed it out of here with that woman."

I scanned the room and groaned. "And you let him leave?"

"I thought your bleeding all over the floor was a more pressing matter." Then Nate backed away from me. "Your wound." He pointed the two-by-four he'd retrieved at my neck. "It's gone."

With my bloodstained hand, I touched my neck, knowing his observation was true. I surveyed the place. The saloon was a wreck. There was a body-sized crack and dent in the wall where Victor had landed. Tables and chairs had been knocked over. Blood was sprayed on almost every wall. Not to mention the half-dead man lying there in the middle of it all. The drunk had covered his own neck wound with his hand, but it only meant blood was running everywhere through his fingers. All he could do was lay there on his back in a bright red pool, wheezing through his mouth like he'd finished running a mile. At least he wasn't dead yet.

"What was that?" Nate asked as he flung his weapon over his shoulder.

"Somethin' that shouldn't be walkin' the earth."

"And you? How'd you heal so fast?"

"I . . ." My head was spinning so much, the only words I could think of were *I was bitten by a vampire*. But I wasn't in the mood to give a lesson on the undead at the moment. "I can heal faster than normal people."

He aimed the piece of wood at the man wheezing in the middle of the floor. "What about him?"

I walked over to the now-silent man. His wide eyes had finally frozen open in death as if asking for the release his mouth couldn't. I shook my head at the large pool of blood around his head. The only bright spot in this mess: flowing blood meant he wouldn't turn. I knelt down and touched the dead man's shoulder. "Ain't nothin' we can do for him now."

"Michigan Central'll be by within the hour," Nate said, his eyes toward the door. "Lay him over the tracks. Train'll take care of the rest. Anybody comes looking for him, it'll look like some drunk had an accident."

I stood there stunned. That plan rolled so easily off his tongue that it sounded like it was something he'd done before.

"What're you waiting for, an invitation?" Nate asked, kneeling beside the man's head. "Grab his feet."

Without thinking, I obeyed. Nate and I carried the man out behind the saloon. Didn't need a lantern to find the tracks since the moon was so bright. I felt kind of bad leaving him there. This was different than all the other victims I'd disposed of. I never thought twice about them after the feeding. But this attack wasn't planned. I didn't know anything about the man except he was in the wrong place at the wrong time and that it was at least partly my fault. I knew what happened to a hungry vamp after laying up for days on end. I knew Victor was crazy and Valerica was terrible at her job.

"You mind telling me what all that was back there?"

Nate's question startled me, breaking the night sounds I'd gotten so used to.

"You tell me," I said, dropping the man's feet on the ground. I stood and stretched my back. "How'd you know about vampires and stakes and such?"

Nate followed suit, situating the man so that his neck rested upon a rail. Then he folded the corpse's arms across its chest. "Is that what you call them? Vampires? A soldier I knew from Louisiana called them something else. Can't remember what. Told us about a woman who stalked his regiment at night, biting the men while they slept."

A woman in Louisiana biting soldiers in their sleep? "Just bit at them?"

He shrugged. "I guess. He didn't describe it like what that man did to you. But I do remember him saying something about trying to stake her. We all thought he was making stuff up to get a discharge. Didn't give it another thought until tonight."

The truth about Simone was at the tip of my tongue. The comfort I felt with Nate at that moment forced it to the surface. And neither a thought nor Simone's voice poured forth telling me to do otherwise. The faint whistle of an approaching train redirected my attention back to the man on the tracks. Nate and I looked toward the east until the ground beneath us began to quiver.

Images flashed across my mind. Valerica running past sand dunes. The rushing of water, the lake, in the background. Angry, Romanian words. Victor's words. A wave of queasiness doubled me over as I tried focusing on Simone's thoughts. But they were absent. Only Victor's poured through as clear as the day was long. I could see even the sand beneath his feet as he ran.

Lord, kill me now.

"Nate, I gotta go."

"Are you okay?"

"I'll be fine once I get my hands on Victor."

He pointed to the man on the tracks. "What about him?"

"He ain't goin' nowhere. I need to take care of Victor once and for all."

I took a step away but then doubled back. "Do me a favor? Pay a call to my house in the mornin'. If I ain't there, know that Victor got me good and I'm either dead or turnin' into what he is. Tell Simone everything that happened tonight. Everything. Don't leave nothin' out. She'll understand. She'll know how to find me. When she tells you where I am, I need you to go there and do to me what you were gonna do to Victor with them stakes, hear?"

And with that, I sprinted away into the darkness using my mind's eye as a guide.

THIRTY

Of course, I found them on the beach in King's dugout. Why? Because this has been my day. My life. Would've been too easy for them to go back to my house in Tolleston or back to their burnt-out shop in Miller's Station. But no. Not only do I gotta get rid of these fools, I'm gonna be haunted by the fact that King was in there dead . . . or worse.

And, of course, Nate didn't do what I asked him to. As soon as I posted myself up on the old thinking dune, Nate was right beside me. He could've at least said something the whole time he was following me here. Or maybe he did and I was too busy fuming and trying to block out Victor's garble to hear him.

"Thought I told you to stay at the saloon."

"Funny," he said as he crouched beside me. "I don't remember having that conversation. What are we looking at?"

"That dugout there. Belongs to King Jones, the fishmonger. Victor and Valerica are in there right now. And if they're there . . ." I squeezed my eyes shut, trying to sort out Victor's thoughts and find King among the mess. But it was all I could do to keep my tears at bay. I refused to acknowledge what my heart knew to be true: King was most likely dead. Which kind of dead, I didn't know. Either one was bad. Either one would be my fault. Couldn't have Nate seeing me come apart, not after my inaction at the saloon. So, I stood and paced, one hand against my forehead and the other in the small of my back.

"Are you alright?" Nate asked.

"I'm fine!" I snapped. "I jus' gotta get my bearin's." That and to slow down the queasiness swelling in my gut. I looked over at the man who'd followed me to what might be his own death. "Sorry 'bout that, Nate. I jus' know somethin' awful done happened to King."

"How did you know they were here?"

"When Victor bit me, our minds got connected. I can see and hear everything he does. Good thing he ain't figured out how to do the same thing to me. If only he'd show me where King is so I can put the poor man outta his misery."

"If you're connected, can you only see what he's doing now, or can you look back and see what happened to the fishmonger?"

I turned my head toward Nate. He caught on awfully quick, accepting the craziness of the whole situation. King thought I was funning with him when I told him about Simone and vampires. Here I am, explaining only a piece of it to Nate and he didn't even flinch. I closed my eyes and focused on Victor's memories as I damn near wrung the skin off my hands. Nothing appeared but a convolution of images that didn't make any sense. A string of curses left my mouth when I didn't see King in any of them.

"His brain's a mess," I said. "I need to get in that dugout, find King, and end this connection with Victor."

"How do you do that?"

"Kill him, I guess."

We could hear the Raduts shouting from inside the dugout. Then they brought their discussion outside. I rose to my feet and started down the dune toward them. I picked up a piece of driftwood on my way, snapped it in two against my leg, and used my bare hands to break off extra pieces until I'd fashioned a couple of stakes. Then I stomped over to them with a stake in each hand. I walked right up behind Victor and cracked him over the head with one of the stakes. That only stunned him for a minute. With Valerica screaming bloody murder, Victor charged at me. This time I was ready for him. I dropped one of the stakes and held the other straight out in front of me with both hands. Drove it right into his body. Except I got him in the stomach, not the heart. I guess it *did* take some practice. Victor stumbled back, grunting and staring at the piece of wood sticking out from him. He roared, then yanked the thing out like it was a splinter in his thumb.

I knew that stake mess wouldn't work.

But then Victor lunged again and sent both of us to the ground before I could pick up the other stake. The weight of the vamp and the hardness of the sand knocked all the wind out of me. I reached up and grabbed Victor by the throat as his jaws snapped at the air in front of my face. With each of his attempts to bite me, my arms slowly gave way, bringing him ever closer to the mark. The rot seeping from his body suddenly filled my nostrils, causing me to gag and turn my face away.

I pushed. I kicked. I writhed on the ground to get him off me. If his goal was to kill me, he'd have to do more than drain me because I'd only come back and hunt these two down until kingdom come.

But then Victor's head snapped back and he fell off me. I scooted away to see Nate stepping over me with that two-by-four in his hands. He swung at Valerica and laid her out beside her husband. A long gash opened on her forehead, but quickly closed, leaving only a thin trail of blood down the middle of her face.

Panting, Nate turned to me and smiled. "You didn't think I was going to stay up there and watch, did you?"

Then Valerica jumped on his back, screeching and pulling on his hair like she was riding a horse. I ran behind them and yanked Valerica from Nate. When she turned to me, I saw the one thing that got my blood boiling. Around her neck was a cross that was bigger than the palm of my hand. A cross that someone had taken the time to carve fancy swirls and patterns into the creamy wood.

African white mahogany wood.

What's the worst thing Valerica had ever done? I had my answer.

I snatched the cross from her neck, pulling her whole body down into the sand. I grabbed her by the bun sitting atop her head. "Where'd you get this? This was King's cross! How'd you get it? Where is he?"

All I heard was a bunch of stuttering foolishness spewing from her mouth.

I dragged her in and around the dugout, all the while cursing her and calling for King. Hot, angry tears flowed down my cheeks as my search for him yielded nothing.

I had planned on setting her free, setting both of us free. Give her choices I never had. Send her back to Romania like she wanted. Here I was believing her—trusting her—when all she was worried about was protecting Victor. Seeing that cross around her neck changed it all. I didn't wanna hear her voice. Deep down, I was to blame. Everything, this whole mess, was my fault.

But I punched her in the mouth anyway. What I wanted now was to never see another Radut again in my life.

While Valerica was rubbing the pain from her face, I went to King's boat and grabbed some rope. I spied Nate walking over to Victor's body. The stake I'd dropped was in his hand. Was surprised the blow to Victor's head had stunned him so. But at least he was just lying there and not attacking anybody. When I returned from the boat, Valerica was still on her knees, pleading her case.

"What will you do to me?" Valerica said as I wound the rope tightly around her body.

"Settin' you free," I said.

I placed Valerica in King's boat then pushed it out into the lake. Valerica kept her eyes on me the whole time she drifted. I wonder if she knew what would happen once she got too far from shore, and her thoughts of being finally free of Victor grew stronger. If she did, her silence meant she either accepted this punishment or thought this was the end she wanted. Her definition of freedom. I don't know how ghouls died, but I hoped Valerica would go insane from the pain until Victor was dead-dead, her head literally exploded, or she'd jump from the boat and drown. Regardless, she'd be a distant memory to me, even if she managed to survive.

Victor!

I ran around to the other side of the dugout to find Victor straddling

Nate's chest. Bent over, the vampire's head bobbed up and down as he drew blood from the left side of Nate's neck. Slowly, I drove the stake in my hand into the base of his neck as a spray of blood exited his throat. He collapsed beside Nate, his mouth and eyes wide open and his curled claws frozen in midair. Finally, the creature was silent. The Raduts had told me all sorts of craziness about what happened to a vampire when it got staked. But Victor didn't disappear into a cloud of smoke or explode. He simply stopped. Guess killing the connection to the brain, and not the heart, killed the vamp. Cutting off the head didn't sound so bad after all.

I fell to my knees beside Nate and held his hand. His neck wound no longer bled but a small puddle of blood caked up in the sand near his head. I smoothed a tangle of curls away from his face and called his name, knowing he wouldn't answer.

"I'm so sorry, Nate."

For a night, he was the only person on this earth who knew what I was—believed what I was—and didn't judge me for it. Didn't think twice about coming to help me either. All this time, the friend I needed was right there in that saloon. With nothing but the rush of the lake behind me filling the air, I planted myself beside Nate's body. The darkness and all the death around me broke the dam in my soul. I stomped my feet against the sand and released my despair in the emptiness of the dunes. Screams clawed their way out of my throat as I beat the earth with my fists. Raged until I was just as empty as the beach. Then I held my knees against my chest and cried. Cried for Nate, for King, for every foolish decision I'd made since teaming up with Simone.

After my purge, I surveyed the chaos on the beach and gathered my thoughts. Needed to clean up before dawn so I wouldn't be caught walking through town with blood all over my blouse from when Victor bit me. I buried the dead vamp up to his neck in sand with his head facing east. If he wasn't dead, he would be when the sun rose. Took me a minute to drag Nate back to my old dugout and roll him into Simone's old hole. I stayed for a good while beside his grave, wishing he could hear how sorry I was for all of this. How I wished he hadn't waited so long to open up to me. Where would I be if I knew the real Nate before the Wiltshires died? But then again, forging a friendship with him would have only put him in Simone's sights. And King. The only reason they killed him was because of me. Valerica would've never known where he was had I not tried to lie about where I lived.

What's the worst thing I'd ever done? After tonight, I don't think I could pick only one.

Thirty-One

I arrived home at dawn. Against my better judgment, I took my time, my feet heavy with everything that had happened the night before. That last look on Nate's face was cemented in my mind. I'll never forget what he did for me. All this time, Simone had been talking about trust. At least now I knew what it really looked like.

So, I occupied my mind by reciting all those countries, continents, and bodies of water Simone had taught me a year ago. Then I started singing all the spirituals I could remember from the Sunday meetings we used to have at Miss Tillie's.

Back in Georgia, a man we all knew as old Brother Rufus once led the makeshift services we held out in the middle of a nearby grove, the only time we were allowed to go that far from the plantation. Brother Rufus would stand on a tree stump, Bible in hand, shouting and foaming at the mouth in the name of the Lord for three straight hours. Would get everybody in such a frenzy that nobody noticed how long we were there. Not that anybody was in any rush to get back to the plantation noway.

I never understood all that Bible talk. Comparing us to the Israelites enslaved in Egypt. Calling some woman Moses who led folks to freedom. If God was so good, what did He let all them people get enslaved for in the first place? Why'd He allow what was happening to us Negroes?

Why were there creatures like vamps in the world? I realized later that Brother Rufus was doing the best he could with scripture, on account he couldn't read it nohow. Wasn't his fault. He was only repeating Massa's nonsense about how we were to accept our circumstances because God had ordained it. The deliverance part must've come from Brother Rufus. I wasn't accepting nothing. Especially not after the night I had.

When I got back home, I drew some water from the Little Calumet River that ran through the Tolleston woods behind the house. Heated up five bucketfuls and poured them into the tin tub in the indoor outhouse. I sat in the soothing water for a good while, my mind shifting between Nate and King. Other than that tidbit Nate had told me about his parents, I didn't know if anyone would miss him, if he still kept in touch with his mama. What about King's poor mama? I'd doomed her to never knowing what happened to her son. And how on earth was I gonna tell Simone that we were no longer connected? All that thinking got my head to hurting and by then, the water had turned ice-cold and I still felt dirty.

Once I drained the tub, I went into the kitchen and grabbed a knife. Rolled up the sleeve of my blouse. I bit my bottom lip and braced for the possibility of pain. But I paused. How did I want this to turn out? If I was cured now that Victor was dead, would anything change? For so long, I'd credited my financial and social success to my peculiar condition. Being a ghoul who practically held the lives of the townsfolk in the palm of my hand led me to think I could do anything. A boldness I'd never imagined—from me, let alone any colored person—had grown like another limb. Could I still be this new, emboldened me as plain old Lavinia?

One deep breath and I slid the blade across my flesh. The pain was sharp and the wound didn't close. I shrieked, emotional from the mix of pain and realization that I was free. Really free. No tethers of any kind keeping me anywhere I didn't wanna be. But what to tell Simone? Did I want to tell her anything? The only way to resolve this was to come clean with Simone and tell her everything that happened with the Raduts, Nate, and King. Everything. Maybe if she knew what I'd gone through, she'd take pity on me.

Dressed in a clean frock and with a bandage wrapped around my forearm, I sat in the parlor to calm myself before going to clean up that mess at the saloon. I released a weary sigh. No way was I gonna get everything done today. And who was I gonna get to help work the saloon now?

"You're back." Simone inched into the room and sat on the sofa, leaving a large space between us. "Where were you?"

I lifted my injured arm and scratched my head. "At the saloon."

"Must have been busy last night. I couldn't get anything from you."

I was surprised she took a second from planning a future with Norquist to attempt digging around in my brain. Nice to know she didn't even notice my injury.

"We need to talk," I said, turning to her. "Some stuff happened yesterday—"

"Me first." Simone took my hands in hers. "What if you didn't have to hunt for me anymore?"

I snorted out a laugh. "What, now you wanna be all independent, too? We both know how that's gonna turn out."

"I mean ever."

"How's that? This got somethin' to do with Norquist comin' 'round here all the time?"

Simone stood and walked toward the dormant fireplace. She leaned against the stone mantel, quietly picking at her fingernails. "Do you think you would be happier if you and King worked out?"

My shoulders fell at the sound of his name. "Don't none of that matter no more."

"But had I not been—what I am—things would be different for you."

"Shoot, wouldn't be no King and me. I'd still be in Georgia in that saloon if you wasn't what you are."

Simone glanced down at the large, handspun rug in the middle of the floor. "I shouldn't be what I am."

I joined her at the mantel. Hot as it was in there, the coolness from the marble sent a chill up my spine. Or my body was sensing something off with this conversation. "Where's all this comin' from? Norquist over here plantin' nonsense in your head or somethin'?"

"It's not nonsense. All this time, we've been talking about redemption and forgiveness. That I could be cured!"

"What on earth d'you tell the man about yourself? He knows you're dead?"

"He knows my soul is dead. And he knows the cure for it."

I cocked my head to the side and raised an eyebrow. "Sounds more like some slick snake oil salesman than a preacher."

"If only you could hear him talk—"

"Oh, Simone! You sound 'bout as silly as the first time we met. That man can't make you any less dead."

She walked over to the bookcase and pulled out the large family Bible that had belonged to the Wiltshires. Fanciest thing they'd owned. It was about as big as the ones you see in churches and bound in white leather with gold curlicues all over the front. Even the page edges were gilded. "This says he can."

I waved her off. I'd actually been reading the Bible as I made my way around the Wiltshires' library. I don't recall nothing in scripture about healing no vamps. Either Norquist was feeding her a bunch of bull or she was hearing what she wanted to hear from him. "You talkin' nonsense now."

Simone flipped through the pages. "There used to be a time you cared about my happiness."

"I did . . . I do. Not so sure I can say the same thing 'bout you, though. You ain't even said nothin' about my arm here."

"Oh, Lavinia. Be happy for me now!" She slammed the book closed, then placed it on the mantel. "He's going to cure me. End all of this. What's it going to hurt?"

This time I grabbed her hands. "What if whatever he's tryin' to talk you into don't work? Then what?"

Her face fell as if she hadn't even considered that possibility. Went back to looking like that little innocent thing I found in Miss Tillie's saloon. "Then . . . I don't know!"

I softened my voice. "Where's all this comin' from? You really that smitten by this man? I didn't think you could be, seein' how your heart ain't even workin'."

She shot me a look like I'd just said the dumbest thing in the world. "Why not? I love you."

I stared into her blue eyes, so pale that they always made me think of ice. There was a coldness to her words that landed on me like a brick. She'd never said it before, and I can't remember the last time I heard anyone direct those words toward me. Not even King. You'd think warm and fuzzy would be the aftereffect. Instead, her lies, her omissions, her selfishness—and she still ain't said nothing about my damn arm—emptied the phrase of any affection I was supposed to feel.

"What he want you to do, Simone?"

She brightened. "Confess my sins."

I laughed. "Confess? Out loud?"

"Well, my priest back home couldn't ever tell anyone what I confessed."

"Norquist's a priest? I thought he was a reverend."

Simone shook her head. "Same thing. Whatever I say will stay with me, him, and God."

"Even if it's a crime? A whole bunch of crimes?"

"I think so."

I released her hands and shook my head. "I don't know, Simone. King didn't know half the stuff you're plannin' on tellin' the reverend, and like you said, he dropped me like a hot potato."

"This is different. He'll have to absolve me. And then, I'll be free of this. *We'll* be free of this."

If only she knew I'd already beaten her to freedom.

"Since you're itchin' to become Mrs. Reverend Norquist, I guess we can go our separate ways now, huh?"

"No one's talking marriage, Lavinia," Simone answered with a smile.

"And when's this hocus-pocus s'posed to happen?"

Simone squealed and raised herself up on her tiptoes. "Tomorrow afternoon!"

I shrugged. What could it hurt? If it don't work, it don't work, which I reckoned would be the case.

A knock at the back door startled us both. I don't know why she was so jumpy. She hadn't gotten two innocent men killed last night. I left Simone in the parlor and went to the back door, and there was King, smiling from ear to ear with four whole catfish wrapped in butcher paper. I clasped my hands over my mouth, stifling a scream. I glanced over my shoulder toward the parlor then ushered him out to the yard.

"What's the matter?" he asked. "You seem surprised to see me."

"I am." Thought you'd been eaten by a vampire, I wanted to say. "I didn't think you were serious 'bout comin' by."

"I said I would. Even brought you that fish I promised." He held the wrapped fish out toward me. "I didn't catch it, though. I've been stay-ing in Chicago with my mother. Bought this from my fishing buddy, Charlie."

"Chicago," I said with a smile. I sighed, feeling some of the weight from last night seep from my neck and down into my toes. "You were in Chicago yesterday. That explains everything."

"Explains what? And what happened to your arm?"

"Nothing." I took the fish and walked to the back door. "Thanks for stoppin' by."

"Well, wait!" he called out. "You said I could call on you today."

I stood on the top of the steps. "Yes. Yes, I did. But my mistress, she got company comin' by, so I got a whole mess of work to do."

"At least let me carry the fish inside for you."

"King, you ain't gotta—"

He had the fish and was in the kitchen before I knew it. I thanked him and tried to get him on his way without being rude.

"Why is *he* here?"

Hearing Simone's voice, I wish I could've melted into the floor. She stood there in the kitchen archway, staring at me like I was butch-ering a pig right there. I lowered my head. At least King can't kick me out this time.

"He was jus' leavin'," I said, pushing him toward the door.

"I thought you said you had a new mistress," King said, his eyes narrowed and aimed in her direction.

"Does it matter?" Simone asked, inching her way into the kitchen.

Thankfully, the rays of sunlight crisscrossing the room kept her from coming any further. "She's done with you, aren't you, Lavinia?"

"Are you, Lavinia?" King asked.

"No!" I said. "Now, look. Why I gotta choose between the two of you? She ain't gon' hurt you, King."

"Only because of the sunlight in here," Simone said as she skulked back toward the parlor. "The minute the sun goes down, he's mine."

"And why do you care, Simone, if Norquist is supposed to cure you? Ain't gotta worry about me or King after that!" I escorted King back outside. "I ain't had a chance to talk to her 'bout runnin' into you at the picnic yesterday."

"Why did you lie about living with her?"

"I didn't lie. I jus' didn't say one way or the other. Didn't think I had to."

"She wants to kill me, Lavinia. Is this what you want? To be beholden to a monster?" He took my hand and walked me away from the house. "Is it just me, or is she like that with everybody you meet?"

I opened my mouth to defend her, but nothing came out. She did want to eat everybody I met. Four of them were already dead. Yet there she was, in the house, waiting for her man to come calling, but I couldn't have anybody. Wonder what she would say if I banned Norquist from the house. Why was I the only one around here having to choose?

"Why don't you leave?" he asked. "You're a free woman. You don't have to live like this anymore."

How right he was! The connection between Simone and me was gone. I could leave and she wouldn't know where I went. She'd have Norquist and all her Tolleston admirers to keep her company whether he cured her or not.

"Tomorrow," I said, curiosity over her supposed healing tomorrow taking over. "Come by tomorrow."

He sighed. "Lavinia . . . Fine. Tomorrow. But I expect today to be the last time I see that thing." He leaned in and whispered, "I know she was the one in the papers, that woman who killed a little girl. I know you were there with her. Get rid of her, or I will."

"After tomorrow, Simone won't matter. Promise."

I watched him walk away with doubt clouding his eyes as he took one last glance at me over his shoulder. He knew the truth. Wasn't sure how I felt about this latest ultimatum, even if it did come from him. What was it with these people who felt the need to force me to do stuff? That it had to be their way or no way? How free did they think I was when they kept telling me what to do?

When I walked into the darkened parlor, I told her everything. About the Raduts' blackmail, their deaths, what happened with Nate, and my lost connection to her. Even told her that King knew about that little girl, though I never admitted it to him. She sat there, listening to the whole thing, not saying a word. Didn't express not one bit of thanks for taking care of our common threat. No sadness over not being connected to me anymore. I couldn't tell what she was thinking, and at this point I didn't care. Apparently, all that mattered to Simone was her happiness. Never mine. Even though I doubted Norquist's hocus-pocus would work, in my heart I prayed it set both of us free.

THIRTY-TWO

Martin and his girlfriend stand at the open door of the jailhouse, like they're waiting on something. I can only guess it's something that will make this night end faster. Bet this is where they took their regular trysts and having to guard me messed with their plans. I stick my face through the bars, catching a quick breeze while listening to drops of rain pattering on the ground.

After not finding whatever he was looking for out there, Martin leans against the doorframe and crosses one foot behind the other. His lady friend remains at the door, picking at her nails like Simone used to do when she was bored. He angles his body toward me and says, "Sounds like you killed Victor Radut."

I frown. "Like I told you earlier, can't kill somethin' that's already dead. And it was Simone who'd killed him first. I jus' put him out of his and everybody else's misery that last time. If I hadn't ended it then, somebody would've done it eventually."

Something outside briefly catches his attention. "But you still killed him."

I stretch my neck. What was he looking at? I strain my ears, listening for the sound of hoofbeats, men shouting for justice, a bubble of light from a mob anxious to carry it out. "And what would you have done if he came after you or your little friend there?"

The reference to the girl bristles him. He takes one last look outside and walks back to his desk. "What about his wife? What happened to her?"

"Don't know," I say with a shrug. "But, there's a way to find out if I'm tellin' the truth."

"How's that?"

I count off the reasons on my fingers. "First, there might be a crazy woman floating out there on Lake Michigan. There might be a dead body buried next to my dugout. Might be a head burnt to a crisp stickin' out of the sand not too far from that. But you gon' need me to show you where they are."

"You'd like that, wouldn't you?" Martin asks. "A reprieve from the executioner."

"What you think?" I ask. "Unless you're okay with killin' an innocent woman."

"If I should decide to go out there and look for these bodies . . ."

I clutch the bars of my cell. Progress. "Then you'd know I was tellin' the truth."

"What about that body you two laid on the train tracks? Was it still there when you went back to the saloon, or do I have to worry about another vampire on the loose?"

A nonbeliever wouldn't ask that question. "Oh, it was still there," I say. "Lookin' for it was the first thing I did 'fore cleanin' up the place that evenin'. Couldn't find the head, though. Coyotes must have got ahold of it. So, you gon' check on the bodies?"

"I'll go," the girl says quietly.

"Get to the part about you killing Miss Arceneau."

"Is anything I'm 'bout to say gon' spur you along? Change your mind 'bout sendin' me to Hammond or lettin' the locals get me for that matter? If you're goin' to look for those bodies, you'd have to wait 'til sunrise. No way you'd find them in the dark. No way you'd find them without me with you, too."

"Maybe," he says, taking a swig from yet another bottle he produces from a drawer in a cabinet at the far end of the jail. How he functions from day to day, I have no idea. "Just maybe."

"I said, I'll go."

Martin and I turn to the girl. I almost forgot she was there, quiet as she was.

"You'll do no such thing," Martin says.

The girl holds out her hand to him. "Come with me then."

He looks to me. "I can't leave. The constable—"

"Will understand. You're investigating a murder."

"Why don't we all go?" I suggest. "You need me to find them."

"How hard could it be? It's on the beach, right?"

"You know how big that beach is?" Martin asks her. Then turning to me, "Nice try, Lavinia. Wouldn't want us to get separated out there."

Charlotte stands and walks over to my cell. "Come on, Martin. She knows exactly where they are, don't you, girl?"

I bite the inside of my mouth, wondering why *this* girl is so keen to go out to the desolate beach and find some dead bodies. And she ain't even heard my whole story. Maybe she's trying to put distance between herself and what her uncles plan to do to me. Maybe she's anxious to have her time with Martin, though I don't know how much good he's gonna be with all that liquor in him. But maybe she's actually taken pity on me and wants to help.

I detail the best route out to King's place where Victor's head should still be smoldering. She leaves with a skip in her step. Whether she finds it or not, what's the worst that could happen?

THIRTY-THREE

The following day, Simone and I sat in our darkened parlor, acting like the other didn't exist. It was Sunday morning, the day Norquist was supposed to make a saint out of Simone. I was only there out of curiosity . . . and anger. I didn't feel like hearing Simone's giddy thoughts about becoming human again. Truth was, I was a bit miffed. If this worked, she'd get to start anew . . . as a sixteen-year-old woman with her whole life ahead of her. Sure, ain't much women could do in 1866. Half the stuff we'd done—other than all the killing—she wouldn't be able to do as a young, married woman. But as a white woman in America? Had a helluva lot more opportunities than I did.

Simone swore we'd still be together, but that didn't matter to me. If this worked, I wouldn't have to choose between her and King. Other than our shared experiences, why would I stay with her? With her as a human, I wasn't stupid enough to believe we would still be equals, especially since I knew her true history. She'd eventually have a husband to care for her anyway. I'd tasted real freedom for far too long to go backward. And with Norquist acting all sweet on her, I'd bet the saloon—which the heifer would probably take back from me, too!—that he'd ask for her hand when it was all done . . . whether she turned or not. I think that was the biggest thorn in my side: her ease at snagging a man when I went through hell and high water for King to start speaking to me again.

Either way, all my stuff, a few dresses and some books I liked, were packed up in my room and ready to go. Even if this didn't work, I was outta here.

Simone sat in the parlor of the house, clad in her lavender walking suit, her hair pinned up to look more grown. Legs crossed at the ankles. Gloved hands folded in her lap. Looked like she was sitting in Sunday service. Every time I glanced in her direction, she'd turn her head or avert her eyes.

"Stop looking at me, Lavinia."

"Not lookin' at you. Saw a fly on the drapes."

"Why are you even here? You don't even believe it'll work."

I shrugged. "Curious." Then I raised my chin. "And I wanna make sure you leave my name out of your little confession."

"I can't do that."

"Meanin' what? After that scene with King the other day, that's the least you could do!"

"But that's not how it works," Simone said with conviction. "You should hear Norquist speak."

"I have. Talks loud enough when he's here. Can prob'ly hear him in the next county over."

Simone turned to me. "No, really. None of what he said was new to me. I had no reason to believe in it until now. Think about it: if poisoned, tainted blood turned me into what I am, wouldn't clean and holy blood cure me?"

"You talkin' about bitin' Norquist?! Jus' 'cause he's a preacher man, don't mean he ain't still a *man*. Everybody got skeletons in their closets. Even him."

"That's the point! Even after all the evil I've done, I can still be saved! Reborn! Changed into a new creature. No longer will I be in the image of the thing that created me, but in the image of God Himself." Simone lifted her eyes and hands as if the Almighty were about to rain forgiveness on her from the ceiling. I didn't disabuse her of her notions. Everybody needs something to believe in, I guess.

"So, in order to be saved . . ." Simone said, stopping in front of the draped windows. Now she was chewing on a glove-covered thumb. She lowered her head and said, "You know they've been reporting on those bodies in the Tolleston woods."

"Yeah," I said warily.

"I told Norquist about them. About how they came to be out there and the strange wounds found on them. He insisted we tell the constable."

My ears flushed with heat. I walked up to Simone. "What exactly did you tell him?"

"I'm sorry, Lavinia—"

I held her shoulders and shook her. "What did you tell him?"

I rushed to the window and pulled the drapes aside slightly so I could look out. Had to wait a bit for my eyes to adjust to the sunlight from the constant dimness of the house. That Norquist sure was a punctual thing. If he said he was gonna come calling at five o'clock, he was there at five o'clock. And there he was, standing on the porch, looking at his pocket watch, waiting until it was time. He rapped on the door several times as I stared at Simone, who avoided my gaze.

"Reverend," I said, finally opening the door. "Come on in."

Simone's face about split open from smiling at the sight of him. He was dressed like he'd just come from church: olive-green frock coat and matching trousers, along with that black coachman's hat he always wore that seemed too big for his little head. With him, he carried a large black bag like the doctors have. He rode around from Chicago to a bunch of little congregations in the area that didn't have no pastor yet. Despite all that traveling and preaching, he still found time to call on Simone several times a week.

After I served tea, I excused myself into the hallway and stood against the front door. You didn't think I was gonna let all this happen without seeing it, did you? I wanted to know how Norquist was gonna pull this off, and if it meant her biting him to get at some holy blood, then I needed to be there to clean up the mess. Plus, I wanted to know what all she was gonna say in this confession of hers. What the constable had to do with this, I didn't know. Did she plan on turning both of us in? She had the wrong one if she thought I was gonna let that happen. All this conversion mess was her idea in the first place, and if penance made her feel better, she could do that alone. I'd be halfway through the Tolleston woods by the time she got up to answer the door if the constable did come. But if Norquist didn't cure her . . . Hopefully King came after I got rid of the two bodies.

Simone and Norquist sat in two Queen Anne chairs with a table and a lit kerosene lamp between the two of them. Norquist was sweating like the dickens in a room I now realized was hot as hell. He was probably wishing they were closer on the couch, either because of his affection for her, or because he unknowingly got a cool breeze from the chill emanating from her dead body. Simone asked him if she should kneel. Norquist patted her folded hands and smiled.

"Whatever you feel comfortable doing is fine." When she chose to stay seated, he continued. "Repeat after me," Norquist said louder. He must've known I was standing out there listening. "'I, a poor, miserable sinner . . .'"

Simone adjusted her sitting position and smiled quickly. "'I, a poor, miserable sinner . . .'"

"'Confess unto Thee all my sins and iniquities . . .'"

Her brow crinkled. "Don't you have to hear them?" She retrieved a folded piece of paper from the pocket of her skirts. "I made a list."

Norquist smiled. "No one on earth can list every sin they've committed, just as no one on earth can stop themselves from sinning. God already knows."

Simone snorted out a nervous chuckle. "I guess that would be impossible. I did find myself making things up when I went to confession as a hu . . . a young girl."

They continued with the confession, which really was her saying nothing other than she was a sinner in need of forgiveness. I wiped my brow. At least my name wouldn't come up. And we wouldn't have to sit here listening to the names of every person she killed and all the stuff we stole. That would take all day. Had a hard enough time pushing it all out of my own brain. Was she actually gonna turn herself in to the constable?

After she "confessed," Norquist forgave her.

"And no penance?" she asked.

"When Jesus said, 'It is finished,'" Norquist said with a smile, "He meant it. No penance required."

Was that it? She didn't look no different. I quietly tsked to myself at the hocus-pocus failure, though I wasn't sure what I expected to happen even if it worked. But Norquist wasn't done. He retrieved the black box he'd brought. Inside he took out another, smaller box with these white little thin round things that looked like paper circles. He said it was bread. Didn't look like no bread I'd ever seen. Then he pulled out a vial with red liquid swishing all around that he poured into a silver cup with no decorations on it whatsoever. He mumbled stuff over the paper circles and the silver cup, making the sign of the cross over them, while calling the circles Jesus's body and the wine Jesus's blood.

I could see Simone trembling as Norquist placed a paper circle on her tongue. The silver cup shook in her hands as she brought it to her lips. And like she did after feeding on someone, she wiped the corner of her mouth with her finger, then licked it clean. Guess some habits don't die.

Simone still didn't look no different. She was still as pale as ever. Wolf teeth still showed a tad on her bottom lip. She gave Norquist a squeeze of thanks, then headed for the front door.

"Wait!" he called out, catching her arm before she opened the door. "The sun is still out!"

"But I'm cured!" Simone declared. "You just said . . ."

"That your sins are forgiven. I didn't mean to insinuate all that physically ails you will be cured. This isn't magic."

Simone didn't listen. As she reached for the doorknob, I ran into the parlor grabbed a throw from the sofa just in case. Slowly, she descended the five or so steps onto the front lawn. The late afternoon sun had already made its trek over most of the sky, leaving the yard in shade. Simone removed her boots and stockings, and then tiptoed through the grass. Stood right up to the line that separated shade from sunlight, and her from turning into a piece of fried fatback. We'd never risked her going out in the daytime at all, let alone in the middle of the afternoon to sit in the shade.

Norquist stood on the porch calling to her as I ran after her with the throw. Simone took one giant step out of the shade and into the full sunlight. She fell to her knees as thin streams of sweet-smelling black smoke—autumn leaves burning came to mind—ascended from her body, even up through her clothes. I knelt beside her and tossed the throw over her exposed face and neck.

"No!" Simone said, shedding the throw. "Let it burn."

She was panting now—breathing—something she ain't never done before. Streams of sweat, not burn marks, covered the back of her neck, and sprouted dark wet patches on her clothes. Then she rolled over on her back and laughed as the sun poured itself on her face.

"It's over," she said, pulling me beside her on the ground. "It worked. I'm free."

I couldn't believe it. The teeth and pale skin, now full of this magic blood Norquist had talked about, were gone. It was as if all the vamp stuff she had in her had gone up in the smoke that left her body. I looked at my arms, half expecting to see smoke coming from me, too.

Norquist, it seems, couldn't believe it either. He fell to his knees right there in the grass, yelling, "It's a miracle!" Funny. If he only knew that it was more than her sins that got cured.

"Lavinia," she said, her voice shaky like she was getting used to her lungs working after so long. "I'm sorry." She swallowed and panted out a few more breaths. "You . . . I will . . . come . . ."

Couldn't hardly see her through all the smoke. All I heard was her panting out the last bits of vamp in her. Soon the ashen smoke thinned into white wisps of vapor. A soft wind, God's breath I reckoned, blew away the smoke. Simone lay there with not a singe mark or burn anywhere on her, not even her dress. A tiny smile teased at the corners of her mouth. Wide blue eyes gazed at the sunlit sky.

"Simone?" I said as I bent over her. I shook her gently. Then I touched her pink cheek. I snatched my hand away. Warmth. For the first time since I'd known her, she was warm to the touch. She didn't even blink. I slapped her face, harder and harder, until Norquist pushed me away.

On his knees, he placed his ear against her mouth, then her chest. I sat on the ground, watching him hold her hand for a moment, placing his thumb on her wrist. He dropped it and checked the other wrist. Then he started pounding on her chest with his fists.

"Stop!" I begged. "What're you doin' to her? You're hurtin' her!"

Norquist stopped. He sat back on his heels, removed his hat, and wiped his brow. His face fell. "She's . . . gone, Lavinia."

"Gone?"

"She's dead."

"But . . . This was s'posed to cure her!"

Norquist let out a sigh, then smoothed his hand over her face, closing her eyes. "It did. Look at her. She's at peace. Free from whatever was torturing her."

"You mean, she's dead . . . for-real dead?"

Norquist turned to me. I couldn't tell if he was sweating or tears had already escaped his eyes. Here I was, still on the ground, looking up at him with the sun behind him like he was God.

A God who suddenly took my Simone away.

THIRTY-FOUR

"I'm sorry, Lavinia," Norquist said after a long silence between us. He stood and helped me to my feet.

Nodding seemed appropriate. Couldn't think of nothing else to say or do. My head bobbing up and down like an idiot. This wasn't what was supposed to happen. She wasn't even supposed to be cured . . . like this. If I'm being honest with myself, I thought we'd go on doing what we'd been doing: me and her charming the pants off everybody, pretending to be full humans. We'd played the part well so far. Had a whole world to conquer and explore. How was I supposed to do it on my own? Without her?

I didn't notice the crowd of neighbors who'd gathered in the yard. Must have heard all the shouting because some of the women had run out with laundry or flour-dusted rolling pins in their hands. A semicircle formed around us. They questioned Norquist, who simply mumbled nonsense. Glad they didn't ask me. What was I gonna say, she ain't a vampire no more? Couldn't blame Norquist for this—out loud. In my heart, I did blame him for this happening because she was upright before this hocus-pocus.

And even deeper in my heart, I knew I was free now, too.

The constable burst through the gathering. His looming figure cast a shadow over Simone's still body. Without saying a word, he walked up to me and grabbed my hands, pinning them behind my back.

"What're you doin'?" I asked as he jostled me. He secured my hands by the wrists, but still felt the need to yank me around for some reason.

"Arresting you for murder, Lavinia."

He was dragging me away from Simone now. "For this? I didn't do this to her. Jus' ask Reverend Norquist." I searched the crowd, but he was nowhere to be found. Coward. Must've lit out when the constable came, leaving me here to explain his mess.

I dug my heels into the ground to no avail. "I didn't kill her! Constable, you know me! Y'all know me! I wouldn't do this!"

The constable, a regular to the saloon, secured the rope around my wrists to his horse's saddle. "I was told you had something to do with those deaths out in the Tolleston woods, the Wiltshires, and that little girl in Crown Point."

"What now?" I asked as if I hadn't heard him correctly.

"I'd come by today to get to the bottom of the accusation, only to find you standing over another dead body. What happened? You killed her to keep her mouth shut?"

"No! It was the reverend!" I tried pulling my hands through the thick, rough rope. Ribbons of red stained my wrists where the restraints were skinning me. Simone accused me of murder. Her murders. That's what she wanted to tell me? That's what she thought would solve our problems? Get rid of me while she rode off into the sunset with that damned Norquist? And here she'd been chiding me all this time about trusting folks. I'd kill somebody right now if I knew it would bring her back . . . all so I could kill her for this shit she pulled.

I was right about one thing: she was making my decision for me. And here I was stressing over what my walking out was gonna do to her.

Looking back, the signs were all there. Should've known I couldn't trust her.

But I had one last card to play.

There among the crowd, was King. Mouth agape, he watched as I stood bound behind the horse. As the constable directed folks to carry

Simone into the house and fetch the undertaker, I shot King doleful eyes. He sidled over to me, careful to keep his sights on the constable and the crowd.

"What did you do?" he whispered through his teeth.

"I didn't do nothin," I said with a shake of my head. "This ain't what it looks like."

"Is she . . . dead? For real?"

I nodded. "And they think I did it."

"Well, didn't you?"

My eyes about popped outta my head. "Of course, not!"

"You didn't kill her for me, did you? When I said get rid of her, I didn't mean—"

"Why would you think I would do that?"

"All the stuff you two did."

"King, listen to me—"

The constable shooed him away before I could answer. I didn't want to leave King thinking I'd killed Simone for him, and his face told me that he found it neither romantic nor touching. He knew the truth. Knew what Simone was. Knew what I'd done for her. No, he had to believe I wouldn't have killed her.

The constable took his time riding out to the jail. I wanted to believe he was being nice, given that I had to walk tied up behind him. But I'm sure his intention was to parade me through the town. Before we got out of the neighborhood, some of the bystanders threw rocks and clumps of dirt at me. King inched away, either fearful the crowd might turn on him, or disgusted by what he thought I'd done. I wished the constable would hurry up so the assault would end and I'd no longer have to hope King was gonna come for me.

Took about an hour, twice as long as normal, to get to the jail, which was on the eastern end of town, the midpoint between my dugout and what used to be my home. I wondered what would become of Simone's body. I wasn't fooling myself that she'd come back and release me from jail like she'd done before, but despite her betrayal, I wished I had a chance to see her one more time. With all the money I'd saved from the saloon, I had enough to do what most wealthy folks did: hire a photographer for one last picture of the dead. Would've propped her up on the sofa in the parlor with her head on my shoulder like she used to do. Would drape that burlap she'd carried all the way from Georgia over her and then insist that she be buried with it. At least I knew they wouldn't embalm her. That cost a pretty penny and nobody knew where I'd stashed all the money we'd made. With no family here, I was sure they'd put her straight in the ground.

I could barely see the jail through my teary eyes. My mind and heart shifted between missing her and hating her for putting me in this position. She was dead-dead, and there wouldn't be no getting outta this one by myself. I'd hang for sure. Like a fool, I tried tapping into her mind. Asking her why she did what she did. If she could answer, I wasn't sure I wanted to hear it. In the end, she didn't choose me.

THIRTY-FIVE

I wipe a tear from my eye. My story replays itself in my mind, but I've never said it out loud before now. My foolishness, my sins, all laid bare for Martin to hear. I don't feel better. I don't feel free. I doubt God is even listening since I've been dealing with all of this by myself.

"He hasn't come to see after you," Martin asks, his voice the quietest I've heard all night. "King. He didn't come. Maybe he'll testify for you when you get to Hammond."

"I can't ask him to do that," I say. I've held onto the bars of my cell as I forced myself to relive these last couple of days. "I don't want him to get caught up in my mess. Y'all will send him right back to Michigan to answer for killing his daddy." Then a thought hit me. "You ain't gonna go after him, are you?"

"Why would I? One nigger killing another in a whole other jurisdiction isn't any concern of mine." He stuffs his jaw with tobacco and jumps from the chair like his butt's on fire. "Rain's letting up."

"Why you so concerned about the rain?" I ask. "You gotta stay here with me anyway, don'tcha? Or do you not care if the town comes and strings up one more nigger?"

He turns his head back toward me and frowns. "Aw, Lavinia. You know I don't think of you like that!"

"Don'tcha? You don't even believe me."

Martin tsks and shifts his weight from one foot to the other. He places his hands on his hips and sighs.

"What am I supposed to make of it? You want me to believe that sweet young woman was some blood-sucking monster?"

I shake my head. "Never called her a monster."

"Sure sounds like what you've been describing for the past several hours."

"What was she supposed to do? She couldn't help what she was, doing what she needed to . . . to be. Is it the mosquito's fault that it needs blood? Even though we hate it, it can't help bitin' us to get what it needs to live. Same thing for Simone."

Martin presses his lips together and then says, "I guess."

"But you don't believe me?"

He shakes his head. "Sorry."

"Ain't you even the least bit curious to see if there is a charred head out on the beach?"

"Not in the least bit."

"And your lady friend out there in the rain? What if she comes back and says she found the charred head?"

Martin raises an eyebrow and tilts his head to the side. "Charlotte will chase a butterfly right off a cliff if you let her. Even if she went, she probably got distracted along the way. If she says there's a charred head on the beach, that just means you killed more folks than we thought. Either way, you're gonna hang for something."

He's back at the door, mumbling about his lady friend's whereabouts. Thunder rumbles in the distance, a low thrum where the storm has traveled. "Good story, though. Can't say the last time I was this entertained." Martin straightens his stance. "I'm going for a piss." He unhooks the dozens of keys on his belt and tosses them onto his desk with a loud clang. Then he clears his throat, adjusts his pants, and walks outside.

Going to take a piss, my eye. Giving his friends one last chance at me.

I walk back to my cot and sit down so hard I hear a soft crack from the wooden legs. I tap the back of my head against the wall, my thick bun of curls crunching in my ears. I try to picture what the end will look like. Will I swing around on that rope, legs kicking like a duck on water? Nearly splitting Victor's neck in two finally stopped him. I wonder if my neck snapping is what'll do me in.

I bite the corner of my bottom lip and close my eyes. *Think, Lavinia. Think!*

Heavy footfalls against the dusty wooden floor alert me to Martin's return.

"That was quick," I say. I hear the thump of a single set of bootheels and a man's moaning.

Charlotte must be back. Probably why he was glued to the night sky. With all that moaning he's doing they must really miss each other when they're away. I keep my eyes closed so as not to see them carrying on like before, especially since there ain't nothing I can do about it. Great. Now I gotta wait until they're done before she tells me what, if anything, she found on the beach. Only a few days ago, they would have been good pickings for Simone. Out here in no-man's-land, guarding a couple of empty cells all alone. Sure, his wife would've missed them. But she can do better than a pair of liars.

"So, did you find that charred head?"

Neither Martin nor the girl answers. I open one eye and see Nate . . . *Nate?*

The constable is in his arms; his face buried against the side of the man's neck I can't see.

I sit up on my cot and wonder if I should warn them that Martin will be back soon. But I notice the constable's arms are limp and dangling at his sides. And there's a whisper of rot and a fresh scent of the beach hanging in the air. Guess that puddle of blood I saw on the beach was Victor's and not his.

The brief smile on my face masks the sad realization that Nate is what he is because of me. I don't know what's worse: knowing I caused his death or knowing I sentenced him to this life. If I deserve to hang for anything, it's this.

"Nate?"

Startled, he raises his face from the man's neck. His beard is wet and red from the constable's blood. He drops the body on the floor like a rag doll and steps over him toward me.

"Lavinia?"

He wipes his mouth on his sleeve. Nate is standing in front of my jail cell. He looks the same way he did the last time I saw him. The ashen pall and sunken eyes I've grown used to seeing in the two vamps I'd known are absent. A bit disheveled from his climb out of the grave, he could've been stopping by to drop off the weekly take like he used to, normal as he appears . . . aside from the blood on his face and clothes.

He stares at me for a moment with a frown on his face like he can't place me. "Why are you here?"

"They say I killed Simone."

"Did you?" He's standing at the cell door asking me questions like he was paying me a visit.

"I didn't kill her," I say. "Preacher man did some voodoo on her and she died."

He wraps his hands around the bars, seeming not to notice that I haven't moved. "What you just saw—"

"Was the worst thing you've ever done?" I sigh and rise to my feet, studying him like he's some child that's come home with a handful of worthless magic beans. I greet him at the bars and place my hands on his.

"Won't be the last time. That's what you gotta do from now on, to get rid of the pains in your stomach."

Nate moves his hands so they are covering mine instead. The grip tightens, posing a question I don't want to answer and he apparently doesn't want to ask. He's looking at me with those dark eyes of his, and for the first time, being this close to him, I can see remnants of his mother where his facial hair has been disturbed.

"You mind fetchin' them keys behind you and lettin' me out?"

Nate complies. The cell door screeches open, and I take in the fact that, at that moment, I'm free. Not a shackle in the world holding me back. Won't be long if I don't get to moving. Once Martin notices I'm gone and the constable ain't just napping at his desk, he'll have the whole town after me. I got no horse, no home. Going back to the dugout wasn't an option, especially after all that I'd told Martin. And I can't give them an excuse to go looking to King for answers, him being the only other Negro around. What I need is time. I look at Nate still holding on to those bars for dear life. As I walk past him, I expect him to attack me right there. He doesn't.

Freedom is right outside that door.

"How'd you come to be here of all places?" I ask, not sure I wanna hear the answer.

He stares into the cell and doesn't answer. Doesn't move. I thought he didn't hear me, but slowly, he turns in my direction. Confusion darkens his face.

"When I woke up, there was a woman wandering around on the beach. She was saying . . . something about a head. But then I . . ." He shakes his head. "Her blood showed me . . . you. In here. I thought—"

"That I'd killed Simone?"

"That you might need me."

I pause at the threshold and think of Simone.

THIRTY-SIX

"Martin!" I whisper when he finally returns from the outhouse. I push my face between the bars of my cell and summon him over with my pointer finger.

"Now what?" he asks, hooking his keys back onto his belt. "I thought your story was done."

Once he gets to my cell, I point toward the wooden cot where, just beyond a pool of thick spittle and my arm bandages on the floor, lies a blanket outlining a slumbering human form.

The taste of metal and pain on my tongue fade as I wipe traces of moisture from my chin.

"There's somethin' in here with me."

Acknowledgments

This book would not be possible without the support and encouragement of many people. A sincere thank you to:

Melissa Danaczko, my wonderful agent, who immediately understood the vision I had for this book. I thank her for putting up with my many, many, many questions, and her tenacity in finding this book a home. The entire Blackstone Publishing team, especially Dan Ehrenhaft for loving this story almost as much as I do and taking the chance on acquiring the book. Alyea Canada and Cole Barnes, my editors, whose amazing expertise helped make the prose shine. To the Blackstone publicity team: Nicole Sklitsis, Rachel Sanders, and Sarah Bonamino for putting together a plan to get this baby out into the world.

To Highland Writers Group, and especially Carla Suson, Bob Moulesong, Rich Elliott, Julie Perkins, Liz Coty, and Loretta Polaski for reading multiple versions of this book and giving such great feedback.

To Midwest Writers Workshop for helping me learn the craft and business of writing. To D.E. Johnson, a former faculty member of Midwest Writers: your words of encouragement all those years ago mattered greatly to me. I don't think you'll ever realize how much!

To my family for being early readers and not caring a bit about all the time I spent writing this.

And despite the genre and topic of the book, I must thank God for the ability to string words together to create a compelling story. Without Him and the many extraordinary people He put in my path along this long journey, none of this would be possible.